The boarding hatch started to close, but not before a running figure darted by and threw a number of tiny silver balls inside. Erv knew what was next. His hands went involuntarily to his ears but he could not shut out the sound. The dull whine grew in pitch until he could no longer hear it. But he could feel it growing, expanding, pressing against the inside of his skull until he was sure his head would explode.

And then it did.

Berkley books by F. Paul Wilson

AN ENEMY OF THE STATE
THE KEEP

F. Paul Wilson

AN ENEMY OF THE STATE

BERKLEY BOOKS, NEW YORK

Grateful acknowledgment is made to the authors listed below; excerpts from their work have been used to open the following chapters:

CHAPTER V: from *The Fall* by Albert Camus © 1956 by Librairie Gallimard, Paris.

CHAPTER VIII: *"Affair with a Green Monkey"* which appeared originally in *Venture*, May, 1957. © 1957 by Theodore Sturgeon. Used here by permission of the author.

CHAPTER XI: from *Capitalism and Freedom* by Milton Friedman © 1962 by The University of Chicago.

CHAPTER XIII: from *The Plague* by Albert Camus © 1947 by Librairie Gallimard, Paris.

CHAPTER XIV: from *The Devil's Dictionary* by Ambrose Bierce © 1957 by Hill and Wang, Inc.

CHAPTER XXI: from *Dune* by Frank Herbert © 1965 by Frank Herbert. Used here by permission of the author.

This Berkley book contains the complete text of the original hardcover edition. It has been completely reset in a typeface designed for easy reading, and was printed from new film.

AN ENEMY OF THE STATE

A Berkley Book / published by arrangement with Doubleday & Company, Inc.

PRINTING HISTORY
Doubleday edition published 1980
Berkley edition / February 1984

ISBN: 0-425-06833-1

A BERKLEY BOOK ® TM 757,375
Berkley Books are published by The Berkley Publishing Group,
200 Madison Avenue, New York, New York 10016.
The name "BERKLEY" and the stylized "B"
with design are trademarks belonging
to Berkley Publishing Corporation.
PRINTED IN THE UNITED STATES OF AMERICA

For my parents

Contents

It appears there will always be unanswered questions about the Great Conspiracy, especially since its chief engineer, Peter LaNague, was not available afterward for questioning. The remarkable depth of his conspiracy's penetration into the fabric of Imperial society left many traceable elements in its wake, and so we have a reasonably clear picture of events during the five-year pre-insurrection period.

But what preceded the conspiracy itself? What started it all? What made Peter LaNague decide that the time was ripe for revolution? Scholars diverge at this point, but the single incident theory appears to be coming into favor in recent texts. The arrival of LaNague on Throne and the cessation of attempts to assassinate Metep VII follow closely on the heels of a small anti-militia riot on Neeka. There was one fatality in that riot—a young woman named Liza Kirowicz. But Kirowicz was her married name. Her maiden name was Boedekker. And there's the rub . . .

from LANAGUE: A BIOGRAPHY
by Emmerz Fent

Prologue

". . . and I say we've had just about enough!"

Liza Kirowicz was in the front row with her husband, cheering, stamping her feet, and shouting with the rest of them. There were about two hundred angry people packed into the hall; the air was hot and reeked of sweat, but no one seemed to take much notice. All were tightly enmeshed in the speaker's word-web.

"It's been well over two standard centuries since we kicked the Earthie militia back to Sol System. They were sucking us dry, taking what we produced and shipping it back to Earth. So our great-great-grandparents revolted and set up the Imperium, supposedly to keep us free. But look at us now: are we any better off? The Imperium has been taxing us since it was formed; and if that wasn't bad enough, it later came around and said Neekan currency was no good—we'd have to pay in Imperial marks. Now, instead of Earthie militia, we have the Imperial Guard all over the planet, to 'protect' us from any possible countermoves by Earth! They must think we're all idiots! The Imperial Guard is here for one reason: to make sure we pay our taxes, and to make sure those taxes go into Metep's coffers on Throne! *That's* why they're here! And I for one have had enough of it!"

Again the audience broke into wild cheering. Jugs were being passed and sampled while coats and inhibitions were being shed. Her lips and finger tips were already starting to tingle, so Liza let the jug pass untasted this time and watched with amusement as her husband Frey took a long pull. They had both been born and bred on Earth, a fact impossible to discern from their appearance. Even their parents would have been hard pressed to recognize their children under the layers of grime and callus.

Like many young couples of their generation, and of generations before them, they had been seduced by the call of pioneer life on the outworlds. Farm workers now, they had been such for almost five local years. Soon they would have enough saved to homestead a tract of their own, and that would mean working even harder. But they were where they wanted to be and loving every minute of it.

The economic situation was far from perfect, however. The standard of living was low on Neeka in the best of times; the taxes that went to the Imperium made things worse. If it hadn't been for those taxes, Liza and Frey would probably have their own place by now. It was galling: taxes were withheld from every pay voucher . . . their pay represented time, and time was life . . . little bits of their lives were being snipped off every pay period and sent to Throne . . . little bits of life trailing off into space.

And now a new levy from Throne: a 2 per cent across the board tax hike to defray further the expenses of the Imperial Guard garrisons on Neeka.

That did it. No more. The garrisons would go. This fellow up on the platform said they didn't need the garrisons and, by the Core, he was right!

Liza felt good. There was an exhilarating warmth spreading evenly throughout her body. She looked at Frey and loved him. She looked at all the weathered, impassioned faces around her and loved them, too. These were real people, solid people, people who were grappling with an alien ecology, aided by a minimal amount of technology and a lot of physical effort. No gentleman farmers here—owner and field hand worked side by side.

The hall had begun to empty, not in an aimless, unhurried dribble, but with a direction. The man on the platform must have said something to activate his listeners—something Liza had missed—because they were pulling on their coats and following him out the double rear doors. Frey pulled her into the surge and she trotted along. They were headed for the local garrison.

The cold night air refreshed her and heightened her perceptions. Shielding her blue eyes against the wind that ran through her auburn hair, Liza glanced at the onyx sky and knew she was no longer an Earthie. The stars looked so *right* tonight. There had been such wrongness up there in the early years after her arrival—the sun had been the wrong shade of fire and the wrong size, the day sky was the wrong shade of blue and by night there were two moons. Both of Neeka's satellites were out tonight; the small, playful Mayna swinging after her remote, austere sister, Palo. Both belonged there. Liza was a Neekan now.

The local garrison was a faceless white block at the corner of the landing pad complex. Two shuttles stood by on the pads ready to scramble the troops up to their orbiting cruiser should the need arise—an eventuality that had become increasingly unlikely with each passing decade since the outworlds' break with Earth, and considered an Imperial fantasy for well over a century. Earth still coveted the outworlds and their resources, but the risk and expense of reclaiming them would be prohibitive.

And so the garrison troopers had it easy. They were reasonably well behaved and their major task throughout their hitch on Neeka was the alleviation of boredom. Until tonight. As the crowd approached, the troopers filed out of the single door on the town side of the building and formed an uneasy semi-circle between the locals and Imperial property. The commander had placed a ringer in the meeting hall to give them early warning should the gathering boil over into a confrontation.

Someone in the crowd started chanting, *"Back to Throne, leave us alone! Back to Throne, leave us alone!"* It was quickly picked up by the rest and all began to stamp their feet in time as they marched and chanted.

Liza had become separated from Frey in the press of bodies and had pushed herself to the front rank in search of him. Once there, however, she quickly forgot about her husband. Her stride was long and determined as she was buoyed along on a wave of fraternity and purpose. They were going to send Metep a message: Yes, Neeka counted itself among the outworlds free from Earth; yes, Neeka counted itself as part of the Imperium. But no more tribute to Metep. No more pieces of life shipped to Throne.

An amplified masculine voice blared from the garrison roof:

"PLEASE RETURN TO YOUR HOMES BEFORE SOMEONE SAYS OR DOES SOMETHING WE'LL ALL REGRET LATER. YOUR FIGHT IS NOT

WITH US. YOU SHOULD CONTACT YOUR REPRESENTATIVES ON THRONE IF YOU HAVE A GRIEVANCE." The message was repeated. "PLEASE RETURN TO YOUR . . ."

The crowd ignored the warning and doubled the volume of its chant: *"Back to Throne, leave us alone!"*

The troopers, edgy and fidgety, held their weapons at ready. Most of them were young, Throners by birth, soldiers by choice due to the sagging job situation on their homeworld. Their training and seasoning to date had consisted of short sessions in holographic simulators. Most of them viewed the locals as stupid dirt-scratchers who spent their lives breaking their backs on reluctant soil because they didn't know any better; but they also knew the locals to be a tough bunch. The troopers had the weapons but the locals had the numbers, and the troopers faced them uneasily.

"COME NO FURTHER!" the voice atop the garrison shouted into the night. "STOP WHERE YOU ARE OR THE GUARD WILL BE FORCED TO FIRE TO PROTECT IMPERIAL PROPERTY!"

The crowd came on. *"Back to Throne, leave us alone!"*

A lieutenant on the ground shouted to his men. "Make certain all weapons are locked onto the stun mode—we don't want any martyrs tonight!" Glancing quickly at the angry mob that was almost upon him, he said, "Fire at will!"

Tight, intense ultrasonic beams began to play against the front ranks of the crowd with immediate effect. Those caught in the wash of inaudible sound began to reel and crumble to the ground as the microvibrations, pitched especially for the human nervous system, wrought havoc on conduction through their neuronal cytoplasm. As the leaders fell twitching and writhing, those being pushed from behind began to trip over their fallen comrades. Soon the entire march was in complete disarray.

With its momentum broken, the crowd backed off to a safe distance and resigned itself to verbal assaults. The troopers turned off their stunners and returned them to the ready position. In a little while, the marchers on the ground began to stir and rise and stagger back to their waiting friends.

All but one.

Liza Kirowicz was not breathing. It would later be discovered that she had been suffering from an unsuspected and, until then, asymptomatic demyelinating disease of the central nervous system. The result was an exaggerated response to the ultrasonic stun beams, resulting in a temporary paralysis of the mid-brain respiratory center. Without oxygen, temporary soon became permanent. Liza Kirowicz was dead.

It was an incident genuinely regretted by both sides as a tragic and unforeseeable accident. But that made little difference to Liza's father when the news finally reached him on Earth a full standard year later. He immediately began searching for a means of retaliating against the Imperium. And when Peter LaNague learned of that search, he knew his time had come round at last.

PART ONE

The Nihilist

The Year of the Tortoise

I

"And how about you? What are *you* rebelling against?"
"Whatta ya got?"

The Wild One

A man would die tonight.

The thin blond man sat in the darkness and thought about that. Long before his arrival on Throne, he had known that lives would be lost, but he had promised—*sworn!*—by all he revered that no man would die by his hand or word. And now, tonight, all that had changed.

He had ordered a man's death. No matter that the man was a killer and would be killed before he could kill again. No matter that it was too late to find another way to stop him, or that a life would be saved as a result.

He had ordered a man's death. And that was ugly.

As Kanya and Josef, shadows among shadows, went through their limbering exercises behind him, the blond man sat motionless and gazed out the window before him. It was not a high window. Cities on the outworlds tended to spread out, not up, and the cities on Throne, oldest of the outworlds, were no exception. It was night and glo-globes below limned the streets in pale orange light as they released the sunlight absorbed during the day. People were moving in steady streams

3

toward Freedom Hall for the Insurrection Day ceremonies. He
and his two companions would soon join them.

The man inhaled deeply, held the air, then let it out slowly,
hoping to ease some of his inner tension. The maneuver failed.
His personal *misho*, sitting on the window sill, responded to
the tension it sensed coiled like a spring within him and held its
trunk straight up from its earthenware container in a rigid
chokkan configuration. Turning his head toward the twisting,
leaping, gyrating shadows behind him, the man opened his
mouth to speak but no words came forth. He suddenly wanted
out of the whole thing. This was not in the plan. He wanted
out. But that was impossible. A course of action had been
started, wheels had been set in motion, people had been placed
in sensitive and precarious positions. He had to follow
through. It would be years before the plan came to fruition,
but the actions of a single man tonight could destroy everything. He had to be stopped.

The blond man swallowed and found his throat dry.

"Time to go."

The shadows stopped moving.

$$\Omega$$

In pre-Imperium days it had been called Earth Hall and the
planet on which it sat had been known as Caelum. Came the
revolution and "Earth" was replaced by "Freedom," Caelum
renamed Throne, seat of the new Outworld Imperium. The
hall's vaulted ceiling, however, remained decorated in the
original pattern of constellations as seen from the motherworld, and it was toward those constellations that the climate
adjusters pulled the hot fetid air generated by the press of
bodies below.

Den Broohnin didn't mind the heat, nor the jostling cele-
brants around him. His mind was occupied with other matters. He kept to the rear of the crowd, an easy thing to do since
everyone else in Freedom Hall was pushing toward the front
for a better look at Metep VII. It was Insurrection Day, anni-
versary of the outworlds' break with Earth.

Broohnin blended easily with the crowd. He stood an
average one-point-eight meters tall and wore his black hair
and beard close-cropped in the current Throne fashion. His
build was heavy, tending toward paunchy; his one-piece casual
suit had a grimy, worn appearance. A single distinguishing
feature was a triangular, thumbnail-sized area of scar tissue on

his right cheek, which could have resulted from a burn or a laceration; only Broohnin knew it had resulted from the crude excision of a patch of Nolevatol rot by his father when he was five years old.

The good citizens around him did not notice that his attention, unlike theirs, was not on the dais. Metep VII, "Lord of the Outworlds," was making the annual Insurrection Day speech, the 206th such speech, and Broohnin was certain that this one would be no different from all the others he had suffered through over the years. His attention was riveted instead on one of the ornate columns that lined the sides of Freedom Hall. There was a narrow ledge between the columns and the outer wall, and although he could detect no movement, Broohnin knew that one of his guerrillas was up there preparing to end the career and the life of Metep VII.

Hollowing out the upper section of one of those columns had been no easy task. Constructed of the Throne equivalent of granite, it had taken a high-energy cutting beam three days to carve out a man-sized niche. The huge amphitheater was reserved for rare state occasions and deserted most of the time; still, it had been nerve-wracking to sneak four men and the necessary equipment in and out on a daily basis.

Yesterday morning the chosen assassin had been sealed into the niche, now lined with a thermoreflective epoxy. He had a small supply of food, water, and air. When the Imperial security forces did an infra-red sweep of the hall on Insurrection Day morning, he went unnoticed.

He was out of the niche now, his joints flexing and extending in joyous relief as he assembled his lightweight, long-focus energy rifle. Today had to be the day, he told himself. Metep had been avoiding the public eye lately; and the few times he did appear, he was surrounded by deflectors. But now, on Insurrection Day, he was allowing himself a few minutes out in the open for tradition's sake. And the assassin knew those moments had to be put to use. Metep had to die . . . it was the only way to bring down the Imperium.

He had no worry for himself. It was Broohnin's contention, and he agreed, that the man who killed Metep would have little fear of official reprisals. The whole Imperium would quickly fall apart and he would be acclaimed a hero at best, or lost in the mad scuffle at worst. Either way, he would come out of the whole affair in one piece—*if* he could kill Metep before the guards found him.

He affixed a simple telescopic sight. The weapon was compatible with the most up-to-date autosighter, but that idea had been vetoed because of the remote possibility that even the minute amount of power used by such an attachment might set off a sensor and alert the security force to his presence. Sliding into a prone position, he placed the barrel's bipod brace on the edge of the narrow ledge. Metep stood sixty meters ahead of him. This would be easy—no adjustments for distance, no leading the target. The proton beam would travel straight and true at the speed of light.

The assassin glanced down at the crowd. The forward part of his body was visible—barely so—only to those at the far side of the hall, and they were all looking at the dais. Except for one . . . he had an odd sensation that whenever he glanced at the crowd, someone down there snapped his or her head away. It couldn't be Broohnin—he was at the back of the hall waiting for Metep's death. No, somebody had spotted him. But why no alarm? Perhaps it was a sympathizer down there, or someone who took him for a member of the security force.

Better get the whole thing over with. One shot . . . that was all it would take, all he would get. Alarms would go off as soon as he activated his rifle's energy chamber and scanners would triangulate his position in microseconds; security forces would move in on him immediately. One shot, and then he would have to scramble back into his niche in the column. But Metep would be dead by then, a neat little hole burned through his brain.

Almost against his will, he glanced again to his right, and *again* experienced the uncanny sensation that someone on the fringe of the crowd down there had just turned his head away. But he could not pinpoint the individual. He had a feeling it could be one of the people near the wall . . . male, female, he couldn't say.

Shrugging uncomfortably, he faced forward again and set his right eye into the sight, swiveled ever so slightly . . . there! Metep's face—fixed smile, earnest expression—trapped in the crosshairs. As he lifted his head from the sight for an instant's perspective, he felt a stinging impact on the right side of his throat. Everything was suddenly red . . . his arms, his hands, the weapon . . . all bright red. Vision dimmed as he tried to raise himself from the now slippery ledge, then it brightened into blazing white light, followed by total, eternal darkness.

A woman in the crowd below felt something wet on her left

cheek and put a hand up to see what it was. Her index and middle fingers came away sticky and scarlet. Another large drop splattered on her left shoulder, then a steady crimson stream poured over her. The ensuing screams of the woman and others around her brought the ceremony to a halt and sent Metep VII scurrying from the dais.

A telescoping platform was brought in from the maintenance area and raised to the ledge. To the accompaniment of horrified gasps from the onlookers, the exsanguinated corpse of the would-be assassin and his unused weapon were lowered to the floor. The cause of death was obvious to all within view: a hand-sized star-shaped disk edged with five curved blades had whirled into the man's throat and severed the right carotid artery.

As the body was being trucked away, an amplified voice announced that the remainder of the evening's program was canceled. Please clear the hall. Imperial guards, skilled at crowd control, began to herd the onlookers toward the exits.

Broohnin stood fast in the current, his eyes fixed on his fallen fellow guerrilla as the crowd eddied past.

"Who did this?" he muttered softly under his breath. Then louder. *"Who did this!"*

A voice directly to his right startled him. "We don't know who's behind these assassination attempts, sir. But we'll find them, have no fear of that. For now, though, please keep moving."

It was one of the Imperial Guard, a young one, who had overheard and misunderstood him, and was now edging him into the outward flow. Broohnin nodded and averted his face. His underground organization was unnamed and unknown. The Imperium was not at all sure that a unified revolutionary force even existed. The incidents—the bombings, the assassination attempts on Metep—had a certain random quality about them that led the experts to believe that they were the work of unconnected malcontents. The sudden rash of incidents was explained as me-tooism: one terrorist act often engendered others.

Still, he kept his face averted. Never too careful. Breaking from the crowd as soon as he reached the cool dark outside, Broohnin headed for Imperium Park at a brisk pace. He spat at the sign that indicated the name of the preserve.

Imperium! he thought. *Everything has "Imperium" or "Imperial" before it!* Why wasn't everyone else on the planet as sick of those words as he was?

He found his brooding tree and seated himself under it, back against the bole, legs stretched out before him. He had to sit here and control himself. If he stayed on his feet, he would do something foolish like throwing himself into the lake down at the bottom of the hill. Holding his head back against the firmness of the *keerni* tree behind him, Den Broohnin closed his eyes and fought the despair that was never very far away. His life had been one long desperate fight against that despair and he felt he would lose the battle tonight. The blackness crept in around the edges of his mind as he sat and tried to find some reason to wait around for tomorrow.

He wanted to cry. There was a huge sob trapped in his chest and he could not find a way to release it.

The revolution was finished. Aborted. Dead. His organization was bankrupt. The tools for hollowing out the column had drained their financial reserves; the weapon, purchased through underground channels, had dried them up completely. But every mark would have been well spent were Metep VII dead now.

Footsteps on the path up from the lake caused Broohnin to push back the blackness and part his eyelids just enough for a look. A lone figure strolled aimlessly along, apparently killing time. Broohnin closed his eyes briefly, then snapped them open again when he heard the footsteps stop. The stroller had halted in front of him, waiting to be noticed.

"Den Broohnin, I believe?" the stranger said once he was sure he had Broohnin's attention. His tone was relaxed, assured, the words pronounced with an odd nasal lilt that was familiar yet not readily identifiable. The man was tall—perhaps five or six centimeters taller than Broohnin—slight, with curly, almost kinky blond hair. He had positioned himself in such a manner that the light from the nearest glo-globe shone over his right shoulder, completely obscuring his facial features. A knee-length cloak further blunted his outline.

"How do you know my name?" Broohnin asked, trying to find something familiar about the stranger, something that would identify him. He drew his legs under him and crouched, ready to spring. There was no good reason for this man to accost him in Imperium Park at this hour. Something was very wrong.

"Your name is the very least of my knowledge." Again, that tantalizing accent. "I know you're from Nolevatol. I know you came to Throne twelve standard years ago and have, in the past two, directed a number of assassination attempts against the life of the current Metep. I know the number of men in your little guerrilla band, know their names and where they live. I even know the name of the man who was killed tonight."

"You know who killed him, then?" Broohnin's right hand had slipped toward his ankle as the stranger spoke, and now firmly grasped the handle of his vibe-knife.

The silhouette of the stranger's head nodded. "One of my associates. And the reason for this little meet is to inform you that there will be no more assassination attempts on Metep VII."

In a single swift motion, Broohnin pulled the weapon from its sheath, activated it, and leaped to his feet. The blade, two centimeters wide and six angstroms thick, was a linear haze as it vibrated at 6,000 cycles per second. It had its limitations as a cutting tool, but certainly nothing organic could resist it.

"I wonder what your 'associates' will think," Broohnin said through clenched teeth as he approached the stranger in a half-crouch, waving the weapon before him, "when they find your head at one end of Imperium Park and your body at the other?"

The man shrugged. "I'll let them tell you themselves."

Broohnin suddenly felt himself grabbed by both arms from behind. The vibe-knife was deftly removed from his grasp as he was slammed back against the tree and held there, stunned, shaken, and utterly helpless. He glanced right and left to see two figures, a male and a female, robed in black. The hair of each was knotted at the back and a red circle was painted in the center of each forehead. All sorts of *things* hung from the belts that circled their waists and crossed their chests. He felt a sudden urge to retch. He knew what they were . . . he'd seen holos countless times.

Flinters!

II

> There used to be high priests to explain the ways of the king—who *was* the state—to the masses. Religion is gone, and so are kings. But the state remains, as do the high priests in the guise of Advisers, Secretaries of Whatever Bureau, public relations people, and sundry apologists. Nothing changes.
>
> from THE SECOND BOOK OF KYFHO

Metep VII slumped in his high-back chair at the head of the long conference table. Four other silent men sat in similar but smaller chairs here and there along the length of the table, waiting for the fifth and final member of the council of advisers to arrive. The prim, crisp executive image had fallen away from the "Lord of the Outworlds." His white brocade coat was fastened only halfway up, and his dark brown hair, tinged with careful amounts of silver, was sloppily pushed off his forehead. The sharply chiseled facial features sagged now with fatigue as he rubbed the reddened, irritated whites of his blue eyes. He was one very frightened man.

The walls, floor, and ceiling were paneled with *keerni* wood; the conference table, too, was constructed of that grainy ubiquitous hardwood. Metep II, designer of this particular room, had wanted it that way. To alter it would be to alter history. And so it remained.

Forcing himself to relax, he leaned back and let his gaze drift toward the ceiling where holographic portraits of his six predecessors were suspended in mid-air. It came to rest on Metep I.

Anyone ever try to kill you? he mentally asked the rugged, lifelike face.

Metep I's real name had been Fritz Renders. A farmer by birth, revolutionary by choice, he had led his ragtag forces in a seemingly hopeless assault against the Earth governorship headquartered here on Throne—then called Caelum—and had succeeded. Fritz Renders had then declared the outworlds independent of Earth, and himself "Lord of the Outworlds." That was 206 years ago today, the first Insurrection Day. The rest of the colonials on other planets rose up then and threw out their own overseers. Earth's day of absentee landlordship over her star colonies was over. The Outworld Imperium was born.

It was an empire in no sense of the word, however. The colonials would not stand for such a thing. But the trappings of a monarchy were felt to be of psychological importance when dealing with Earth and the vast economic forces based there. The very name, Outworld Imperium, engendered a sense of permanence and monolithic solidarity. Nominally at least, it was not to be trifled with.

In actuality, however, the Imperium was a simple democratic republic which elected its leader to a lifelong term—with recall option, of course. Each leader took the title of Metep and affixed the proper sequential number, thereby reinforcing the image of power and immutability.

How things had changed, though. The first council meeting such as this had taken place in the immediate post-revolutionary period and had been attended by a crew of hardbitten, hard-drinking revolutionaries and the radical thinkers who had gravitated to them. And that was the entire government.

Now look at it: in two short centuries the Outworld Imperium had grown from a handful of angry, victorious interstellar colonials into a . . . business. Yes, that's what it was: A business. But one that produced nothing. True, it employed more people than any other business in the outworlds; and its gross income was certainly much larger, though income was not received in free exchange for goods or services, but rather through taxation. A business . . . one that never showed a profit, was always in the red, continually borrowing to make up deficits.

A rueful smile briefly lit Metep VII's handsome middle-aged face as he followed the train of thought to its end: lucky for this business that it controlled the currency machinery or it would have been bankrupt long ago!

His gaze remained fixed on the portrait of Metep I, who in his day had known everyone in the entire government by face and by name. Now . . . the current Metep was lucky if he knew who was in the executive branch alone. It was a big job, being Metep. A high-pressure job, but one with enough power and glory to suit any man. Some said the position had come to hold more power than a good man would want and an evil man would need. But those were the words of the doom-and-gloomers who dogged every great man's heels. He had power, yes, but he didn't make all the decisions. All the civilized out-worlds, except for a few oddball societies, sent representatives to the legislature. They had nominal power . . . nuisance value, really. The real power of the outworlds lay with Metep and his advisers on the Council of Five. When Haworth arrived, the true decision-makers of the Imperium would all be in this one room.

All in all, it was a great life, being Metep. At least until recently . . . until the assassination attempts had started. There had been one previous attempt on a Metep—back when the legal tender laws were being enforced by Metep IV—but that had been a freak incident; a clerk in the agriculture bureau had been passed over at promotion time and laid all blame on the presiding Metep.

What was going on here and now was different. Tonight was the third attempt in the past year. The first two had been bombs—one in his private flitter, and then another hidden in the main entrance from the roof pad of the palatial estate occupied by every Metep since III. Both had been found in time, thank the Core. But this third attack, the one tonight . . . this one had unnerved him. The realization that a man had been able to smuggle an energy weapon into Freedom Hall and had actually been in position to fire was bad enough. But add to that the manner in which he was stopped—his throat sliced open by some grotesquely primitive weapon—and the result was one terrified head of state.

Not only was some unknown, unheralded group trying to bring his life to an end, but another person or group, equally unknown and unheralded, was trying to preserve it. He did not know which terrified him more.

Daro Haworth, head of the Council of Five, entered then, bringing the low hum of conversation around the table and Metep VII's reverie to an abrupt halt. Born on Derby, educated on Earth, he was rumored in some quarters to wield as much power on Throne and in the Imperium as the Metep himself. That sort of talk irked Metep VII, whose ego was unsteady of late. But he had to admit that Haworth possessed a deviously brilliant mind. Given any set of rules or regulations, the man could find a loophole of sufficient size to slip through any program the Metep and his council desired. Moved by neither the spirit nor the letter of any constitutional checks and balances, he could find ways to make almost anything legal—or at least give it a patina of legality. And in those rare instances when his efforts were thwarted, he found the legislature more than willing to modify the troublesome law to specification. A remarkable man.

His appearance, too, was remarkable: deeply tanned skin set against hair bleached stark white, a decadent affectation he had picked up during his years on Earth and never lost. It made him instantly identifiable.

"Afraid I don't have anything new to tell you on that dead assassin, Jek," Haworth said, sliding into the chair directly to the Metep's right. Like all members of the Council of Five, he called Metep VII by the name his parents had given him forty-seven standard years ago: Jek Milian. Other cronies who had known him way back when and had helped him reach his present position used it, too. But only in private. In public he was Metep VII—to everyone.

"Don't call him an 'assassin.' He didn't succeed so he's not an assassin." Metep straightened in his chair. "And there's nothing new on him?"

Haworth shook his head. "We know his name, we know where he lived, we know he was a dolee. Beyond that, it's as if he lived in a vacuum. We have no line on his acquaintances, or how he spent his time."

"Damn dolees!" was muttered somewhere down the table.

"Don't damn them," Haworth said in his cool, cultured tones. "They're a big vote block—keep a little money in their pockets, give them Food Vouchers to fill their bellies, and there'll be no recall . . . ever. But getting back to this would-be assassin. We *will* get a line on him; and when we do, it will be the end of the group behind these assassination attempts."

"What about that thing that killed him?" Metep asked. "Any idea where it came from? I've never seen anything like it."

"Neither have I," Haworth replied. "But we've found out what it is and it's nothing new. Couple of thousand years old, in fact." He hesitated.

"Well?" The entire table was listening intently.

"It's a *shuriken*, used on old Earth before the days of atmospheric flight." A murmur arose among the other four councilors.

"A relic of some sort?" Metep said.

"No. It's new . . . manufactured only a few years ago." Again the hesitation, then: "And it was manufactured on Flint."

Silence, as deep and complete as that of interstellar space, enveloped the table. Krager, a short, crusty, portly old politico, broke it.

"A Flinter? Here?"

"Apparently so," Haworth said, his delicate fingers forming a steeple in front of him on the table. "Or somebody trying to make us think there's a Flinter here. However, judging by the accuracy with which that thing was thrown, I'd say we were dealing with the real thing."

Metep VII was ashen, his face nearly matching the color of his jacket. "Why me? What could a Flinter possibly have against me?"

"No, Jek," Haworth said in soothing tones. "You don't understand. Whoever threw the *shuriken* saved your life. Don't you see that?"

What Metep saw was a colossal reversal of roles. The man who thought himself the gamemaster had suddenly become a pawn on a board between two opposing forces, neither identified and both totally beyond his control. This was what was most disturbing: he had no control over recent events. And that, after all, was why he was Metep—to control events.

He slammed his palm down on the table. "Never mind what I see! There's a concerted effort on out there to kill me! I've

been lucky so far, but I'm not supposed to be relying on luck
. . . I'm supposed to be relying on skilled security personnel.
Yet two bombs were planted—"

"They were found," Haworth reminded him in a low voice.

"Yes, found." Metep VII lowered his voice to match the
level of his chief adviser's. "But they shouldn't have been
planted in the first place! And tonight tops everything!" His
voice began to rise. "There should have been no way for anyone to get an energy weapon into Freedom Hall tonight—but
someone did. There should have been no way for him to set up
that weapon and sight in on me—but he did. And who stopped
him before he could kill me?" His eyes ranged the table. "*Not*
one of my security people, but someone, I'm now told, from
Flint! *From Flint!* And there shouldn't even *be* a Flinter on
Throne without my knowing about it! My entire security setup
has become a farce and I want to know why!"

His voice had risen to a scream by the time he finished and
the Council of Five demonstrated concerned respect for his
tantrum by pausing briefly in absolute silence.

Haworth was the first to speak, his tone conciliatory, concerned. "Look, Jek. This has us frightened as much as you.
And we're as confused as you. We're doing our best to
strengthen security and whip it into shape, but it takes time.
And let's face it: we're simply not accustomed to this type of
threat. It's never been a problem before."

"Why is it a problem now? Why me? That's what I want to
know!"

"I can't answer that. At least not yet. In the past, we've
always been able to funnel off any discontent in the direction
of Earth, always been able to point to Sol System and say,
'There's the enemy.' It used to work beautifully. Now, I'm
not so sure."

"It still works." Metep VII had regained his composure
now and was again leaning back in his chair.

"To a certain extent, of course it does. But apparently
there's someone out there who isn't listening." Haworth
paused and glanced at the other members of the council.
"Somebody out there thinks *you're* the enemy."

III

Never initiate force against another.
That should be the underlying principle of your life. But should someone
do violence to you, retaliate without
hesitation, without reservation, without quarter, until you are sure that he
will never wish to harm—or never be
capable of harming—you or yours
again.

from THE SECOND BOOK OF KYFHO
(Revised Eastern Sect Edition)

Nimble fingers ran through his hair, probed his clothes and
shoes. Finding him void of further weaponry, they released
him.

"That's Josef to your right"—the male figure bowed
almost imperceptibly at the waist—"and Kanya to your
left"—another bow. "Kanya is personally responsible for the
death of your assassin back there in Freedom Hall. I'm told
her skill with the *shuriken* is without parallel."

It's over was the only thought Broohnin's mind could hold
at that moment. If Metep was able to hire protection of this
caliber, then all hope of killing him was gone.

"How did he do it?" Broohnin said when he was finally

able to speak. "What did he have to pay to get Flinters here to do his dirty work for him?"

The blond man laughed—Broohnin still could not make out any facial features—and there was genuine amusement in the sound.

"Poor Den Broohnin! Can't quite accept the fact that there are people other than himself who do not have a price!" The voice took on a sterner tone after a brief pause. "No, my petty revolutionary, we are not here at Metep's bidding. We are here to destroy him. And by 'him' I do not mean the man, but everything he represents."

"Lies!" Broohnin said as loudly as he dared. "If that was true you wouldn't have interfered tonight!"

"How can a man who has built up such an efficient little terrorist group right under the noses of the Imperial Guard be so naïve about the Imperium itself? You're not dealing with a monarchy, my friend, despite all the showy trappings. The Outworld Imperium is a republic. There's no royal bloodline. Metep VII's term is for life, granted, but when he's gone his successor will be elected, just as he was. And should Metep VII be assassinated, a temporary successor will be in his place before the day is out."

"No! The Imperium will collapse! The people—"

"The people will be terrified!" the stranger said in harsh, clipped tones. "Your ill-conceived terrorism only serves to frighten them into clamoring for sterner laws and harsher measures against dissent. You only end up strengthening the very structure you wish to pull down. *And it must cease immediately!*"

The stranger paused to allow his words to penetrate. Then: "The only reason you remain alive at this point is because I have some small use for certain members of your organization. I am therefore giving you a choice: you may fit yourself into my plan or you may return to Nolevatol. Should you choose the former, you will meet me in the rearmost booth of the White Hart Tavern on Rocklynne Boulevard tomorrow night; should you choose the latter, you will be on an orbital shuttle by that time. Choose to oppose me and you will not survive one standard day."

He gave a short, quick bow and strolled back the way he had come. The Flinters disappeared into the darkness with a whisper of sound and Broohnin was suddenly alone once more under his tree. It was as if nothing had happened. As if the entire exchange had been a hallucination.

He had a sudden urge to move, to get where the lights were bright and there were lots of people around. Thoughts swirled through his consciousness in a confused scramble as his pace graduated from a walk to a loping run from the park. There were Flinters on Throne . . . they were here to bring down the Imperium . . . that should have been a cause for rejoicing but it wasn't. Reinforcements had arrived but they might as well be aliens from another galaxy as Flinters.

No one knew anything for sure about Flinters beyond the fact that every member of their culture went about heavily armed and was skilled in the use of virtually every weapon devised by man throughout recorded history. They kept to themselves on their own little world and were rumored to hire out occasionally as mercenaries. But no one could ever document where or when. No traders were allowed to land on Flint —all commerce was conducted from orbit. The Flinters had no relations with Earth and did not recognize the Imperium as the legitimate government of anything. A sick society, by all accepted standards, but one that had proven viable and surprisingly unaggressive.

Broohnin slowed his pace as he reached the well-lit commercial district. Only a few people dawdled about. Even here in Primus, seat of the Imperium and capital of the most cosmopolitan of the outworlds, people went to bed early. News of an attempted assassination on Metep had driven them off the streets even sooner. Dolees were an exception, of course. Excitement of any sort stimulated them, and since they had nothing ahead of them the next day, they could stay out to all hours if they wished. Sometimes that meant trouble. Violent trouble. An unfortunate outsider, or even one of their own, could be beaten, vibed, or blasted for a few marks or just to alleviate the bleakness of their everyday existence.

On any other night Broohnin would have felt uneasy to be weaponless as he passed through knots of bored young dolees. The possibility that a Flinter might be watching him from the shadows erased all other fears, however. The youths ignored him, anyway. He was on the dole himself, sheltered and warmed by rent and clothing allowances, fed via Food Vouchers. And he was scruffy enough to pass for one of them. When he finally reached his side-street, one-room flat, he sealed the door behind him and flopped on the thin pneumatic mattress in the corner. And began to shake.

He was no longer faceless. Playing the guerrilla, the unseen terrorist, striking from the shadows and running and striking again was exciting, exhilarating. He could remain a shadow, an anonymous symbol of revolt. He could go down to the public vid areas and mingle with the watchers as reports of his latest terrorist acts were replayed in all their holographic splendor.

But that was over now. Someone knew his name, where he came from, and all he had done. And what one man could learn, so could others.

Flinters! He couldn't get over it. Why was Flint involving itself in the overthrow of the Imperium? Its attitude toward interplanetary matters had always been strict non-involvement. Earth and the rest of Occupied Space could fall into the galactic core for all Flint cared. Why were Flinters here now?

And that other one . . . the blond man. He was no Fiinter. His accent hovered on the brink of recognition, ready to fall into place. But not yet. That was not what was bothering Broohnin, however. The most deeply disturbing aspect of the scene back in Imperium Park was the realization that the blond man seemed to be in command of the Flinters. And nobody tells Flinters what to do. They have utter contempt for all would-be rulers and barely recognize the existence of the rest of humanity . . . with the possible exception of the residents of the planet Tolive—

Tolive! Broohnin rose to a sitting position. *That* was the blond man's accent—he was a Tolivian! And that was the connection between him and the Flinters. Outworld history lessons from his primary education trickled back to him as the associations multiplied.

The key was Kyfho, a staunchly individualistic, anarcho-capitalist philosophy born on Earth before the union of the Eastern and Western Alliances. Its adherents became outcasts on the crowded collectivist motherworld, forming tight, tiny enclaves in an attempt to wall out the rest of the world. An impossible task. The all-pervasive world government seeped through every chink in their defenses and brought the movement to near extinction.

The interstellar colonization program saved it. Any sufficiently large group of prospective colonists meeting the given requirements of average age and rudimentary skills was given free transportation one way to an Earth-class planet. It was understood that there would be no further contact with Earth and no rescue should the colony run into trouble. A sink-or-swim proposition. Earth had its hands full managing the awesome mass of its own population, the solar system colonies, and its own official star colonies. It could afford neither the talent nor the expense of playing guardian to a host of fledgling interstellar settlements.

The response was overwhelming. The followers of every utopian philosophy on Earth sent delegations to the stars to form the perfect society. Splinter colonies, as they came to be known, were sent off in every direction. Wherever an exploration team had discovered an Earth-class planet, a splinter group was landed. Tragically and predictably, many failed to survive a single turn around the primary. But a significant percentage hung on and kept on, making mankind an interstellar race in the truest sense.

The program served two purposes. It gave divergent philosophies a chance to test their mettle . . . if they thought they had the answers to humanity's social ills, why not form a colonial group, migrate to a splinter world, and prove it? The program's second purpose directly benefited the newly unified Earth state by unloading a host of dissidents on the stars, thereby giving it some time to consolidate its global reach. The plan worked beautifully. The troublemakers found the offer irresistible and Earth once more became a nice place for bureaucrats to live. It was such an easy and efficient solution . . . but one that Earth would pay for dearly in the future.

By the time the splinter colony program was getting started, the Kyfho adherents had mitosed into two distinct but cordial factions. Each applied separately for splinter colony status and each was approved. The first group, composed of rationalists and intellectual purists, was a quiet, introspective lot, and named its planet Tolive. The second group wound up on a harsh, rocky planet called Flint. Its members had been raised for the most part in the Eastern Alliance and had somehow blended Kyfho with remnants of old Asian cultures; each adherent had become an army unto him- or herself.

Like most splinter colonies, both groups had major problems and upheavals during their first century of existence, but both survived with their own form of the Kyfho philosophy intact. It had been that philosophy which kept both planets aloof when the rest of the splinter colonies joined Earth in the establishment of an outworld trade network, and subsequently spared them the necessity of joining in the revolution that broke Earth's resultant economic stranglehold on those very same outworlds. Neither Tolive nor Flint had taken any part in the formation of the Outworld Imperium and had ignored it during its two centuries of existence.

But they were not ignoring it now, as Den Broohnin was well aware. Flint and Tolive were actively involved in bringing down the Imperium. Why? There would always be a philosophical link between the two cultures, a bond that the rest of the outworlds could neither share nor understand. Perhaps it was something in that very philosophy which was bringing them into the fray. Broohnin knew nothing about Kyfho . . . did not even know what the word meant.

Or was it something else? The blond stranger seemed to have eyes everywhere. Perhaps he knew some secret plans of Metep and his Council of Five that would explain the sudden appearance of Flinters and Tolivians on Throne. Something big must be in the wind to make them reverse their centuries-old policy of non-involvement.

Broohnin dimmed the light and lay back on the mattress. He was not going to leave Throne, that was certain. Not after all the effort he had invested in Metep's downfall. Nor was he going to risk being killed by some bizarre Flinter weapon.

No, he was going to be at the White Hart tomorrow night and he was going to be all ears. He was going to agree to any conditions the blond man wanted and was going to play along as long as it seemed to suit his own purposes. For if nothing else, Den Broohnin was a survivor.

VOLUME I   NUMBER 1

THE ROBIN HOOD READER

Look to the Skies!

A
TAX
REFUND
IS
COMING

Look to the Skies!

─── *The Economic Weather Eye* ───

PRICE INDEX (using the 115th year of the
Imperium—when the Imperial
mark became mandatory legal
tender—as base year of 100)   154.6

MONEY SUPPLY (M3)   949.4

UNEMPLOYMENT LEVEL   7.6%

	Imperial Marks	Solar Credits
GOLD (Troy ounce)	226.2	131.7
Silver (Troy ounce)	10.3	5.9
Bread (1 kg. loaf)	.62	1.81

IV

No state shall . . . make anything but
gold and silver coin a tender in payment of debts. . . .

THE CONSTITUTION OF
THE UNITED STATES

"What *are* these things?"

"Flyers. Nobody seems to know where they came from but
they're all over the city. I thought they'd amuse you."

After Metep had the courtesy of first look, Haworth passed
other copies of the flyer across the table to the rest of the
Council of Five. The mood around the table had relaxed considerably since Metep's outburst. Expressions of deep concern
for his safety had mollified the leader and it was decided to
lower further his already low public profile.

"Robin Hood, eh?" Krager said, smiling sardonically as
he glanced over the flyer. He looked to Haworth. "Wasn't
he . . . ?"

"An old Earth myth, right," Haworth replied with a nod.
"He robbed from the rich and gave to the poor."

"I wonder which of the rich he plans to rob?"

"Not from me, I hope," Bede, the slim Minister of Transportation, said with a laugh. "And what's this little insignia
top and bottom? Looks like an omega with a star in it. That

23

supposed to mean something?''

Haworth shrugged. ''Omega is the last letter in the Greek alphabet. If this is some revolutionary group, it might mean the Last Revolution or something equally dramatic. 'The Last Revolution of the Star Colonies.' How does that sound?''

''It doesn't sound good,'' Metep said. ''Especially when they appear on the night of an assassination attempt.''

''Oh, I doubt there's a link,'' Haworth said slowly. ''If there were, the flyers would have been printed up in advance proclaiming your death. This mentions nothing about death or disaster. Probably a bunch of Zem addicts, but I'm having security check it out anyway.''

Bede's brow was furrowed. ''Isn't omega also the ohm, symbol for resistance? Electrical resistance?''

''I believe it is,'' Krager said. ''Perhaps this Robin Hood group—it may be one man for all we know—considers itself some sort of resistance or revolutionary group, but the message in this flyer is totally economic. And well informed, too. Look at that price index. Sad but true. It takes 150 current marks to buy now what 100 marks bought back in the 115th year. That's a lot of inflation in eighty years.''

''Not really,'' Haworth said, looking up from the notes before him on the table.

''That's Earthie talk,'' Krager said, an ill-concealed trace of annoyance in his tone. ''The Earthies are used to inflation by now—''

''Earth has recently brought her economy under control and—''

'' —but we outworlders are still suspicious of it.'' The older man had raised his voice to cut off Haworth's interjection and had perhaps put unnecessary emphasis on the word ''we.'' Haworth's Earth-gained education still raised hackles in certain quarters of the Imperium.

''Well, we'd all better *get* used to it,'' Haworth said, oblivious to any implied slur, ''because we're all going to be living with it for a long time to come.''

Amid the mutterings up and down the table, Metep VII's voice broke through. ''I take it, then, the new economic projections are in and that they're not good.''

''Not good at all,'' Haworth said. ''This downtrend is not one of the cyclic episodes the outworld economy has experienced from time to time in the past half dozen decades. We are in a slow, steady decline in exports to Earth with no slackening of our import growth rate. I don't have to tell any of you how serious that is."

They all knew. Knew too well.

"Any bright ideas on how we can turn it around—besides more inflation?" It was Krager speaking, and his tone had yet to return to neutral.

"Yes, as a matter of fact. But I'll get to that later. Those of you who have kept up to date know that we're caught in the middle of two ongoing trends. Earth's rigid population controls are paying off at last; their demand for grain and ore is decreasing, and at a faster rate than anyone expected. Outworld populations on the other hand, are expanding beyond our ability to keep up technologically. So our demand for Sol system hardware keeps growing."

"The answer is pretty obvious, I think," Metep VII said with bland assurance. "We've got to pump a lot more money into our own technical companies and make them more competitive with Earth's."

"How about an outright subsidy?" someone suggested.

"Or an import tax on Earth goods?" from another.

Haworth held up his hands. "This has to be a backdoor affair, gentlemen. A subsidy will have other industries wailing for some of the same. And an import tax will upset the whole economy by sending technical hardware prices into orbit. Jek's right, however. We have to pump money into the right industries, but discreetly. Very discreetly.

Krager again: "And where do we get it?"

"There are ways."

"Not by another tax, I hope. We're taking an average of one out of every three marks now—seven out of ten in the higher brackets. You saw what happened on Neeka when we announced that surcharge. Riots. And that dead girl. Not here on Throne, thank you!"

Haworth smiled condescendingly. "Taxes are useful, but crude. As you all know, I prefer adjustments in the money supply. The net result is the same—more revenue for us, less buying power for them—but the process is virtually undetectable."

"And dangerous."

"Not if handled right. Especially now while the Imperial mark still has some strength in the interstellar currency markets, we can shove a lot more currency out into the economy and reap the benefits before anyone notices. The good citizens will be happy because they'll see their incomes go up. Of course prices will go up faster, but we can always blame that on unreasonable wage demands from the guilds, or corporate profiteering. Or we can blame it on Earth—outworlders are always more than ready to blame Earth for anything that goes wrong. We have to be careful, of course. We have to prime the pump precisely to keep inflation at a tolerable level."

"It's at 6 per cent now," Krager said, irritated by Haworth's didactic tone.

"We can push it to 10."

"Too dangerous!"

"Stop your nonsensical objections, old man!" Haworth snarled. "You've been living with 6 per cent inflation—causing it, in fact!—for years. Now you balk at 10! Who are you play-acting for?"

"How dare—" Krager was turning red and sputtering.

"Ten per cent is absolutely necessary. Any less and the economy won't even notice the stimulus."

Metep VII and the rest of the Council of Five mulled this dictum. They had all become masters of economic manipulation under Haworth's tutelage, but 10 per cent . . . that marked the unseen border of monetary no-man's land. It was double-digit inflation, and there was something inherently terrifying about it.

"We can do it," Haworth said confidently. "Of course, we have Metep IV to thank for the opportunity. If he hadn't rammed through the legal tender laws eighty years ago, each outworld would still be operating on its own currency instead of the Imperial mark and we'd be helpless. Which brings me to my next topic . . ."

He opened the folder before him, removed a sheaf of one-mark notes, and dropped them on the table.

"I'd like to take the legal tender laws one step further."

Metep VII picked up one of the marks and examined it. The note was pristine, bright orange and fresh out of the duplicator, with the satin gloss imparted by the specially treated *keerni* wood pulp used to make it still unmarred by fingerprints and creases. Intricate scrollwork was printed around the perimeter on both sides; a bust of Metep I graced the obverse while a large, blunt *1* dominated the reverse. Different polymer sheets had been tried and discarded when the legal tender laws were introduced during the last days of Metep IV's reign, but the *keerni* paper held up almost as well and was far cheaper. He lifted the bill to his nose—smelled better, too.

"You're not thinking of going totally electronic like Earth, I hope," he asked Haworth.

"Exactly what I'm thinking. It's the only way to truly fine-tune the economy. Think of it: not a single financial transaction will be executed without the central computer knowing about it. We talk of subsidizing certain industries? With a totally electronic monetary system we can allot so much here, pull away just enough there . . . it's the only way to go when you're working with interstellar distances as we are. And it's worked for Earth."

Metep VII shook his head with deliberate, measured slowness. Here was one area of economic knowledge in which he knew he excelled over Haworth.

"You spent all that time on Earth, Daro," he said, "and got all that fine training in economic administration. But you've forgotten the people you're dealing with here. Outworlders are simple folk for the most part. They used to barter exclusively for their needs until someone started hammering coins out of gold or silver or whatever else was considered valuable on that particular colony. Metep IV damn near had a full-scale revolt on his hands when he started to enforce the legal tender laws and make the Imperial mark the one and only acceptable currency in the outworlds."

He held up a one-mark note. "Now you want to take even this away and change it to a little blip in some computer's memory bank? You intend to tell these people that they will no longer be allowed to have money they can hold and count and pass back and forth and maybe bury in the ground somewhere?" Metep VII smiled briefly, grimly, and shook his head again. "Oh no. There's already a maniac fringe group out there trying to do away with me. That's more than enough, thank you. If we even hinted at what you suggest, I'd have every man and woman on the outworlds who owns a blaster coming after me." He lifted a copy of *The Robin Hood Reader* in his other hand. "The author of this would be predicting my death rather than a tax refund. No, my friend. I have no intention of being the only Metep overthrown by a revolution."

He rose from his seat and his eyes came level with Haworth's. "Consider that idea vetoed."

Haworth looked away and glanced around the table for a

hint of support. He found none. Metep had veto power at council meetings. He also knew outworld mentality—that was how he became Metep. The matter was, for all intents and purposes, closed. He looked back to Metep VII, ready to frame a graceful concession, and noticed a puzzled expression on the leader's face. He was holding the two sheets of paper —the mark note in his left hand, *The Robin Hood Reader* in his right—staring at them, rubbing his thumbs over the surface of each.

"Something wrong, Jek?" Haworth asked.

The Metep raised each sheet in turn to his nose and sniffed. "Have there been any thefts of currency paper?" he asked, looking up and fixing Krager with his stare.

"No, of course not. We guard the blank paper as well as we guard the printed slips."

"This flyer is printed on currency paper," Metep VII stated.

"Impossible!" Krager, who was Minister of the Treasury, reached for one of the flyers on the table. He rubbed it, sniffed it, held it up to gauge the glare of light off its surface.

"Well?"

The old man nodded and leaned back in his form-fitting chair, a dumbfounded expression troubling his features. "It's currency paper all right."

Nothing was said for a long time. All present now realized that the author of the flyer that had been so easily dismissed earlier in the meeting was no fevered radical sweating in a filthy basement somewhere in Primus City, but rather a man or a group of men who could steal currency paper without anyone knowing. And who showed utter disdain for the Imperial mark.

V

"I sometimes think of what future historians will say of us. A single sentence will suffice for modern man: he fornicated and read the papers."

J. B. Clammence

The White Hart had changed drastically. The thin blond man whose name was Peter LaNague noticed it as soon as he entered. The décor was the same: the rich paneling remained, the solid *keerni* bar, the planked flooring . . . these were as inviolate as the prohibition against women customers. During the five standard years since he had last visited Throne and had supped and drunk in the White Hart, there had been no physical alterations or renovations.

The difference was in the mood and in the level of sound. The regulars didn't realize it, but there was less talk around the bar these days. No one except LaNague, after a five-year hiatus, noticed. The diminution of chatter, the lengthening of pauses, both had progressed by tiny increments over the years. It was not just that the group's mean age had progressed and that familiarity had lessened what they had left to say to one another. New faces had joined the ranks while some of the older ones had faded away. And yet the silence had crept along on its inexorable course.

The process was less evident in the non-restricted bars. The presence of women seemed to lift the mood and add a certain buoyancy to a room. The men wore different faces then, responding to the opposite sex, playing the game of being men, of being secure and confident, of having everything under control.

But when men got together in places where women could not go, places like the White Hart, they left the masks at home. There was little sense in trying to fool each other. And so a pall would seep through the air, intangible at first, but palpable by evening's end. Not gloom. No, certainly not gloom. These were not bad times. One could hardly call them good times, but they certainly weren't bad.

It was the future that was wrong. Tomorrow was no longer something to be approached with the idea of meeting it head on, of conquering it, making the most of it, using it to add to one's life. Tomorrow had become a struggle to hold one's own, or if that were not possible, to give up as little as possible as grudgingly as possible with as tough a fight as possible.

All men have dreams; there are first-order dreams, second-order dreams, and so on. For the men at the bar of the White Hart, the dreams were dying. Not with howls of pain in the night, but by slow alterations in aspiration, by a gradual lowering of sights. First-order dreams had been completely discarded, second-order dreams were on the way . . . maybe a few in the third-order could be preserved, at least for a little while.

There was the unvoiced conviction that a huge piece of machinery feeding on hope and will and self-determination, ceaselessly grinding them into useless power, had been levered into motion and that no one knew how to turn it off. And if they were quiet they could, on occasion, actually hear the gears turning.

LaNague took a booth in a far corner of the room and sat alone, waiting. He had been a regular at the bar for a brief period five years ago, spending most of his time listening. All the intelligence gathered by the investigators Tolive had sent to Throne over the years could not equal the insight into the local social system, its mood, its politics, gathered in one night spent leaning against the bar with these men. Some of the regulars with long tenures gave him a searching look tonight, sensing something familiar about him, and sensing too that he wanted to be alone.

If LaNague had judged the man correctly—and he hoped he had—Den Broohnin would walk through the front door momentarily. He would have to be handled carefully. Reason would be useless. Fear was the key: Just the right amount would bring him into line; too much and he would either run or attack like a cornered animal. A dangerous man, an explosive man, his co-operation was imperative if the plan was to maintain its schedule. But could his berserker tendencies be controlled? LaNague didn't know for sure, and that bothered him.

He reviewed what he knew about Broohnin. A native of Nolevatol's great farm lands, he had grown up with little education, spending most of his daylight hours trying to pull a crop from the alien soil of his family's farm. Friction between the boy and his father began and grew and culminated in young Den Broohnin fleeing the family farm—but only after beating his father senseless. He somehow made it to Throne where years on the streets of Primus toughened and seasoned him in the ways of city life.

Somewhere along the line he had come to the conclusion that the Imperium must fall and that he was the one to bring it down—by any means. For Broohnin the murder of the reigning Metep seemed the most direct way to accomplish this. That course of action had to be stopped, for it threatened to ruin all of LaNague's plans.

Ω

When Broohnin entered, the already low level of chatter at the bar lowered further as it does when any outsider ventures near an insular group such as this. He knew his uneasiness showed. His lips were tight behind his beard as his eyes scanned the room. He spotted a blond stranger waving from the corner. Conversation gradually returned to its previous level.

With every muscle in his body tense and ready to spring at the first sign of danger, Broohnin stalked warily to the booth and slid in opposite LaNague.

He was now truly seeing the stranger for the first time. He had spoken to a shadowy wraith last night; the figure before him now was flesh and blood . . . and not exactly an imposing figure. A thin, angular face with an aquiline nose dividing two green eyes, intense, unwavering, all framed with unruly almost kinky, blond hair. Long neck, long limbs, long tapered fingers, almost delicate. Alarmingly thin now without the bulk of last night's cloak, and dressed only in a one-piece shirtsuit and a vest, all dark green.

"Where are your friends?" Broohnin asked as his eyes roamed the room.

"Outside." The stranger, who already held a dark ale, signaled the barman, who brought the tray he had been holding aside. He placed before Broohnin a small glass of the colorless, potent liquor made from hybrid Throne corn with a water chaser beside it.

Broohnin ran the back of his hand across his mouth in an attempt to conceal his shock: this was what he drank, just the way he drank it. Any hope he had held of dealing with this man on an equal footing had been crushed beyond repair by that one little maneuver. He was completely outclassed and he knew it.

"Am I supposed to be impressed?"

"I certainly hope so. I want you to be in such complete and total awe of my organization and my approach to a . . . change . . . that you'll drop your own plans and join me."

"I don't see that I have much choice."

"You can go back to Nolevatol."

"That's hardly a choice. Neither is dealing with your Flinter friends." He lifted his glass. "To a new order, or whatever you have in mind."

The stranger hoisted his ale mug by the handle, but did not drink. He waited instead until Broohnin had swallowed his sip of liquor, then made his own toast.

"To *no* order."

"I'll drink to that," Broohnin said, and took another burning pull from his glass while the other quaffed half a mugful. That particular toast appealed to him. Perhaps this wouldn't turn out too badly after all.

"LaNague is the name," the stranger said. "Peter La-Nague." He brought out a small cube and laid it on the table. "The Flinters gave me this. It creates a spheroid shell that distorts all sound waves passing through its perimeter. Radius of about a meter. It's quite unlikely that anyone here would be much interested in our conversation, but we'll be discussing some sensitive matters, and with all the assassination attempts lately"—a pause here, a disapproving twist of the thin lips—"I don't want some overzealous citizen accusing us of sedition."

He pressed the top of the cube and suddenly the chatter

from the bar was muted and garbled. Not a single word was intelligible.

"Very handy," Broohnin said with an appreciative nod. He could think of dozens of uses immediately.

"Yes, well, the Flinter society is obsessed with the preservation of personal privacy. Nothing really new technologically. Only the pocket size is innovative. Now . . ."

"When does the Imperium fall?" Broohnin's interjected question was half facetious, half deadly earnest. He had to know.

LaNague answered with a straight face. "Not for years."

"Too long! My men won't wait!"

"They had better wait." The words hung in the air like a beckoning noose. Broohnin said nothing and kept his eyes on his glass as he swirled the colorless fluid within. The moment passed and LaNague spoke again.

"Most of your men are Throners, I believe."

"All but myself and one other."

"A very important part of my plan will require a group such as yours. It will help if they're natives. Will they co-operate?"

"Of course . . . especially if they have no other choice."

LaNague's head moved in a single, quick, emphatic shake. "I'm not looking for that kind of co-operation. I called you here because you seem to be an intelligent man and because we are both committed to bringing the Outworld Imperium to an end. You've developed an underground of sorts—an infrastructure of dedicated people and I don't think they should be denied the chance to play a part. But you and they must play according to my plan. I want to *enlist* your aid. The plan requires informed, enthusiastic participation. If that is beyond you and your cohorts, then you'll not participate at all."

Something was wrong here. Broohnin sensed it. Too much was being withheld. Something did not ring true, but he could not say where. And there was an air of—was it urgency?—about the slight man across the table from him. Under different circumstances he would have played coy and probed until he had learned exactly what was going on. But this fellow had Flinters at his beck and call. Broohnin wanted no part of any games with them.

"And just what is this plan of yours? What brings a Tolivian to Throne as a revolutionary?"

LaNague smiled. "I'm glad to see I didn't underestimate your quickness. The accent gave me away, I suppose?"

"That, and the Flinters. But answer the question."

"I'm afraid you're not in a position of confidence at this point. Be secure in the knowledge that the stage is being set to bring down the Imperium with a resounding crash—but without slaughter."

"Then you're a dreamer and a fool! You can't smash the Imperium without taking Metep and the Council of Five out of the picture. And the only way those fecaliths will be moved is to burn a few holes in their brain pans. *Then* see how fast things fall apart! Anything else is wasted time! Wasted effort! Futility!"

As he spoke, Broohnin's face had become contorted with rage, saliva collecting at the corners of his mouth and threatening to fly in all directions. His voice rose progressively in volume and by the end of his brief outburst he was shouting and pounding on the table. He caught himself with an effort, suddenly glad LaNague had brought the damper box along.

The Tolivian shook his head with deliberate slowness. "That will accomplish nothing but a changing of the guard. Nothing will be substantially different, just as nothing is substantially different now from the pre-Imperium days when Earth controlled the outworlds."

"You forget the people!" Broohnin said, knowing he sounded as if he were invoking an ancient god. "They know that everything's gone wrong. The Imperium's only two centuries old and already you can smell the rot! The people will rise up in the confusion following Metep's death and—"

"The people will do nothing! The Imperium has effectively insulated itself against a popular revolution on Throne—and only on Throne would a revolution be of any real significance. Insurgency on other worlds amounts to a mere inconvenience. They're light years away and no threat to the seat of power."

"There's no such thing as a revolution-proof government."

"I couldn't agree more. But think: more than half—*half!*— the people on Throne receive all or a good part of their income from the Imperium."

Broohnin snorted and drained his glass. "Ridiculous!"

"Ridiculous—but true." He began ticking off points on the fingers of his left hand: "Dolees, retirees, teachers, police and ancillary personnel, everyone in or connected to the armed forces"—then switched to his right—"Sanit workers, utility workers, tax enforcers/collectors, prison officials and all who

work for them, all the countless bureaucratic program shuf-
flers . . .'' He ran out of fingers. ''The list goes on to nau-
seating length. The watershed was quietly reached and quietly
passed eleven standard years ago when 50 per cent of Throne's
population became financially dependent on the Imperium. A
quiet celebration was held. The public was not invited.''

Broohnin sat motionless, the rim of his glass still touching his lower lip, a slack expression on his face as LaNague
watched him intently. Finally, he set the glass down.

''By the Core!'' The Tolivian was right!

''Ah! The light!'' Lanague said with a satisfied smile. ''You
now see what I meant by insulation: the state protects itself
from being bitten by becoming the hand that feeds. It insin-
uates itself into the lives of as many of its citizens as possible,
always dressed in the role of helper and benefactor but always
leaving them dependent on it for their standard of living. They
may not wind up loving the state, but they do wind up relying
on it to increasing degrees. And chains of economic need are
far harder to break than those of actual physical slavery.''

Broohnin's voice was hoarse. ''Incredible! I never
thought—''

''The process is not at all original with the Outworld Imperium, however. States throughout history have been doing it
with varying degrees of success. This one's been slyer than
most in effecting it.''

As he turned off the sound damper and signaled the waiter
for another round, the conversation drifting over from the bar
became mildly intelligible. After the drinks had been delivered
and the shield was operating again, LaNague continued.

''The Imperium has concentrated its benefits on the citizenry of Throne to keep them in bovine somnolence. The
other outworlds, with Flint and Tolive as notable exceptions,
get nothing but an occupation force—pardon me, 'defense
garrison' is what it's called, I believe. And why this disparity?
Because outraged citizens on other planets can be ignored;
outraged Throners could bring down the Imperium. The logical conclusion: to bring down the Imperium, you must incite
the citizens of Throne to outrage against the state. Against *the
state!* Not against a madman who murders elected officials
and thus creates sympathy for the state. *He* then becomes the
enemy instead of the state.''

Broohnin slumped back in his seat, his second drink untouched before him, a *danse macabre* of conflicting emótions whirling across his mind. He knew this was obviously a crucial moment. LaNague was watching him intently, waiting to see if he would accept an indirect approach to felling the Imperium. If he still insisted on a frontal assault, there would be trouble.

"Have I made myself clear?" LaNague asked, after allowing a suitable period of brooding silence. "Do you still think killing Metep will bring down the Imperium?"

Broohnin took a long slow sip of his drink, his eyes fixed on the glass in his hand, and hedged. "I'm not sure what I think right now."

"Answer honestly, please. This is too important a matter to cloud with face-saving maneuvers."

Broohnin's head shot up and his gaze held LaNague's. "All right—no. Killing Metep will not end the Imperium. But I still want him dead!"

"Why? Something personal?" LaNague appeared struck by Broohnin's vehemence.

"No . . . something very general. He's there!"

"And is that why you want the Imperium overthrown? Because it's there?"

"Yes!" Silence followed.

"I'll accept that," LaNague said after a moment's consideration. "And I can almost understand it."

"What about you?" Broohnin asked, leaning forward intently. "Why are you here? And don't tell me it's something personal—you've got money, power, and Flinters behind you. The Gnomes of Tolive wouldn't get involved in something like this unless there was some sort of profit to be made. What's their stake? And how, by the Core, are we going to pull this off?"

LaNague inclined his head slightly in acknowledgment of the "we" from Broohnin, then reached into his vest and withdrew three five-mark notes.

"Here is the Imperium's insulation. We will show the higher-ups and all who depend on it just how thin and worthless it really is. Part of the work has already been done for me by the Imperium itself." He separated the oldest bill and handed it to Broohnin. "Read the legend in the lower right corner there."

Broohnin squinted and read stiltedly: " 'Redeemable in gold on demand at the Imperial Treasury.' "

"Look at the date. How old is it?"

He glanced down, then up again. "Twenty-two years." Broohnin felt bewildered, and simultaneously annoyed at being bewildered.

LaNague handed over the second bill. "This one's only ten years old. Read *its* legend."

" '*This is legal tender for all debts, public and private, and is redeemable in lawful money at the Imperial Treasury.*' " Broohnin still had no idea where the demonstration was leading.

The third bill was handed over. "I picked this one up today —it's the latest model."

Broohnin read without being prompted. " '*This note is legal tender for all debts public and private.*' " He shrugged and handed back all three mark notes. "So what?"

"I'm afraid that's all I can tell you now." LaNague held up the oldest note. "But just think: a little over two standard decades ago this was, for all intents and purposes, *gold*. This" —he held up the new bill—"is just paper."

"And *that's* why you're trying to topple the Imperium?" Broohnin shook his head in disbelief. "You're crazier than I am!"

"I'll explain everything to you once we're aboard ship."

"Ship? What ship? I'm not going anywhere!"

"We're going to Earth. That is, if you want to come."

Broohnin stared as the truth hit him. "You're not joking, are you?"

"Of course not." The tone was testy. "There's nothing humorous about going to Earth."

"But why would—" He stopped short and drew in a breath, narrowing his eyes. "You'd better not be bringing Earthies into this! If you are, I'll wring your neck here and now and not an army of Flinters will save you!"

LaNague's face reflected disgust at the thought of complicity with Earth. "Don't be obscene. There's a man on Earth I must see personally. On his response to a certain proposal may well hinge the entire success or failure of my plan."

"Who is he? Chief Administrator or some other overgrown fecalith?"

"No. He's well known, but has nothing to do with the government. And he doesn't know I'm coming."

"Who is he?"

"I'll tell you when we get there. Coming?"

Broohnin shrugged. "I don't know . . . I just don't know. I've got to meet with my associates tonight and we'll discuss it." He leaned forward. "But you've got to tell me where all this is leading. I need something more than a few hints."

Broohnin had noted that LaNague's expression had been carefully controlled since the moment he had entered the tavern. A small repertoire of bland, casual expressions had played across his face, displayed for calculated effect. But true emotions came through now. His eyes ignited and his mouth became set in a fierce, tight line.

"Revolution, my dear Broohnin. I propose a quiet revolution, one without blood and thunder, but one which will shake this world and the entire outworld mentality such as no storm of violence ever shall. History is filled with cosmetic revolutions wherein a little paint is daubed on an old face or, in the more violent and destructive examples, a new head set on an old body. Mine will be different. Truly radical . . . which means it will strike at the root. I'm going to teach the outworlds a lesson they will never forget. When I'm through with the Imperium and everything connected with it, the people of the outworlds will swear to never again allow matters to reach the state they are in now. Never again!"

"But how, damn you?"

"By destroying these"—LaNague threw the mark notes on the table—"and substituting this." He reached into another pocket of his vest and produced a round metal disk, yellow, big enough to cover a dead man's eye, and heavy—very heavy. It was stamped on both sides with a star inside an ohm.

Ω

The circle was to meet at the usual place tonight. Broohnin always referred aloud to the members of his tiny revolutionist cadre as "my associates." But in his mind and in his heart they were always called "the Broohnin circle." It was a varied group—Professor Zachariah Brophy from Outworld U.; Radmon Sayers, an up-and-coming vid-caster; Seph Wolverton with the communications center; Gram Hootre in the Treasury Department; Erv Singh at one of the Regional Revenue Centers. There were a few fringe members who were in and out as the spirit moved them. The first two, Zack and Sayers, had been out lately, protesting murder as a method; the rest seemed to be going along, although reluctantly. But then, who else did they have?

There was only one man on the rooftop: Seph Wolverton.

"Where are the others?"

"Not coming," Seph said. He was a big-boned, hard-muscled man; a fine computer technician. "No one's coming."

"Why not? I called everyone. Left messages. I told them this was going to be an important meeting."

"You've lost them, Den. After last night, they're all convinced you're crazy. I've known you a long time now, and I'm not so sure they're wrong. You took all our money and hired that assassin without telling us, without asking our approval. It's over, Den."

"No, it's not! I started this group! You can't push me out—"

"Nobody's pushing. We're just walking away." There was regret in Seph's voice, but a note of unbending finality, too.

"Listen. I may be able to work a new deal. Something completely different." Broohnin's mind was racing to stay ahead of his tongue. "I made a contact tonight who may be able to put a whole new slant on this. A new approach to stopping the Imperium. Even Zack and Sayers won't want to miss out."

Seph was shaking his head. "I doubt it. They're—"

"Tell them to give it a chance!"

"It'll have to be *awfully* good before they'll trust you again."

"It will be. I guarantee it."

"Give me an idea what you're talking about."

"Not yet. Got to take a trip first."

Seph shrugged. "All right. We've got plenty of time. I don't think the Imperium's going anywhere." He turned without saying good-by and stepped into the drop chute, leaving Broohnin alone on the roof. He didn't like Seph's attitude. He would have much preferred angry shouts and raised fists. Seph looked at him as if he had done something disgusting. He didn't like that look.

Broohnin looked up at the stars. Whether he wanted to or not, it appeared he would be going to Earth with LaNague. There was no other choice left to him, no other way to hold on to the tattered remnants of "the Broohnin circle." He would use LaNague to pull everyone back together, and then take up again where he had left off. Once he got a feel for LaNague he was sure he could find ways to maneuver him into a useful position.

Off to Earth . . . and why not? Who could pass up a free trip like that anyway? Few outworlders ever got there. And right now he was curious enough about what was going on in that Tolivian head to go just about anywhere to find out.

VOLUME I ⊕ NUMBER 2

THE ROBIN HOOD READER

A Shot in the Arm

The duplicators at the Imperial Mint are working overtime
these days, turning out new mark notes at an alarming rate.
The idea is to give our sagging economy a "shot in the
arm," which is what deliberate inflation of the money supply
is called in Bureaucratese. The theory holds that the extra
marks in circulation will increase consumer buying power,
which will in turn increase production, which will lead to
greater employment, resulting in a further increase in buying
power, and so on.

Sounds good, but it doesn't work that way. With more marks
suddenly available to buy existing goods, the prices of those
goods go up. And stay up. Which means more marks are
needed.

Let's continue the medical analogy: it's like treating a
steadily weakening patient who's bleeding internally by
giving him a shot of Zemmelar and nothing else. True, he
feels better for a while, but he's still bleeding. After the
Zemmelar wears off, he's weaker than before. So you give
him another jolt of Zem and he feels better again, but for a
briefer period this time. He continues to weaken. Before
long, he's lost. Even if the internal bleeding halts spontaneously, he's too weak to respond . . . and he's now a
hopeless Zemmelar addict anyway.

The Economic Weather Eye

PRICE INDEX (using the 115th year of the Imperium—when the Imperial mark became mandatory legal tender—as base year of 100)		155.2
MONEY SUPPLY (M3)		942.6
UNEMPLOYMENT LEVEL		7.6%

	Imperial Marks	Solar Credits
GOLD (Troy ounce)	227.0	131.6
Silver (Troy ounce)	10.4	5.9
Bread (1 kg. loaf)	.62	1.83

VI

Nor law, nor duty bade me fight.
Nor public men nor cheering crowds.
A lonely impulse of delight
Drove to this tumult . . .

Yeats

Vincen Stafford hung lazily suspended alongside the *Lucky Teela* with only a slim cord restraining him from eternity. As Second Assistant Navigator, the fascinating but unenviable duty of checking out all the control module's external navigation equipment fell to him. The job required a certain amount of working familiarity with the devices, more than the regular maintenance crew possessed. Only someone in the Navigator Guild would do. And since Stafford had the least seniority imaginable—this was his first assignment from the guild—he was elected.

Although finished with the checklist, he made no move to return to the lock where he could remove his gear and regain his weight. Instead he floated free and motionless, his eyes fixed on the ring of cargo pods encircling the control module . . . a gently curving necklace of random, oddly shaped stones connected by an invisible thread, reflecting distant fire.

The outworld-Earth grain run was ready to move. The area here at the critical point in the gravity well of Throne's star was used as a depot for Earth-bound exports from many of the agricultural worlds. The cargo pods were dropped off and linked to each other by intersecting hemispheres of force. When the daisy chain was long enough to assure sufficient profit from the run, the control module and its crew were linked up and all was set to go.

This run would not be completely typical, however. There were two passengers bound for Earth aboard. Unusual. Few if any outworlders outside the diplomatic service had contact with Earth. The diplomats traveled in official cruisers, all others traveled any way they could. The two passengers within had to be wealthy—passage to Earth, even on a grain run, was not booked cheaply. They didn't look rich, those two . . . one dark of clothing, beard, and mood, the other blond and intense and clutching a small potted tree under his arm. An odd pair. Stafford wondered.

He realized he was wasting time. This was his maiden voyage in a navigational capacity and he had to be in top form. It had taken a long time for the guild to find him this post. After spending the required six standard years in intense encephaloaugmented study until he had become facile in every aspect of interstellar flight—from cosmology to subspace physics, from the intricacies of the proton-proton drive to the fail-safe aspects of the command module's thermostat—he was ready for the interstellar void. Unfortunately the void was not ready for him. The runs were not as frequent as they used to be and he had spent an unconscionably long time at the head of the list of applicants waiting for an assignment.

Vincen Stafford did not ask much of life. All he wanted was a chance to get in between the stars and earn enough to support himself and his wife. Perhaps to put away enough to eventually afford a home of their own and a family. No dreams of riches, no pot of gold.

When he had almost despaired of ever being assigned, word had come; he was now officially a spacer. His career had begun. He laughed inside the helmet as his cord reeled him toward the *Teela*'s lock. Life was good. He had never realized how good it could be.

Ω

"Why the bush? You carry it around like you're related to it."

"It's not a bush," LaNague said. "It's a tree. And one of my best friends."

If the remark was meant to be amusing, Broohnin did not find it so. He was edgy, fidgety, feeling mean. The *Lucky Teela* had dropped in and out of subspace three times in its course toward Earth, accompanied by the curious, much-investigated but little-explained wrenching nausea each time.

LaNague did not seem to mind, at least outwardly, but for Broohnin, who had not set foot on an interstellar ship since fleeing Nolevatol, each drop was an unnerving physical trial, causing the sweat to pour off him as his intestines tried to reach the outside world through both available routes simultaneously. In fact, the entire trip was a trial for Broohnin. It reminded him of that farmhouse on Nolevatol where he grew up, a tiny island of wood in the middle of a sea of grain, no one around but his mother, his brother, and that idiot who pretended to be a father. He had often felt like this on the farm . . . trapped, confined, with nothing outside the walls. He found himself wandering the corridors of the control ship incessantly, his palms continually moist, his fingers twitching endlessly as if possessed of a life of their own. At times the walls seemed to be closing in on him, threatening to crush him to currant jelly.

When his mental state reached that stage—when he could swear that if he looked quickly, without warning, to his right or left he could actually catch a trace of movement at the edges of the walls, always toward him, never away—he popped a couple of Torportal tablets under his tongue, closed his eyes, and waited. They dissolved rapidly, absorbed through the sublingual mucosa and into the venous circulation almost immediately. A few good pumps of his heart and the active metabolite was in his brain and at work on the limbic system, easing the tension, pushing back the walls, allowing him to sit still and actually carry on a coherent conversation . . . as he was doing now.

He wondered how LaNague could sit so calmly across the narrow expanse of the tight little cabin. Space was precious on these freight runs: the chairs on which they sat, the table on which LaNague's tree stood, all had sprung from the floor at the touch of an activator plate; the bed folded down from the wall when needed; all identical to Broohnin's quarters across the hall. A common-use toilet and washroom were located down the corridor. Everything was planned for maximal usage of available space, which meant that everything was cramped to a maddening degree. Yet LaNague seemed unperturbed, a fact which would have infuriated Broohnin to violence were he not presently in a drugged state. He wondered if LaNague used any psychotropics.

"That's Pierrot," LaNague was saying, indicating the tree which stood almost within Broohnin's reach on the table aftward and between them. "He started as a *misho* many years ago and is now a stunted version of the Tolivian equivalent of the flowering mimosa. He shows he's comfortable and at ease now by assuming the *bankan* position."

"You talk like it's a member of the family or something."

"Well . . ." LaNague paused and a hint of a mischievous smile twisted his lips upward. "You might say he *is* a member of my family: my great-grandfather."

Not sure of just how he should take that, Broohnin glanced from LaNague to the tree. In its rich brown, intricately carved *fukuro-shiki-bachi* earthenware container, it stood no taller than the distance from the tip of a man's middle finger to the tip of his elbow. The foliage consisted of narrow, five-fingered fronds, spread wide and lined with tiny leaves, all displayed in a soft umbrella of green over its container. The trunk was gently curved to give an over-all picture of peace and serenity.

A thought occurred to Broohnin, a particularly nasty one that he found himself relishing more and more as it lingered in his mind. He knew he was physically superior to LaNague, and knew there were no Flinters aboard. There was no further reason to fear the Tolivian.

"What would you do if I uprooted your precious little tree and broke it into a pile of splinters?"

LaNague started half out of his chair, his face white. When he saw that Broohnin had not yet made an actual move toward Pierrot, he resumed his seat.

"I would mourn," he said in a voice that was dry and vibrated with—what? Was it fear or rage? Broohnin couldn't tell. "I might even weep. I would burn the remains, and then . . . I don't know. I'd want to kill you, but I don't know if I would do it."

"You won't allow Metep to be killed, but you'd kill me because of a stinking little tree?" Broohnin wanted to laugh in the other man's face, but the coldness in LaNague's voice gave him pause. "You could get another."

"No. I couldn't. There is only one Pierrot."

Broohnin glanced over to the tree and was startled by the change in its appearance. The finger-like fronds had pulled close together and the trunk was now laser-beam straight.

"You've startled Pierrot into the *chokkan* configuration," LaNague said reproachfully.

"Perhaps I'll break *you* into splinters," Broohnin replied, turning away from the disturbing little tree that changed shape as mood dictated, and focusing again on LaNague. "You've no Flinters to do your dirty work now . . . I could do it easily . . . break your back . . . I'd enjoy that."

He was not saying this merely to frighten LaNague. It would feel *good* to hurt him, damage him, kill him. There were times when Broohnin felt he must destroy something, anything. Pressure built up inside him and fought madly for release. Back on Throne, he would wander through the dimmest areas of the dolee zones when the pressure reached unbearable levels, and woe to the poor Zemmelar addict who tried to assault him for the few marks he had. The ensuing scuffle would be brief, vicious, and unreported. And Broohnin would feel better afterward. Only the Torportal in his system now kept him from leaping at LaNague.

"Yes, I believe you would," LaNague said, totally at ease. "But it might be a good idea to wait until the return trip. We're on our way to Sol System, don't forget. You'd be taken into custody here and turned over to the Crime Authority once we reached the disengagement point. And the Crime Authority of Earth is very big on psycho-rehabilitation."

The inner rage abruptly dissolved within Broohnin, replaced by shuddering cold. Psycho-rehab started with a mindwipe and ended with a reconstructed personality.

"Then I'll wait," he said, hoping the remark did not sound as lame as he felt. There followed a protracted, uncomfortable pause—uncomfortable, it seemed, only for Broohnin.

"What's our first step once we get to Earth?" he asked, forcing himself to break the silence. The whole idea of a trip to Earth to lay groundwork for a revolution in the outworlds bothered him. Bothered him very much.

"We'll take a quick trip to the southern pole to confirm personally a few reports I've had from contacts on Earth. If those prove true—and I'll have to see with my own eyes before I believe—then I'll arrange a meeting with the third richest man in Sol System."

"Who's that?"

"You'll find out when we meet him."

"I want to know *now*!" Broohnin shouted and sprang from

his chair. He wanted to pace the floor but there was no room for more than two steps in any direction. "Every time I ask a question you put me off! Am I to be a part of this or not?"

"In time you will be privy to everything. But you must proceed in stages. A certain basic education must be acquired before you can fully understand and effectively participate in the workings of my plan."

"I'm as educated as I need to be!"

"Are you? What do you know about outworld-Sol System trade?"

"Enough. I know the outworlds are the bread basket for Sol System. It's grain runs like the one we're on right now that keep Earth from starving."

"*Kept* Earth from starving," LaNague said. "The need for an extraterrestrial protein source is rapidly diminishing. She'll soon be able to feed her own and these grain runs will become a thing of the past before too long. The outworlds will no longer be Earth's bread basket."

Broohnin shrugged. "So? That'll just leave more for the rest of us to eat."

LaNague's laugh was irritating in its condescension. "You've a lot to learn . . . a *lot* to learn." He leaned forward in his chair, his long-fingered hands slicing the air before him as he spoke. "Look at it this way: think of a country or a planet or a system of planets as a factory. The people within work to produce something to sell to other people outside the factory. Their market is in constant flux. They find new customers, lose old ones, and generally keep production and profits on an even keel. But every once in a while a factory makes the mistake of selling too much of its production to one customer. It's convenient, yes, and certainly profitable. But after a while it comes to depend on that customer too much. And should that customer find a better deal elsewhere, what do you think happens to the factory?"

"Trouble."

"Trouble," LaNague said, nodding. "Big trouble. Perhaps even bankruptcy. That's what's happening to the outworlds. You—I exclude Tolive and Flint because neither of those two planets joined the outworld trade network when Earth was in command, preferring to become self-supporting and thus sparing ourselves dependency on Sol-System trade—you members of the Outworld Imperium are a large factory with one product and one customer. And that customer is learning how to live without you. Before too long you'll all be up to your ears in grain which everyone is growing but no one will be buying. You won't be able to eat it fast enough!"

"Just how long is 'before too long'?"

"Eighteen to twenty standard years."

"I think you're wrong," Broohnin said. Although he found the idea of a chaotic economic collapse strangely appealing, he could not buy it. "Sol System has always depended on the outworlds for food. They can't produce enough of their own, so where else can they get it?"

"They've developed a new protein source . . . and they're not feeding as many," LaNague said, leaning back in his chair now.

The pollution in the seas of Earth had long ago excluded them from ever being a source of food. What could be grown on land and in the multilevel warehouse farms was what humanity would eat. Yet as the population curve had continued on its ever-steepening upward climb, slowing briefly now and then, but moving ever upward, available land space for agriculture shrank. As the number of hungry mouths increased and took up more and more living space, Earth's Bureau of Farms was strained to its utmost to squeeze greater and greater yields out of fewer and fewer acres. The orbiting oneils helped somewhat, but the crush of people and the weight of their hunger surpassed all projections. Synthetic foods that could be processed in abundance were violently rejected; palatable staples could not be supplied in sufficient quantities.

And so the outworld trade network was formed. The colonies were recruited and made over into huge farms. Since a whole ring of grain pods could be dropped in and out of subspace almost as cheaply as one, the outworld-Sol System grain runs were begun and it appeared that a satisfactory solution had at last been found.

For a while, it worked. Came the outworld revolution and everything changed. Sol System still received grain from the outworlds, but at a fair market price. Too broke to start settling and developing new farm colonies, Earth turned inward and began setting its own house in order.

First step was genetic registry. Anyone discovered to have a defective, or even potentially defective, genotype—this included myriad recessive traits—was sterilized. Howls and threats of domestic revolution arose, but the Earth government was not to be moved this time. It gave the newly formed Bureau of Population Control police powers and expected it to use them.

An example was made of Arna Miffler: a woman with a genotype previously declared free of dangerous traits. She was young, childless, single, and idealistic. She began a campaign of protest against the BPC and its policies, a successful one in its early stages, one that was quickly gathering momentum. At that time, the BPC re-examined Arna Miffler's genotype and discovered a definite trait for one of the rare mucopolysaccharide disorders. She was arrested at her home one night and led off to a BPC clinic. When released the next morning, she was sterile.

Lawyers, geneticists, activists who came to her aid soon learned that their own genotypes, and those of their families, were undergoing scrutiny. As some of Arna's supporters here and there were dragged off to BPC clinics and sterilized, the protest movement faltered, then stalled, then died. It was quite clear that the Bureau of Population Control had muscle and was not afraid to use it. Resistance was reduced to a whisper.

It rose to a scream again when the next step was announced: reproduction was to be limited to the status quo. Two people were only allowed to engender two more new people. A male was allowed to father two children and no more; a female was allowed to deliver or supply ova for two children and no more. After the live birth of the second child, each was to report for voluntary sterilization.

The option for sterilization after fathering or mothering a second child was about as voluntary as Earth's voluntary tax system: comply or else. The genotype of every newborn was entered into a computer which cross-analyzed each parent's genetic contribution. Once the analysis indicated the existence of a second child derived from a certain genotype, that individual's number was registered and he or she was immediately located and escorted to the nearest BPC clinic, where a single injection eliminated forever the possibility of producing another viable gamete.

The BPC looked on this approach as a masterful compromise. Each citizen was still allowed to replace himself or herself via a child, something many—too many—considered an inalienable right. But no more than self-replacement was permitted. Fathering or mothering a child was a capital offense, the male or the female parent being chosen for death by lot in order to "make room" for the newborn child.

The population thus decreased by attrition. Death from disease, although rare, still whittled away at the numbers. Accidental deaths did the same at a faster rate. Children who died after birth—even if they were only seconds old—could not be replaced. The one-person/one-child rule was adhered to dogmatically. Special tax incentives were offered to those who would submit to sterilization before giving rise to new life, higher taxes levied on those who insisted on reproduction.

It worked. After two centuries of harsh controls, the motherworld's population was well into an accelerating decline. There were still food riots now and again in a megalopolis, but nowhere near as frequently as before. There was breathing space again; not much, but after what the planet had been through, it seemed like wide open spaces.

"Sol System is rapidly approaching a break-even point," LaNague was saying, "where its population will be such that the existing farm land, the oneils, and the new protein source will be sufficient to feed everyone. That's when it will stop importing grain from the outworlds. That's when the Imperium will fall apart. What we do in the next few days, weeks, and years will decide whether anything is to be saved at all."

Broohnin said nothing as he stood by his chair and considered what he had been told. LaNague made sense, much as he hated to admit it. Everything was going to fall apart one way or another. That seemed certain now. The two men could at least agree on that point.

But as for saving something? He and LaNague would be at odds on that score. Broohnin wanted nothing spared in the final collapse.

VII

You can see it in their eyes as they sit and move the levers that work the gears of the State. They look at you and know there really is a free lunch. And when they reach to tear off a piece of your flesh, do you bite the hand that feeds on you? Or do you, like so many of your fellows, ask if the maggot likes you rare, medium, or well done?

from THE SECOND BOOK OF KYFHO

A drop of blood formed at the puncture site after the needle was removed from LaNague's thumb. The technician dabbed it away and smeared the area with stat-gel to halt any further bleeding.

"That should do it, sir. But let's just run a little check to make sure." She tapped a few numbers into the console on her left, then pointed to a small funnel-like opening at the front of the console. "Put your thumb in there."

LaNague complied and a green light flashed on the counter. "Works?"

The technician nodded. "Perfectly. You are now an official part of the Sol-System credit network."

"I may not appear so on the surface," LaNague said with a wry twist to his mouth, "but inside I am filled with boundless ecstasy."

Broohnin watched the technician smile. It was a nice smile; she was a pretty girl. And LaNague's remark went right by her. Broohnin turned back to the huge transparent plate that made up the greater part of the outer wall of the way station. Earth hung outside.

The *Lucky Teela* had completed its last subspace jump ahead of schedule and had emerged north of the rotating disk of planets, gas giants, and debris that made up Sol System. The grain pods were deposited in orbit around Earth and the two passengers transferred to the *Bernardo de la Paz*, an orbiting depot for people and freight run by the Lunarians. People seemed to be scarce at the moment: except for a group of vacationers outward bound for Woolaville on the winter border of Mars' northern ice cap, Broohnin and LaNague had most of the way station to themselves.

LaNague's first step had been to establish credit for himself before their descent to the planet below. He had given a pile of Tolivian ags to the station's exchequer official in order to establish a balance in Earth's electronic monetary system. The silver coins had been eagerly accepted, converted into Solar credits, and entered into the computer network. A coded signature device had been implanted into the subcutaneous fat pad of his right thumb with an eighteen-gauge needle. As long as his balance lasted, he could buy anything legally available on Earth. A light on consoles similar to the one beside the pretty technician would flash red when he exhausted it.

"Ingenious little device, wouldn't you say?" LaNague remarked, admiring his thumb as he joined Broohnin at the viewing wall. "I can't even feel it in there."

Broohnin tore his eyes away from the planet below. "What's so ingenious? All I have to do is cut off your thumb and I'm suddenly as rich as you are."

"They're ahead of you there, I'm afraid. The little device is sensitive to extreme alterations in blood flow . . . I imagine that's why they asked me if I had Raynaud's disease. Even a tourniquet left in place too long will deactivate it."

Broohnin returned his attention to the view wall. As ever, LaNague was unflappable: he had already considered and discarded the possibility of someone cutting his thumb off. Someday, Broohnin promised himself, he would find a way to break that man. The only time he had been able to pierce the Tolivian's shield was when he had threatened his damned miniature tree. And even that was out of reach now in the quarantine section of the way station. But someday he would get through. Someday . . .

Right now he stood transfixed by the motherworld whirling outside the window.

"Think of it," LaNague said at his shoulder. "Down there is where humanity first crawled out of the slime and started on its trek to the stars."

Broohnin looked and saw something like a blue Nolevatol thornberry, mottled brown with rot and streaked with white mold. He wanted to jump.

Ω

LaNague's thumb was quickly put to good use after they shuttled down to the Cape Horn spaceport. Their luggage was stored, a two-man flitter rented. It was only after they were airborne and headed further south that Broohnin realized the precariousness of his position.

"Think you're pretty smart, don't you?" he told LaNague.

"What's that supposed to mean?"

"Your thumb. It makes you rich and me penniless. You're free to move, I have to follow. You wanted it that way." He felt rage growing within him even as he spoke.

"Never thought of it, actually." LaNague's face was guileless. "I just couldn't see opening two accounts when we're only going to be here for a day or so. Besides"—he held up his right thumb—"this is not freedom. It's the exact opposite. The Earth government has used these implants and the electronic credit network to enslave its population more effectively than any regime in human history."

"Don't try to change the subject—"

"I'm not. Just think what that implant does to me. Every time I use it—to rent this flitter, to buy a meal, to rent a room—my name, the amount of money I spent, what I spent it on, the place of purchase, the time of purchase, all go into the network!" He thrust his thumb toward Broohnin's face. "And this is the only legal money on the entire planet! Coins and paper money have been outlawed—to use any leftovers is illegal. Even barter is illegal. Do you know what that means?"

Surprised by LaNague's vehemence, Broohnin fumbled for an answer. "I—"

"It means your life is one big holovid recording to anyone who wants to know and has connections. It means that somewhere there's a record of every move you make every day of your life. Your entertainment tastes can be deduced from where you spend your leisure time, your sexual preferences from any devices you might buy, your taste in clothes, your favorite drink, your confidences, your infidelities!"

LaNague withdrew his hand and lay his head back into the upper portion of the padded seat. His eyes closed as he visibly relaxed. After a while he exhaled slowly but kept his lids shut, basking in the dying rays of the sinking sun as they played off the sharp planes of his face.

Finally: "If you really want, I'll set up a small credit balance for you when we get to the peninsula."

"Forget it," Broohnin replied, hating the meekness he heard in his voice. "Where are we going?"

LaNague opened his eyes. "I punched in a course for the South Pole, but we'll never reach it. They'll stop us long before we get near it."

The flitter took them across Drake Passage, over the tip of the Antarctic Peninsula, and along the western shore of the Weddell Sea. The concepts of "east" and "west" steadily lost meaning as they traveled toward the point where even "south" held no meaning, where every way was north.

Darkness swallowed them as they cut through the cold air above the monotonous white wastes of the Edith Ronne Ice Shelf. When all around him had become featureless darkness, Broohnin finally admitted to himself that he was frightened. He doubted either of them could survive an hour down there in that cold and wind if the flitter went down.

"This was a stupid idea," he muttered.

"What was?" LaNague, as usual, seemed unperturbed.

"Renting this flitter. We should have taken a commercial flight. What if we have a power failure?"

"A commercial flight wouldn't take us where we have to go. I told you before—I have to see this new protein source myself before I'll really believe it."

"What protein are you going to find on an ice cap? Everything's frozen!" This trip was becoming more idiotic by the minute.

"Not everything, I'll bet," LaNague said, craning his neck forward as he scanned the sky through the observation bubble. He pointed upward and fifteen degrees off the flitter's port bow. "Look. What do you think those are?"

Broohnin saw them almost immediately. Three long, narrow ellipses of intensely bright light hung in the black of the sky, motionless, eerie.

"How high you think they are?" LaNague asked.

Broohnin squinted. They looked *very* high, almost fixed in the sky. "I'd say they were in orbit."

"You're right. They're in a tight polar orbit."

"Orbiting lights?"

"That's sunlight."

"By the Core!" Broohnin said in a breathy voice. He knew what they were now—mirrors. Orbiting solar reflectors were almost as old in practice as they were in concept. They had been used by wealthy snow belt cities in the pre-interstellar days to reduce the severity of their winter storms. But the advent of weather modification technology had made them obsolete and most of them had been junked or forgotten.

"I've got it!" he said. "Someone's melted enough ice to be able to plant crops at the South Pole!"

LaNague shook his head. "Close, but not quite. I doubt if there's enough arable soil under the ice to plant a crop. And if there were, I certainly wouldn't feel impelled to see it with my own eyes. What I've—"

The traffic control comm indicator on the console flashed red as a voice came through the speaker.

"Restricted zone! Restricted zone! Turn back unless you have authorized clearance! Restricted zone! Restricted—"

"We going to do it?" Broohnin asked.

"No."

He fumbled with the knobs on the console. "Can't we turn it off then?" The repetitious monotone of the recorded warning was getting on his nerves. When the volume control on the vid panel did nothing to lessen the droning voice, Broohnin raised his hand to strike at the speaker. LaNague stopped him.

"We'll need that later. Don't break anything."

Broohnin leaned back and bottled his growing irritation. Covering his ears with his hands, he watched the solar mirrors fatten in the middle, growing more circular, less ellipsoid. As the flitter continued southward, they became almost too bright to look at.

The cabin was suddenly filled with intolerably bright light, but not from the mirrors. A police cutter was directly above them, matching their air speed. The voice from the traffic control comm finally cut off and a new one spoke.

"You have violated restricted air space. Proceed 11.2 kilometers due south and dock in the lighted area next to the sentry post. Deviation from that course will force me to disable your craft."

LaNague cleared the pre-programmed course and took manual control of the flitter. "Let's do what the man says."

"You don't seem surprised."

"I'm not. This is the only way to get to the South Polar Plateau without getting blasted out of the air."

The cutter stayed above them all the way to the sentry station and remained hovering over their observation bubble even after they had docked.

"Debark and enter the sentry station," the voice said from the speaker. Without protest, LaNague and Broohnin broke the seal on the bubble, stumbled to the ground, and made a mad dash through the icy wind to the door of the station. The sentry joined them a moment later. He was young, personable, and alone. Broohnin considered the odds to be in their favor, but LaNague no doubt had other ideas.

Ω

It was much roomier in the cab of the sentry's cutter. Broohnin stretched out his legs and started to doze.

"Keep awake!" LaNague said, nudging him. "I want you to see this, too."

Broohnin struggled to a more upright sitting position and glared at the Tolivian. He felt tired, more irritable than usual, and didn't like anyone nudging him for any reason. But his annoyance faded quickly as he remembered LaNague's masterful handling of the sentry.

"Are all Earthies that easy to bribe?" he asked.

There was no humor in LaNague's smile. "I wouldn't be surprised if they were. Those two coin tubes I gave him were full of Tolivian ags, and each ag contains one troy ounce of .999 fine silver. With silver coins, that sentry can operate outside the electronic currency system. The official exchange rate is about six solar credits per ag, but the coins are each worth ten times that in the black market. And believe me, Earth's black market is second to none in size and diversity."

Broohnin remembered the way the sentry's eyes had widened at the sight of the silver coins. The man had looked as if he were about to lick his lips in anticipation. He had hardly seemed to hear LaNague as he explained what he wanted in return for the coins.

"Black market prices are higher," Broohnin said. "Why bother with it?"

"Of course they're higher. That's because they've got something to sell. Look: all prices and wages are fixed on Earth, all goods are rationed. Whatever makes it to the market at the official price disappears in an instant, usually into the hands of friends and relatives of the people with political connections. These people sell it to black marketeers, who sell it to everyday people; the price goes up at each stop along the way."

"That's my point—"

"No. You've *missed* the point. The price of a three-dimensional display module for a home computer is 'X' Solar credits in the government-controlled store; it's a fixed bargain price, but the store never has any. So what good is a fixed price? The black marketeer, however, has plenty of them, only he wants 'double-X' Solar credits for each. It's an axiom of Kyfhon economics: the more rigidly controlled the economy, the bigger and better the black market. Earth's economy is run completely from the top, therefore there's hardly a thing you cannot buy in Earth's black market. It's the biggest and best there is!

"The black market here also means freedom from surveillance. You can buy anything you want without leaving a record of what, where, and when. Of *course* the sentry was easy to bribe! It costs him nothing to let us take this ride, and look what he got in return!"

The sentry had not come along. There was no need to. He had searched them for weapons and cameras; finding none, he had sealed them into the cutter and programmed a low-level reconnaissance flight into the craft's computer. The two outworlders would get a slow fly-by of the area that interested them, with no stops. Anyone monitoring the flight would detect nothing out of the ordinary—a routine fence ride. The chance of the cutter's being stopped with the outworlders aboard was virtually nil. The sentry was risking nothing and gaining a pocketful of silver.

The solar mirrors were now almost perfect circles in the night sky, intolerably bright. LaNague pointed to a soft glow ahead on the horizon.

"That's it. That's got to be it!"

The glow grew and spread left and right until most of the horizon ahead of them was suffused with a soft yellow haze. Suddenly they were upon it and in it and sinking through wispy clouds of bright mist. When those cleared, they could see huge fields of green far below them. A sheer wall of ice was behind them, swinging away to each side in a huge crystal arc.

"By the Core!" Broohnin said softly. "It's a huge valley cut right out of the ice!"

LaNague was nodding excitedly. "Yes! A huge circular cut measuring thirty kilometers across if my reports are correct —and they haven't failed me yet. But the real surprise is below."

Broohnin watched as their slow descent brought them toward the floor of the valley. The fine mist that layered over the top of the huge man-made depression in the South Polar Plateau diffused the light from the solar mirrors, spreading it evenly through the air. Acting as a translucent screen, it retained most of the radiant heat. The valley was one huge greenhouse. Looking down, Broohnin saw that what had initially appeared to be a solid carpet of green on the valley floor was actually a tight grove in some sort of huge, single-leafed plants. Then he saw that the plants had legs. And some were walking.

"It's true!" LaNague whispered in a voice full of wonder. "The first experiments were begun centuries ago, but now they've finally done it!"

"What? Walking plants?"

"No. Photosynthetic cattle!"

They were like no cattle Broohnin had ever seen. A vivid bice green all over, eight-legged, and blind, they were constantly bumping into and rubbing against each other. He could discern no nose, and the small mouth seemed suited only to sucking water from the countless rivulets that crisscrossed the valley floor. The body of each was a long tapered cylinder topped by a huge, green, rear-slanting rhomboidal vane averaging two meters on a side. All the vanes, all the countless thousands of them, were angled so their broad surfaces presented toward the solar mirrors for maximum exposure to the light . . . like an endless becalmed regatta of green-sailed ships.

"Welcome to Emerald City," LaNague said in a low voice.

"Hmmmm?"

"Nothing."

They watched in silence as the sentry's cutter completed its low, slow circuit of the valley, passing at the end over herds of smaller green calves penned off from the rest of the herd, held aside until they were large enough to hold their own with the adults. The cutter rose gently, leaving the valley hidden beneath its lid of bright mist.

"Didn't look to me like one of those skinny things could feed too many people," Broohnin remarked as the wonder of what they had seen ebbed away.

"You'd be surprised. The official reports say that even the bones are edible. And there are more hidden valleys like that one down here."

"But what's the advantage?"

"They don't graze! Do you realize what that means? They don't take up land that can be used for growing food for people; they don't eat grains that can be fed to people. All they need is water, sunlight, and an ambient temperature of 15 to 20 degrees."

"But they're so thin!"

"They have to be if they're going to be photosynthetic. They need a high surface-area-to-mass ratio to feed themselves via their chlorophyll. And don't forget, there's virtually no fat on those things—what you see is what you eat. As each green herd reaches maturity, they're slaughtered, the derived protein is mixed with extenders and marketed as some sort of meat. New ones are cloned and started on their way."

Broohnin nodded his understanding, but the puzzled expression remained on his face. "I still don't understand why it's being kept a secret, though. This is the kind of breakthrough I'd expect Earth to be beating its chest about all over Occupied Space."

"It doesn't want the outworlds to know yet. Earth realizes that those green cows down there could spell economic ruin for the outworlds. And the longer they keep the outworlds in the dark about them, the worse shape they'll all be in when grain imports are completely cut off."

"But why—?"

"Because I don't think Earth has ever given up hope of getting the outworlds under its wing again."

"You going to break the news?"

"No."

They flew in silence through the polar darkness for a while, each man digesting what he had just seen.

"I imagine that once the word gets out," LaNague said

finally, "and it should leak within a few standard years, the
Earthies will move the herds into the less hospitable desert
areas where they can probably expect a faster growth rate. Of
course, the water requirement will be higher because of increased evaporation. But that's when Earth's need for im-
ported grain will really begin to drop . . . she'll be fast on her
way to feeding all her billions on her own."

The lights of the sentry station appeared ahead.

"Speaking of all these billions," Broohnin said, "where are
they? The spaceport wasn't crowded, and there's nothing
below but snow. I thought you told me every available centi-
meter of living space on Earth was being used. Looks like
there's a whole continent below with no one on it. What kind
of residue you been giving me?"

"The coast of the South Polar continent is settled all
around, and the Antarctic Peninsula is crowded with people.
But from what I understand, inland settlements have been discouraged. It's possible to live down there," he said, glancing
at the featureless wastes racing by below the cutter. "The
technology exists to make it habitable, but not without exten-
sive melting of the ice layers."

Broohnin shrugged. He managed to make it a hostile
gesture. "So?"

"So, a significant ice melt means significant lowland flood-
ing and there are millions upon millions of people inhabiting
lowlands. A few thousand square kilometers of living space
down here could result in the loss of millions elsewhere in the
world. Not a good trade-off. Also, 80 per cent of Earth's fresh
water is down there. So Antarctica remains untouched."

The cutter slowed to a hover over the sentry station, then
descended. As they prepared to debark, LaNague turned to
Broohnin.

"You want to see billions of people, my friend? I'll show
you more than you ever imagined. Our next stop is the Eastern
Megalopolis of North America. By the time we're through
there, you'll *crave* the solitude of the cabin you occupied on
the trip in from the outworlds."

VIII

> . . . human beings cease to be human
> when they congregate and a mob is a
> monster. If you think of a mob as a
> living thing and you want to get its
> I.Q., take the average intelligence of
> the people there and divide it by the
> number of people there. Which means
> that a mob of fifty has somewhat less
> intelligence than an earthworm.
>
> *Theodore Sturgeon*

"You sure you know where you're going?"

"Exactly. Why?"

"It's not the type of neighborhood I'd expect to see the 'third richest man in Sol System' in."

"You're right. This is a side trip."

The press of people was beyond anything Broohnin had ever imagined. They were everywhere under the bleary eye of the noonday sun, lining the streets, crowding onto the pavement until only the hardiest ground-effect vehicles dared to push their way through. There were no fat people to be seen, and the streets themselves were immaculate, all a part of the ethics of starvation wherein everything must be recycled. The air was thick with the noise, the smell, the *presence* of packed human-

61

ity. And even behind the high, cheap, quickly poured apartment walls that canyonized the street, Broohnin was sure he could feel unseen millions.

"I don't like it here," he told LaNague.

"I told you you wouldn't."

"I don't mean that. There's something wrong here. I can feel it."

"It's just the crowds. Ignore it."

"Something is *wrong!*" he said, grabbing LaNague's arm and spinning him around.

LaNague looked at him carefully, searchingly. "What's bothering you?"

"I can't explain it," Broohnin said, rubbing his damp palms in fearful frustration. There was sweat clinging to his armpits, his mouth felt dry, and the skin at the back of his neck was tight. "Something's going to happen here. These people are building toward something."

LaNague gave him another long look, then nodded abruptly. "All right. I know better than to ignore the instincts of a former street urchin. We'll make this quick, then we'll get out of here." He looked down at the locus indicator disk in his palm, and pointed to the right. "This way."

They had returned to the tip of the South American continent and dropped off their flitter at the Cape Town Spaceport. From there a stratospheric rammer had shot them north to the Bosyorkington Spaceport, which occupied the far end of Long Island, formerly called the Hamptons. Three hundred kilometers west northwest from there by flitter brought them to the putrescent trickle that was still called the Delaware River, but only after carrying them over an endless, unbroken grid of clogged streets with apartments stretching skyward from the interstices. Everything looked so carefully planned, so well thought-out and laid out . . . why then had Broohnin felt as if he were descending into the first ring of Hell when their flitter lowered toward the roof of one of the municipal garages?

LaNague had purchased a locus indicator at the spaceport. They were big sellers to tourists and people trying to find their roots. It was a fad on Earth to locate the exact spot where a relative had lived or a famous man had been born or had died, or a historical event had occurred. One could either pay homage, or relive that moment of history with the aid of holograms or a sensory-cognitive button for those who were wired.

"What are we looking for if not your rich man?" Broohnin

asked impatiently. The tension in the air was making it difficult to breathe.

LaNague did not look up from his locus indicator. "An ancient ancestor of mine—man named Gurney—used to live in this area in the pre-stellar days. He was a rebel of sorts, the earliest one on record in my family. A lipidlegger. He defied his government—and there were many governments then, not just one for all Earth as there is now—out of sheer stubbornness and belligerence." He smiled at a private thought. "Quite a character."

They walked a short distance further to the north. There seemed to be fewer people about, but no less tension. LaNague didn't seem to notice.

"Here we are!" he said, his smile turning to dismay as he looked around, faced with the same monotonous façades of people-choked apartments that had oppressed them since leaving the municipal garage.

"Good. You found it. Let's go," Broohnin said, glancing about anxiously.

"This used to be a beautiful rural area," LaNague was saying, "with trees and wildlife and mist and rain. Now look at it: solid synthestone. According to my co-ordinates, Gurney's general store used to be right here in the middle of the street. This whole area used to be the Delaware Water Gap. How—"

A sound stopped him. It was a human sound, made by human voices, but so garbled by the overlapping of so many voices that no words were distinguishable. Its source was untraceable . . . it came from everywhere, seamlessly enveloping them. But the emotion behind the sound came through with unmistakable clarity: rage.

All around them, people began to flee for their homes. Children were pulled off the street and into apartment complex doorways that slid shut behind them. LaNague dove for the door of a clothing store to their left but it zipped closed before he could reach it and would not open despite his insistent pounding. As Broohnin watched, the storefront disappeared, fading rapidly to a blank surface identical to the synthestone of the apartment walls around it. LaNague appeared to be trying to gain entry to a solid wall.

"What's going on?" Broohnin yelled as the din of human voices grew progressively louder. He could not localize the source to the north of them, approaching rapidly.

"Food riot," LaNague said, returning to Broohnin's side.

"Sounds like a big one. We've got to get out of here." He pulled a reference tablet the size of a playing card from his vest pocket and tapped in a code. "The garage is too far, but there's a Kyfhon neighborhood near here, I believe." The surface of the tablet lit with the information he had requested. "Yes! We can make it if we run."

"Why there?"

"Because nobody else will be able to help us."

They ran south, stopping at every intersection while La-Nague checked his locus indicator. The bustling stores they had passed only moments before had disappeared, glazed over with holograms of blank synthestone walls to hide them from the approaching mob. Only a rioter intimately familiar with this particular neighborhood would be able to locate them now.

"They're gaining!" Broohnin said breathlessly as they stopped again for LaNague to check their co-ordinates. After nearly two decades of living on Throne, his muscles had become acclimated to a gravitational pull approximately 5 per cent less than Earth's. The difference had been inconsequential until now because his activity had been limited to sitting, dozing, and strolling. Now he had to run. And he felt it.

LaNague, who weighed about seven kilos less on Earth than he did on Tolive, found the going easy. "Not much further. We should be—"

The mob rounded the corner behind them then and rushed forward with a roar. An empty, hapless g-e vehicle parked at the side of the street slowed their momentum for a moment as a number of rioters paused to tear it to pieces. The strips of metal pulled from the vehicle were used to assault any store windows they could find behind their holographic camouflage. The windows were tough, rubbery, and shatterproof. They had to be pierced and torn before entry could be gained.

LaNague and Broohnin stood transfixed with fascination as they watched a clutch of rioters attack what seemed to be a synthestone wall, their makeshift battering rams and pikes disappearing into it as if no wall existed. And none did. With a sudden shout, those in the forefront pushed their way into the wall image and disappeared. They must have found the hologram projector controls immediately because the camouflage evaporated and the crowd cheered as the wall became a storefront again . . . a furniture outlet. Its contents were passed out to the street bucket-brigade style and smashed with roars of approval.

"That's not food!" Broohnin said. "I thought you called this a food riot."

"Just a generic term. Nobody riots for food any more. They just riot. Theories have it that the crowding makes a certain type of person go temporarily berserk every so often."

And then the crowds began to move again. Blind, voracious, swift, deadly.

Broohnin found his fear gone, replaced by a strange exhilaration. "Let's join them!" The carnage, the howling ferocity of the scene had excited him. He wanted a chance to break something, too. He always felt better when he did.

"They'll tear you to pieces!" LaNague said, shoving him into motion away from the mob.

"No, they won't! I'll be one of them!"

"You're an outworlder, you fool! They'll see that immediately. And when they're through with you, nobody'll be able to put you back together again. Now run!"

They ran. The mob was not after them in particular, but it followed them. Nor was the riot confined to a single street. As they passed various intersections, LaNague and Broohnin could see extensions of the crowd to the right and left. Fires had been set and smoke began to thicken in the air.

"Faster!" LaNague shouted. "We could get ringed in! We're dead if that happens!"

It was unnecessary advice. Broohnin was running at maximum effort. His muscles screaming in protest as the smoke put an extra burden on his already laboring lungs. LaNague had slowed his pace to stay with him and yell encouragement. Broohnin resented the ease with which the skinny Tolivian loped beside him. If worse came to worse, he would throw LaNague to the mob which was now only a scant hundred meters behind them, and gaining.

"Not much further!" LaNague said. "Don't quit now!" He glanced down at the indicator in his palm. "That should be it straight ahead!"

Broohnin saw nothing different at first, then noticed that the street after the next intersection was a different color . . . yellow . . . and there were still people in the street . . . children . . . playing. There were men on the corners. Women, too. And they were all armed.

The Kyfhons stood in small placid groups, watching the two fleeing outworlders with mild interest. Except for the long-range blasters slung across their shoulders and the hand blasters on their hips, they looked like all the other Earthies seen since landfall. It was only when it became obvious that LaNague and Broohnin were going to cross onto the yellow-colored pavement that they sprang to life.

A dozen blasters were suddenly pointed in their direction. Broohnin glanced at the children who had stopped playing —some of the older ones had small hand blasters drawn and ready, too. LaNague swung out his arm and slowed Broohnin to a walk, then trotted ahead of him. The Tolivian held his hands in front of him, out of Broohnin's sight. He seemed to be signaling to the group of Kyfhons on the right-hand corner. They glanced at each other and lowered their weapons. One stepped forward to have a quick conversation. There were brief nods, then LaNague turned to Broohnin.

"Hurry! They'll give us sanctuary."

Broohnin quickly followed LaNague onto the yellow pavement. "Where do we hide?" His words were barely audible between gasping respirations.

"We don't. We just lean against the wall over here in the shade and catch our breath."

"We're not getting off the street?"

LaNague shook his head. "That would mean entering someone's home. And that's asking too much."

The mob surged forward, its momentum constant, irresistible, spilling out of the confines of the narrow street and into the intersection. The Kyfhons had reslung or reholstered their weapons and now stood in clusters, eying the onrushing wave of humanity in attitudes of quiet readiness.

Although LaNague seemed calm beside him, Broohnin was unable to relax. He leaned back with his palms flat against the wall, panting, ready to spring away when he had to. And he was sure he'd have to soon. That mob was rolling and it wasn't going to be stopped by a few adults and kids with blasters. It was going to tear through here, yellow pavement or no, and destroy everything in its path.

As it happened, Broohnin was only half right. The mob did not stop, but neither did it pour into the Kyfhon street. It split. After filling the intersection, half of the rioters turned to the right, half to the left. Not a single foot crossed onto the yellow pavement.

Den Broohnin could only stare.

"Told you we'd be safe," LaNague said with a smug air.

"But why? There's not enough firepower in this street to even nick a mob like that, let alone stop it!"

LaNague looked up at the overhanging buildings. "Oh, I wouldn't say that."

Broohnin followed his gaze. The roofs, and every window at every level, were lined with Kyfhons, and each of them was armed. Looking back to the mob that was still surging and dividing at the end of the street, he saw not the slightest hint of reluctance or hesitation in the rioters as they skirted the yellow pavement. It seemed to be taken for granted that this neighborhood was untouchable. But how—?

"Over the years, I imagine a lot of rioters died before people got the message," LaNague said, answering the unspoken question. "It's called 'a sense of community'—something that's been long forgotten on Earth, and even on the outworlds. We Kyfhons are set apart from others by our attitudes and values. We form a close-knit family . . . even to the point of having secret hand signals so we can recognize each other. I used one to gain sanctuary today." He gestured toward the mob that was finally beginning to thin. "We're not interested in traffic with people who don't share our values, and so we're driven together into neighborhoods like this one, or to planets like Tolive and Flint. But it's a self-imposed exile. Our ghetto walls are built from the inside."

"But does the Crime Authority allow—"

"The Crime Authority is *not* allowed in here! The motto of Eastern Sect Kyfhons is 'A weapon in every hand, freedom on every side.' They police their own streets, and have let it be known for centuries that they protect their own. Public temper tantrums like the one that almost ran us over are not tolerated on their streets. The word has long been out: Do what you will to your own community, but risk death if you harm ours."

Broohnin had finally caught his breath and now pushed himself away from the wall. "In other words, they get away with murder."

"It's called self-defense. But there are other reasons they're left alone. For instance: didn't you wonder why there were no Crime Authority patrols in the air trying to quell the riot? It's because life is still a surplus here. If a few rioters get killed, that's fewer mouths to feed. The same logic applies to any rioters foolish enough to invade neighborhoods like this.

"As for criminals who might belong to the Kyfhon communities, the justice meted out here against their own kind is swifter and often harsher than anything that goes on in the Crime Authority prisons. And finally, from a purely pragmatic viewpoint, you must remember that these people grow up learning how to fight with every part of their body and with every weapon known to man." LaNague smiled grimly. "Would you want to walk in here and try to arrest someone?"

"They're like a bunch of Flinters," Broohnin muttered, glancing around and feeling the same uneasiness he had experienced in Throne's Imperium Park steal over him again.

"They are!" LaNague said, laughing. "They just never moved to Flint. After all, Flinters are just Eastern Sect purists in ceremonial garb who have a planet all to themselves. Just as Tolivians are Western Sect Kyfhons with their own planet."

"Where do these Western Sect types keep themselves on Earth?"

LaNague's smile faltered. "Most of them are gone. We—they never took to violence too well . . . gobbled up . . . destroyed. Tolive is just about the only place left where Western Sect Kyfho is practiced." He turned away. "Let's go."

After speaking briefly to a small knot of the adults on the corner, obviously thanking them, he moved toward the now deserted street, motioning Broohnin to follow.

"Come. Time to see the rich man."

Ω

They were three kilometers up in the cloud-cluttered sky, heading southeast at full throttle. The Bosyorkington megalopolis had been left behind, as had the coastal pile-dwelling communities and the houseboat fleets. Nothing below now but the green algae soup they still called the Atlantic Ocean.

"He live on a boat?"

LaNague shook his head.

"Then where're you taking us?" Broohnin demanded, his gaze flicking between the map projected on the flitter's vid screen and the rows of altocumulus clouds they were stringing like a needle through pearls. "There's nothing out here but water. And we'll never reach the other side."

LaNague checked the controls. "Watch up ahead."

Broohnin looked down toward the ocean.

"No," LaNague told him. "Ahead. *Straight* ahead."

There was nothing straight ahead but clouds. No . . . there was something . . . they speared into a patch of open air, and there it was, straight ahead as LaNague had said: a sprawling Tudor mansion with a perfect lawn and rows of English hedges cut two meters high and planted in devious, maze-like patterns. All floating three kilometers in the sky.

"Ah!" LaNague said softly at Broohnin's side. "The humble abode of Eric Boedekker."

IX

"Competition is a sin."
John D. Rockefeller, Sr.

Eric Boedekker's home sat in a shallow, oblong, six-acre dish
rimmed with batteries of anti-aircraft weapons. The general
public looked on the skisland estates as mere toys for the
obscenely rich, totally devoid of any practical value. The general public was wrong, as usual.

"Looks like a fort," Broohnin said as they glided toward it.

"It is."

Members of the uppermost layers of Earth's upper-upper
class had long ago become regular targets of organized criminal cartels, political terrorists, and ordinary people who were
simply hungry. Open season was declared on the rick and they
were kidnaped and held for ransom at an alarming rate. The
electronic currency system, of course, eliminated the possibility of monetary ransom, and so loved ones were held captive
and returned in exchange for commodities useful in the black
market, such as gold, silver, beef.

Huge, low-floating skislands had long been in use as vacation resorts, guaranteeing the best weather at all times, always
staying ahead of storms and winter's chill. Seeing the plight of

the very rich, an enterprising company began constructing smaller skislands as new homes for them, offering unparalleled security. The skisland estates could be approached only by air, and were easily defensible against assault.

There were a few drawbacks, the major one being the restriction from populated areas, which meant any land mass on the planet. Huge gravity-negating fields were at work below the skislands and no one knew the effects of prolonged exposure to the fields on human physiology. No one was volunteering, either. And so the skislands were all to be found hovering over the open sea.

A holographic message was suddenly projected in front of LaNague's flitter. Solid-looking block letters told them to approach no further, or risk being shot from the sky. A vid communication frequency was given if the occupants wished to announce themselves. LaNague tapped in the frequency and spoke.

"This is Peter LaNague. I desire a personal meeting with Eric Boedekker on a matter of mutual interest."

There was no visual reply, only a blank screen and a curt male voice. "One moment." After a brief pause, the voice spoke again. "Audience denied."

"Tell him I bring word from Flint!" LaNague said quickly before the connection could be broken, then turned to Broohnin with a sour expression. " 'Audience denied'! If it weren't so vital that I see him, I'd—"

A bright crimson light began blinking on and off from the roof of a squat square structure to the left of the main buildings. The male voice returned, this time with a screen image to go with it . . . a young man, slightly puzzled, if his expression was a true indicator.

"You may land by the red flasher. Remain in your flitter until the escort arrives to take you inside."

Ω

They walked idly about the great hall of the reconstructed Tudor mansion, waiting for Boedekker to appear. After being carefully scanned for anything that might conceivably be used as a weapon, they had been deposited here to await the great man's pleasure.

"He doesn't appear to be in much of a hurry to see you,"

Broohnin said, staring at the paintings framed in the gold leaf ceiling, the richly paneled walls, the fireplace that was functional but unused—nobody on Earth burned real wood any more.

LaNague appeared unconcerned. "Oh, he is. He's just trying hard not to show it." He ambled around the hall, thin arms folded across his chest, studying the collection of paintings which seemed to favor examples of the satyr-and-nymph school of art.

"Boedekker's probably one of your heroes, isn't he?" Broohnin said, watching LaNague closely for a reaction. He saw one he least expected.

LaNague's head snapped around; his thin lips were drawn into an even thinner line by anger. "Why do you say that? Are you trying to insult me? If you are—"

"Even *I've* heard of Eric Boedekker," Broohnin said. "He single-handedly controls the asteroid mining industry in Sol System. He's rich, he's powerful, he's big business . . . everything you Tolivians admire!"

"Oh. That." LaNague cooled rapidly. He wasn't even going to bother to reply. Broohnin decided to push him further.

"Isn't he the end product of all the things you Tolivians yammer about—free trade, free economy, no restrictions whatsoever? Isn't he the perfect capitalist? The perfect Tolivian?"

LaNague sighed and spoke slowly, as if explaining the obvious to a dim-witted child. It irked Broohnin, but he listened.

"Eric Boedekker never participated in a free market in his life. He used graft, extortion, and violence to have certain laws passed giving him and his companies special options and rights of way in the field of asteroid mineral rights. He used the Earth government to squash most of the independent rock jumpers by making it virtually impossible for them to sell their ore except through a Boedekker company. Nothing you see around you was earned in a free market. He doesn't eliminate his challengers in the market place by innovations or improvements; he has his friends in the government bureaus find ways to put them out of business. He's a corruptor of everything a Tolivian holds dear! He's an economic royalist, not a capitalist!"

LaNague paused to catch his breath, then smiled. "But there's one Earth law even he hasn't been able to circumvent, despite every conceivable scheme to do so: the one person/one child law.''

"I would think that'd be the easiest to get around."

"No. That's the one law that can have no exceptions. Because it affects everyone, applies to everyone the same. It has been held as an absolute for as long as any living human can remember. If you allowed one person to have one extra child—no matter what the circumstances—the entire carefully structured, rigidly enforced population control program would fall apart once word got out."

"But he has two children . . . doesn't he? What's he want another for?"

"His first born was a son, another Eric, by his second wife. When they were in the process of dissolving their marriage, they fought over custody of the child. With Boedekker pulling the strings, there was no chance that the wife would keep the boy, even though by Earth law he was rightfully hers because she had him by intrauterine gestation. In a fit of depression, the woman poisoned herself and the child.

"He fathered a second child, a girl named Liza, by his third wife. Liza was gestated by extrauterine means to avoid potential legal problems should the third marriage break up—which it did. She grew to be the pride of his life as he groomed her to take over his mining empire—"

"A girl?" Broohnin said, surprise evident on his face. "In charge of Boedekker Industries?"

"The pioneer aspects of outworld life have pushed women back into the incubator/nest-keeper role, and it'll be a while before they break out of it again. But on Earth it's different. Anyway, Liza met a man named Fred Kirowicz and they decided to become outworlders. It was only after they were safely on Neeka that she sent her father a message telling him what he could do with Boedekker Industries. Eric tried everything short of abducting her to get her back. And eventually he might have tried that had she not been accidentally killed in a near-riot at one of the Imperial garrisons on Neeka."

"I remember that!" Broohnin said. "Almost two years ago!"

"Right. That was Eric Boedekker's daughter. And now he has no heir. He's been trying for an exemption from the one person/one child rule ever since Liza ran off, but this is something his money and power can't buy him. And he can't go to the outworlds and father a child because the child will then be considered an outworlder and thus forbidden to own property in Sol System. Which leaves him only one avenue to save his pride."

Eric Boedekker entered at the far end of the room. "And what avenue is that, may I ask?" he said.

"Revenge."

Like most Earthies, Eric Boedekker was clean-shaven. Broohnin judged his age to be sixty or seventy standards, yet he moved like a much younger man. His attire and attitude were typical of anyone they had seen since their arrival from the outworlds. Only his girth set him apart. The asteroid mining magnate's appetite for food apparently equaled his appetite for power and money. He took up fully half of an antique love seat when he sat down, and gestured to two other chairs before the cold fireplace.

"Neither of you appears to be a Flinter," he said when Broohnin and LaNague were seated across from him.

"Neither of us is," LaNague replied. "I happen to be a Tolivian and have been in contact with representatives from Flint."

"May I assume that Flint has changed its mind in regard to my offer last year?"

"No."

"Then we have nothing further to discuss." He began to rise from the seat.

"You wanted the Outworld Imperium crushed and destroyed, did you not?" LaNague said quickly. "And you offered the inhabitants of Flint an astonishingly large sum if they would accomplish this for you, did you not?"

Boedekker sat down again, his expression concerned, anxious. "That was privileged information."

"The Flinters brought the offer to a group with which I am connected," LaNague said with a shrug. "And I'm bringing it back to you. I can do it for you, but I don't want your money. I only want to know if you still wish to see the Outworld Imperium in ruins."

Boedekker nodded twice, slowly. "I do. More than anything I can think of. The Imperium robbed me of my only surviving child. Because of it, I have no heir, no way to continue my line and the work I've begun."

"Is that all? You want to bring down a two-hundred-year-old government because of an accident?"

"Yes!"

"Why didn't you try to bring down the Earth government when your first child died?"

Boedekker's eyes narrowed. "I blamed my wife for that. And besides, no one will ever bring the Earth bureaucracy down . . . one would have to use a planetary bomb to unravel that knot."

"There must be more to it than that. I'll have to know if I'm to risk my men and my own resources—a lot of my plan depends on you."

"You wouldn't understand."

"Try me."

"Do you have any children?"

"One. A daughter."

Boedekker's expression showed that he was as surprised as Broohnin. "I didn't think revolutionaries had families. But never mind . . . you should then be able to understand what it's like to groom a child all her life for a position and then have her run off to be a farmer on the edge of nowhere!"

"A daughter isn't a possession. You disowned her?"

"She didn't care! She kept saying . . ." His voice drifted off.

"She tried for a reconciliation?"

Boedekker nodded. "She wanted me to come out and visit her as soon as they had a place of their own." Tears began to well in his eyes. "I told her she'd be dead and buried out there before I ever came to visit."

"I see," LaNague said softly.

"I want to see that pompous ass, Metep, and his rotten Imperium dead and forgotten! Buried like my Liza!"

Broohnin watched and marveled at how LaNague had turned the conversation to his advantage. He was the guest of an extraordinarily powerful man, yet he was in complete control of the encounter.

"Then it shall be done," LaNague replied with startling offhandedness. "But I'll need your co-operation if I'm to succeed. And I mean your *full* co-operation. It may cost you everything you own."

It was Boedekker's turn to shrug. "I have no one I wish to leave anything to. When I die, my relations will war over Boedekker Industries, break it up and run home with whatever pieces they can carry . I'll be just as happy to leave them nothing at all. BI was to be my monument. It was to live long after I was gone. Now . . ."

"I'm offering you the downfall of the Imperium as your monument. Interested?"

"Possibly." He scrutinized LaNague. "But I'll need more than grandiose promises before I start turning my holdings over to you. Much, *much* more."

"I don't want your holdings. I don't want a single Solar credit from you. All you'll have to do is make certain adjustments in the nature of your assets, which need never leave your possession."

"Intriguing. Just what kind of adjustments do you have in mind?"

"I'll be glad to discuss them in detail in private," LaNague said with a glance at Broohnin. "In don't wish to be rude, but you haven't reached the point yet where you can be privy to this information."

Broohnin shot to his feet. "In other words, you don't trust me!"

"If you wish," LaNague replied in his maddeningly impassive voice.

It was all Broohnin could do to keep from reaching for the Tolivian's skinny throat and squeezing it until his eyes bulged out of their sockets. But he managed to turn and walk away. "I'll find my own way out!"

He didn't have to. An armed security woman was waiting on the other side of the door to the great hall. She showed him out to the grounds and left him to himself, although he knew he was constantly watched from the windows.

It was cold, windy, and clear outside the house, but Broohnin found his lungs laboring in the rarefied air. Yet he refused to go back inside. He had to think, and it was so hard to think through a haze of rage.

Walking as close to the edge as the meshed perimeter fence would allow, he looked out and down at the clouds around the skisland. Every once in a while he could catch a glimpse of the ocean below through a break. Far off toward the westering sun he could see a smudge that had to be land, where people like him were jammed so close together they had to go on periodic sprees of violence—short bursts of insanity that allowed them to act sane again for a while afterward. Broohnin understood. Understood perfectly.

He looked back at the mansion and its grounds, trying to imagine the incomprehensible wealth it represented. He hated the rich for having so much more than he did. Another glance in the direction of the megalopolis that had so recently endangered his life and he realized he hated the poor, too . . . because he had always found losers intolerable, had always felt an urge to put them out of their misery.

Most of all, he hated LaNague. He would kill that smug Tolivian on the way back. Only one of them would return to the outworlds alive. When they made their first subspace jump he'd—

No, he wouldn't. The Flinters would be awaiting LaNague's return. He had no desire to try to explain the Tolivian's death at his hands to them!

He cooled, and realized he didn't trust LaNague. There were too many unanswered questions. If Tolive and Flint were going to be spared in the coming economic collapse as LaNague said they would, why were they involved in the revolution? Why didn't they just sit back and refuse to get involved as they had in the past, and just let things take their course?

And then there was the feeling that LaNague was maneuvering him toward something. It was all so subtle that he had no idea in which direction he was being nudged . . . but he felt the nudge. If LaNague was in such complete control of everything, why was he spending so much time with Broohnin? What did he have in mind for him?

"Mr. LaNague awaits you at the flitter dock."

Broohnin spun sharply at the sound of the voice behind him. It was the same female guard who had led him out.

"Something wrong?" she asked.

He ignored her and began walking toward the dock.

Ω

"You'll be taking the *Penton & Blake* back alone," LaNague told him.

Broohnin was immediately suspicious. "What about you?"

"I'm taking the *Adzel* back to Tolive. I've business to attend to there before I return to Throne."

Both men sat staring out the view wall of the *Bernardo de la Paz* way station as the globe of Earth passed above them. La Nague ue had retrieved his tree from the quarantine section and sat with it on his lap.

"And what am I to do until then?"

"You'll be contacted shortly after your return."

"By Flinters?"

LaNague smiled at Broohnin's concern, but it was not a jeering grimace. He seemed relaxed, at ease, almost likable. The thought of returning to his homeworld seemed to have changed him into a different person.

"Flinters make up only a small part of my force on Throne. And they must stay out of sight." He turned toward Broohnin and spoke in a low voice. "Have you ever heard of Robin Hood?"

"Does he live in Primus City?"

LaNague's laughter was gentle and full of good humor. "In a way, yes! You'll become intimate friends, I think. And if all goes well, people will come to think of you and he as one and the same."

"What's that supposed to mean?" Broohnin found this new, easy-going side of LaNague disconcerting, and harder to deal with than the dour, reserved, omniscient conspiratorial mastermind he had been traveling with since their departure from Throne. Which was real?

"All in good time." He rose to his feet. "My ship leaves before yours. Have a good trip. I'll see you again on Throne."

Broohnin watched the Tolivian stroll away with his damned tree under his arm. It was obvious that LaNague thought he was going to use him. That was okay. Broohnin would be quite happy to play along for a while and wait for his chance. He'd let LaNague live as long as he was useful. When the time was right, Broohnin would step in and take over again. And then he would settle with LaNague once and for all.

PART TWO

The Anarchist

The Year of the Tiller

X

The world little knows or cares the storms through which you have had to pass. It asks only if you brought the ship safely to port.

Joseph Conrad

The first time had been a frantic headlong dive to ease a mutual hunger of desperate dimensions, begun and ended so quickly that it had already become a dim memory. The second was more exploratory, a fruitful search for familiar responses, familiar patterns of give and take. And the third was a loving, leisurely welcome home that left them both drained and content.

"Been too long, Peter," Mora said.

"Much."

They huddled in deep-breathing silence for a while, then Peter spoke. "You haven't asked me about the trip."

"I know. I thought it could wait."

"Afraid we'd fight again?"

Peter could feel her head nodding in the dark next to him. "I was sure of it. With the new year beginning, I wanted us to enter it *in* arms instead of *at* arms."

He smiled and held his wife closer. "Well, it's here and so are we. And this is the only way to start a new year."

"You were gone when the Year of the Tortoise began. That was a lonely time. And you won't be here for the Year of the Malak either."

"But I'm here now and we can discuss the rest in the morning. No talk now."

Mora fell asleep first, her head on his shoulder. Peter, despite his fatigue, lay awake awhile longer, listening to the rumble of the storm-whipped surf outside. It was so good to be home. So comfortable. So safe. He knew he could not bring himself to leave again. Let someone else take care of things on Throne from now on. He'd had enough. Next Year Day and every other day in between would find him here in his little house on the dunes. Then the dream would stop.

That decision made, he drifted off to sleep.

The first one was a woman. She slipped through the open bedroom door and slinked across the room toward the bed, a large cloth-wrapped bundle in her arms. After peering carefully at his face to be sure that it was him, her eyes lit with maniacal rage and she dumped the contents of her bundle over him. Thousands of orange and white Imperial mark notes fell like a poisonous snow. She turned and called soundlessly over her shoulder, and soon a steady stream of strangers trailed through the door, all with hate-filled eyes, all with bundles and bushels of mark notes that they emptied over him. He could only move his head back and forth. Mora was gone. He had been left alone to face this silent, murderous crowd. And still they came, and the pile of mark notes covered his face, and he could no longer breathe, and he was dying, dying, suffocated by Imperial marks . . .

Peter awoke in a sitting position, drenched with sweat. It had happened again. The dream had pursued him across half of Occupied Space. That did it! He was through. Tomorrow he'd tell the Trustees to find someone else to handle the revolution.

$$\Omega$$

"Come *on*, Daddy! Hurry, please!"

Children, he thought, trudging up the celadon dune in the wake of his seven-year-old daughter. You go away for a year and a half and you don't recognize them when you come back, they've grown so. And they're a little shy with you at first. But by the next day, they treat you like you were never away.

"I'm coming, Laina." She stood at the top of the dune, slim and sleek and straight and fair, staring seaward, her blond hair streaming in the stiff onshore breeze. Something began to squeeze his larynx and knot the muscles of his jaw as he watched her. *She's growing up without me.* He continued up the dune, not daring to stop.

The wind slapped at him when he reached the top. The weather did nothing to lighten his mood . . . one of those gray days with a slippery slate sky dissolving into a molten lead sea, small white clouds like steam obscuring the junction. Another two steps and he could see the beach: Laina hadn't been exaggerating.

"Daddy, it's really a malak, isn't it?"

"So it is!" Peter muttered, staring at the huge blunt-headed mass of fish flesh, inert and lifeless on the sand near the high water mark. "Last time this happened was when I was about your age. Must be at least thirty meters long! Let's go down for a closer look."

As Laina leaped to run down the dune, Peter scooped her up and swung her to her shoulders, her bare legs straddling the back of his neck. She liked to ride up there—at least she had before he left—and he liked the contact. Needed it.

Sea wind buffeted their ears and salt mist stung their eyes as they approached the decaying form.

"A sieve malak, leviathan class," he told her, then sniffed the air. "And starting to stink already. Before they were all killed off, there used to be creatures like this on Earth called baleen whales. But whales weren't fish. Our malaks are true fish."

Laina was almost speechless with awe at the immensity of the creature. "It's so big! What killed it?"

"Could've died of old age out at sea and drifted in, but I don't see much evidence of the scavengers having been at it. Probably got confused by the storm last night and wound up beached. I read somewhere that all the insides get crushed when a malak is beached . . . killed by its own weight."

"Must eat a whole lotta other fish to make it grow so big."

"Actually it doesn't eat other fish at all." He walked her closer to the huge mouth that split the head, their approach stirring up a flight of scale-winged keendars from their feast on the remains. "See those big plates of hairy bone along the upper jaw . . . looks like a comb? That's the sieve. As they swim along, these malaks strain sea water through their sieve and eat all the tiny animals they trap in the hairs. Mostly it's stuff called plankton.''

He let Laina down on the sand so she could run up for a closer look. She wasn't long—the stench from the cavernous maw was too strong to allow a leisurely inspection.

"What's plankton?" she asked as she returned to his side. "I never heard of that before."

"Let's go back up on the dune where the smell isn't so bad and I'll tell you all about it."

Hand in hand they plodded through the damp, yielding blue granules to a point overlooking the waterline, yet beyond the carcass' fulsome stench, and watched the screaming, circling keendars for a quiet moment.

"Still interested in plankton?" Receiving a nod, Peter spoke in a slow, almost reminiscent manner, gearing his explanation to a child's mind, yet keeping it up at a level where Laina would have to reach a bit.

"Plankton is the basic food of the sea. It's billions of tiny little creatures, some plants, some animals, but all very, very tiny. They gather in huge batches out at sea, some just drifting others wiggling a little whip-like arm called a flagellum to push them here and there.

"All they really do is live and die and provide food for most of the ocean. They probably think they know just where they're going, never realizing that all the time the entire plankton patch is being pushed about at the whim of wind and current. They get gobbled up by huge sieve malaks that can't see what they're eating, and the plankton don't even know they've been eaten till it's over and done with."

"Poor plankton!" Laina said, concern showing in her face.

"Oh, they're happy in their own way, I suppose. And while the malaks are cutting huge swaths out of their ranks, they just go on whipping the old flagella about and having a grand time. Even if you tried to tell them of the malaks and other sea creatures that constantly feed off them, they wouldn't believe you."

"How come you know so much about plankton?"

"I've studied it up close," Peter said, thoughts of Earth flashing through his mind.

Laina eyed the long baleen combs on the malak's jaw. "Glad I'm not a plankton."

"If I have my way," Peter said, putting his arm protectively around his daughter, "you never will be." He stood up and gave the inert leviathan one last look. "But it's nice to know that malaks die, too. Let's go. Your mother'll have the morning soup ready and we don't want cold soup."

Backs to the ocean, they walked along the blue dune toward the house, wind spasms allowing a murmur or two of small talk to drift back to the beach where keendars were crying the sound that had given them their name and pecking morsels from the malak's landward eye, glazed and forever sightless.

Ω

"You're going back, aren't you," Mora said as they sat in the Ancestor Grove under Peter's great-grandfather tree. He hadn't told her of his pre-dawn resolution to stay, and was glad. The light of day quickly revealed the many flaws in plans that had seemed so simple and forthright in the darkness. He had to go back. There was no other way.

"I must." Leaning against the tree, a much larger version of Pierrot, gave him the strength to say it. On the day of his great-grandfather's death, a hole had been dug into the root ball of this tree and the coffinless remains interred there. Throughout the remainder of the following year, the tree had absorbed nutrients from the decomposing body, incorporating them into itself, growing taller on the unique organic fertilizer. The seeds that formed on the tree's branches the following spring were saved until the birth of the next LaNague child. And on that day, the day of Peter LaNague's birth, two of those seeds were planted—one in the Ancestor Grove, and one in an earthenware pot that would remain cribside as the child grew.

The Tolivian mimosa, it had been learned, possessed a unique ability to imprint on a human being. A seedling—called a *misho*—in constant exposure to a growing child will become attuned to that particular child, sensitive to and reflective of his or her moods. The art of branch and root pruning, necessary to limit the tree's size, is carefully taught as the child grows. Raising a child with a personal *misho* was a common practice on Tolive, but hardly universal. Mora's family considered it a silly custom and so she was never given her own tree, and now could never have one since codevelopment was necessary for imprinting. She could never understand the indefinable bond between her husband and Pierrot, nor the growing bond between Laina and her own *misho*, but she could see that it seemed to add an extra dimension to each of them and felt poorer for never having experienced it herself.

Peter looked at his wife in the midday light. She hadn't changed, not in the least. The deep, shining, earthy brown of her hair caught the gold of the Tolivian sun and flung it back. The simple shift she wore did little to hide the mature curves enclosed within. She appeared at ease as she reclined against him, but he knew that was a façade.

"The gloves ready?" he asked, making small talk.

"A hundred pairs. They've been ready for a long time." She looked away as she spoke.

"And the coins?"

"Being minted as fast as possible. But you know that."

Peter nodded silently. He knew. He had seen the reports around the house. Mora was a supervisor at the mint. The star-in-the-ohm design was hers, in fact.

"You could still get out of it," she said abruptly, twisting toward him.

"I could. But would you want to live with me if I did?"

"Yes!"

"I don't think I'd be good company."

"I don't care! You know how I feel. This revolution is all a huge mistake. We should just sit back and let them all rot. We've no obligation to them. They built the fire—let them burn!" Mora was not alone in her opinion; quite a few Tolivians were uncomfortable with the idea of fomenting a revolution.

"But we'll burn, too, Mora. And you know that. We've been over this a thousand times, at least. When the Imperium economy crumbles—and it's already started to—they'll go looking for ways to bolster the mark. The only way for a bankrupt economy to do that is to find a huge new market, or to confiscate a hoard of gold and silver and use it to make its currency good again. Tolive is known to be the largest hoarder of precious metals in Occupied Space. They'll come to us and they won't be asking, they'll be demanding—with the full force of the Imperial Guard ready to back up any threat they care to make."

"With Flint on our side we could hold them off!" Mora said eagerly. "And then the Imperium will fall apart on its own. All we have to do is hold them off long enough!"

"And then what? With the Imperium gone, Earth will step in and take over the outworlds without a single energy bolt being fired. With everything in chaos, Earth will act as if it's doing everyone a favor. But this time they'll make sure none of the outworlds gets free again. This time they'll not allow maverick planets like Tolive and Flint to remain aloof. And with our own resources already drained by a drawn-out battle with the Imperium, we'll have no chance at all against the forces Earth will array against us. There *must* be a revolution now if there's to be a free Tolive for Laina."

"You don't know that Earth'll take us over!" Mora said, warming to their habitual argument. "You want to cut all the outworlds free of the Imperium so they can go their own ways. But do you have the right to do that? Do you have the right to cut people free like that? A lot of them won't want it, you know. A lot of people are scared to death of freedom. They *want* somebody hanging over them all the time, wiping their noses when they're sad, paddling their rumps when they diverge from the norm."

"They can have it, if they wish! They can set up their own little authoritarian enclaves and live that way if it pleases them. I don't care. Just don't include me, my family, my planet, or anybody else who thinks that's no way to live! We have a right to try to preserve a place for the safety and growth of the people, ideas, and things we value!"

Despite her anguish, Mora could not bring herself to disagree with him then, for she believed what he believed, and valued what he valued. Tears came to her eyes as she pounded her small fists futilely against the ground at the base of the tree.

"But it doesn't have to be you! Somebody else can go! It doesn't have to be *you!*"

Wrapping his arms around her, Peter held her close, his lips to her ear, aching to tell her what she wanted to hear, but unable to. "It has to be me. The Charter, the Sedition Trust, they've all been LaNague family projects for generations. And it so happens that the destruction of the Imperium, which we all knew would someday be necessary, has fallen to me."

He rose and pulled her gently to her feet, keeping his arm around her. "I'll walk you home. Then I've got to go see the Trustees."

Mora was quiet for a while as they walked through the sun-dappled tranquillity of the Ancestor Grove. Then: "You should stop by the Ama Co-operative on your way to the Trustees. Adrynna's been sick."

Sudden fear jolted him. "She's dying?"

"No. She recovered. But still, she's old and who knows . . . ? She may not be here when you get back."

"I'll stop in first thing this afternoon."

Ω

Peter was consistently struck by the smallness of the Ama Cooperative whenever he visited it, probably because all his impressions of the asymmetrical collection of squat buildings where the teachers of Kyfho dwelt were gathered during his childhood. He was announced via intercom from the courtyard and granted immediate entry. Everyone knew who he was and knew his time on the planet was short. He found his ama, his lifelong intellectual guide and philosophical mentor, in her room, gazing out the window from her low chair.

"Good day, Ama Adrynna," he said from the doorway.

She swiveled at the sound of his voice, squinting in his direction. "Come into the light where I can have a good look at you." Peter obliged, moving toward the window, where he squatted on his haunches next to her. She smiled, cocking her head left, then right. "So it's you after all. You've come to say good-by to your old ama."

"No. Just hello. I'm on my way to the Trustees and thought I'd stop in and see you. Heard you've been sick or something like that."

She nodded. "Something like that." She had aged considerably but had changed little. Her hair, completely white now, was still parted in the middle and pulled down each side of her face in two severe lines. The face was tightly wrinkled, the mouth a mobile gash, the body painfully lean. Yet her eyes were still the beacons of reason and unshakable integrity that had inspired him throughout his youth and continued to fuel him to this day.

He had seen little of her in the past decade. As a member of the amae, Adrynna spent her days teaching and defining the Kyfho philosophy, and he had progressed beyond the stage where he relied on her counsel. He had taken what she had taught him and put it to use. Yet a large part of whatever he was and whatever he would be derived from the years he had spent at her knee. Tolive, the outworlds, humanity, and Peter LaNague would be so much poorer when she was gone.

"The Trustees, eh?" Adrynna continued, her eyes narrowing. "The Sedition Trust is now your plaything, Peter. Whatever the Trustees think or say or do means nothing now that the revolution mechanism has been set in motion. Only the man in charge on Throne has the final say. And that man is you, Peter. For many generations, countless Tolivians have denied their heirs a single ag by willing all their possessions to the Sedition Trust upon their deaths. Their beliefs, their fortunes, the products of their lives ride to Throne with you, Peter LaNague.''

"I know." No one had to tell him. The burden of that knowledge weighed on him every day. "I won't fail them, Adrynna."

"What you mean by failure and what I mean by failure may be two different things. You know the quote by that old Earthie writer, Conrad, about bringing ships to port? Then you know that he was not talking about Tolive. *This* world cares about the storms through which you'll have to pass. Our concern for your mission is not limited to its success. We will want to know *how* you succeeded. We will want to know what moral corners you had to cut, and will want 'None' for an answer.''

"You taught me well. You must know that.''

"I only know one thing," the old woman said in a voice ringing with her fierce conviction, "and that is that the revolution must be conducted in accordance with the principles of Kyfho if it is to have any real meaning. There must be no bloodshed, no violence unless it is defensive, *no* coercion! We must do it our way and our way alone! To do otherwise is to betray centuries of hardship and struggle. Above all else: Kyfho. Forget Kyfho in your pursuit of victory over the enemy, and you will become the enemy . . . worse than the enemy, for he doesn't know he is capable of anything better.''

"I know, Adrynna. I know all too well.''

"And beware the Flinters. They may be Kyfhons, but they follow a degraded version of the philosophy. They have embraced violence too tightly and may overreact. Watch them, as we will watch you.''

He nodded, rose, and kissed her forehead. It was hardly a comforting thought to know that his actions would be under such close scrutiny. But it was hardly a new thought, either—it had come with the territory.

The Trustees were his next stop: three people who, like many before them, had been elected guardians of the fund begun by the LaNague family in the early days of the colony.

There being no government to speak of on Tolive, the matter of undermining a totalitarian state had been left to the efforts of individuals, and would be backed by that fund: the Sedition Trust. No one had envisioned an Outworld Imperium then—it had always been assumed that Earth would be the target of the Trust. And until recently, the job of Trustee—decided by votes from all contributors—had been a simple bookkeeping task. Now it was different. Now they held the purse strings on the revolution.

Yet Adrynna, in her offhanded manner that cut as quick and true as a vibe-knife, had pointed out something Peter had overlooked. The revolution as it was set up was really a one-man operation. Peter LaNague would make the moment-to-moment decisions and adjust its course as he went along. With the Trustees light years away, Peter LaNague was the revolution.

Adrynna must have had the most say in his being chosen as the agent provocateur—an ama knew her student better than a parent knew a child. Of course, out of deference to the founding family of the Sedition Trust, the same family that had spent generations honing a charter for a new organization which would rise from the ashes of the revolution, a LaNague would always have first consideration for the task if he or she were willing . . . and capable . . . and of the necessary fiber. The task was rife with possibilities for abuse—from simple malfeasance to outright betrayal of the cause—and could not be entrusted to someone merely because of lineage.

Peter LaNague had apparently met all the criteria. And when offered the job, had accepted. He had been working as a landscaper, a task that kept his hands busy but had allowed his mind long periods in which to roam free. He had known the call was coming and had developed myriad ideas on how to assault the Imperium's weak points. Circumstances, the Neeka incident, and Boedekker's subsequent proposal to the Flinters had narrowed him down to a devious strategy that would strike at the heart of the Imperium. It had all been so clean and simple then, so exciting in the planning stage. Now, in the midst of the sordid details of actually bringing the plan to fruition, he found he had lost all of his former enthusiasm. He wanted it over and done with.

All three Trustees were waiting for him when he arrived at the two-story structure that sat alone on the great north-western plain of Tolive's second-largest continent, the building people called "Sedition Central." It was to these men and this building that the Flinters had come with news of what Eric Boedekker had offered them in exchange for the Imperium's demise. Peter LaNague's life had been radically altered by that information.

After greetings and drink-pouring, Peter and the Trustees seated themselves in an open square. Waters, senior Trustee, brought the talk around to business.

"We've all heard your report and agree that the killing of the assassin was justified and unavoidable."

"If there had been another way, I would have tried it," Peter said. "But if we hadn't moved immediately, he would have murdered Metep. It was a life for a life."

"And the agreement with Boedekker? He's actually staking his fortune on you?"

Peter nodded. "He's risking little. The necessary conversions merely change the nature of his assets. They never leave his control."

"But if you're successful, he'll be ruined," said Connors, the most erudite of the Trustees. "He must know that! He certainly didn't reach his present position by taking this kind of risk!"

"He doesn't care about his present position. He wanted to build a monolithic financial empire and center it around his family. But he's lost his family, and the Earth government won't let him start another. My plan gives him the opportunity to use his own empire to destroy another empire, the one that destroyed the last hope of his dream becoming reality. He agreed."

"Then that's it!" Waters said. "It's all set!"

"Yes . . . yes, I think so."

"What about this Broohnin you mention?" It was Silvera, youngest of the three and an eminent architect before she became a Trustee. "He worries me."

"Worries me, too," Peter said. "But I think—I hope—I've dazzled him enough to keep him off balance for a while."

"He does sound dangerous," Connors added. "Violent, too."

"He's a wild card—as dangerous as they come and as unpredictable. But I can't bring the revolution through in the necessary time period without his contacts. I don't like him, I don't trust him, but without his co-operation there can be no revolution."

The three Trustees considered this in silence. Only Connors had further comment.

"Is your five-year limit that strict? Can't we afford a year or two extra to slip our own people into sensitive positions?"

"Absolutely not!" Peter replied, shaking his head vigorously. "The economic situation is going to deteriorate rapidly on its own. If we allow seven, or even six years before we bring the house down, there may be nothing left to salvage. We figure that twenty years from now the Imperium, even if left alone, will be in such disarray that Earth could move in unchallenged. What we need is quick collapse and quick reconstruction before Earth is able to make its move. We can do it on a five-year schedule. On a seven-year schedule, I doubt we could move fast enough to keep the Earthies out." He held up the fingers of his right hand. "Five years. No more. And only four are left."

Connors persisted: "Couldn't we use Broohnin's organization without him?"

"Possibly. But that could be risky. We might be suspected of collusion with the Imperium. If that happened, we'd get no co-operation at all. Broohnin has valuable contacts in most of the trade guilds, in the Imperial communications centers, in the Treasury itself. Plus, there's a minor vid personality and a professor at the University of the Outworlds who might prove useful. They're peripherally associated with Broohnin's group, not necessarily out of approval of his methods, but because he's the only resistance they've got. I need Broohnin to reach them."

"I see then we have no choice," Connors said resignedly. "But it *feels* wrong, and that bothers me."

"You're not alone."

Ω

Despite her best efforts to stanch them, tears were brimming and spilling over Mora's lower eyelids. She faced away from the smooth, flat expanse of the spaceport grid and the orbital shuttle patiently waiting on it.

"I don't want you to go," she said against her husband's chest. "Something's going to happen, I know it."

"The Imperium's going to come crashing down," Peter said with all the confidence he could muster. "That's what's going to happen."

"No. To you. Something bad. I can feel it. Let somebody else go."

"I can't."

"You can!" She lifted her head and looked at him. "You've done your share—more! All the groundwork is laid. It's just a matter of time from now on. Let somebody else finish it!"

Peter shook his head sadly. There was nothing in Occupied Space he wanted more than to stay right where he was. But that couldn't be.

"It has to be me, Mora. It's my plan. I've got to handle it, I've got to be there myself."

"There must be some other person you can trust!" Mora's tears were drying in the heat of growing anger. "Surely you don't think you're the only one capable of overseeing the revolution. You can't tell me that!"

"I must know! I can't sit light years away and entrust this to someone else. It's too delicate. The future of everything we've worked for is at stake. I can't walk away. I want to—but I cannot!"

"But you can walk away from me! And from Laina! Is that so much easier?"

"Mora, please! That's not fair!"

"Of course it's not fair! And it's not fair that your daughter won't see you for years now! Maybe never again! She was so upset about your leaving again that she wouldn't even come down to the spaceport! And as for my having a husband—" She pulled free of his arms.

"Mora!"

"Maybe Laina had the right idea!" She was backing away from him as she spoke. "Maybe we both should have stayed home and let you come here all by yourself. We're both second place in your life now anyway!" She swung around and began walking away.

"Mora!" Peter heard his voice break as he called after his wife. He started to follow her but stopped after two steps. She was beyond gentle reasoning now. They were two stubborn people who shared a life as fierce in its discord as in its love-making. He knew from long experience that it would be hours before the two of them could carry on a civil conversation . . . and there were no hours left to him on Tolive. There were complex interstellar travel connections to be made and he had to leave now. If he tarried too long, his arrival on Throne could be delayed as long as a standard month.

He watched her until she rounded a bend in the corridor, hoping she would look back, just once. She never did.

Peter LaNague entered the boarding tube that would drop him at the waiting shuttle. Dealing with Den Broohnin, keeping the Flinters in line, masterminding a revolution that still hinged on too many variables, that if successful would significantly alter the course of human history . . . none of these disturbed his *wah* as much as an argument with that stubborn, hot-tempered, and occasionally obnoxious creature called Mora, who could make his life so miserable at times, and yet make it all so worth while. He would never understand it.

It helped somewhat when he glimpsed her standing on the observation tower, gripping the railing with what he knew must be painful intensity, watching the shuttle, waiting for lift-off. It helped, but it failed to loosen the knot that had tightened to the fraying point in the center of his chest, nor did it lighten the lead cast that sat where his stomach had been.

He could not allow himself to dwell on Mora, nor on Laina. They were a part of his life that had to be completely walled off if he were to function effectively on Throne. As the shuttle rose toward the stars, he cast Mora as Fortunato, played Montresor himself, and began the brickwork.

It hurt.

THE ROBIN HOOD READER

Good News

Average wages increased a full five per cent (5%) in the past standard year. More outworlders are earning more than ever before.

Bad News

Inflation hit a full eight per cent (8%) last year. Subtract this from the five per cent (5%) average increase in wages and you're left with a bit of a deficit. In other words, despite an increase in wages, your buying power is now three per cent (3%) less than last year. Sorry.

Worse

Because the schedule of progressive tax rates has not been corrected for inflation, more and more outworlders are moving into the upper income brackets and paying upper bracket taxes. Now, if you've read the above, you know that increased income no longer means increased buying power. And now that tax time is here, you'll find your buying power further diminished by the fact that you will be giving more of those hard-earned marks to the Imperial Tax Service.

The Economic Weather Eye

PRICE INDEX (using the 115th year of the Imperium—when the Imperial mark became mandatory legal tender—as base year of 100)   160.2

MONEY SUPPLY (M3)   995.7

UNEMPLOYMENT LEVEL   7.9%

	Imperial Marks	Solar Credits
GOLD (Troy ounce)	244.3	130.5
Silver (Troy ounce)	11.2	6.0
Bread (1 kg. loaf)	.69	1.80

XI

> The free man will ask neither what his country can do for him nor what he can do for his country.
>
> *Milton Friedman*

It was just another warehouse on the outskirts of Primus City, no different from the dozens of others surrounding it. The name across the front wall, ANGUS BLACK IMPORTS, told the passer-by nothing about the company or what lay within. It could house crates of vid sets, racks of open-seamed clothing ready for autofitting, or seafood delicacies from planets like Friendly or Gelk. Just another warehouse. LaNague wanted it that way.

Tonight was the first step in the active phase, the first blow against the empire, the first physical act of sedition. The principals were all present, along with a few extraneous characters who were there to see them off and wish them well. Faces that had been new three months ago could be seen here and there across the wide, empty interior of the warehouse . . . LaNague had come to know them all intimately since his return from Tolive, gaining their confidence, and they gaining his. Singly, then in pairs, then in a group, they approached him as he entered the warehouse carrying a box under his arm.

Zachariah Brophy, professor of economics at the University

of the Outworlds, was the first. Very tall, bony, knobby, and sixtyish, he raised a knotted fist toward LaNague's face.

"Either you let me go along or I flatten you right here and now!"

LaNague laughed. "Sorry, Doc, but we don't have a holo-suit to fit you, and I'm afraid some of your former students would recognize you even if we did."

"Aahh!" he sighed with exaggerated despondency, un-folding his fist and laying the open hand on the younger man's thin shoulder. "You've been telling me no all along. I guess now I'll have to believe you."

LaNague had developed a genuine affection for the older man, loved his wit, his intelligence, his integrity. And Doc Zack, as his students had called him for years, reciprocated warmly. Apparently he saw many things he liked in LaNague, the same things he had sought and found lacking in Broohnin. He made no secret of his relief at the fact that LaNague had superseded him.

"Why don't you try your hand at one of the flyers," LaNague suggested. "We've fallen behind schedule because of all the calling cards we've been duplicating for tonight. You can draft up the next *Robin Hood Reader* while we're out playing the part."

"Fair enough. At least I'll get to be one of the Merry Men one way or another." He squeezed LaNague's shoulder where his hand rested. "Good luck tonight." He turned and made his way toward the bank of duplicators against the rear wall.

Radmon Sayers was next, stopping briefly on his way out. He was portrait handsome with the perfect features and metic-ulous grooming that befitted a vid personality. His sleek black hair reflected the ceiling lights as it lay plastered against his scalp in the latest fashion. His eyes were less calculating and more genuinely lively tonight.

"It's really going to happen, isn't it!" he said, rubbing gloved hands together in barely suppressed glee.

"Did you think all these preparations were for some elab-orate hoax?" LaNague replied evenly, trying to keep annoy-ance out of his voice. He had found Sayers aloof and hard to like. He gave news reports on one of the smaller independent vid systems on Throne. He was good—able to project sincer-ity, objectivity, and concern as well as anybody else in the business, but was condemned to relative obscurity by the fact that most of Throne's population watched the Imperial Vid

System, which had long ago commandeered the best wave-lengths and transmitted with the strongest signal. His obscurity, however, was destined to be short-lived if LaNague had his way.

"No, of course not," Sayers said. "But still, it's hard to believe that tonight I've been involved in making some news instead of just reading it. That'll be nice for a change. Very nice."

"You've got your diversion set?"

Sayers nodded. "We'll monitor the official channels, as usual. When we hear them talking about the hijack, I'll delay the remote crew until it starts to rain."

"Good. Just watch the time."

There were further words of encouragement to say to the tense men who were gathered around the large, enclosed flitter lorry sitting in the middle of the warehouse floor. Computer experts, communication technicians, Flinters, street toughs, all gravitated toward the one who would make them into wanted men tonight. Only Broohnin hung back, conspicuous by his lack of enthusiasm.

"All right," LaNague said after a while. "It's full dark outside by now and time to go. But first, I want you all to wear these."

He opened the box he had been carrying under his arm and began handing out pairs of transparent, gossamer-light gloves.

"What're these?" someone asked.

"They serve two purposes. First of all, they protect all of you from any chance of leaving epidermic clues behind. All the Imperial investigators have to do is find one of your skin cells when they go over the hijacked ships tomorrow—and believe me, they'll go over them as they've never been gone over before—and they'll have your genotype, which they'll try to match against every type on record. Some of you had to have a genotype recording made when you applied for the sensitive jobs you're in. If one of your cells is identified, you're as good as caught.

"The second reason for wearing these gloves has to do with the fine little pattern of whorls you'll notice on the palmar surface. The gloves are made of a micropore material that will let sweat and skin oils through . . . enough to leave good fingerprints."

A sudden murmur of protest arose from the group, but LaNague quelled it by raising his hand.

"Don't worry. They won't be your fingerprints. They'll be my great-grandfather's. He knew the revolution would come someday, and knew he wouldn't be around to see it. So his dying request was that someone wear gloves like these at some time during the revolution, just so he could say he had a hand in the downfall of the Imperium."

The ensuing laughter lightened the mood as the men, fifteen of them, filed quickly and spiritedly into the flitter. LaNague felt no lightness, however. His palms were moist and he had a pain crawling up the back of his head from his neck—this was the first overt move and everything had to be just right. But he hid his fears well, pretending to have everything under control, exuding confidence and competence he did not feel.

Josef acted as pilot on the way out; another would return the ship after the Merry Men were dropped off. The wide warehouse doors opened and allowed the flitter to slide out into the night. It flew low and slow until past the Primus City limits, then rose to thirty meters where it could pick up speed and be safe from interfering treetops.

"Everyone have their projectors secured?" LaNague asked once they had reached cruising speed. There was a murmured assent from the group crowded into the cargo area. "All right. Let's try them."

The holosuit was a whimsical concoction, designed for imaginative types who found stimulation in role-playing. The most popular models were sexual in nature, but those to be employed tonight had been specially modified. They were the standard six-piece models consisting of two wrist bands, two ankle bands, a belt, and a skull cap. When activated, they formed a holographic sheath around the wearer, a costume of light that could make him appear to be anything he chose—a male, a female, a demon, a lover. Anything, depending on what had been programmed into the unit.

The suits flickered to life one by one, causing their wearers to fade from view, replaced by lean and wolfish outlaws garbed in leather and Lincoln green, topped by jaunty, feathered caps. To any of their contemporaries, the men in the command flitter would be as alien in appearance as creatures from another galaxy. A few adjustments had to be made, especially on one man's skull cap which failed to activate, leaving his own head and shoulders exposed. This was quickly remedied, bringing his appearance into line with his companions'.

"This is stupid!"

It was Broohnin. He had already doused his holosuit and leaned sullenly against the wall opposite LaNague, scowling through his beard.

"I expected that from you," LaNague replied without missing a beat. "Care to give us grounds for your opinion? We've got time to listen."

Broohnin swaggered into the middle of the group. It was obvious that he still considered himself the unacknowledged leader, despite the fact that LaNague was giving the orders. He was keeping to his role of the tough, hard-hitting, no-quarter revolutionary. It had worked before, and there was no reason why it shouldn't work now.

"We're just playing games with these funnysuits! This is no masquerade ball—this is the real thing! We're not going to get prizes for how good we look; we're just going to get stunned and maybe even blasted into a couple of pieces by the fecaliths guarding this shipment. We have to hit them *hard!* Make them remember us! Let them know we mean business! Make them leave the lights on at night when they go to sleep! Never let them forget we're out here, ready to strike at any time, without warning!"

"Then you think we should forget disguise and mount a frontal assault?" LaNague said, unmoved by the oratory.

"Absolutely!"

"What about the multiple cameras in each of the ships we're going after tonight? Our images will be transmitted to the Imperial Guard the instant we board the first currency ship. We'll all be marked men after that!"

"Don't board!" Broohnin snarled. "Blow them to bits! *Then* let the cameras try to take our pictures!"

"There are men on board each of those ships. They'll be killed."

"They're Imperial lackies—they take the pay, they take the chances. This time they lose."

"And what of your own man on board the second ship. You intend to blow him up, too?"

"Of course not! We'll get him off first, then blow the rest."

The momentum of the argument was swinging toward Broohnin. He offered easy solutions, hard and fast victory. But he had left an opening for LaNague.

"You realize, don't you, that as the only survivor, your man will become an instant fugitive. Every Imperial Guardsman on Throne will be hunting him as an accomplice in the slaughter of their comrades. Do you wish that on him?"

Broohnin paused for an instant, and in that instant he lost his audience. LaNague had shown that he had considered the problem from more sides than his burlier counterpart; and while it might be said that he seemed to be overly concerned for the well-being of the men guarding the targeted currency shipment, it was also obvious that he was equally concerned about the men who would be at his side during tonight's raid.

But LaNague would not let it go at that. He had to win these men firmly to his side. So firmly, that if it came to a choice between Peter LaNague and Den Broohnin, the men would choose LaNague.

"There's more to these holosuits than a mere masquerade ball, I assure you," he said, ostensibly speaking to Broohnin, but letting his gaze rest in turn on each and every man in the flitter. "We need to protect our identities—that's our primary requirement for success. If we can't move about freely on Throne, we've lost our usefulness. Another thing: there's always a chance that one or even all of us might someday be captured; how we're treated then will depend a lot on how we treat the crews of the transports tonight, and how we treat all Imperial Guardsmen in the future. Remember that. So—if we intend to leave live witnesses behind, we need disguises. And if we intend to use disguises, *why not make a point with them!*"

He paused to let this sink in. He was marking a trail of logic and he wanted no one to lose his way. All eyes were on him. Even Broohnin's.

"The Robin Hood motif was not chosen capriciously. As most of you remember, he was a mythical do-gooder on Old Earth who supposedly robbed from the rich and gave to the poor. But that's the sanitized, government-approved version of the legend. Anyone reading between the lines will see that Robin Hood was the archetypical tax rebel. He robbed from the rich, yes—but those rich happened to be King John's tax collectors. And he gave to the poor—but his beneficiaries were those who had been looted by the tax collectors. He merely returned their own property.

"So what we're going to do tonight," he said, lowering his voice to a conspiratorial undertone, "is replay history. Metep is King John, we're Robin Hood and his Merry Men, and tonight we rob from the very rich—the Imperial Treasury. By the end of tonight, the poor—the public, that is—will be the recipients of our good deed." He smiled. "I doubt the message will be lost on them."

LaNague's smile was returned by the faces around him. He debated whether or not to delve into the other reason for his resurrection of Robin Hood. This was probably not the time or place for it . . .

Josef's voice cut through his thoughts and made the decision for him: *"We're over the drop-off spot. Going down."*

Ω

It was tax time on Throne. For two months, the good citizens would be required to figure out how much they owed the Imperium for the preceding year, subtract from that what they had already given over in withholding taxes, and remit the difference. The Imperium called it "a voluntary tax system." Those who refused to pay, however, were fined or jailed.

Throne's population was clustered on a single large land mass, with Primus City occupying the central plateau, four thousand kilometers from each coast. Inhabitants of the central regions sent their taxes directly to Primus City. Regional Revenue Centers collected the extorted marks on the coasts and shipped them inland to the Treasury Bureau for culling and replacement of old currency. From there it disappeared into the insatiable maw of the Imperium bureaucracy.

A three-ship convoy was on its way now from the west coast Regional Revenue Center, laden with currency as it flew over the barren hinterlands between the coast and the central plateau. The transports were well armed and manned with members of the Imperial Guard. This was purely routine, however, since no one had ever even attempted to hijack a currency transport since the runs began.

Ω

Erv Singh waited for the lurch. If he had timed everything right, the circuits would be overloading just about now. He waited, and it came. A gentle tug, imperceptible to someone who wasn't looking for it. But it was there, and it meant that Mother Gravity was firming up her grip on the ship. He watched the altimeter start to slip, gave the anti-grav generator a little more juice to no avail. The warning light flashed red. They were sinking. Right on schedule.

"Ship Two to Leader," he said into the communicator

panel. "We're getting heavy here. No a-g response. I think we've got an overload."

"Hit the auxiliary, Ship Two," came the calm reply.

"Will do." He phased in the backup a-g generator, but there was no boost in altitude. After a sufficient trial: "Sorry, Leader, but we're still getting heavier. Up to zero-point-four-five normal mass now and sinking. I think we'd better turn back."

"You'll never make it, Two. Not at the rate you're putting on mass. Better look for a place to put down and see what's wrong."

"Right. Shouldn't be too hard to find." Erv Singh knew it wouldn't be too hard at all. He had the place all picked out. He just hoped everybody below was insulated by now. "Looks like a good clearing half a kilometer ahead. How does she scan?"

The reply was delayed for a few prolonged heartbeats. *"Nothing but big rocks and bush. No movement, no major heat sources, not even any minor lifeforms. Looks safe. You go down and we'll keep cover overhead."*

"What's up?" One of the guards had come up from the rear. "Why we going down?"

"No life. We're almost to normal mass," Erv told him.

"Hey, Singh—you mean you can't even fly from the back burgs to Primus without a breakdown? Some pilot!"

Erv looked suitably annoyed. "You want to take over? I'd take baby-sitting all that money any day to trying to fly this piece of junk!"

"Don't get excited, Erv," the guard said. "There's nothing to look at back there anyway. It's all crated and it's all very dull."

"Then get back there before it runs away."

Singh overrode the guidance cassette and took manual control of Ship Two, settling it gently into a clearing ringed by the deciduous, red-leafed brush indigenous to Throne's hinterlands. The two companion ships in the convoy circled warily overhead. After releasing the safety locks on the a-g generator inspection ports from his command center, Singh opened the hatch and strolled out for a look. After shining a hand lamp into two of the ports, he turned and hurried back inside.

"I'm down to stay, Leader," Erv said, returning to his communicator.

"That bad?"

"Everything's burned up."

"Look like sabotage?"

"I wouldn't know sabotage if I saw it. All I know is I can't fix it." There was silence at the other end. Erv allowed sufficient time for thought, then made his own suggestion, a pre-planned red herring. "Why don't you guys stay up there and keep watch while we wait for another ship from the center. I can transfer my cargo over and then you can all be on your way."

"No," came the reply after a brief pause. *"Take too long."* Erv knew what was going through the convoy leader's head: it was to have been a quick and simple run tonight: leave early, get to the Primus Treasury, unload, and spend a night on the town. If they wasted half the night waiting for a replacement ship, there'd be no fun and games in Primus City. *"We're coming down."*

"You think that's wise?"

"Let me worry about that. The area scans clean. We'll off-load your consignment and divide it up between Ships One and Three. Then we'll head for the Treasury while you wait for a lift."

"Thanks a lot, Leader." Erv refrained from showing the relief he felt, knowing that his every move was being recorded. The bait had been taken.

"Sorry, Ship Two, but somebody's got to stay with her."

Erv waited at the hatch until the other two cargo flitters were down. In strict compliance with regulations, he ordered one of the three guards in the cargo bay to man the external weapons control panel, then opened the rear of the ship, letting the loading ramp slide toward the ground. The same procedure began on the other ships and soon the men were transferring the cargo from Ship Two to the other two, pushing float-dollies down the ramps, across the dirt and grass, and into the waiting holds.

The men moved warily at first, on guard against any would-be hijackers. But as the work progressed and the scanners picked up no suspicious activity in the surrounding area, they relaxed and talked and joked among themselves. The talk concerned the near-superhuman feats they would perform tonight once they were let loose in Primus; the jokes were mostly at the expense of Erv and his crew, teasing them about what they were going to miss.

Ship Two was soon emptied of her cargo of currency, every last crate of it squeezed into the companion ships. As his own crew sat inside the barren hold, grousing about being left behind, Erv stood at his boarding hatch, watching, listening. He saw the other crews begin to board their own ships, and heard a shout from the man at the weapons console behind him:

"We've got activity outside, Erv! Lifeforms! A whole bunch of them coming out of nowhere! Almost on top of us!"

"Close up quick!" Erv yelled in reply. "But whatever you do, don't fire—you'll hit the other ships!"

The boarding hatch started to slide closed, but not before a running figure darted by and threw something. There were metallic pings as a number of tiny silver balls danced along the ship's deck and bounced off the walls. Erv knew what was next. His hands went involuntarily to his ears, but no matter how tightly he pressed against them, he could not shut out the sound that started as a dull whine and grew in pitch until he could no longer hear it. But he could feel it growing, expanding, pressing against the inside of his skull until he was sure his head would explode. And then it did.

$$\Omega$$

The heat inside the thermoreflective dome had quickly reached a stifling level. Its rough, irregular outer surface would scan cold and inert—no heat, no movement, no life. Inside was another matter. The respiratory heat of fifteen bodies had nowhere to go. The men sat still and silent in the dark while LaNague watched the clearing through a peep lens in the wall. He saw the first ship, Ship Two, the one with their man aboard, land jarringly a few meters away, saw the pilot step outside and go through the motions of peering into the inspection ports, saw him return to the cabin of his ship.

The remaining two ships soon joined their companion on the ground and the unloading process began. It had been decided to let the employees of the Imperium do the heavy work; that would allow the Merry Men more time before reinforcements arrived from Primus. When Ship Two was empty, LaNague split a handful of pea-sized metallic globes between Kanya and Josef.

"Whatever you do," he whispered, "don't drop them."

The warning was superfluous. LaNague and the two Flinters had practiced short sprints for the past week in preparation for this moment, and all three were aware that the sonibombs in their hands were impact-activated—one good bump and they went off.

"Holosuits on," he said to the others. "Check the man on your right, making sure his gloves are on and his holosuit is fully functional."

A vague glow lit the interior of the dome as the holosuits came on. When everyone was checked out, LaNague split a seam and the "rock" opened. The next few moments were a blur of tense, feverish activity. He and the Flinters ran full tilt into the center of the triangle formed by the three ships. Surprise was on their side, as was the fact that the ships were so situated that each was in the other's line of fire. They were all set to defend against attacks from the air and from the ground, but not from within their own perimeter. Each runner reached his assigned ship and hurled a handful of sonibombs through the hatchway before it could be closed off, then dove for the ground. All before a shot could be fired.

The transports were shielded from any external ultrasonic barrage. But a single thirty-second sonibomb going off within the small confines of the ship was enough to render anyone on board unconscious. Handfuls of the little weapons were used to reduce the chance of a miss-throw, and all went off on impact with the deck or rear wall. The Merry Men outside remained unaffected because the bombs weren't focused and the sound waves dissipated rapidly in the open air. None of the crewmen managed to escape his ship, but in case one did, a few of the Merry Men stood ready with stun rifles.

As soon as it was evident that there would be no resistance, the Merry Men divided up into pre-arranged work groups. Some began hauling the unconscious crewmen out of Ships One and Three, dragging them to Ship Two and stretching them out on the deck there. Others carried sacks of small leaflets from the "rock" to the cargo holds of the two operable ships. Still others went to the control areas and began blasting the monitoring equipment. LaNague had assigned Broohnin to the last group, realizing that the man must be allowed to destroy something or else he would go berserk. One of the Merry Men passed, carrying a blaster rifle. LaNague recognized Broohnin's gait and followed him into Ship Three.

Broohnin went to the main communications console and waved into the receiver. Then he lifted his blaster and melted the panel with a tight proton beam. The last thing seen by the communications hand on the other end of that monitor was an oddly dressed man raising a blaster toward his face. The alarm would go out immediately and flitterfuls of Imperial Guardsmen would be mobilized and sent careening in their direction. Although no expression could be read through the holomask, LaNague could see that Broohnin was thoroughly enjoying himself as he stalked the length of the ship destroying the monitor eyes. LaNague was content to let him vent his fury as he wished until one of the crewmen rolled over at Broohnin's feet and started to rise to his hands and knees.

"Don't!" LaNague shouted as he saw Broohnin lower the blaster muzzle toward the man's head. He leaped over and pushed his arm aside.

No words passed between the two men as they stood locked in position over the wavering form of the crewman. Broohnin could not see the face of the man who had interfered with him, but there could be no doubt in his mind as to who it was. Further conflict was made moot by the crewman's abrupt collapse into unconsciousness again. LaNague did not release Broohnin's wrist until the inert form had been dragged from the ship.

"If I ever see anything like that again," he said, "you'll spend the rest of the revolution locked in a back room of the warehouse. I will *not* tolerate murder!"

Broohnin's voice trembled with rage as he replied in kind. "If you ever touch me again, I'll kill you!"

Peter LaNague did what he then considered the bravest act of his life. He turned his back on Broohnin and walked away.

After all the unconscious crewmen had been stretched out in Ship Two, the hatches were closed and locked, but not before a steel-tipped longbow arrow, with "Greetings from Robin Hood" emblazoned on the shaft, had been driven into the cushion on the pilot's seat. The Merry Men then hurriedly boarded the two functional transports and took to the air. After inserting a pre-programmed flight cassette into the control console, the new pilot of each ship sat back and watched the instruments.

The two Treasury Transports took separate courses, one to the northeast, another to the southeast. The flight cassettes, which had been carefully programmed meter by meter the previous week, would keep the ships moving as low and as fast as possible, each taking a divergent route to Primus. They could be traced and located, but not with any great ease or accuracy. And no one would be expecting them to head for Primus, the very seat of the planet's major police and militia garrisons.

"All right," LaNague said, now that Ship One was underway, "let's get to work."

Most of the men had turned their holosuits off by now; all leaped to the task of tearing open the crates of orange currency slips and dumping the contents onto the floor of the cargo hold. The flattened, empty crates were passed to a man at the boarding hatch who threw them out toward the darkened grasslands not far below. To the north on Ship Three, Broohnin, Kanya, and Josef were directing a similar task.

When all the currency had been dumped into a huge pile in the center of the hold, the men stood back and surveyed the mass of wealth.

"How much do you think?" someone said in an awed voice to anyone who was listening.

"About thirty million marks," LaNague replied. "And about the same amount in the other ship." He bent and lifted one of the sacks that had been loaded earlier. "Time to add the calling cards."

The men each grabbed a sack and emptied the thousands of tiny white slips of paper within onto the pile of marks, creating a mound of orange cake with white icing. Then they began kicking at the mount and throwing handfuls of it into the air until currency and calling cards were evenly mixed.

LaNague looked at the time. "Sayers ought to have his remote crew just about ready to move out now." The first dump was designated for the neighborhood outside the vid studio. He hoped Sayers had been able to stall long enough.

Eternities passed before the ship began to rise and the control panel buzzed warning that the flight cassette was coming to its end. They were at Primus City limits, and the pilot took manual control.

"Open the loading hatch," LaNague said.

Slowly, the rear wall of the cargo bay began to rise. When the opening was a meter high, LaNague called a stop and it held that aperture. A cool wind began to whirl through the hold as the men awaited word from the pilot. Then it came:

"First target below!"

Reluctantly at first, and then with mounting enthusiasm, they began kicking piles of mark notes mixed with their own private calling cards out the opening.

It began to rain orange and white.

Ω

His first thought was that he had finally cracked . . . the boredom had finally worn away his sanity until he was now beginning to hallucinate.

Well, why not? Vincen Stafford thought uneasily. *After all, here I am in the dead of night, standing in the middle of my vegetable patch.*

The little garden had become an important part of Stafford's life lately. He had been getting fewer and fewer assignments on the grain runs, and had actually been bumped off the last one. Two small orders had been consolidated into one and he had been left hanging due to lack of seniority. The runs seemed to be coming fewer and farther between . . . hard to believe, but that was the way it was.

At least he had the house. After navigating six consecutive runs, he had applied to a bank for a mortgage and had been approved. The single-level cottage on a synthestone slab behind him was the result. Not much, but it was a place to start, and it was home.

Then the runs had slowed up. Good thing his wife had that part-time night job, or things really would have been tight. He hadn't wanted Salli to take it at first, but she'd said she needed something to do while he was shuttling between the stars. She didn't want to sit home alone. But look who was staying home alone now! Very alone, since he had yet to make any fast friends in the neighborhood. That was why the garden had become so important. The loneliness and the boredom of waiting for an assignment had driven him to try his hand at growing a few vegetables, especially with produce prices being what they were. He had planted a few legumes and tubers last week and they had just started to sprout.

So here he was, out in the dark, standing over his newborn vegetable plants like an overprotective parent. But the garden gave him peace, eased that empty gnawing feeling that followed him around like a shadow. It sounded crazy, so he kept it to himself. Just as he would have to keep this hallucination to himself . . . he could swear it was raining mark notes.

He turned around. By the light pouring from the rear windows of his house he could see that there was money all over the back yard. He bent over to see if it just might be real . . . if it could be touched. It could. It was real—old bills, new bills, ones, fives, ten-mark notes were spilling from the sky. And something else . . .

He reached down and picked up one of the small white slips of paper that fell with the currency.

> YOUR TAX REFUND
> AS PROMISED.
> ROBIN HOOD AND HIS MERRY MEN

Stafford looked up and saw nothing. The rain of money had stopped. He had never heard of Robin Hood . . . or had he? Wasn't there an old story about someone with that name? He'd have to ask Salli when she got home.

As he walked about the yard, picking up what later totaled one hundred and fifty-six marks, he idly wondered if it might be stolen money. They weren't in any dire financial trouble, but the extra cash would certainly come in handy, especially with a new house to care for.

Even if he never spent it, Stafford thanked Robin Hood, whoever he might be, for brightening up a dull evening.

VOLUME II ☧ NUMBER 3

THE ROBIN HOOD READER

You Can't Afford to Own Money!

Inflation for the past ten-month standard year has now been officially rated at 8% (which means that the *real* rate of inflation is at least 11%). DUMP YOUR MONEY, FOLKS! That 100 marks you put in the savings account last year is now worth significantly less. What's that you say—what about the interest?

Let's give Metep's mob the benefit of the doubt and assume that the inflation rate really was 8% last year. This means that the 100 marks you put in the savings account ten months ago is now worth only 92. But you collected 6 marks' interest. Harrah! Of course, you realize that you owe around 25% of that in taxes, leaving you a net of 4.5 marks interest.

To sum up: that 100 marks you put away in hopes of watching it grow into a fortune in an interest-bearing account has now shrunk to 96.5 marks. There's only one solution. Get your money and . . .

BUY! BUY! BUY! BUY!

— *The Economic Weather Eye* —

PRICE INDEX (using the 115th year of the Imperium—when the Imperial mark became mandatory legal tender—as base year of 100) **165.7**

MONEY SUPPLY (M3) 1032.3

UNEMPLOYMENT LEVEL 8.1%

	Imperial Marks	Solar Credits
GOLD (Troy ounce)	261.1	130.3
Silver (Troy ounce)	12.9	5.9
Bread (1 kg. loaf)	.74	1.78

XII

Pity the poor, diseased politician. Imagine: to spend your days and expend your efforts making rules for others to live by, thinking up ways to run other lives. Actually to strive for the opportunity to do so! What a hideous affliction!

from THE SECOND BOOK OF KYFHO

"How many times are they going to show that sequence?" Metep VII catapulted himself out of his seat as he spoke and stalked about the small, darkened room, irritation evident in every move.

Daro Haworth's reply was languid, distracted. "As long as they can get an audience for it." His eyes were intent on the large, sharply focused vid globe in the center of the room. "Don't forget, they have an exclusive on this: they were the only ones on the street with a remote crew when the rains came."

"Which is just a little too pat, don't you think?"

"We had security look into it. There's a logical explanation. They monitor the official frequencies just like the other two vid services, and heard the hijack alarm along with everybody else. But they've got a small budget with no remote crew on stand-by, so they were way behind their competition in getting to the scene. It so happened they were just about to take to the air when the money started to fall. A good example of how inefficiency can pay off once in a while.''

Radmon Sayers' familiar face filled the vid globe. Orange mark notes fluttered all around him, interspersed occasionally with flashes of white, all so real and seemingly solid that a viewer with a large holo set would be tempted to reach out and grab a handful. Sayers' expression was a mixture of ecstatic delight and barely suppressed jubilation.

"Ladies and gentlemen," he said from within the globe, "if someone had told me about this, I'd have called him a liar. But here I am in the street outside our studio, and it's raining money! No, this is not a stunt and it's not a joke. There's money falling from the sky!"

The camera panned up the side of a building to the dark sky yielding orange and white slips of paper out of its otherwise featureless blackness, then jumped to a wider angle on Sayers. He was holding one of the white slips. Behind and around him, people could be seen scurrying about, snatching up money from the street.

"Do you remember those crazy little flyers we've been seeing around town for the past half-year or so? *The Robin Hood Reader?* One of the early ones promised a tax refund—'Look to the skies,' it said, if I remember correctly. Well . . . I think I may be standing in the middle of that tax refund right now."

He held up the white piece of paper and the camera angle closed in on it, virtually thrusting his magnified hand into the room. The printing on the slip was clear: *"Your tax rebate as promised. Robin Hood and his Merry Men."* For those who could not read or whose reception might be poor, Sayers read the inscription.

"So it looks like this Robin Hood fellow kept his promise," he said as the rain of paper tapered off to nothing. "There was an unconfirmed report of one of the Imperial Treasury convoys being hijacked this evening. If that's true, and this is the stolen money, then I fear Mr. Hood and his Merry Men are in big trouble."

The camera angle widened to a full-length shot of Sayers and the street. People could be seen standing here and there around him, faces upward, expectantly watching the sky, wads of bills clutched tightly in their hands. He went over to a middle-aged woman and put his arm around her shoulder. She obviously recognized him and smiled at the camera.

"Let's ask this woman what she thinks of this whole affair."

"Oh, I think it's just wonderful!" she cooed. "I don't know who this Robin Hood fellow is, but he's welcome in my neighborhood any time!"

"But the money may be stolen."

Her smile faltered. "From who?"

"From the government, perhaps."

"Oh, that would be too bad. Too bad."

"What if the government confirmed that it was the same money that was hijacked from the Imperial Treasury ships and asked that all good citizens turn in the money they had picked up tonight . . . would you comply?"

"You mean would I give it back?"

"Yes."

"Of course I would!" Her expression was utterly deadpan as she spoke; then she smiled; then she began to giggle.

"Of course." Sayers, too, allowed a smile to play about his lips. He stepped away from the woman and faced the camera. "Well, it looks as if the monetary monsoon is over. This is Radmon Sayers saying good night from a scene that neither these people around me nor the Imperial Treasury officials are likely to forget for a long time. By the way, it might not be a bad idea to take a look outside your own window. Perhaps Robin Hood is delivering *your* tax refund right now."

The globe faded to gray and then the head of another vidcaster appeared. Haworth touched a groove in the arm of his chair and the globe went dark.

"We all look like fools!" Metep said, still wandering the room. "We'll have to make a real example of these dogooders when we catch them!"

"That won't be too easy, I'm afraid."

"And why not?"

"Because they didn't leave a single clue to their identities behind. A sweep of those ships turned up countless sets of fingerprints—all identical, all unregistered, all obviously phony—but not a single epidermis cell other than the crews'. And of course their use of holosuits during the entire affair precludes visual identification."

"Identifying them shouldn't be the problem!" Metep shouted. "We should have them in custody!"

"Well, we don't, and there's no use ranting and raving

about it. They pulled some very tricky maneuvers last night, the trickiest being the finale when they had everyone pursuing empty transports halfway back to the west coast."

"Idiots! We all look like idiots!"

"Yes, I'm afraid we do," Haworth said, rising to his feet and rubbing both hands up over his eyes and through the stark white of his hair. "But not as idiotic as we're going to look when the results of Krager's programs for voluntary return of the money are in. A 'patriotic gesture,' he called it! The old fool!"

"Why? I think it's a good idea. We may even get a few million back."

"We'll get nothing back except a few token marks, and then we'll really look like idiots!"

"I think you're wrong."

"Really? What would you do if you just found a tax-free bonus lying in your back yard, and knew it was stolen from the same people who had recently taken a sizable piece of your income in taxes? How would you respond when those people asked for their money back, and they didn't know exactly who had it? What would you do?"

Metep considered this. "I see what you mean. What'll we do?"

"Lie. What else? We'll announce that more than 90 per cent of the money had been returned and that only a greedy, disloyal few have failed to return the money that rightfully belongs to their fellow citizens."

"Sounds good. A little guilt is always good for the common man."

Haworth's smile was sardonic. "Assuming they'll feel guilty." The smile faded. "But there's a lot about this Robin Hood character—if he's actually an individual at all—that bothers me. What's he up to? He doesn't call for your death or violent overthrow of the Imperium. He just talks about money. There's no heated rhetoric, no obvious ideology. Just money."

"That bothers you? Not me! I prefer what he's doing to threatening my life. After all, he could have robbed a military base and been dropping neutrons on us."

"It bothers me because I don't know where he's heading. And I sense there's method to his madness. He's got a goal in mind and I can't see what it is. Perhaps he'll let us know in his newsletter."

"Which we've already outlawed, naturally. Anyone caught in possession of a *Robin Hood Reader* from now on will be arrested and interrogated."

"And that's another thing that bothers me. We lend Robin Hood a certain mystique by officially declaring him and his silly little flyers illegal."

"But we have no choice. He's committed armed robbery. We can't ignore that!"

Haworth didn't appear to be listening. He had walked to the wall and turned it to maximum transparency. The northern half of Primus City lay spread out before him.

"How many people do you think got a handful or two of money last night?" he asked Metep.

"Well, with two ships and sixty million marks . . . has to be thousands. Many thousands."

"And only a tiny fraction of those giving the money back." He turned to Metep VII. "Do you know what that means, Jek? Do you know what he's done?"

Metep could only shrug. "He's robbed us."

"Robbed us?" Haworth's expression could not disguise his contempt for his superior's obtuseness. "He's turned thousands of those people out there into accomplices!"

Ω

"My compliments to you, sir!" Doc Zack said, raising a glass of iced grain alcohol toward LaNague as they sat alone in one of the small offices that lined the rear of the Angus Black warehouse. "You have not only thumbed your nose at the Imperium, you've also succeeded in extracting joyful complicity from the public. A master stroke. Long live Robin Hood!"

LaNague raised his own glass in response. "I'll drink to that!" But he only sipped lightly, finding the native Throne liquors harsh and bitter. He preferred Tolive's dry white wines, but importing them in quantity would be a foolish extravagance. He didn't need any ethanol now anyway. He was already high. *He had done it!* He had actually done it! The first overt act of sedition had come off flawlessly, without a single casualty on either side. Everyone was intact and free.

There had been a few tense moments, especially after they had made the money drops over the various sectors of Primus City and the Imperial Guard cruisers were closing in. Dropping them down to street level, the pilots had run a zigzag course toward the city limits. At a pre-determined point, the transports were halted in the dolee section of the city, all the crew poised at the cargo and boarding hatches. With touch-down, everyone jumped out and scattered. The pilots were the last to leave, having been assigned the duty of plugging in a final flight cassette designed to take the pursuing cruisers on a merry chase. LaNague's pilot must have been delayed inside, because Ship One was a full three meters off the ground before he appeared at the boarding hatch. But without a second's hesitation, he leaped into the air and hit the street running. Everyone melted away—into alleys, into doorways, into wait-ing ground cars. Within the space of a few heartbeats, the hi-jacked transports had arrived, discharged their human cargo, and departed, leaving the streets as they had been before, with no trace of their passing.

And now all were safe. Yes, he had done it. It was an ex-hilarating feeling. And an immense relief.

"But what happens to Broohnin now that Robin Hood has arrived?"

"He remains a part of the revolution," LaNague replied. "I promised him that."

"You always keep your promises?"

"Always. I promised Broohnin a front row seat at the Im-perium's demise if he would turn over his Throne contacts to me, and if he didn't interfere in my plans. I intend to keep that promise."

"Den is a sick man, I'm afraid."

"Then why were you a member of his group?"

Doc Zack laughed. "A member of his group? Please, sir, you insult me! He contacted me after a few of my critical remarks about the Imperium's shortsighted policies reached the public. We met a few times and had a few disjointed con-versations. It was refreshing to talk to someone who was as anti-Imperium as myself—the halls of academe on Throne are filled with yea-sayers who fear for their positions, and who thus follow the safest course by mouthing the proper attitudes and platitudes. But I could see that violence was just a hair's breadth away from Broohnin's surface and so I kept my distance."

"And Radmon Sayers? How did he and Broohnin make contact?"

"That I don't know, but I get the impression they knew

each other in their younger days, before Broohnin became obsessed with overthrowing the Imperium and Sayers became a public face. But enough of Broohnin and Sayers and myself. Tell me, my friend," Zack said, leaning back in his chair and luxuriating in the mellow mood induced by his third glass of spirits. "Isn't there a lot more to this Robin Hood pose than meets the eye? I mean, I can see drawing on archetypes and so on, but this goes beyond that."

"Just what do you mean? Specifically." LaNague was quite willing to tell the professor, but wanted to see if the man could draw an accurate conclusion on his own.

"As I see it, the Robin Hood gambit provides the average out-worlder with a flesh and blood human being as a focus, a conduit for his discontent. Through the persona of Robin Hood he can conceptualize his aggressions and vicariously act them out. Isn't that what you have in mind?"

LaNague laughed. "Maybe. I don't think in those terms, Doc. My initial idea was to provide something concrete for the outworlder to respond to. He lives a tough life and doesn't have much room left in the hours of his day for abstractions. He won't respond to an idea anywhere near as quickly as he'll respond to another man. Robin Hood will hopefully provide him with that man."

"But what of the final act? You're going to have to set things up so the outworlder—at least the ones here on Throne—will have to make a choice between Metep and Robin Hood. How are you going to arrange that?"

"I'm not sure yet," LaNague said slowly. "I'll have to see how things develop. Any definite plans I make now will undoubtedly have to be altered later on . . . so I'm not making any."

"And me—when do I get to play my part?"

"Not for a while yet. We first have to build Radmon Sayers' reputation up a little, to make sure you get the kind of coverage your part will deserve." He glanced at the glowing figures on the wall clock. "His ratings will begin a long and steady climb as of tonight."

"You going to feed him some exclusives, or what?"

"No . . . he's going to find a very loyal friend in the central ratings computer."

Doc Zack nodded with gleeful insight. "Ah, yes! So you're putting Seph to work tonight."

"He should be at it right now."

Ω

He had a clearance for the building, but without an official work requisition, he'd have a tough time explaining his presence in this particular section. Viewer preferences were tabulated here, and adjustments made accordingly. Every vid set manufactured on Throne contained a tiny monitoring device that informed the rating computer when the set was on and to which program it was tuned. The presence of the device was no secret, and it was quite legal to have it removed after purchase of the set. But few people bothered. The Imperium said it was there to better tune programming to the current tastes of the public, so why not leave it in the set and forego the trouble and expense of having it removed?

Everyone knew the value of the vid as a propaganda weapon; that was self-evident, and so any attempts at overt propaganda would be routinely ignored. Since it licensed every transmitter, it would be a simple matter for the Imperium to impose its will directly and forcefully on the vid companies. But this was not necessary. The Imperium had many friends in all the media, seen and unseen, who liked to be considered part of the inner circle, who liked to help in any way they could in molding and mobilizing public opinion. Certain themes would begin to recur in dramas, or even comedies; certain catchwords and catch phrases would be mouthed by popular newsreaders and personalities. Soon public opinion would begin to shift; imperceptibly at first, then by slow degrees, then in a giant leap, after which it would never occur to anyone that he had ever thought any differently. Vid addicts were totally unaware of the process; only those who ignored the pervasive entertainment machine could see what was happening, but their cries of warning went unheeded. No one liked to admit that he or she could be so easily manipulated.

Seph Wolverton locked himself in with the central ratings computer and began removing a plate over an inspection port. Here was the starting point for all public influence operations. This particular section of the central computer tallied the number of sets tuned to a given program at a given time. A crucially important operation, since the best way to reach people through the vid was to reach them via the programs they liked best.

Seph laid a small black box in the palm of his hand. It popped open at a touch and revealed two compartments. One was empty; the other held a tiny sphere, onyx black. He had spent weeks programming that little sphere. Now it was time to put it to work.

He attached a light plate to his forehead and turned it on. A world of tiny geometric shapes, arranged in seemingly incomprehensible patterns and matrices, opened up before his eyes as he thrust the upper half of his body into the inspection port. Using an insulated, socket-tipped tool in his right hand, he removed a black sphere from the matrix of spheres and replaced it with the one he had brought with him. The old one was placed in the box for safekeeping and the inspection port closed. Soon he was back in the corridor and on his way to a section of the building in which he belonged.

The new chip would soon be at work, subtly altering the delicate magnetic fields the computer used to store new information and retrieve old. Seph had formed a crossover in the matrix that would funnel a percentage of the impulses from *"Sugar! Sugar!"*—a popular late-night comedy about a praline-crazed dwarf and his misadventures on and between the outworlds—over to the Radmon Sayers news report. Sayers would be experiencing an expected boost in ratings now anyway, due to his coverage of "the money monsoon." That would be short-lived, however, since no news program could normally hold out against *"Sugar! Sugar!"* for long. What Seph Wolverton had done tonight would convince the people who monitored such things that perhaps Radmon Sayers was on his way to becoming the new fair-haired boy of the newsreaders, and that perhaps it might be wise if one of the larger networks offered him a spot in a better time slot, one that would take full advantage of the man's obvious drawing powers.

Seph glanced at the row of vids in the monitoring station as he passed. Yes, there was Sayers now, halfway through his show.

". . . and on the business scene: The Solar Stock Exchange experienced a mild selling panic today when it was learned that Eric Boedekker, the wealthy asteroid mining magnate, has dumped every single share of stock, common and preferred, in every one of his many portfolios. He has been doing it gradually for the past few months through numerous brokers, and he has been selling the stocks for cash. This amounts to billions of Solar credits! No one knows if he's reinvesting it elsewhere. But fearing that the notoriously shrewd and ruthless Boedekker might know something they do not, a large number of smaller investors sold their own holdings today, causing a precipitous dip in many stock prices. The situation seems to have stabilized at this time, however, after numerous assurances from many investment councilors and brokerage houses that investor concern is unwarranted, that Earth's economy is sounder than it has ever been. Eric Boedekker has remained steadfastly unavailable for comment throughout the entire affair.

"On the home front: Throne . . . authorities have yet to track down any of the culprits in last night's daring hijack of an Imperial Treasury currency shipment, and the subsequent dumping of that shipment into the air over Primus City. Police say they have some good leads as to the identity of Robin Hood and his Merry Men, as the hijackers call themselves, but are not commenting yet on the nature of those leads.

"Last night, this reporter was an eyewitness to the now infamous 'money monsoon,' and for those of you who may have missed that particular vidcast, and its various replays during the course of today's programming, here it is again . . ."

THE ROBIN HOOD READER

The Rule of 72

This is a handy little pearl to carry around in your head
while trying to find your way through an inflation-ridden
economy like ours. It instantly gives you an idea as to when
the money in your pocket is going to lose half of its present
value, and allows you to plan accordingly.

Example: if inflation is constant at 3%, you merely divide
72 by three and get 24. This means that 24 years of 3%
inflation will cut the spending power of that 100 marks in
your pocket to 50. It means the price of everything will
double every 24 years.

Not so bad, you say? Let's try 6%. That rate of inflation will
double prices (or cut your money's spending power, however you wish to look at it) every dozen years.

You can live with that, you say? All right, try this: the new
official inflation rate (remember, they lie) is now 12%.
That's TWELVE PER CENT! It means that all the ridic-
ulously high prices you see around you now will double in
six (6) years! And I foresee 24% in the near future. Mull
that . . .

The Economic Weather Eye

PRICE INDEX (using the 115th year of the
Imperium—when the Imperial
mark became mandatory legal
tender—as base year of 100)   171.3

MONEY SUPPLY (M3)   2002.7

UNEMPLOYMENT LEVEL   8.5%

	Imperial Marks	Solar Credits
GOLD (Troy ounce)	275.9	130.4
Silver (Troy ounce)	13.8	6.0
Bread (1 kg. loaf)	.78	1.77

XIII

". . . when you see the misery it
brings, you'd need to be a madman, or
a coward, or stone blind to give in to
the plague."

Dr. Rieux

LaNague sat silent and unmoving, listening to dissension
brewing . . . and so soon. But the deaths of four good men
could do that.

"Retaliate!" Broohnin said, standing in the center of the
office. "We've got to retaliate!"

For once, LaNague found himself ready to agree. Perhaps it
was what he had seen a few hours ago, perhaps it was the long
day and the sleepless night that lay behind him. Whatever the
cause, something dark within him was demanding revenge and
he was listening.

No . . . he couldn't allow himself the luxury of giving in to
that seductive siren call. But four lives! Gone! And so early
on. They were only three quarters through the Year of the
Tiller and already four lives lost. All his fault, too.

Everything had been going according to plan during the
three months since the first hijack. Robin Hood had been
keeping a low profile, with only the *Reader* to keep him in the
public consciousness. Distribution of the *Reader* had been going well, too, experiencing a dramatic increase in interest and

123

circulation since being outlawed after the "money monsoon." Metep and the Council of Five were making all the expected moves as the economy picked up speed in its downward spiral, right on schedule. The time finally arrived when the Imperium needed another jolt to its complacency. Another raid by Robin Hood and his Merry Men. Another "money monsoon."

It wasn't going to be quite so easy this time, of course. Currency shipments to and from the Central Treasury were now escorted by heavily armed cruisers. There would be no simple way to relieve the Imperium of its flat money en route. So the obvious conclusion was to hit the currency transports before they linked up to their escorts and became an armed convoy. Hit them before they ever left the ground.

The East Coast Regional Revenue Center was chosen as target this time. It was located in the port city of Paramer, and handled smaller volumes of currency due to the fact that most of the population and industry on Throne were concentrated around and to the west of Primus City. But the amounts funneled through it were more than adequate for the purposes of Robin Hood and his Merry Men.

The tax depot was hit with precise timing—the strike had to occur immediately after the transports were loaded and before the escort cruisers arrived. Sonic weapons were again used, then the two loaded transports were manned with four Merry Men each and programmed with flight cassettes that would take one ship over Paramer itself, and the other north to the smaller Echoville. LaNague would have preferred to make another run over Primus City, but it was too far away . . . they never could have flown the transports from Paramer to the center of the continent without being intercepted. It was probably just as well; it wouldn't do to have the east coast towns feel slighted.

While the transports made their deliveries into the air over the two target towns, LaNague, Broohnin, and the Flinters manned four speedy little sport flitters, ready to act as interceptors if the escort cruisers happened to appear ahead of schedule. They had been scheduled to arrive from the Imperial garrison to the south, but unknown to LaNague and the rest, an unexpected change had been made in the plans: they had been routed to a repair station in Paramer itself. They would depart from the repair station directly to the tax depot.

And so it was with growing concern that LaNague and his lieutenants awaited the arrival of the cruisers, ready to fly into their faces and lead them away from the transports. It would be dangerous, but their smaller craft had speed and maneuverability on their side and could outrun anything in the sky. They didn't know that while they were waiting, the escort happened upon the transport assigned to Paramer just as it was making its final pass over the center of the town. The chase was short, the battle brief, the transport a ball of flaming wreckage by the time it slammed into the sea.

"They were only doing their duty, Den," Radmon Sayers said, watching Broohnin carefully.

"And it's our duty to even the score! If we don't they'll know they can kill as many of us as they want whenever they get the chance. We owe it to ourselves and to those four dead men!"

"We all knew what we were risking when we started out last night," LaNague said, fatigue putting an edge on his voice. "We all knew there was a chance some of us might not come back one of these times. This happened to be the night. It was just bad luck—rotten, stinking, lousy luck that the tight routine the escort cruisers have followed for months was altered last night."

"Luck?" Broohnin sneered. "Tell those dead men about luck!" He turned to Doc Zack and Sayers. "I say we retaliate! I want a vote on it right now!"

"Forget it, Den," Doc said in a low voice. "That's not what we're about here."

"Then what *are* we about?" Broohnin asked, piercing them with his fierce gaze. "Where's all this leading us? What have we done so far besides play a few games and lose a few lives? Are we any closer to ending the Imperium? If we are, show me how and where and I'll shut up!"

"That was not your original demand," Doc Zack said softly, maintaining his professional cool. "You want us to turn killer. We decline. I'd like to be sure you understand that before we go on to other topics."

Broohnin's beard hid most of his expression, but what could be seen of his mouth was a thin, tight line. "And I just want *you* to understand," he said, stabbing his fingers at Sayers and Doc, "that I'm not going to die for *him!*" The finger went toward LaNague on the last word. After a final glare at all present, he wheeled and strode from the room.

"He's right," LaNague said after he was gone. "I *am* responsible for those deaths. Those men were following my orders when they died. If I had checked just a little more carefully last night, they'd be out on the warehouse floor celebrating now.'' He rose from his seat and walked over to where Pierrot sat on a shelf, its drooping leaves reflecting his master's mood. ''If I hadn't come here and started this whole thing, they'd still be alive. Maybe I should have stayed on Tolive.''

He was speaking more to himself than to anyone else. The other two occupants of the cubicle realized this and allowed him a few moments of silence.

''Den did have a point at the last there,'' Zack said finally. ''Where is all this leading? It's all very dramatic and great copy for guys like Radmon, but where is it taking us?''

''To the end of the Imperium.''

''But how? I'd like to know. I'd like to go to bed at night and know that something I've done that day has pushed us closer to getting this very weighty piece of government off our backs. But that's not happening. I mean, I seem to be doing a lot, and it's all antigovernment, but I don't see any dents in the Imperium. I see no cracks in the foundation, no place to drive a wedge in. We're winning psychological victories, but every morning I wake up and find we're still at square one.''

''Fair question,'' Sayers said. ''We're big boys, and we can be trusted. I think we deserve to know where you're leading us.''

LaNague turned and faced them. He wanted to tell them, wanted to unburden himself to someone. He desperately wished Mora were at his side at that very moment. He had a pounding in both his temples and a pain at the back of his head that felt like a muscular hand had arisen from his neck and clamped the back of his skull in a death grip. Tension headaches were no strangers, but this one was one of the worst he could remember. He almost felt he could chase it away if he could tell these two good men what he had in mind for their world. But he couldn't risk it. Not yet. Not even Josef and Kanya knew.

''You're right, both of you,'' he said. ''But you'll have to trust me. I know that's a lot to ask,'' he said quickly, sensing the objections forming on their lips, ''it's the way I have to work it. The fewer people who know exactly where all this is heading, the less chance of someone telling all when and if one of us is captured. And don't kid yourselves—a simple intravenous injection and any one of us, no matter how strong-willed he thinks he is, will answer any question without the slightest hesitation.''

''But there's no sign of progress!''—Zack said. ''Not the slightest indication that we're getting anywhere!''

''That's because the real work is going on behind the scenes. You don't see any progress because that's the way I want it. I don't want anyone getting tipped off too soon. Everything's going to happen at once. And when it does, believe me, you'll know it. Trust me.''

There was silence again, and again Zack broke it. ''If you weren't a Tolivian, and if I didn't know what I know about the Kyfho philosophy's code of honor, I'd say you were asking too much. But frankly, my friend, you're all we've got at the moment. We have to trust you.''

''Well, I don't know all that much about the Kyfho philosophy,'' Sayers said, ''but I agree you're all we've got.'' He looked past LaNague to Pierrot. ''You've always got that tree around. Does that have something to do with Kyfho?''

LaNague shook his head. ''No. Just an old friend.''

''Well, it looks like he needs water.'' Sayers didn't understand why LaNague seemed to think this was funny, and so he continued speaking over the Tolivian's laughter. ''What does Kyfho mean, anyway? It's not a word with any meaning in Interstellar.''

''It's not a word, really,'' LaNague said, marveling inwardly at how much a little laughter could lighten his mood. ''It's an acronym from one of the Anglo tongues on Old Earth. The philosophy was first synthesized on preunification Earth by a group of people in the Western Alliance. It could only have been formed in the Western Alliance, but as it experienced slow and limited growth, it was picked up and modified by people in the Eastern Alliance. Modern Kyfho is now a mixture of both variants. The acronym was derived from the title of the first book—a pamphlet, really—in which Kyfho was expounded, a supposedly scatalogical phase that meant 'Don't Touch.' Does either of you understand Anglo?''

Sayers shook his head. ''Not a word.''

''I used to know a little when I was in the university,'' Doc said, ''but I remember almost nothing. Try me anyway.''

''All right. The title was KEEP YOUR FUCKING HANDS OFF. Mean anything to you?''

"Not a thing."

"Nor to me. But it supposedly summed up the philosophy pretty well at the time."

"The important thing," Zack said, "is that we trust you. The next question is, when do I get to do my bit?"

"Very soon. Especially now that our public personality here," he indicated Sayers, "has been moved into the limelight. I forgot to congratulate you, by the way, Radmon."

"Nothing more that I deserve," Sayers said, beaming. His ratings had risen steadily thanks to the computer fix and to the follow-the-leader phenomenon that causes people who hear that lots of other people are watching a certain program to start watching it too, thus inducing still more people to start watching it, and so on in a geometric progression. The result was an offer of a spot on the early evening news show of one of the larger vid services, thereby assuring him a huge audience. The ratings computer would now have to be returned to its untampered state.

"I'm all set to go," Zack said. "Have been for months on end now. Just give me the word."

"Take the first step."

"You mean change the course name?"

"Right. But don't show them your lesson plans until they're good and mad. Hit them with those when they're in the wrong mood and the regents will be sure to cancel your course."

"And then will they be sorry!"

"I don't care if the regents are sorry or not. I want Metep to be sorry."

Sayers stood up and walked toward the door of the cubicle. "And I'll be sorry if I don't get home and get some sleep. Tonight's my first appearance on the new show and I need my beauty rest. Good luck to us all."

Ω

". . . and the big news of the day remains the story from Paramer concerning an aborted attempt to repeat the famous Robin Hood caper of three months ago. The end result this time, however, was death, with an Imperial cruiser intercepting and shooting down the hijacked Treasury transport in the air over the port city. But not before the Merry Men had completed their mission—an estimated twenty-five million marks hurled into the sky over Paramer, with the same Robin Hood calling cards as the last time. Four bodies were found in the transport wreckage, burned beyond recognition. The Imperial Guard, it appears, takes its work seriously. Let all would-be tax rebels take a lesson from that.

"More news from Earth tonight on the strange behavior of Eric Boedekker, the wealthy asteroid mining magnate. It seems he has just sold the mineral rights to half of his asteroid holdings to his largest competitor, Merritt Metals, for a sum that probably exceeds the gross planetary products of some of our brother outworlds. The mineral rights to the rest of the Boedekker asteroids are reportedly up for sale, too. Anyone interested in buying a flying mountain . . . ?"

THE ROBIN HOOD READER

HIT THE BANKS!

Notice how many banks are encouraging second mortgages lately? How they're telling you to borrow on your current home and use the money for renovations or added conveniences or vacations? Suspicious? Do you feel that the bankers must know a whole lot more about money than you do and there must be a catch?

Well, you're right—there is a catch, only this time the bankers will get caught. With construction at a virtual standstill, they've got all this money lying around in the savings accounts of people who have either not been reading these flyers, or ignoring them. (They'll learn!) The banks want to lend it out. So do yourself a favor: borrow it. Sure, they'll charge you 11%, but with inflation officially running at 14% now, every 100 marks you pay back next year will only be worth 86 of the marks you borrow today. You thus get the spending power of this year's marks and pay back the bank with impaired marks in subsequent years. (Remember the Rule of 72!) And as inflation worsens, you'll be paying the bank back with increasingly worthless paper. Ah, but what to do with this borrowed money? Watch this space, and . . .

BORROW! BORROW! BORROW!

The Economic Weather Eye

PRICE INDEX (using the 115th year of the Imperium—when the Imperial mark became mandatory legal tender—as base year of 100)   179.7

MONEY SUPPLY (M3)   2061.2
UNEMPLOYMENT LEVEL   9.0%

	Imperial Marks	Solar Credits
GOLD (Troy ounce)	282.1	130.8
Silver (Troy ounce)	14.6	5.9
Bread (1 kg. loaf)	.83	1.74

The Year of the Malak

XIV

BRAIN: In our civilization, and under
our republican form of government,
brain is so highly honored that it is
rewarded by exemption from the cares
of office.

Ambrose Bierce

The confrontation had been considerably delayed by a computer programmer who either meant well or didn't pay too much attention to what she was doing. Any aware and upright programmer, conscious of job security, would have immediately reported Dr. Zachariah Brophy's change in the title of his first-year economics course from *Economics: The Basics* to *Economics: Our Enemy, the State.*

And so it was not until the printed course booklet was issued to all the students at the University of the Outworlds that Doc Zack's little act of provocation came to light. Reaction was mixed. The course was immediately booked solid, but that only meant that fifty students were interested; it hardly reflected the view of the campus at large. The university was state-supported—grounds, buildings, materials, and a full 75 per cent of tuition was paid for by the Imperium. Even room and board at the university dorms was state-funded. This could have resulted in a free, open forum for ideas, where no point of view was proscribed. Could have, but did not.

There was a long waiting list for seats in the University of the Outworlds; students who made the slightest ripple, such as objecting too loudly to course content and narrow viewpoints among the faculty, soon found it most difficult to obtain passing grades in key courses. And without those passing grades, their educational support was withdrawn. They had to drop out and join the great unwashed, monitoring the courses and taking examinations via the vid. It always happened within the first months of a term to the few free spirits who had managed to slip in with the new class. And it only took the academic demise of a couple of those to enlighten the survivors to the facts of life at the University of the Outworlds: co-operate and graduate.

Doc Zack's move was something else. This was not a questioning voice speaking out of order; this was no mere breach of academic etiquette. This was a red handkerchief fluttering in the faces of the regents and those to whom they had to answer. And what was worse, the offending course title was now in the hands of every student at the university. The semester was about to begin. Something had to be done, and quickly!

They canceled the course. A message was sent to each student who had possessed the temerity to enroll in a course entitled *Economics: Our Enemy, the State* informing him or her that a new course would have to be chosen to fill that time spot. The names on the class list were placed in a special file of students who would bear watching.

But Doc Zack had his own lists and he sent word to the students who had signed up for his class, and to favored students from past years, that he would be giving the first lecture as scheduled in the course catalogue. Anyone who was interested was welcome to come and listen. Radmon Sayers was also informed of the time and location of the lecture, but by a mere circuitous route. He would see to it that Dr. Zachariah Brophy's first and last lecture of the new semester would have a much larger audience than the regents or anyone else anticipated.

Ω

"I'm not exactly overwhelmed by the turnout this morning," Doc Zack said, strolling back and forth across the front of the classroom in his usual speaking manner, looking as cadaverous as ever. "But I guess it would be hoping too much to see a standing-room-only crowd before me. I know that the prices of everything are keeping two jumps ahead of salary increases, and that many of you here are risking your places in this glorious institution just by being here. For that I thank you, and commend your courage."

He craned his neck and looked around the room. "I see some familiar faces here and some new ones, too. That's good." One of the new faces sat in the last row. He was young enough to pass for a student, but the square black vid recorder plate he held in the air, its flat surface following Zack wherever he went, gave him away as something more. This would be Sayers' man, recording the lecture. Zack took a deep breath . . . time to take the plunge.

"What we're going to discuss here today may not seem like economics at first. It will concern the government—our government, the Imperium. It's a monster story in the truest, Frankensteinian sense, of a man-made creature running amuck across the countryside, blindly destroying everything it touches. But this is not some hideous creature of sewn-to-gether cadavers; this creature is handsome and graceful and professes only to have our best interests at heart, desiring only to help us.

"Where most of its power lies is in the economy of our land. It creates the money, controls its supply, controls the interest rates that can be charged for borrowing it, controls, in fact, the very value of that money. And the hand that controls the economy controls you—each and every one of you. For your everyday lives depend on the economy: your job, the salary you receive for working that job, the price of your home, the clothes on your back, the food you eat. You can no more divorce a functioning human being from his or her ambient economy than from his or her ambient air. It's an integral part of life. Control a being's economic environment and, friend, you control that being.

"Here on the outworlds, we live in a carefully controlled economy. That's bad enough. But what's worse is that the controlling hand belongs to an idiot."

He paused a moment to let that sink in, glancing at the recorder plate held aloft at the rear of the room, noting that it was aimed in such a way that if it happened to include any of the students in its frame, only backs of heads would be visible.

"Let's take a look at this handsome, ostensibly well-

meaning, idiotic monster we've created and see what it's doing
to us. I think you'll soon see why I've subtitled this course.
Our Enemy, the State. Let's see what it does to help those of
us who can't seem to make ends meet. I won't start in on the
Imperial Dole Program—you all know what a horrendous
mess that is. Everybody has something bad to say about the
dole. No . . . I think I'll start with the program that's been
most praised by the people within the government and press:
the Food Voucher Program.

"As it stands now, a man with a family of four earning
12,000 marks a year is eligible for 1,000 marks' worth of food
vouchers to supplement his income and help feed his family.
That's okay, you say? You don't mind some of your taxes
going to help some poor working stiff make ends meet? That's
lucky for you, because nobody asked you anyway. Whether
you like it or not, approve of it or not, he's going to get the
1,000 marks.

"But putting that aside, did you realize that the Imperium
taxes this man 2,200 marks a year? That's right. It takes 2,200
marks out of his pocket in little bits and pieces via withholding
taxes during each pay period. And the withholding tax is a
very important concept as far as the government is concerned.
It is thereby allowed to extract the income tax almost pain-
lessly, and to force the employer to do all the accounting for
the withholding tax free of charge, despite the fact that slavery
has never been allowed in the outworlds. It needs the withholding tax, because if the Imperium tried to extract all the
year's income taxes at once it would have the entire citizenry
out in the streets with armfuls of rocks . . . it wouldn't last a
standard year.

"But back to our food voucher recipient: his 2,200 marks
are collected each year, sent to the Regional Revenue Center,
and from there shipped to the Central Treasury in Primus City
—if Robin Hood doesn't get it first." This brought a laugh
and a smattering of applause from the class. "Now don't
forget that everybody who handles it along the way gets paid
something for his time—from the lowliest programmer to
the Minister of the Treasury, everyone takes a chunk. Then
the money has to be appropriated by the legislature into the
Bureau of Food Subsidization, and the case workers have to
decide who's eligible, and how much the eligibles should get,
and somebody has to print up the vouchers, and somebody
has to run the maintenance machinery to keep the floors of the

Bureau of Food Subsidization clean and so on, ad nauseam. Everybody along the line gets paid something for his or her efforts.

"In the end, our lowly citizen gets his thousand marks' worth of food vouchers, but in the process, not only has his 2,200 marks in taxes been consumed by the bureaucracy, but an additional 830 marks of *your* taxes as well! A total of 3,030 marks! That's right: it costs 3.03 marks in taxes for our enemy, the Imperium, to give a single mark's worth of benefits. And has anyone along the line suggested that we just cut this poor citizen's taxes by a thousand marks? Of course not! That would save us all a net of 2,000 marks, but it would also mean cutting appropriations, and fewer do-nothings in the Revenue Service and the Bureau of Food Subsidization, and who knows where else. The men who run these bureaus and run these outworlds don't want that. And they have the say and we don't. And that's why the Imperium is our enemy, because it is filled with these men."

Zack paused briefly here for breath and to allow himself to cool. He always got worked up talking about the excesses and idiocy of the Imperium, and had to be careful not to say more than he meant to.

"And so you can see why you have to understand the working of a large and powerful government if you are to understand modern economics. The Food Voucher System is only a very obvious example. There are economic machinations going on within the Imperium which are far more subtle and far more sinister than the buffoonery of the Bureau of Food Subsidization, and we shall delve into those at a later date. But first we must teach you all some of the rudiments of free market economics, a realm of economic theory that has been the victim of de facto censorship in teaching centers from here to Earth for centuries. We'll begin with von Mises, then—"

Noticing alarmed expressions on the faces of some of the students, and sensing that the focus of their attention had suddenly shifted to a point somewhere behind him, Zack turned around. Two university security men stood in the doorway.

"We have a report of an unauthorized class being conducted here," the burly one on the right said. "Are you a member of the faculty, sir?"

"Of course I am!"

"And what course is this?"

"Economics 10037: *Our Enemy, the State.*"

The guard on the left, taller but equally well muscled, frowned disapproval and scanned the readout on his pocket directory. "Didn't think so," he said, glancing at his partner. "There's no such course."

"What's your name?" said the burly one.

"Zachariah Brophy, Ph.D."

Again the pocket directory was scanned. Again a negative readout. "No one on the faculty by that name."

"Now wait just a minute! I've been teaching here for twenty years! I'll have you know—"

"Save it, pal," the burly one said, taking Zack's elbow. "We're going to escort you to the gate and you can find yourself somewhere else to play school."

Zack pulled his arm away. "You'll do no such thing! I demand that you call the regents' office and check that."

"This is a direct link to the regents' computer," the taller guard said, holding up his pocket directory. "The information out of here is up to the minute—and it says you don't belong here. So make it easy for all of us and come quietly."

"No! I won't go anywhere quietly! This is supposed to be a university, where all points of view can be heard, where inquiring minds can pick and choose among a variety of ideas. I won't be stifled!" He turned to the class. "Now, as I was saying—"

The two guards behind him could be seen glancing at each other and shrugging. Each stepped forward and, grabbing an elbow and an armpit, dragged Doc Zack backward from the classroom.

"Let me go!" Zack shouted. He dug his heels into the floor, struggled to free his arm but to no avail. As a last desperate hope, he turned to the class. "Some of you help me, please! Please! Don't let them take me away like this!"

But as they dragged him out through the door and around the corner and down the hall, no one moved, and that was what hurt most of all.

Ω

". . . now I think you all know that it's not my policy to editorialize. I merely report the news the way it happens. But I believe that what we've just seen is so extraordinary that I must comment upon it. The exclusive eyewitness recording of the expulsion of Professor Zachariah Brophy from the campus of the University of the Outworlds that was just replayed was obtained because I had heard that this renegade professor was determined to give his treasonous course despite the fact that his superiors had canceled it. I sent a recorder technician to the classroom to see just how the regents would handle such an incident, and you have seen the results yourselves tonight.

"I must say that I, as a citizen of the Imperium, am proud of what I have just seen. Enormous amounts of our tax marks are spent yearly to keep the University of the Outworlds one of the top institutions of learning in Occupied Space. We cannot allow a few malcontents to decide that they are wiser than the board of regents and to teach whatever they see fit, regardless of academic merit. We especially cannot allow someone like Professor Zachariah Brophy, impressive as his credentials might be, to denigrate the Imperium, which supports the university, and therefore denigrate the university itself by his unfounded and inflammatory criticism!

"I support freedom of speech to the fullest, but when it's being done on my time and being supported by my tax dollars, then I want some control over what's being said. Otherwise, let Professor Brophy take his podium to Imperium Park and give his message to whoever wishes to gather and listen. And to anyone else who tries to waste the taxpayers' money by trying to besmirch the Imperium at their expense, let this be a warning."

The final segment of the recording, wherein Doc Zack was dragged kicking and pleading from the classroom, was rerun, and then Radmon Sayers' face filled the screen again.

"And now, new word from Earth on the mysterious behaviour of Eric Boedekker, the wealthy asteroid mining magnate, who has just sold the remainder of his asteroid mineral rights to a consortium of prospectors for an undisclosed but undoubtedly enormous sum. Still no hint as to what he's doing or plans to do with all that credit.

"And on Neeka—"

Metep VII touched a stud on the armrest of his chair and the holovid globe went dark. "That Sayers is a good man," he told Haworth, who sat an arm's length away to his left.

"Think so?"

"Sure. Look how he defended the regents. That could have been a very embarrassing recording. It would take nothing to exploit it into an example of repression of academic freedom, freedom of speech, creeping fascism, or whatever other nonsense you want. But Sayers turned it into a testimonial to the way the regents and the Imperium are ever on guard against misuse and abuse of educational taxes. He turned it into a plus for us and kept Brophy a miscreant instead of elevating him to a martyr.''

"You think he's on our side, then?"

"Definitely. Don't you?"

"I don't know." Haworth was pensive. "I really don't know. If he were really on our side, I don't think he would have shown that recording at all."

"Come now! He's a newsman! He couldn't pass up a story like that!''

"Yes, that's very obvious. But it all seems too pat. I mean, how did he happen to know that Brophy would be giving that lecture against the orders of the regents?''

"Probably one of the students told him."

"Possible. But do you realize that even if the regents had left Brophy to his own devices and let him give his course as originally scheduled with no interference, only a few thousand would have heard him over the closed-circuit vid? And if it weren't for Sayers, only twenty or thirty would have heard him today. But now, after showing that recording on the prime time news, Professor Brophy's message has reached millions. Millions!''

"Yes, but it was a silly message. There are a dozen stories like that going around every month about waste in government. Nobody pays them too much mind.''

"But the contempt in his voice," Haworth said, frowning. "The utter contempt . . . it came across so strongly."

"But it doesn't matter, Daro. Sayers negated any points that old bird managed to score by painting him as a tax waster and a disloyal employee.''

"Did he? I hope so. Maybe he made Brophy look silly to you and me, but what about all those sentimental slobs out there? How did Brophy look to them? Are they going to remember what Radmon Sayers said about him, or is the one thing that sticks in their minds going to be the image of a skinny old man being forcibly dragged from view by a couple of young, husky, uniformed guards?''

Ω

"And what was all that supposed to prove?" Broohnin asked as Radmon Sayers' face faded from the globe.

"It proves nothing," LaNague replied. "Its purpose was

merely to plant a seed in the backlot of the public mind to let it know what kind of power the Imperium has.''

"I'm not impressed. Not a bit. We could have had a full-scale riot on the campus if we had planned it right. The Imperial Guard would have been called out and then Sayers would have really had something to show on his news show!''

"But the effect wouldn't have been the same, Den," Zack said from his seat in the corner. "There's big competition for on-campus placement at U. of O., and people seeing the students out on the grounds rioting would only resent the sight of rare opportunity being wasted. They'd want the Imperial Guard to step in; they'd cheer them on. And people would get hurt, which is what we're trying to avoid.''

"We could see to it that a lot of the Guard got hurt!" Broohnin said with a grin. "And if a few students got banged up, all the better. I mean, after all, you wanted to show the oppressive powers of the Imperium. What better evidence than a few battered skulls!''

Zack shook his head in exasperated dismay and looked at LaNague. "I give up. You try.''

LaNague didn't relish the task. He was beginning to think of Broohnin as more and more of a lost cause. "Look at it this way: the Imperium is not an overtly oppressive regime. It controls the populace in a more devious manner by controlling the economy. And it controls life within its boundaries as effectively via the economy as with a club. The indirection of the Imperium's controls makes us forget that it still has the club and is holding it in reserve. The only reason we don't see the club is because the Imperium has found ways to get what it wants without it. But as soon as necessity dictates, out it will come. And it will be used without hesitation. We didn't want the club brought out today, because that would mean bloodshed. We just wanted the public to get a peek into the sack where it's kept . . . just a reminder that it's there.''

"And it was relatively painless," Zack said, rubbing his axillae. "The worst I got out of it was a couple of sore armpits.''

"But what the public saw," LaNague continued, "was an elderly man—''

"Not so elderly!''

"—who is a renowned professor, being pulled from the classroom by force. He wasn't destroying the campus or disrupting the educational process. All he was doing was standing and talking—teaching!—a group of students. And for that he was dragged away by two uniformed men. And believe me, there's something in the sight of uniformed henchmen laying their hands on a peaceful civilian that raises the hackles of outworlders."

"But what did they do? There've been no protests, no cries of outrage, no taking to the streets? Nothing!"

"Right!" LaNague said. "And there won't be, because it was a minor incident. Doc Zack wasn't arrested and he wasn't beaten to a pulp. But he was silenced and he was dragged away by force. And I think people will remember that."

"And so what if they do?" Broohnin said, as belligerent as ever. "The Imperium isn't weakened one erg."

"But its image is. And that's enough for now."

"Well, it's not enough for me!" Broohnin rose and wandered aimlessly around the room, pulling something from his pocket as he moved. LaNague watched him pop whatever it was under his tongue—he guessed it to be a mood elevator —and stand and wait for it to take effect. Yes, Broohnin was definitely on the brink. He would have to be watched closely.

"Hear about the meeting?" Zack said into the tension-filled silence.

"What meeting?" LaNague said.

"Metep and the Council of Five. Word's come down that they've called a special hush-hush super-secret enclave next week. Even Krager's cutting his vacation short and coming back for it."

"Sounds important. Anybody know what it's about?"

Zack shrugged. "Ask Den . . . One of his people picked it up."

Broohnin turned and faced them. The anger lines in his face had smoothed slightly. His voice was calm, even. "Nobody's sure exactly what it's about, but Haworth's behind it. He wants the meeting and he wants it soon."

That troubled LaNague. "Haworth, eh?"

"Something wrong with that?" Zack asked.

"It's probably nothing of any real importance, but there's always the chance that Haworth has come up with some sort of brainstorm to temporarily pull them out of the current crunch . . ."

"I thought you had all exits covered," Broohnin said, barely hiding a sneer. "Afraid Haworth'll slip something past you?"

"With a man like Haworth around, it doesn't pay to get

overconfident. He's shrewd, he's sly, he's smart, and he's ruthless. I'll be anxious to see what comes out of this meeting."

"I'd worry along with you if I could," Zack said. "But since you're the only one who knows where all this is taking us, I'm afraid you're going to have to sleep with those worries alone." He paused, watching LaNague closely. "I do have a few ideas about your plan, however, gathered from what I've seen and heard during the past year."

"Keep them to yourself, please."

"I will. But do you actually think there's any way Haworth or anybody else can turn this whole thing around?"

LaNague shook his head. "No. The Imperium has started its descent and only magic can save it."

"Well, let's just hope Haworth doesn't know any magic," Zack said.

"He might. But just in case they run dry of things to say at the meeting, I think Robin Hood should be able to find a way to keep the conversation going."

THE ROBIN HOOD READER

THE LESSON OF THE GOLD OUTIE

You don't see them in circulation any more—Gresham's Law took care of that—but just sixty years ago, real gold coins were used for money. Exempt from the Legal Tender Laws because it was a symbol of our independence from Earth, each gold outie contained one Troy ounce of gold and was worth about 25 Imperial marks.

A one-ounce gold coin for 25 marks? The price is now 279!

Which brings us to the subject of price vs. value. The Metep mob is trying to confuse the two so you won't know that it is solely to blame for the current inflationary spiral.

Consider: A good quality, natural fiber business jumper cost about 25 marks six decades ago. Today, although there's no fabric shortage and they're certainly not better made, suits of comparable quality cost 250 marks. That's *PRICE*.

Sixty years ago all you needed to buy a business suit was a single gold outie. Today, you can still buy a high-quality suit for a single gold outie. That's *VALUE*.

The Lesson: MONEY SHOULD HAVE VALUE.

Now, you should no longer have to ask what to do with any cash you can scrape up or borrow. Buy gold, silver, platinum, etc!

The Economic Weather Eye

PRICE INDEX (using the 115th year of the Imperium—when the Imperial mark became mandatory legal tender—as base year of 100) 200.3

MONEY SUPPLY (M3) 2195.5

UNEMPLOYMENT LEVEL 9.6%

	Imperial Marks	Solar Credits
GOLD (Troy ounce)	309.3	131.3
Silver (Troy ounce)	18.0	6.1
Bread (1 kg. loaf)	.88	1.70

XV

"It's no good, Vin. He's not coming."

"Yes, he is. He's *got* to come!"

As persistent and patient and straight as a tree rooted in the soil, Vincen Stafford stood with his arm around his wife's shoulders and waited in the back yard of what had once been their house. It stood locked, barred, and empty behind him as he watched the sky. Better to stare into the empty blackness above them than to stare into the empty bleakness of the structure behind. The house had become the symbol of all his failures and of all the things that had failed him. He couldn't bear to look at it.

The drop-off in grain runs to Sol System had started it all, causing him to be bumped from one scheduled flight after another due to his lack of seniority. Finally, he had been laid off. The Imperial Grain Export Authority had let him down —promising him full-time employment when he signed on, and then leaving him grounded. That was bad, but he knew he could make it through on his unemployment benefits from the Spacers Guild. Salli had a part-time job and they had a little money in the bank. It would be tight, but they could squeak

143

through until something broke loose for him.

But the only things that broke loose were prices. Everything except grain seemed to cost more—food, clothing, transportation, everything. Only his mortgage payment had remained fixed. The bank had tried to get him to refinance at a higher interest rate but he had resisted, despite the advice of the *Robin Hood Reader* to borrow all he could and invest it in gold and silver. That, he now realized, had been his biggest blunder. As daily living expenses went up, he and Salli had found it harder and harder to scrape together the mortgage payments each month. Their savings were soon gone and the bank was soon penalizing them for late payments.

Then catastrophe: the Spacers Guild cut his benefits in half due to the drain put on its finances by heavy layoffs. Then the benefits stopped all together; the Spacers Guild had arbitrarily cut him off in order to concentrate benefits on the senior members. Even his union had let him down.

Vin and Salli had immediately tried to refinance the house, but the bank was no longer interested. Mortgage money had dried up and there was none to spare for an out-of-work interstellar navigator. They put the house on the market, but with so little mortgage money around, nobody was buying at the current inflated prices. They missed payments; the bank foreclosed. They were locked out of their own home.

Vincen Stafford was now at the lowest point of his entire life. He and Salli lived in a shabby one-room apartment in the dolee section of town . . . and why not? He was on the dole. When they weren't screaming at each other, they sat in stony silence across the room from each other. Only tonight had brought them together. Robin Hood was coming.

"He's not going to show, Vin," Salli said. "Now let's go home."

"Home? We have no home. It was taken from us. And he *is* coming. Just wait a little longer. You'll see."

Robin Hood was just about the only thing on this world or any other that Vincen Stafford had left to hold onto. When the first "money monsoon" had come, he had turned in the money he had collected. At that time it seemed like the right thing to do . . . after all, the money belonged to the Imperium. And when he analyzed it to any depth, he admitted that he had hoped his name would show up somewhere on a list of exemplary citizens and he would have a crack at the next grain run out, seniority or no. But that hadn't happened. He hadn't made a single run since. His friends had laughed at his naïveté then, and he cursed himself for it now. What he wouldn't give to have those mark notes in his hand right now. A year and a half could make a lot of changes in a man.

If only he'd listened to that newsletter and followed its advice. He knew a couple of men his age who had done just that—refinanced their homes, borrowed to the limit of their credit, and invested it all in gold and silver and other precious metals. One had used the profits from the soaring prices of the commodities to supplement his income and keep him in the black and in his home. Another had let the bank repossess his home and had moved into an apartment. He was now sitting on a pile of gold coins that was growing more and more valuable every day while the bank was stuck with a house it couldn't sell.

Vincen Stafford wasn't going to get caught looking the other way this time. Robin Hood and his Merry Men had robbed a currency shipment this morning; if they held true to form, there'd be money raining down soon.

"This is ridiculous!" Salli said. "I'm going back to the apartment. You heard what they said on the vid. He's not coming."

Stafford nodded in the darkness. "I heard what they said. But I don't believe it." Police authorities had been on the air all day telling the public that Robin Hood and his Merry Men were now robbing tax collections and keeping the money for personal uses, showing themselves for the common thieves and renegades they really were. Anyone waiting for another "money monsoon" would be bitterly disappointed! But Stafford didn't believe it. Couldn't—wouldn't believe it.

One of the stars winked out overhead, then another to its left. Then the original star came on again.

"Wait!" he told Salli, reaching for her arm. "Something's up there!"

"Where? I don't see anything."

"That's the whole idea."

When the first mark notes began slipping down into sight, a great cheer was heard all over the neighborhood . . . Stafford and his wife were not alone in their nocturnal vigil.

"Look, Vin!" Salli said excitedly. "It's really happening. I can't believe it! It's money!" She began scrambling around the yard, picking up the mark notes, disregarding the white calling cards. "Come on, Vin! Help!"

Vincen Stafford found himself unable to move just yet. He merely stood with his face tilted upward, tears streaming down his cheeks, silent sobs wracking his chest.

At least there was still *somebody* left you could count on.

Ω

". . . and it appears that Robin Hood and his Merry Men have lowered their sights, physically and figuratively. After more than seven months of inaction since the costly east coast caper, with only the caustic, omnipresent *Robin Hood Reader* as evidence of his continued presence among us, Robin Hood has struck again. A ground effect vehicle, carrying a large shipment of fresh currency from the Central Treasury to the North Sector branch of the First Outworld Bank of Primus, was waylaid on the streets of the city early this morning.

"The death of four of his Merry Men last year should have made Robin Hood more cautious, but he appears to be as daring as ever. The vehicle was stopped and its guards overpowered in the bright light of morning before a crowd of onlookers. The shipment of currency was quickly transferred to two sport flitters which took off in different directions. No one was hurt, no witnesses could identify any of the perpetrators due to the holosuits they wore, and no evidence was left behind other than the customary arrow with the inscribed shaft.

"As news of the robbery spread, people rushed out into their streets and yards, anticipating a rain of mark notes. But none came; the authorities began to suspect that either Robin Hood was now stealing taxpayer money for personal gain, or that the caper was the work of clever imitators.

"People steadfastly waited all day. So did the Imperial Guard. But alas! No Robin. The majority of hopefuls went home, but a large number of the faithful hung on into the dark. However, it began to look like the police were right. There would be no money monsoon tonight.

"And then it happened. After a year-and-a-half-long drought, the skies of Primus City opened up at 17.5 tonight and began to pour marks down on the parched populace. The fall was much lighter than on the previous occasion—sixty million had been hurled into the air then; tonight's precipitation amounted to approximately one fourth of that. But from the cheers and shouts of joy that arose from every quarter of the city, it is evident that anything was welcomed by the citizens of Primus City.

"If this reporter might be permitted a comment or two: I find it reprehensible that so many of our fellow citizens demean themselves by standing and waiting to receive stolen money from this Robin Hood charlatan. There are no solutions to be found in thievery and cheap showmanship. The real solutions lie with the Imperium's leaders. We should seek solutions there, not in the dark skies of night.

"And now to other news:

"Word from Earth shows that Eric Boedekker, the wealthy asteroid mining magnate, is still at it. Having disposed of his extraterrestrial holdings, he has now sold all of his Earthside property—millions of square meters' worth of land on all of the planet's five continents. And if you think land is getting expensive here on the outworlds, you should look into the prices on Earth! Eric Boedekker has now amassed a liquid fortune that must be unparalleled in the financial history of the human race. No indication as yet as to just what he's doing with it. Is he reinvesting it or just keeping it in a huge account? The entire interstellar financial community is buzzing with curiosity.

"And speaking of buzzing, insiders here on Throne are doing a little of their own as they speculate on the sudden premature return of Treasury Minister Krager from his Southland vacation. Is something afoot in the inner circles of the Imperium? We'll see . . ."

Ω

"Gentlemen," Haworth said, standing behind his chair to the right of Metep VII, "we are in trouble. Big trouble."

There were no groans of protest or resignation. The Council of Five knew the Imperium was in trouble, and each member knew that he didn't have a single idea as to how to remedy the situation. All they could come up with as a group were the same things they had been doing all along, only more so. All looked to Haworth now for some glimmer of hope.

"You've all read the report I sent to each of you by special courier last night—at least I hope you have. You all know now why our grain imports have been falling off. My sources on Earth are reliable. If they say the Earthies have developed photosynthetic cattle, then, believe me, it's true."

"All right," said Cumberland of the Bureau of Agrarian Resources. "I read the report and I'll grant that it's possible. And I can see how it affects my department and all the farmers under me. But I don't see why it's such bad news for everybody else."

"Domino effect," Haworth replied. "If we export less and less grain, which is just about all the outworlds have that Sol System wants, then we cut a significant chunk out of total outworld productivity. Which means less income for us to tax. The result is that the Imperium has less money to work with.

"But it doesn't stop there. The drop in profits to the agrarian worlds means that they're going to start cutting their work forces. That means an increase in unemployment roles, which inevitably leads to an increase in the number of former workers going on the dole where they become tax consumers instead of taxpayers.

"Which means that the Imperium's expenses are going up while its income is going down. Naturally, we just increase the money supply to meet our needs. But our needs have been such that the money supply has increased too rapidly and we're caught in a period of steep inflation. This increases the viciousness of the circle: inflation wipes out savings, so people don't save. That leaves the banks with no money to lend, and that means no construction, no growth. Which leads to more unemployment and more people on the dole. Which means we have to spend more money. Inflation is also allowing more and more people to meet criteria for participation in other programs such as Food Vouchers." He shook his head. "The Food Voucher Program is chewing up marks as fast as we can turn them out. Which adds to the inflation which adds to . . . well, you get the idea."

Cumberland nodded. "I see. Then we'll just have to control the rate of inflation."

Haworth smiled and Krager laughed aloud from the far end of the table. "That would be nice. We just hit a 21 per cent annual rate, although publicly of course, we're only admitting to 15. To slow inflation, the Imperium has to stop spending more than it takes in in taxes. We either have to increase taxes, which is out of the question, or we have to start cutting the Imperial budget." He turned his smirking visage toward Cumberland. "Shall we start with the farm subsidies?"

"Impossible!" Cumberland blustered and blanched

simultaneously. "Those subsidies are depended on by many small farmers!"

"Well? Where shall we start cutting? The dole? Food Vouchers? With more people than ever on public assistance, we'd be risking wide-scale food riots. And it's because I fear there may be some civil disorder in the near future that I don't advise cutting defense budgets."

"I suggest we freeze the money supply for the next half year," Krager said. "There'll be some fallout, naturally, but we've got to do it sometime, and it might as well be now."

"Oh no, you don't!" It was Metep VII speaking. He had bolted upright in his chair at Krager's suggestion. "A freeze would swing us into a depression!" He looked to Haworth for confirmation.

The younger man nodded his white-haired head. "A deep one, and a long one. Longer and deeper than any of us would care to contemplate."

"There! You see?" Metep said. "A depression. And during *my* term of office. Well, let me tell you, gentlemen, that as much as I desire a prominent place in the annals of human history, I do not wish to be known as the Metep whose administration ushered in the first great outworld depression. No, thank you! There'll be no freeze on the money supply and no depression as long as *I* sit in this chair. There has to be another way and we have to find it!"

"I don't think another way exists," Krager said. "As a matter of fact, we're now getting to the point over at Treasury where we're seriously talking about changing the ratio of small bills to large bills. Maybe even dropping the one-mark note altogether. We may even get to the point of issuing 'New Marks,' trading them one to ten for 'old marks.' That would at least cut duplicating expenses, which gives you a pretty good idea of how fast the money supply is expanding."

"There's no way out if we persist in limiting ourselves to simple and obvious solutions," Haworth said into the ensuing verbal commotion. "If we freeze, or even significantly slow, the growth of the money supply, we face mass bankruptcy filings and soaring unemployment. If we keep going at this pace, something's bound to give somewhere along the line."

Metep VII slumped in his chair. "That means I'm to be 'the Depression Metep' for the rest of history, I guess. Either way, I lose."

"Maybe not." Haworth's voice was not raised when he said it, but it cut cleanly through the undertone of conversational pairs around the table and brought all talk to an abrupt halt.

"You've got an idea? A way out?"

"Only a chance, Jek. No guarantees, and it will take lots of guts on all our parts. But with some luck, we may get a reprieve." He began strolling around the conference table as he spoke. "The first thing we do is start to inform the public about Earth's new protein source, playing it up not as a great biological advance, but as a sinister move to try and ruin the outworld economy. We'll create a siege mentality, ask everyone to sacrifice to fight the inflation that Earth is causing. As a stopgap, we'll impose wage-price controls and enforce them rigidly. Anyone trying to circumvent them will be portrayed as an Earthie-lover. If legal penalties don't scare them into compliance, social pressure will. And we'll play the unions off against the businessmen as usual."

"That's not a reprieve!" Krager said, turning in his seat as Haworth passed behind him. "That's not even a new trial— it's just a stay of execution, and a short one at that! It's all been tried before and it's never solved anything!"

"Kindly let me finish, won't you?" Haworth said as calmly as he could. The latent hostility between the Chief Adviser and the Minister of the Treasury was surfacing again. "What I'm proposing has never been attempted before. If we succeed, we will be heroes not only in the outworld history spools, but in the recorded history of humanity. I'm calling it Project Perseus."

He scanned the table. All eyes were on him, watching him with unwavering attention. He continued strolling and speaking.

"We've been monitoring multiple radio sources concentrated in the neighboring arm of this galaxy. We've been at it ever since our ancestors settled out here. There's no doubt that their origin is intelligent and technologically sophisticated. We've sent a few probe ships into the region but they were lost. It's cold, black, and lonely out there and a single probe ship hunting for life is like loosing a single member of a hymenoptera species into the atmosphere of a planet which supports a single flower on its surface, and waiting to see if the bug can find the flower. But if a whole hiveful of the insects is freed into the air at carefully calculated locations, chances of success are immeasurably better. So that's what we're going to

do: build a fleet or probe ships and contact whoever or whatever is out there.''

They all must have thought he was crazy by the looks on
their faces. But Daro Haworth had expected that. He waited
for the first question, knowing ahead of time what it would be
and knowing that either Cumberland or Bede would ask it.

It was Cumberland. ''Are you crazy? How's that going to
get us out of this?''

''Through trade,'' Haworth replied. ''By opening new
markets to us out there. The latest calculations show that
there's another interstellar race in the Perseus arm, outward
from here. It lives a damnable number of light years away, but
if we try, we can reach it. And then we'll have billions of new
customers!''

''Customers for what?'' Metep said. ''The only thing we've
got to trade in any quantity is grain. What if they don't eat
grain? Or even if they do—and that's unlikely, I'm sure—
what makes you think they'll want to buy ours?''

''Well, we've got plenty of grain at the moment,'' Cumberland said. ''Let me tell you—''

''Forget about grain!'' Haworth shouted, his face livid.
''Who am I talking to—the most powerful men in the outworlds or a group of children? Where is your vision? Think of
it! An entire interstellar race! There has to be a million things
we can exchange—from art to hardware, from Leason crystals
to chispen filets! And if we don't have it, we can ship it out
from Earth. We could arrange trade agreements and be sole
agents for whatever alien technology is found to have industrial uses. We could corner any number of markets! The
outworlds could enter a golden age of prosperity! And''—he
smiled here—''I don't think I have to remind you gentlemen
what that could mean to each of us in the areas of political
clout and personal finances, do I?''

The undertone began again as each man muttered cautiously at first to his neighbor, then with growing enthusiasm.
Only Krager had a sour note to sing.

''How are we going to pay for all this? To build and equip a
fleet of probe ships will take an enormous sum of money.
Billions and billions of marks. Where are we supposed to get
them?''

''The same place we get all the other billions of marks we
spend but don't have—the duplicators!''

Krager began to sputter. ''But that will send inflation into

warp! It'll go totally out of control! The mark is already
weakened beyond repair. Why it's still holding up in the Interstellar Currency Exchange, I can't fathom. Maybe the
speculators haven't figured out how bad off we are yet. But
this probe ship idea will completely ruin us!"

"That's why we've got to act now!" Haworth said. "While
the mark still has some credibility on the Exchange. If we wait
too long, we'll never be able to get enough credit to purchase
the drive tubes and warp units necessary for the probe fleet.
The mark has been holding up better than any of us ever expected. That indicates to me that the people active in the Interstellar Currency Exchange have faith in us and think we can
pull ourselves out of this."

"Then they're dumber than I thought they were," Krager
muttered.

"Not funny," Haworth said. "And not fair. You forget
that Project Perseus will also create jobs and temporarily
stabilize the tax base in the interim." He walked back to his
place at Metep's side. "Look: it's a gamble. I told you that
before I broached the subject. It's probably the biggest gamble
in human history. The future of the entire Imperium and all
our political careers is riding on it. If I thought there was
another way out, believe me, I'd try it. Personally, I don't give
a damn about getting in touch with the aliens in the Perseus
arm. But right now, it's our only hope. If we succeed, then all
the extra inflation caused by Project Perseus will be worth
while and eventually compensated by the new avenues of trade
we'll establish."

"Suppose we fail?" Metep said. "Suppose there's something out there that gobbles up probe ships. Suppose they find
nothing but the ruins of a dead civilization!"

Daro Haworth shrugged with elaborate nonchalance. "If
we fail, every outworlder will spit when he hears our names
five years from now. And in perhaps a dozen years, Earth will
reinstate her claim to the outworlds."

"And if we do nothing?" Metep asked, afraid of the
answer.

"The same, only the spitting stage won't be reached for
perhaps ten years, and the return of Earthie control won't occur for twenty. Face it, gentlemen: this is our only chance. It
may not work, but I see no other alternative. We're all to
blame; we've all—"

"I won't take the blame for this mess!" Krager shouted.

"I've warned you all along, all of you, that someday—"

"And you went right along, too, old man." Haworth's lips twisted into a sneer. "You okayed all the increases in the money supply. You made noises, but you went along. If your objections had had any real conviction behind them, you would have resigned years ago. You flew with us, and if we go down, you'll crash with us!" He turned to the others. "Shall we vote, gentlemen?"

Ω

It was the first time LaNague could remember being happy to see Broohnin. He and Doc Zack and Radmon Sayers had waited in the warehouse office into the hours toward dawn. The money drop earlier in the evening had gone off as smoothly as the heist that morning. Things were looking up all over, at least as far as his plans for the revolution were concerned. Everything was going according to schedule, and going smoothly. Too smoothly. He kept waiting for a kink to develop somewhere along the line, waiting and hoping that when it appeared he would be able to handle it. The meeting tonight between Metep and his Council of Five could possibly produce a kink, but that was unlikely. There was no way out for the Imperium now. No matter what they did, no matter what they tried, they were unaware of the purpose of Boedekker's activities on Earth. The Imperium was going to crumble, that was for certain. The Boedekker aspect of the plan would enable LaNague to control the exact moment of its fall, its rate of descent, and its force of impact. The Boedekker aspect would ensure an impact of such force that no trace of the cadaver would remain.

"What's the word from the meeting?" LaNague asked as Broohnin entered the office.

"Nothing!" Broohnin said, scowling through his beard. "A complete waste of time. You wouldn't believe what they wound up deciding to do after hours in hush-hush conference."

"Spend more money, of course," Zack said.

Sayers nodded. "Of course. But on what?"

"Probe ships!" Broohnin looked around at the uncomprehending faces. "That's right—probe ships. I told you you wouldn't believe it."

"What in the name of the Core for?" Sayers asked.

"To find aliens. Haworth wants to jump over to the next

arm of the galaxy and sell stuff to aliens. He says they're over there and they can save the Imperium."

As Zack and Sayers began to laugh, Broohnin joined in. The three of them whooped and roared and pounded the arms of their chairs until they noticed that LaNague was not even smiling. Instead, he was frowning with concern.

"What's the matter, Peter?" Sayers said, gasping for breath. "Have you ever heard of a more ridiculous idea?"

LaNague shook his head. "No. Never. But it may ruin everything."

"But how could—"

LaNague turned away from the vidcaster toward Broohnin. "When does construction start?"

"Immediately, from what I can gather."

"Is it going to be a military or civil project?"

"Civil. They're going to run it through the Grain Export Authority."

"And monitoring?"

Broohnin looked at him questioningly. LaNague's intensity was alarming. "I don't—"

"Communications! The probes have to have a place to report back to, a nerve center of some sort that'll co-ordinate their movements."

"That'll be the GEA comm center, I guess. That's where all the grain pods reported to as they assembled for a run. It's got all the necessary equipment."

LaNague was up and pacing the room. "Have you got any contacts in there?" Seeing Broohnin nod, he went on. "How many?"

"One."

"Get more! Slip our people onto the duty roster in the communications area. We need people on our side in there."

"That's not going to be easy. With the grain runs falling off, they've cut the comm staff. Not enough work to go around."

"If we have to, we'll bribe our way onto the staff. Beg, plead, threaten . . . I don't care what you do, but get us enough people in that comm center to keep it covered at all times!"

"But why?" Sayers asked.

"Because I want to be the first to know what those probe ships find. And if I don't like what they find, I'm going to see to it that the information takes an awful long time getting to the Council of Five.''

Doc Zack spoke from his seat. "You don't really think finding aliens to trade with could open up a large enough market to offset what the Imperium's already done to the economy, and what the cost of this probe ship program will do on top of that, do you? Let me say as an authority on economics that there isn't the slightest chance of success."

"I realize that," LaNague said from the middle of the room.

"Then why the sudden panic? Why tell us that it could ruin everything when you know it can't."

"I'm not worried about them trading with whatever aliens are out there. I'm worried about them stumbling into something else—the one thing that might turn everything we've worked for around; the one thing that's always helped the Meteps and the Imperiums of history out of slumps. And you of all people, Doc, should know what I'm talking about."

Doc Zack's brow furrowed momentarily, then his eyes widened and his face blanched.

"Oh, my!"

THE ROBIN HOOD READER

THE THREE LAWS OF POSITRONIC CITIZENSHIP

1) A citizen may not injure the State, or, through inaction, allow the State to come to harm.

2) A citizen must obey orders given it by the State except when such orders conflict with the First Law.

3) A citizen must protect its own existence as long as such protection does not conflict with the First or Second Law.

If you do not respond positively to all of the above, report immediately to your local public library for rewiring.

Library? Yes, library. More on them next time.

The Economic Weather Eye

PRICE INDEX (using the 115th year of the
               Imperium—when the Imperial
               mark became mandatory legal
               tender—as base year of 100)   219.7

MONEY SUPPLY (M3)   2612.4

UNEMPLOYMENT LEVEL   14.9%

	Imperial Marks	Solar Credits
GOLD (Troy ounce)	502.1	133.2
Silver (Troy ounce)	29.6	6.3
Bread (1 kg. loaf)	1.08	1.71

PART THREE

"Above All Else: KYFHO"

The Year of the Sickle

XVI

Do you wish to become invisible?
Have no thought of yourself for two
years and no one will notice you.
Old Spanish Saying

"Meat?" Salli cried, her gaze shifting back and forth between the roast on the table and her husband. "How did you get it?"

"Bought it." Vincen Stafford was smiling. For the first time in two years he was feeling some pride in himself.

"But how? You just can't get meat any more, except in—"

He nodded. "Yeah. The black market."

"But they don't accept Food Vouchers. And we don't have any money."

"Yes, we do. I signed up as a pilot for Project Perseus today."

"You mean that probe ship thing? Oh no, Vin! You can't mean it! It's too dangerous!"

"It's the only thing I know how to do, Salli. And it pays thirty thousand marks a year. They gave me half in advance for signing."

"But you'll be out there all alone . . . nobody's ever been out there before."

"That's why I got such a premium for signing. It's nothing to pilot those one-man ships. All the skill's in the navigation.

And that's what I do best. It was made for me! I've got to take it.'' The light in his face faded slightly. "Please understand. We need the money . . . but more than that, I need this job.''

Salli looked up at her husband. She knew he needed the job to feel useful again, to feel he had control over something in his life again, even if it was just a tiny probe ship in the uncharted blackness between the galactic arms. And she knew it would be useless to argue with him. He had signed, he had taken the money, he was going. Make the best of it.

She rose and kissed him.

"Let's get this roast cooking."

Ω

". . . and once again there's news from Earth about Eric Boedekker, the wealthy asteroid mining magnate. It seems that he has now sold his fabulous skisland estate to a high bidder in one of the most fantastic auctions in memory. As far as anyone can tell, the estate was the last of the Boedekker holdings to be liquidated, and the former owner is now living in seclusion, address unknown.

"Thus, one of the largest fortunes in human history has been completely liquidated. Whether it sits in an account for future use or has been surreptitiously reinvested remains a tantalizing question. Only Eric Boedekker knows, and no one can find him.

"And here on the outworlds, Project Perseus is proceeding on schedule. A crew for the fleet of ships has been picked from the host of heroic applicants—most of whom were underqualified—and all that is necessary now is completion of the tiny probe ships themselves . . ."

Ω

It was the same old argument, over and over again. Broohnin was sick of it. So was everyone else. LaNague still refused to let them know where it was all heading. He was promising them the full story by the end of the year, but Broohnin wanted it now. So did Sayers and Doc Zack. Even the Flinters looked a little uncertain.

"But what have we *done?*" Broohnin said. "The Imperium's inflating itself out of business. But Doc says that'll take another ten years. We can't wait that long!"

"The Imperium will be out of business in two," LaNague said, calmly, adamantly. "There won't be a trace of it left on

Throne or on any other outworld."

"Doc says that's impossible." Broohnin turned to Zack. "Right, Doc?" Zack nodded reluctantly. "And Doc's the expert. I'll take his word over yours."

"With all due respect," LaNague said, "Doc doesn't know certain things that I know, and without that information, he can't make an accurate projection. If he had it, he'd concur with two years or less as a projected time of collapse."

"Well, give it to me, then!" Zack said. "This is frustrating as hell to sit around and be in the dark all the time."

"At the end of this year, you'll know. I promise you."

From the look on Doc Zack's face, that wasn't what he wanted to hear. Broohnin stepped back and surveyed the group, withholding a smile of approval. He saw LaNague's hold on the movement slipping. His rigid rules of conduct, his refusal to let anyone know the exact nature of his plan for revolution, all were causing dissension in the ranks. Which meant that Broohnin had a chance to get back into the front of everything and run this show the way it should be run.

"We fear Earthie involvement, LaNague." One of the Flinters had spoken. Broohnin had to squint to see whether it was the male or the female. With the bunned hair and red circles on their foreheads, and their robes and weapons belts, they looked like twins. He noticed the swell of the speaker's chest. It had been Kanya.

"Yes," Sayers said. "I'm sure Earth's planning right now when and how to move in and take over."

"I'm sure it is," LaNague said, concentrating his reply on the silent, standing forms of Josef and Kanya. "But Earth will also be projecting a ten- to twelve-year period before the Imperium smothers in its own mark notes. When it crumbles two years from now, they'll be caught off guard. By the time they get organized, their chance will be gone."

Doc Zack was speaking through clenched teeth. "But what can you do that will cause it to crumble so quickly?"

"You'll know at the end of the year."

The meeting broke up then, with the frustrated participants leaving separately, at intervals, via different exits. All that had been decided was that the next Robin Hood robbery should be put off for a while until a new device the Flinters had ordered from their homeworld could be smuggled in. The Flinters had made their own arrangements for delivery, which was expected any day. It would give the Merry Men a totally new approach to robbery. Conventional methods were out now, due to the heavy guard that had been placed on anything that even looked like a currency shipment. The Imperial Guard had been caught looking the other way due to the long interval between the second and third heists. It appeared they did not intend to be caught again.

Broohnin watched the two Flinters as they stood by the front exit, waiting for their turn to depart. For all the fear they inspired in him, Broohnin found the Flinters infinitely fascinating. He saw them not as people but as weapons, beautifully honed and crafted, staggeringly efficient. They were killing machines. He wished he could own one. Pulling his courage together, he sauntered over to where they stood.

"You two have any plans for the evening?" They looked at him but made no reply. "If not, maybe we could get together over a few drinks. I've got some things I'd like to discuss with you both."

"It was previously agreed," Josef said, "that we would not allow ourselves to be seen together outside of the warehouse unless we lived together."

"Oh, that was LaNague's idea. You know what an old woman he is! Why not come down to the—"

"I'm sorry," Josef said, "but we have other plans for the evening. Sorry." He touched his belt and activated a holosuit that covered his Flinter garb with the image of a nondescript middle-aged man. Kanya did the same. They turned and left without so much as a "Next time, perhaps."

Broohnin watched them stroll down the darkening street. There were no other pedestrians about. At night the streets had become the property of the barbarians of Primus City—the hungry, broke, and desperate, who jumped and stole and ran because there was nothing else left to them, were bad enough; but then there were those who had found themselves beaten down, humbled, and debased by life, who had retreated once too often and now needed proof that they were better than somebody—anybody. They needed to force someone to his or her knees and for just a moment or two see another human being cringe in fear and pain before them. To taste power over another life before they snuffed it out was, in some twisted way, proof that they still had control over their own. Which they didn't.

Broohnin shook his head as he watched the two bland, weak-looking figures walk into the darkness, looking like so much fresh meat for anyone hungry for a bite. Pity the jumper who landed on those two.

On an impulse, he decided to follow them. What did Flinters do in their spare time? Where did they live? He was not long in finding out. Kanya and Josef entered a low-rent apartment building not far from the warehouse district. He watched for a while, saw a third floor window on the east wall fill with light before it was opaqued. Fantasizing for a moment, he idly wondered if weaponry and combat were as much a part of their sex play as the rest of their daily life. He cut off further elaboration on the theme when he noticed a standard size flitter lift off from the roof of the apartment building. As it banked to the right, he could see two figures within, neither one identifiable, but definitely a pair. He wondered . . .

With no flitter at his disposal, Broohnin was forced to stand helplessly and watch them go. They were probably off to pick up that new device for the next Robin Hood heist. He would have liked to have seen how they smuggled things onto Throne so easily. It was a technique that could prove useful to him some time in the future. As it was, he was stuck here on the street. It was all LaNague's fault, as usual. He should have seen to it that they were all provided with their own personal flitters. But no. Broohnin wasn't allowed to have one because Broohnin was on the dole and, as far as the records showed, could not afford a personal flitter. To be seen riding around in one all the time would attract unwanted attention.

One thing he could do, though, was go into the apartment building and see if Kanya and Josef were still there. He crossed the street, entered, and took the float-chute up to the third floor. From where he had seen the lighted window earlier, he deduced the location of their apartment. Steeling himself, he approached the door and pressed the entry panel. The indicator remained dark, meaning either that no one was within, or that whoever was in did not want to be disturbed.

With a sigh of relief, he turned away and headed for the floatchute. An unanswered door was hardly evidence that Kanya and Josef had been in that flitter, but at least it didn't negate the possibility. The next thing to do was to go up to the flitter pad on the roof and wait. If they returned tonight, perhaps he could get some idea as to where they had been. What he intended to do with the information, he didn't know. Nothing, most likely. But he had no place to go, no one waiting for him anywhere, no one he wanted to be with, and knew no one who wanted to be with him. He might as well spend the night here on the roof as within the four walls of his room on the other side of town.

The wait was not a long one. He had found himself a comfortable huddling place in the corner of the roof behind the building's own solar batteries, discharging now to light the apartment below, and had just settled in for his vigil when landing lights lit the roof pad from above. It was the flitter he had seen earlier, and after it had locked into its slot, the figures of two familiar middle-aged men emerged.

The first one looked carefully around him. Satisfied that there was no one else on the roof, he nodded to the other and they removed two boxes from their craft, one large and rectangular, the other small and cubical. Carrying the larger box between them with the smaller resting atop it, they pushed through the door to the drop-chute and disappeared.

And that was that. Broohnin sat and bitterly questioned what in the name of the Core he was doing there alone on a roof watching two disguised Flinters unload a couple of boxes from their flitter. He knew no more now about their smuggling procedure than he did before. Bored and disgusted, he waited until he was sure the Flinters were safely behind the door to their apartment, then took the dropchute directly to street level and headed for the nearest monorail stop.

Ω

The wracking total-body parasthesia that enveloped him during the lift into real space as his nervous system was assaulted from all sides was an almost welcome sensation. Vincen Stafford had made the first long jump in his probe ship. The nausea that usually attended entering and leaving subspace passed unnoticed, smothered by a wave of exultation. He was alive again. He was free. He was master of reality itself.

After a few moments of silent revelry, he shook himself and got to work, taking his readings, preparing the beacon to be released and activated. It would send out an oscillating subspace laser pulse in the direction of the radio sources in the Perseus arm; in real space it would send a measured radio beep. Stafford considered the latter mode useless since his subspace jumps would take him far ahead of the radio pulses, but if that was the way the people running the brand-new Imperial Bureau of Interstellar Exploration and Alien Contact wanted it, that's the way they would get it.

The subspace laser beacon was a good idea, however. If the target radio sources really did belong to another interstellar race, and that race was advanced enough to have developed subspace technology, the beacons he and his fellow probe pilots would be dropping off in a predictable zigzag pattern would blaze an unmistakable trail through the heavens for anyone with the equipment to follow. Hopefully, some member of that race would plot out the course of one of the probes and send a welcoming party to wait for it when it lifted into real space at the end of one of the jumps.

Stafford thought about that. If the aliens happened to choose his ship to contact, the responsibility would be awesome. The entire future of the relationship between humankind and the aliens could be marred or permanently estranged by some inadvertent bungle on the part of a hapless probe pilot. He didn't want to be that pilot. He could do without the glory of first contact. All he wanted was to do his job, do it well, and get back to Throne and Salli in one piece.

In one piece. That was the crux of the matter. He would be making a lot of jumps . . . far more in the following months than he would during years as a navigator on the grain runs. Warping down was always a hazard, even for the most experienced spacer. He was tearing open the very fabric of reality, accentuating the natural curve of space to an acute angle, and leaping across the foreshortened interval, reappearing again light years away from his starting point. Probe ships were small, fragile. Sometimes they didn't come out of subspace; sometimes they became lost under the curve of space, trapped forever in featureless, two-dimensional grayness.

Stafford shuddered. That wouldn't happen to him. Other probes had traveled out here between the arms and not come back. But he would. He had to. Salli was waiting.

$$\Omega$$

"The old 'little black box' ploy, ay?" Doc Zack said from the corner seat that had become unofficially his whenever they met in the warehouse office.

"Yes," said LaNague, smiling, "but like no little black box you've ever seen."

"What's it do?" Sayers asked.

"It's a time machine."

"Now just a minute," Zack said. "The Barsky experiments proved time travel impossible!"

"Not impossible—impractical. Barsky and his associates found they could send things back in time, but they couldn't correct for planetary motion in the cosmos. Therefore, the object displaced past-ward invariably wound up somewhere else in space."

Sayers shook his head as if to clear it. "I remember reporting on that at one time or another, but I can't say I ever fully understood it."

Broohnin was paying little attention to the conversation. He was more interested in the whereabouts of the larger box the Flinters had unloaded from their flitter last night. They had brought the small one in with them, and that was what had triggered this meaningless discussion of time travel. But where was the big one?

"Let me put it this way," LaNague was saying. "Everything occupies a locus in time and space, correct? I think we can take that as given. What the Barsky apparatus does is change only the temporal locus; the spatial locus remains fixed."

Sayers' eyebrows lifted. "Ah! I see. That's why it ends up in interstellar space."

"Well, *I* don't see," Broohnin snapped, annoyed that his wandering thoughts had left him out. "Why should sending something back in time send it off the planet?"

LaNague spoke as patiently as he could. "Because at any given instant, you occupy a 'here' and a 'now' along the space/time continuum. The Barsky device changes only the 'now.' If we used it to send you back ten years into the past, your 'now' would be altered to 'then,' but you'd still be 'here' in space. And ten years ago, Throne was billions of kilometers away from here. Ten years ago, it hadn't reached this point in space. That's why they could never bring any of the temporally displaced objects back. Barsky theorized that this was what was happening, but it wasn't until the Slippery Miller escape that he could finally prove it."

Broohnin vaguely remembered the name Slippery Miller, but could not recall any of the details. Everyone else in the room apparently could, however, by the way they were nodding and smiling. He decided not to look like an idiot by asking about it.

"Well, if you've got any ideas of sending me or anyone else back into time with that thing, you can just forget it." He consciously tried to make it sound as if he were standing up for the group against LaNague. "We're not taking any chances like that for you or anybody!"

LaNague laughed in his face, and there was genuine amusement in the sound rather than derision, but that didn't blunt its sting. "No, we're not planning to send any people back in time. Just some of the Imperium's money."

Ω

It was strictly understood that after Broohnin had completed his little mission, he was to return the flitter to LaNague. No joy-riding. If he broke one of the air regs, he'd be hauled in, and not only would he have to answer a lot of questions about how a dolee came to be in possession of a nice new sporty flitter, but he might also be linked with LaNague. That was something to be avoided at all costs.

But Broohnin didn't consider this a joy ride. And even if he had, the displeasure of Peter LaNague was hardly a deterrent. He had delivered the Barsky temporal displacer in the tiny black box to Erv Singh on the west coast, and had passed on LaNague's instructions. Erv's next currency run wasn't until the following week; he'd have to wait until that time before he could place the box according to plan. He'd contact Broohnin as soon as everything was set. That done, the rest of the night lay free ahead of Broohnin. He had been approaching the Angus Black Imports warehouse when the idea struck him that now was a perfect time to check up on the Flinters. The nature of the other box they had unloaded that night on the roof of their apartment still nagged at him. Something about the way they had handled it pestered him, like an itchy patch of skin out of reach in the middle of his back.

He had a little trouble finding their apartment building from the air, but after following the streets as he had walked them, he reached a familiar-looking roof. And yes, the Flinters' flitter was still there. Broohnin circled around in the darkness until he found a resting place for his craft on a neighboring roof. He'd give it an hour. If there was no sign of the Flinters by then, he'd call it a night. No use making LaNague wait too long.

He waited the full hour, and then a little bit longer. The extra time spent in watch had not been a conscious decision. He had popped a torportal under his tongue to ease his restlessness in the cramped flitter seat and had nodded off. Only the stimulus of flickering light seeping through the slits between his eyelids roused him to full consciousness. A flitter was rising off the neighboring roof. It was the same one the Flinters had used last night. As it moved away into the darkness, its running lights winked off. Now Broohnin was really interested.

Leaving his own running lights off, he lifted his craft into the air and climbed quickly to a higher altitude than he thought the Flinters would be using. Without their running lights to follow, Broohnin would lose them before they had traveled a few kilometers. His only hope was to get above and keep them silhouetted against the illumination given off by Primus City's ubiquitous glo-globes. As long as they stayed over the urban areas, he could follow above and behind them without being seen. If they moved over open country, he would have to think of something else.

They stayed over the city, however, and headed directly for Imperium Park at its center. Broohnin began to have some trouble over the park since its level of illumination was drastically less than the dwelling areas. It was only by chance that he noticed them setting down in a particularly dense stand of trees. Broohnin chose a less challenging landing site perhaps two hundred meters east of them and sat quietly after grounding his craft, unsure of what to do next.

He desperately wanted to see what two Flinters could be up to in the middle of Imperium Park in the dead of night, but he didn't want to leave the safety of the flitter. If the streets of Primus City were on their way to becoming nighttime hunting grounds, Imperium Park was already far into the jungle stage. Once he stepped out onto the ground, he was fair game for whoever was walking about. Not that Broohnin couldn't handle himself in a fight with one or even two assailants. He carried a vibe-knife and knew how to use it to damaging effect. It was just that nowadays the jumpers hunted in packs in the park, and he had no illusions about his fate should he stumble onto one of those.

He only hesitated briefly, then he was out in the night air, locking the flitter entry behind him. All things considered, the odds were probably in his favor for coming through the jaunt unscathed. The section of the park in which he had landed was on high ground where the underbrush was the thickest. There were no natural paths through here and it would not be considered prime hunting area for any of the packs.

He pushed his way carefully through the brush until he felt

he had traveled half the distance to the Flinters, then he got down on his belly and crawled. And crawled. His chest and abdomen were bruised and scratched, and he was about to turn back, thinking he had wandered off course, when his right hand reached out and came in contact with nothing but air. Further tactile exploration brought his surroundings into clearer focus; he was on the edge of a low rocky bluff. Below him and to the right he heard grunting and groaning. Craning his head over the edge, he spied the Flinters' craft.

A hooded lamp provided faint illumination for the scene, but enough for Broohnin to discern two figures pushing and pulling at a huge slab of rock. With a prolonged agonized chorus of guttural noises from two bodies straining to the limits of their strength, the rock began to move. Intensifying their efforts, the Flinters rolled it up on its edge in one final heave, revealing a rectangular hole. After a panting, laughing pause as they leaned against the up-ended stone, they returned to the flitter and the large box that lay on the ground beside it . . . the same box Broohnin had seen them unload on the roof the other night.

Each of them removed a small white disk from his or her belt—even with their holosuits deactivated, Broohnin could not tell Kanya from Josef at this distance—and pressed it into a slotted opening in the side of the crate in turn. Then the white disks went back into the weapons belts. Carefully, almost gingerly, they carried the crate to the hole under the rock, placed it within and covered it with a thin layer of dirt. With less effort and fewer sound effects, they toppled the stone back over the hole.

Then the two Flinters did something very strange—glancing once at each other, they stepped away from the rock and stood staring at it. From their postures, Broohnin could not be sure whether he was reading guilt or grief or both. He almost slipped from the bluff in a vain attempt to get a glimpse of their faces. What was going on down there anyway? What was in that crate and why was it being buried in Imperium Park? If security was all they were looking for, there were certainly better places to hide it out on the moors. And why was LaNague having all this done without telling the group?

The questions plagued Broohnin as he returned through the brush to his flitter, and left the front of his mind only long enough for him to make the dash from cover to the flitter and to get into the air as quickly as possible. As he rose into the night, a thought occurred to him: what if LaNague didn't know about that box either?

Ω

LaNague stopped at the door to his apartment and rubbed his temples with both hands. Another headache, but a mild one this time. As the plan reached the ignition point, they seemed to be bothering him less frequently, and were less severe when they struck. And the dream . . . months had passed since it had troubled his sleep. Everything seemed to be falling into line as predicted, everything coming under control.

There were still variables, however. Boedekker was the biggest. What if he balked? LaNague grimaced in annoyance at the thought as he placed his palm against the entry plate which was keyed to him, Kanya, and Josef. The door slid open and he stepped through. Boedekker so far had followed his instructions to the letter, at least as far as LaNague could tell. He had liquidated anything of value that he owned, and other indicators showed that he was following through with the secondary aspects of his part in the play. Boedekker could still go his own way, and that bothered LaNague. The man was out of reach. He didn't want to trust him, but he had no choice.

He let the door slide closed behind him but did not move into the room just yet. He felt good, despite the headache. This bouyancy of mood was a fairly recent development, a slow process over the past year. At first the knowledge that the fate of the otworlds was falling more and more completely into his hands had weighed on him like half a dozen G's. Billions of people were going to be affected to varying degrees across the light years of Occupied Space. Even Earth would not escape unscathed. The agrarian outworlds were already on their way into a deep depression, and by the time the Imperium came apart, they'd be back to a barter economy and would hardly notice its demise. But the people on Throne . . . their entire social structure would be destroyed almost overnight.

Mora's angry words came back to him—what right did he have to do this? The question used to trouble him fiercely, despite his standard answer: self-preservation. But it troubled him no more. It was all a moot point now, anyway. The plan was virtually to the point of no return. Even if Mora could show up and convince him that he had been in error all along, it would be too late. The juggernaut had begun to roll and could not be stopped. Its course could be altered, modified to a degree, its moment of impact adjusted—that was the purpose of LaNague's continued presence on Throne—but no one, not even LaNague, could stop it now. The realization had a strangely exhilarating effect on him.

Odd he should think of Mora now. He had been managing to keep her at the far end of his mind except when making a holo for her or viewing one from her. The communications were too brief, too few, and too long in coming. He missed her. Not as much as he had at first, though. Perhaps he was getting used to life without her . . . something he had once considered impossible.

Walking over to where Pierrot sat on the window sill, he touched the moss at the tree's base and noted that it felt dry. Due for some water soon, probably a root-pruning, too. Soon . . . he'd get to it soon. The trunk was halfway between *chokkan* and *bankan*, which was neutral, but the leaves seemed duller than usual. Closer inspection revealed a few bare inner branches with peeling bark—a sure sign of localized death.

Was something wrong with Pierrot? Or was the tree reflecting some sort of inner rot afflicting LaNague himself? That was one of the drawbacks of having an imprinted *misho*—there was always a tendency to read too much into its configuration, its color, its state of health. It did prompt introspection, though, and a little of that was never bad. But not now. There were too many other things on his mind.

He broke off the dead wood and threw it into the molecular dissociator that stood in the corner. The appliance was not the extravagance it seemed. LaNague made a point of disintegrating everything that was not part of a normal household's garbage. There was another dissociator at the warehouse in which all debris from production of *The Robin Hood Reader* and other sundry subversive activities was eventually destroyed. He would not have the revolution tripped up by a wayward piece of refuse.

He turned toward the sink for Pierrot's water and froze as he caught a glimpse of movement in the doorway that led to the bedroom.

"Peter, it's me."

"Mora!" Conflicting emotions rooted him to the spot. He should have been overjoyed to see her, should have leaped across the room to embrace her. But he wasn't and he didn't.

Instead, he felt resentment at her presence. She had no right showing up like this . . . she was going to interfere . . .

"But how?" he said when he found his voice.

"I came on a student visa. I'm supposedly going to do research at the U. of O. library. Kanya let me in this morning." Her brow furrowed. "Is something wrong?"

"No."

"I was watching you with Pierrot. He's your only friend here, isn't he?"

"Not really."

"You look older, Peter."

"I am."

"Much older." Her frown turned into a smile that failed to mask her hurt and concern at his remoteness. "You almost look your age."

"Where's Laina?"

She drifted toward him, cautiously, as if fearing he'd bolt from her. "With your mother. She's too young to join the Merry Men."

It took a while for the implications of what she had said to filter through to LaNague's befuddled brain. But when it did: "Oh no! Don't even consider it!"

"I've been considering it since you left." She moved closer, gently touching his arms with her hands, sending shock waves through him, cracking the paralysis that held him immobile. "I was wrong . . . this is the only way out for Tolive . . . for Laina . . . for our way of life . . . and the minting's done . . . the coins are ready to be shipped . . ."

"No! There's chaos coming to Throne. I don't want you here when everything comes apart. Too dangerous!" He wouldn't want her here even if it were safe.

Mora kissed him gently, tentatively, on the lips. "I'm staying. Now, are we going to stand here and argue, or are we going to catch up on two and a half years of deprivation?"

LaNague replied by lifting her up and carrying her into the adjoining room. He could no longer deny his hunger for her. He'd send her home later.

Ω

Vincen Stafford prepared to eject another beacon into the starry void. How many was this, now? He'd have to check his records to be exactly sure. It was all becoming so mechanical and routinized—jump, release a beacon, jump, release a beacon, jump . . . even the jumps themselves seemed to be less traumatic. Was there such a thing as acclimation? He shrugged. He'd never heard of it, but maybe it happened. And if it did or didn't, so what? He was more than halfway to the Perseus arm. If he reached it without being contacted, he could turn back and go home. So far, so good.

There was a buzz behind him. He turned and saw his communicator light flashing. Someone—or something—was trying to contact him. Opening the circuit gave rise to no audio or visual signal. That meant the incoming message was not on the standard frequency. Stafford was liking this less and less every second. Reluctantly, he activated the search mechanism. It would lock in on the frequency of the incoming signal when it located it.

It didn't take long. The vidscreen suddenly lit with a face like nothing Stafford had ever seen. No, wait . . . there was something vaguely familiar there . . . the snout, the sharp yellow teeth, the bristly patches of fur around the ears . . . canine. Yes, that was it. The creature was definitely dog-faced. But not like any dog he ever wanted in the same room with him. He was glad the probe ship was equipped with only flat-screen reception. A holograph of that thing would be downright frightening. No torso features were visible but that was okay.

"Greetings," the image said in Interstellar that was garbled and gutturalized far beyond the capability of a human throat.

"Who—who are you?" Stafford blurted inanely. "Where are you?"

"I am an emissary of the Tark nation"—at least it sounded like "Tark," a barking sound with a harsh initial consonant— "and my craft is approximately two of your kilometers aft of you."

"You speak our language." Stafford was reaching for the aft monitor. He wanted to see what kind of welcoming party had been sent to intercept him. An intensified image of a bulky ovoid filled the screen. At first he thought the emissary had understated the distance, but the readout showed a large mass two kilometers aft. Stafford took another look. That was no peaceful envoy ship. He had no idea what alien weaponry might look like, but he saw all sorts of tubes pointed in his direction and there was a definite feeling about the ship that said it wasn't built for mere information-gathering duties. It reminded him of a Sol-System dreadnought. But then, maybe they were just being careful. In their position, he'd probably come armed to the teeth, too.

"Of course," the Tark replied. "We've been keeping watch on your race for quite some time. We are not so timid as you: as soon as we had sufficient evidence of an interstellar race in your arm of the galaxy, we investigated."

"Why didn't you contact us?"

"We saw no need. Your race is obviously no threat to the Tark nation, and you are much too far away to be of any practical use to us."

"What about trade?"

"Trade? I am not familiar with the term." He looked down and seemed to be keying a reference into a console to his right.

Stafford couldn't resist prompting him. "An exchange of goods . . . and knowledge."

"Yes, I see now." He—for no good reason, Stafford had automatically ascribed a male gender to the creature—looked up. "Once again, we do not see any purpose in that. Your race does not appear to have anything that interests us sufficiently at this point." The subject of trade apparently bored the Tark and he turned to another. "Why do you invade Tarkan space? You made certain that we would intercept you. Why?"

"To offer trade with us."

The Tark gave a sharp, high-pitched yelp. Laughter? Annoyance? "You must understand—we do not trade with anyone. That would involve an exchange, requiring Tarks to give up one thing in order to gain another."

"Of course. That's what trade is all about."

"But Tarks are not weak. We do not surrender what we have. If you had something we truly desired, we would take it."

"You don't understand . . . " Stafford began to say, but heard his voice trail off into silence. Perspiration had been collecting in his axillae since the comm indicator had buzzed; it was now running down over his ribs. They didn't understand, not at all. And to think that he had dreaded being in the contact ship for fear of unintentionally offending the aliens. This was worse. These creatures seemed devoid of anything approaching a concept of give and take. They were beyond offending.

The face on the screen had apparently come to a decision. "You will shut down your drive mechanism and prepare to be boarded."

"Boarded! Why?"

"We must be assured that you are not armed and that you pose no threat to the Tark nation."

"How could I threaten that monstrosity you're riding?" Stafford said, glancing at the aft monitor. "You could swallow me whole!"

"Shut down your drive and prepare for boarding! We will—"

Stafford switched off the volume. He was frightened now and needed to think, something he couldn't do with that growling voice filling the cabin. He felt a sharp tug on the ship and knew that a tractor beam or something very similar had been focused on him. He was being drawn toward the Tark dreadnought. In a brief moment of panic, he stood frozen in the middle of his tiny cabin, unable to act, unable to decide what to do next.

He was trapped. His real space propulsion system was the standard proton-proton drive through a Leason crystal tube. But small. Too small to break free of the tractor beam. Activating it now would only serve to move him through space pulling the dreadnought behind him, and that futile gesture would last only as long as his fuel or the Tark commander's patience. If the latter ran out first, his probe ship might become a target for those banks of weapons which could easily reduce it to motes of spiraling rubble.

There was the warp capacity, of course. It could be used for escape, but not now . . . not when he was in the thrall of a tractor beam and in such close proximity to a mass as large as the Tark ship. The thought of attempting a subspace drop under those circumstances was almost as frightening as the thought of placing himself at the mercy of the Tarks.

No, it wasn't. A quick look at the canine face that still filled his comm screen convinced him of that. Better to die trying to escape than to place his life in that creature's hands.

He threw himself into the control seat and reached for the warp activator. If the tractor beam and the dreadnought's mass sufficiently disturbed the integrity of the probe ship's warp field, it would be caught between real space and subspace. The experts were still arguing over just what happened then, but the prevailing theory held that the atomic structure of that part of the ship impinging on subspace would reverse polarity. And that, of course, would result in a cataclysmic explosion. It was a fact of life for every spacer. That was why the capacity of the warp unit had to be carefully matched to the mass of the ship; that was why no one ever tried to initiate a subspace jump within the critical point in a star system's gravity well.

He released the safety lock and placed his finger on the activator switch. A cascade of thoughts washed across his mind as he closed his eyes and held his breath . . . *Salli* . . . if the ship blew, at least he'd take the Tarks with him . . . *Salli* . . . was this what had happened to the few probe ships that had been sent this way in the past and were never heard from again? . . . *Salli* . . .

He threw the switch.

THE ROBIN HOOD READER

YOU CAN DEPEND ON THE IMPERIAL LIBRARY LIKE YOU DEPEND ON THE IMPERIUM!

For the real truth, go straight to the source: go down to the local library branch and peruse the spools you require on the premises, or have them keyed to your home vid. You can depend on the Imperial Library system.

Really? Take a look at this excerpt from an old memo sent to all the librarians in the Imperial Bureau of Libraries:

RE: THE WIZARD OF OZ. Only the specially revised edition of L. Frank Baum's classic fantasy is recommended for purchase by regional and school branches of the Imperial Library. The reason should be obvious to anyone reading the original closely. The state, in the person of the Wizard, is portrayed as fraudulent, incompetent, ineffectual, and impotent. The Lion, the Scarecrow, and the Tin Woodsman [citizens] are seen on a pilgrimage to the Wizard [the state] in quest of qualities they already possess in abundance. Conclusion: the state is supercilious.

We don't want our children exposed to that kind of thinking! In the revised version, the Wizard imbues them with Courage, Intelligence, and Heart *before* they tackle the Evil Witch, thus enabling them to succeed.

YOU CAN DEPEND ON THE IMPERIAL LIBRARY LIKE YOU DEPEND ON THE IMPERIUM!

— *The Economic Weather Eye* —

PRICE INDEX (using the 115th year of the Imperium—when the Imperial mark became mandatory legal tender—as base year of 100)   257.6

MONEY SUPPLY (M3)   3103.4

UNEMPLOYMENT LEVEL   17.1%

	Imperial Marks	Solar Credits
GOLD (Troy ounce)	933.3	134.0
Silver (Troy ounce)	41.1	6.2
Bread (1 kg. loaf)	1.15	1.70

XVII

When two coins are equal in debt-paying value but unequal in intrinsic value, the one having the lesser intrinsic value tends to remain in circulation and the other to be hoarded or exported.
Gresham's Law (original version)

Bad money drives out good.
Gresham's Law (popular version)

Mora not only refused to return to Tolive, she insisted on coming along on the next Robin Hood caper.

"Give me one good reason," she said, looking from her husband to Zack, to the Flinters, to Broohnin. "One good reason why I shouldn't go to the mint with you."

None of them wanted her along, but the non-Kyfhons objected to her presence solely on the basis that she was a woman. They had all come to know Mora well during the past week, and she had charmed every one of them, including Sayers, who was absent today. Even Broohnin's sourness mellowed when she was around. But this was man's work, and although neither Zack nor Broohnin verbalized it internally or externally, each felt that the significance of their mission was somehow diminished if a woman joined them.

The Flinters objected because she was a non-combatant, no more, no less.

LaNague's objection rested on different grounds. Her presence made him feel uncomfortable in some vague way that he found impossible to define. He felt as if he were being scrutinized, monitored, judged. Mora made him feel . . . guilty somehow. But of what?

"I'm a big girl, you know," she said when no one accepted her challenge. "And as long as firing a weapon or damaging another person is not involved, I can keep up with the best of you."

Zack and Broohnin glanced at each other. With the exception of Flint and Tolive, sexual equality was an alien concept on most outworlds. Men and women had reached the stars as equals, but women had become nest-keepers again as the overall technological level regressed on the pioneer worlds. They would soon be demanding parity with men, but there was no movement as yet. Mora knew this. She obviously chose her words to goad Zack and Broohnin, and to remind the Flinters and her husband of their heritage.

"You'll fly with me," LaNague said, bringing the dispute to a close. He knew his wife as she knew him. By now each would recognize when the other had reached an intransigent position.

"Good. When do we leave?"

"Now. We've already wasted too much time arguing. And timing is everything today."

Erv Singh had called Broohnin the day before to report that he had finally been able to place the Barsky box in a vault filled with old currency waiting to be destroyed. He mentioned that the vault was unusually full. LaNague explained the reason for that to his wife as their flitter rose into the air over Primus City.

"The one-mark note has finally been rendered obsolete by inflation; the Treasury Bureau is trying to cut expenses by phasing it out. Supply of the larger denomination bills is being upped. When the good coins started disappearing, that was an early warning sign. But now, even the most obtuse Throner should get the message that something is seriously wrong when small bills are no longer produced."

They flew toward the dying orange glow of the sun as it leaned heavily on Throne's horizon, over Imperium Park and the surrounding structures that housed the bureaucratic entrails of the Imperium itself, and then over the city's dolee zone, a sector that was expanding at an alarming rate, on to a huge clearing fifty kilometers beyond the limits of Primus City. An impregnable block of reinforced synthestone occupied the middle of that clearing, like an iceberg floating still in a calm sea, nine tenths of its structure below the surface.

LaNague brought his craft to rest in a stand of trees on a hill overlooking the site; the second flitter followed him down. Broohnin emerged first, followed by Zack and the two Flinters. Kanya was carrying an electronic timer of Flinter design, unequaled in precision. She set it on the deck of LaNague's flitter and removed a round white disk from her belt.

"What's that?" Broohnin asked. Something in the man's voice made LaNague turn and look at him. He had worn a bored and dour expression all day. Now he was suddenly full of life and interest. Why?

"A timer," Kanya said. She did not look up, but concentrated on fitting the disk, which could now be seen to have a red button in its center, into the circular depression atop the timer.

"No . . . that." He pointed to the disk.

"That's the trigger for the Barsky box."

"Do they all look like that? The triggers, I mean."

"Yes." Kanya looked up at him. "Why do you ask?"

Broohnin suddenly realized that he was under close scrutiny from a number of sources and shrugged nervously. "Just curious, that's all." With visible effort, he pulled his eyes away from the trigger and looked at LaNague. "I still don't understand what's going to happen here. Go over it again."

"For me, too," Mora said.

"All right." LaNague complied for his wife's benefit more than Broohnin's, who he was sure knew exactly what was going to happen. He wondered what was cooking in that bright but twisted mind now. "When activated, the Barsky box in the vault will form an unfocused temporal displacement field in a rough globe around itself. Anything encompassed by that field will be displaced exactly 1.37 nanoseconds into the past."

"That's all?" Mora said.

"That's enough. Don't forget that Throne is not only revolving on its axis and traveling around its primary; it's also moving around the galactic core along with the other star systems in this arm, while the galaxy itself is moving away from the location of the Big Bang. So it doesn't take too long for Throne to move the distance from here to Primus City."

Mora frowned briefly and chewed on her lower lip. "I'd hate to even begin the necessary calculations."

"The Flinters have formulae for it. They've been experimenting with the Barsky apparatus as a means of transportation." LaNague smiled. "Imagine listing an ETA at point B *before* the time of departure from point A. Unfortunately, they've been unable to bring anything through alive. But they're working on it."

"But why the timer?" Mora asked.

"Because the box has to be activated at the precise nanosecond that Throne's axial and rotational attitudes come into proper alignment. The Flinters have it pin-pointed at sometime between 15.27 and 15.28 today. No human reflex can be trusted to send the signal at just the right instant, so an electronic counter is employed."

Mora still looked dubious. She pulled her husband away from the flitter.

"It'll work," LaNague told her, glancing back over his shoulder as he moved and watching Broohnin, whose eyes were fixed again on the white trigger mechanism.

"What if there's someone in the vault?" Mora asked when they were out of earshot.

"There won't be," LaNague assured her. "The workday is over down there. Everybody's gone."

"No guards?"

"A few."

"How do you know where they'll be when you activate the Barsky device? What if one of them gets sucked into the field?"

"Mora," LaNague said, trying to keep his tone even, "we've only got one device and it has to be activated soon . . . tonight."

"Why? Why can't we wait until we're sure no one's going to get killed down there?"

"Because the money in that vault is tagged for destruction. And when they burn it, they're going to burn the Barsky box along with it. We only have one Barsky box!"

"Then let's wait until later . . . just to be sure."

"We'll never be sure!" Impatience had passed into exasperation. "We can't see inside the vault, so we can't be sure it's unoccupied. And the device has to be activated between 15.27 and 15.28 tonight or not at all, because proper alignment won't occur again for another three days!"

"Is it so important then? Do you have to get this money out? Why not just forget about it this time."

LaNague shook his head. "I need one more Robin Hood episode to keep his reputation up and his name before the public eye. And with all currency shipments so heavily guarded now, this is the only way I can make one last big strike."

Mora's voice rose to a shout. *"But somebody could be in that vault!"* The others by the flitter turned to look at her.

"Then that's too bad," LaNague said, keeping his own voice low. "But there's nothing I can do about it." He turned and strode back toward the flitter. It had happened as he knew it would—Mora was interfering in his work. It hadn't taken her long to get involved. For a while it had actually seemed that she would keep to herself and stay out of his way. But no—that would have been too much to ask! The more he thought about it, the more it enraged him. What right did she—?

He was half the distance to the flitter when he realized that there was a sick cold sphere centered in the heat of his anger, and it was screaming for him to stop. Reluctantly—very reluctantly—he listened. Perhaps there was another way after all.

As he approached Broohnin and the Flinters, he said, "I want you to take the other flitter and strafe the entrance to the mint."

"With hand blasters?" Broohnin asked, startled.

LaNague nodded. "You're not out to cause damage, but to create a diversion—to pull the inside guards toward the entrance and away from the vaults. One pass is all you should need, then head for Primus as fast as you can. By the time they can mobilize pursuit, you should be lost in the dolee sector."

"Count me out," Broohnin said. "That's crazy!"

LaNague put on what he felt was his nastiest sneer. "That figures," he said in a goading tone. "You rant and rave about how everything in my plan is too soft and too gentle, but when we give you a chance for some action, you balk. I should have known. I'll ask the Doc. Maybe he'll—"

Broohnin grabbed LaNague's arm. "No you don't! You don't replace me with a teacher!" He turned to the Flinters. "Let's go."

As the flitter rose and made a wide circle to the far side of the mint, LaNague felt an arm slip around his back. "Thank you," Mora said.

"We'll see if this works," he said, not looking at her.

"It will."

"It had better." He felt utterly cold toward Mora. Perhaps she had been right, but that did not lessen his resentment of her interference.

The flitter with Broohnin and the Flinters was out of sight now on the other side of the mint, gaining momentum at full throttle. Suddenly, it flashed into view, a silver dot careening over the barracks straight toward the squat target structure. Alarms were already going off down there, LaNague knew, sending Imperial Guardsmen to their defense positions, and the mint guards into the corridors as the vaults within began to cycle closed automatically. There were small flashes briefly brightening the entranceway to the mint, and then the flitter was gone, racing toward Primus City and anonymity.

LaNague checked the time—it was 15.26. He pressed the trigger in the center of the white disk, arming it. The timer would do the rest.

When the precise nanosecond for firing arrived, the timer pulsed the trigger, which in turn sent a signal to the Barsky box in the vault, activating it. The money in the vault, along with small amounts of synthestone from the walls and floors, abruptly disappeared. The package traveled 1.37 nanoseconds into the past and appeared in the air over Primus City at the exact locus the treasury vault was destined to occupy 1.37 nanoseconds from then.

$$\Omega$$

". . . although officials are more tight-lipped than usual, it does appear that the 'money monsoon' that occurred earlier this evening consisted of obsolete currency stolen from the vaults of the mint itself. From what we can determine, the mint was briefly harassed by a lone flitter in the early evening hours; guards reported that the money was in the vault before the incident, and discovered to be missing when the vaults were reopened approximately an hour after the flitter had escaped. The particular vault in question is thirty meters underground. The walls were not breached and no tunnel has been found. The rain of one-mark notes carried no white calling cards this time, but there is no doubt in anyone's mind that Robin Hood has struck again. The Bureau of the Treasury has promised a full and thorough investigation of the matter . . ."

Ω

"Money, money, money!" Mora was saying as they sat in the apartment, watching Radmon Sayers on the vid. "That's all you seem to care about in this revolution. There's more to a government—good or bad—than money!"

"Not much. In any government, dictatorial or representational, the politicos spend 95 per cent of their time taking money from one place and shuttling it to another. They extort money from the citizenry and then go about the tasks of passing bills to appropriate to this group, grant to that group, build here, renovate there."

"But legislation for freedom, rights—"

"That's all decided at the outset, when the government is formed. That's when there's the most freedom; from then on it's a continuous process of whittling down the individual's franchise and increasing the state's. There are exceptions, of course, but they're rare enough to qualify as aberrations. Look back in the Imperium: one, perhaps two, pieces of legislation a year are involved purely with extension or abridgment—usually the latter—of freedom. What the public never realizes is that it really loses its freedom in the countless appropriations passed every day to create or continue the countless committees and bureaus that monitor human activities, to make countless rules to protect us from ourselves. And they all require funding."

"Money again."

"Correct! Keep a government poor and you'll keep it off your back. Without the necessary funds, it can't afford to harass you. Give it lots of money and it will find ways to spend it, invariably to your eventual detriment. Let it control the money supply and all the stops are out: it will soon control you! I shouldn't have to tell you this."

"But what of culture?" Mora spread her fingers in a gesture of frustration. "Whatever culture the outworlds were beginning to develop is dying now. What are you going to do about that? How does that fit into your plan? How're you going to tie that into economics?"

"I'm not even going to try. I don't want an outworld culture! That connotes homogenization, something the Imperium has been attempting to do. If everyone is the same, it's much easier for a central government to make rules for its subjects. I don't want one outworld culture—I want many. I want human beings to stretch themselves to the limit in every direction. I don't want anyone telling anyone else how to live, how to think, what to wear. I want diversity. It's the only way we'll keep from stagnating as a race. It almost happened to us on Earth. If we had remained on that one little planet, we'd be a sorry lot by now, if any humans at all still existed. But you can't have diversity in a controlled society. If you control the economy, you control lives; you have to bring everyone down to the lowest common denominator. You have to weed out the oddballs, stifle the innovators. Do that on all the outworlds and pretty soon you'll have your 'outworld culture.' But would you want to participate?"

Mora hesitated before answering, and in the interval the vidphone chimed. LaNague took the call in the next room. He recognized Seph Wolverton's face as it filled the screen.

"News from the probe fleet," he said without salutation. "Contact made halfway to the Perseus arm. Hostile. Very hostile from the report."

LaNague felt his stomach lurch. "Who knows?"

"Nobody except you, me, and the man who decoded the subspace call, and he's with us."

LaNague sighed with minimal relief. It was a bad situation, but it could have been much worse. "All right. Send a message back as pre-arranged. He's to return directly to Throne, with no further contact until he's in the star system, and even then he's only to identify his craft and answer no questions until he is picked up by an orbital shuttle and brought down for debriefing. See that the probe's message is erased from the comm computer. No one is to know the contents of that message. Clear?"

Wolverton nodded. "Clear."

LaNague cut the connection and turned to see Mora staring at him from the doorway.

"Peter, what's the matter? I've never seen you so upset."

"The probes have made contact with a hostile alien culture

out toward the Perseus arm.''

"So?"

"If word of this gets to Metep and Haworth and the others, they'll have the one lever they need to keep themselves in power and maybe even save their skins: war.''

"You're not serious!''

"Of course I am! Look through history—it's a tried and true method for economically beleaguered regimes to save themselves. It works! Hostile aliens would push humans together out of fear.''

"But hostile aliens are not a war.''

LaNague smiled grimly. "That could be arranged. Again: not the first time it's happened. All Metep and the Council of Five would have to do is send a 'trade envoy' with a half-dozen cargo ships out toward the Perseus arm, ostensibly to open peaceful relations. If these aliens are as aggressive as the contact probe pilot seems to think, they'll either try to take possession of whatever enters their sphere of influence, or will feel directly threatened by the approach of human craft—either way, there's bound to be bloodshed. And that's all you need. 'The monsters are coming! They ambushed unarmed cargo ships in interstellar space. Guard your wives and children.' All of a sudden we've got to put aside our petty differences, close ranks, and defend humanity. The Imperium may be rotten and teetering, but it's the only government we've got right now, so let's not switch horses in midstream . . . And so on.'' He shut off the torrent of words with visible effort.

Mora stared at her husband. "I've never seen you so bitter, Peter. What's happened to you these past three years?''

"A lot, I suppose.'' He sighed. "Sometimes I wonder if I'm still me. But it's opposition to the men who are the Imperium—and after all, the Imperium doesn't have a life of its own; it's just people—that lets you see that there's not much beneath their reach. They'll go to any lengths, including interstellar war, just to save their careers and their places in history. The lives lost, the trauma to future generations, the chaos that would follow . . . they wouldn't care. It would all fall on the shoulders of the next generation. They'd be out of it by then.''

He lapsed briefly into silence, and finally came to a decision.

"I'm going to send Boedekker his signal. It's a little earlier in the game than I had planned, but I really don't have much choice. I want things in pieces by the time that pilot gets back. And even then, I must see to it that no one connected with the Imperium learns about the aliens in the Perseus arm."

"It's almost Year Day," Mora said softly.

"For Tolivians, yes. The Year of the Dragon begins in a few days. I suppose it will be a Dragon year for Throners, too . . . they'll be feeling his fiery breath soon. Very soon."

The Year of the Dragon

XVIII

> . . . no government, so called, can
> reasonably be trusted for a moment,
> or reasonably supposed to have honest
> purposes in view, any longer than it
> depends wholly on voluntary support.
>
> from NO TREASON
> by *Lysander Spooner*

"Good evening, this is Radmon Sayers. It does not seem
possible that there could be anyone watching right now who is
not already aware of the catastrophic events that have rocked
the length and breadth of Occupied Space today. But just in
case someone has been unconscious since the early hours of
the morning, I will recap:

"The Imperial mark has crashed. After holding fairly
steady for years at an exchange rate of two marks per Solar
credit, the Imperial mark began a steady decline at 5.7 hours
Throne time. As most of you know, the Interstellar Currency
Exchange never closes, but all trading in Imperial marks was
suspended at 17.2 hours Throne time this evening when it hit a
terrifying low of eighty marks per Solar credit. There is no telling how far its official trade value would have fallen had not
trade been suspended.

"The precipitating factors in the selling panic have not yet been pin-pointed. All that is known at this time is that virtually every brokerage firm involved with the Exchange received calls this morning from multiple clients, all with sizable accounts in Imperial marks, informing them to sell every mark they possessed, no matter what the going rate happened to be. And so billions of marks were dumped on the market at once. The brokers say that their clients were quite insistent: they wanted no further Imperial marks in their portfolio and were willing to take losses to divest themselves of them. The Exchange authorities have promised a prompt and thorough investigation into the possibility that a conspiracy has been afoot to manipulate the exchange rate for profit. So far, however, no one has been found who has made a windfall profit from the crash.

"In an extemporaneous speech on the vid networks, Metep VII assured the people of Throne and all the other outworlds that there is nothing to fear. That all we can do is keep calm and have faith in ourselves and in our continued independence from Earth. 'We've had hard times before and have weathered them,' Metep said. 'We shall weather them again . . .' "

Ω

"Was Eric Boedekker behind all this?" Doc Zack asked as LaNague darkened the holovid and Sayers' face faded from the globe. The inner circle was seated around the vid set in LaNague's apartment.

"Yes. He's been selling everything he owns for the past three years or so, and converting the credit to marks. Thousands of accounts under thousands of names were started during that period, with instructions to the brokers to buy Imperial marks every time their value dipped."

"And thereby creating an artificial floor on their value!" Zack said.

"Exactly."

"But for all Eric Boedekker's legendary wealth," Zack said, "I don't see how even he could buy enough Imperial marks to cause today's crash. I mean, there were hundreds of billions of marks sold today, and as many more waiting to be disposed of as soon as trading on them opens again. He's rich, but nobody's *that* rich."

"He had help, although the people involved didn't know

they were helping him. You see, Boedekker made sure to call
public attention every time he sold off one of his major assets.
His financial peers thought he was crazy, but they kept a close
eye on him. He had pulled off some major coups in the past
and they wanted to know exactly what he was doing with all
that accumulated credit. And they found out. You can't keep
too many things secret down there on Earth, and the ones who
really wanted to know found out that he was quietly, anony-
mously, buying up Imperial marks whenever he could. So they
started buying up marks, too . . . just to be safe. Maybe
Boedekker knew something they didn't; maybe something was
cooking in the outworlds that would bring the Imperial mark
up to trading parity with the Solar credit. I sent him the 'sell'
signal last week and he's been getting ready ever since.''

"Ah, I see!" Zack said. "And when *he* dumped—"

"—*they* dumped. From there it was a cascade effect.
Everybody who was holding Imperial marks wanted to get rid
of them. But nobody wanted to buy them. The Imperial mark
is now worth one fortieth of its value yesterday, and would
probably be less than a hundredth if trading had not been
suspended. It's still overpriced.''

"Brilliant!" Doc Zack was shaking his head in admiration.
"Absolutely brilliant!"

"What's so brilliant?" Broohnin said from his reclining
position on the floor. For a change, he had been listening intently to the conversation. "Is this the spectacular move
you've promised us? So what? What's it done for us?"

Zack held up a hand as Lanague started to reply. "Let me
answer him. I think I see the whole picture now, but correct
me if I'm wrong." He turned to Broohnin. "What our friend
from Tolive has done, Den, is turn every inhabitant of Throne
into a potential revolutionary. All the people who have come
to the conclusion that the Imperium is inimical to their own interests and the interests of future generations of outworlders
have been constrained to go on supporting the Imperium
because their incomes, either wholly or in part, have depended
on the Imperium. That is no longer a consideration. The
money the Imperium has been buying their loyalty with has
now been reduced to its true value: nothing. The velvet cover-
ings are off; the cold steel of the chains is now evident.''

"But is that fair?" Mora said. She and the Flinters had been
silent until now. "It's like cutting off a flitter's power in mid-

air. People are going to be hurt."

"It would have happened with or without us," LaNague told her brusquely. "If not now, then later. Boedekker has only allowed me to say when; he didn't really change the eventual outcome."

"And don't forget," Zack said more gently, "that the people getting hurt bear a great deal of the blame. They've allowed this to go on for decades. The people of Throne are especially guilty—they've allowed the Imperium to make too many decisions for them, run too much of their lives, buy them off with more and more worthless fiat money. Now the bill's come due. And they've got to pay."

"Right," LaNague said. "This could not have happened if outworlders had refused to allow the Imperium to debase the Imperial mark. If the mark had had something real backing it up—if it had represented a given amount of precious metal or another commodity, and had been redeemable for that, if it had been something more than fancy printed *keerni* paper, then there would have been no crash, no matter how many Imperial marks Eric Boedekker bought and dumped on the Interstellar Currency Exchange."

"Why not?" Broohnin said.

"Because they would have real value, intrinsic value. And that's not subject to much speculation. People have been speculating in the mark for years now, watching for fluctuations in exchange rates, taking a little profit here and there, but knowing all the time that it really had no intrinsic value, only what had been decided on by the money lenders and traders."

"But what does Boedekker get out of all this?" Zack asked. "He doesn't seem like the type to give up his fortune just to ruin the Imperial mark."

"He gets revenge," LaNague said, and explained about Liza Kirowicz. "With no direct descendant to hand his fortune to, he lost all desire to keep adding to it. And don't worry—I'm sure he's got plenty of credit left in his Earth accounts, plus I'm sure he probably sold a good number of marks short before the crash."

"But I still don't see where all the Robin Hood business ties in," Broohnin said, combing his fingers through the coiled blackness of his beard. "One doesn't lead to the other."

"There's an indirect connection," LaNague replied. "We'll

let the people of Throne find out what's really happened to them, and then we'll offer them a choice: Metep or Robin Hood.''

Ω

"What are we going to *do*?" Metep VII wandered in a reverberating semi-circle around the east end of the conference table, alternately wringing his hands and rubbing them together. His perfect face framed eyes that were red-rimmed and hunted-looking. "I'm ruined! I'm not only broke, I'm now destined to go down in history as the Metep who killed the mark! What are we going to do?"

"I don't know," Haworth said softly from his seat. Metep stopped his pacing and stared at him, as did everyone else in the room. It was the first time they could remember Daro Haworth without a contingency plan.

"You don't know?" Metep said, stumbling toward him, panic flattening and spreading his facial features. "How can you say that? You're *supposed* to know!"

Haworth held Metep's gaze. "I never imagined anything like this happening. Neither did anyone else here." His eyes scanned the room, finding no sympathy, but no protest either. "It was a future possibility, a probability within a decade if we found no new markets for outworld goods. Bu no one could have predicted this. No one!"

"The Earthies did it," Krager said. "They're trying to take over the outworlds again."

Haworth glanced at the elderly head of the Treasury and nodded. "Yes, I think that's the approach we'll have to take. We'll blame it on Earth. Should work . . . after all, the Exchange is based on Earth. We can say the Imperial mark has been the victim of a vicious manipulation in a cynical, calculated attempt by Sol System to reassert control over us. Yes. That will help get the anger flowing in some direction other than ours."

"All right," Cumberland said, shifting his bulk uneasily in his chair. "That's the official posture. But what really happened? I think that's important to know. Did Earth do this to us?"

Haworth's head shake was emphatic. "No. First of all, the outworlds have fallen into debt to Earth over the past few years, and the credit has always been tallied in marks—which means that our debt to them today is only 2 or 3 per cent of what it was yesterday. Earth lost badly on the crash. And second, I don't think anyone in the Sol System government has the ingenuity to dream up something like this, or the courage to carry it through."

"You think it was just a freak occurrence?"

"I'm not sure *what* I think. It's all so far beyond the worst nightmare I've ever had . . ." Haworth's voice trailed off.

"In the meantime," Krager said sarcastically, "while you sit there in a blue funk, what about the outworlds—Throne in particular? All credit has been withdrawn from us. There's been no formal announcement, but the Imperium is now considered bankrupt throughout Occupied Space."

"The first thing to do is get more marks into circulation," Haworth said. "Immediately. Push the duplicators to the limit. Big denominations. We've got to keep some sort of commerce going."

"Prices will soar!" Krager said.

"Prices are soaring as we talk! Anyone holding any sort of useful commodity now isn't going to part with it for Imperial marks unless he's offered a lot of them, or unless he's offered something equally valuable in trade. So unless you want Throne back on a barter economy by week's end, you'd better start pouring out the currency."

"The agrarian worlds are practically on barter now," Cumberland said. "They'll want no part—"

"Let the agrarian worlds fall into the Galactic Core for all I care!" Haworth shouted, showing emotion for the first time since the meeting had begun. "They're useless to us now. There's only one planet we have to worry about, and that's Throne. Forget all the other outworlds! They can't reach us, and the sooner we put them out of our minds and concentrate our salvage efforts on Throne, the better we'll be! Let the farmers out there go on scratching their dirt. They can't hurt us. But the people here on Throne, and in Primus City especially . . . they can cause us real trouble."

"Civil disorder," Metep said, nodding knowingly, almost thankfully. Riots he could understand, cope with. But all this economics talk . . . "You expect major disturbances?"

"I expect disturbances—just how major they'll be depends on what we do in the next few weeks. I want to try to defuse any riots before they start; but once they start, I want plenty of manpower at our disposal." He turned to Metep. "We'll need an executive order from you, Jek, ordering withdrawal of all Imperial garrisons from all the other outworlds. We can't afford to keep them supplied out there anyway, and I want them all gathered tight around us if things get nasty."

There was a chorus of agreement from all present.

Haworth glanced up and down the table. "It's going to be a long, hot summer, gentlemen. Let's try to hold things together until one of the probe ships makes contact with the aliens in the Perseus arm. That could be our only hope."

"Any word yet?" Metep said.

"None."

"What if we never hear anything from them?" Cumberland asked. "What if they never come back?"

"That could be useful, too."

Ω

"Fifty marks for a loaf of bread? That's outrageous!"

"Wait until tomorrow if you think fifty's too much," the man said laconically. He stood with his back against a blank synthestone wall, a hand blaster at his hip, his wares—unwrapped loaves of bread—spread on a folding table before him. "Probably be fifty-five by then."

Salli Stafford felt utterly helpless, and frightened. No one had heard from Vin or any of the other probe pilots; no one at Project Perseus knew when they were coming back. Or *if* they were coming back. She was alone in Primus City and could daily see signs of decay: lengthening, widening cracks in its social foundations. She needed Vin around to tell her that everything would be all right, that he would protect her.

She needed money, too. She had read in one of *The Robin Hood Readers* that came out just after the bottom had dropped out of the mark that she should immediately pull all her money out of the bank and spend every bit of it. She didn't hesitate. Vin had grown to have unwavering faith in whoever was behind those flyers, and Salli had finally come around to believing in him, too. Especially after that long wait in their old back yard, when she had laughed at Vin's almost childish faith, and then the money had come down. She wasn't going to waste time laughing this time; she was down at the bank first thing the next morning, withdrawing everything that was left from Vin's advance for joining the probe fleet.

That had been a month ago, and it was the smartest thing she had ever done in her life. Within the first three days after the crash of the Imperial mark, fully half the banks in Primus had closed. They didn't fail—the Imperium prevented that by seeing to it that every depositor was paid the full amount of his or her account in nice, freshly minted paper marks—they simply ran out of depositors.

Salli followed up her foresight with shortsightedness that now seemed incredibly stupid. Instead of spending the entire ten thousand marks she had withdrawn on commodities, as *The Robin Hood Reader* had suggested, she waffled and spent only half. The rest she hid in the apartment. She now saw the error of that—prices had risen anywhere between 1,000 and 2,000 per cent in the intervening weeks. Steri-packed vegetables and staples she could have picked up for five marks then—and she had considered that exorbitant—were now going for fifty or sixty, with people thankful they could find them. It was crazy! The four thousand marks she had hidden away then would have bought her fifty thousand marks' worth of food at today's prices. She cursed herself for not following Robin Hood's advice to the letter. Everyone in Primus now knew from personal experience what he had said back then. Nobody held onto cash any more; it was spent as soon as it was in hand. The only things worth less were Food Vouchers . . . retailers laughed when you brought them in.

Salli was afraid. What was going to happen when her money ran out? She had called Project Perseus but they had said they could not release Vin's second fifteen thousand until he had returned. She shrugged as she stood there on the street. What was fifteen thousand any more? Nothing!

"You gonna buy, lady?" the man asked, his eyes constantly shifting up and down the street. His legs straddled a large box of currency and he mentally took the measure of every passerby.

"Will you take anything else?"

His eyes narrowed. "Gold, silver, platinum if you've got any. I can let you take it out in trade or I can give you a good bundle of marks depending on what you've got."

"I—don't have any." She didn't know what had made her ask. She didn't really want bread. It was being made out in the hinterlands on isolated farms and there were no preservatives being used because there were none to be had. Bread like that went stale too fast to be worth fifty marks to a woman living alone.

He looked her up and down, his gaze seeming to penetrate her clothing. "Don't bother to offer me anything else you've got," he sneered. "I've got more offers for that every day than I could handle in a lifetime."

Tears sprang into Salli's eyes as she felt her face redden. "I didn't mean that!"

"Then why did you ask?"

Salli couldn't answer. She had been thinking about the future—the near future, when her money ran out. How was she to get by then? Her employer had told her he couldn't give her a raise, that his business had fallen off to the point where he might have to close up shop and go home.

As she turned away, the man called after her. "Hey, look, I'm sorry, but I've got a family of my own to feed. I've got to fly out and pick this up on my own. The freight unions aren't running till they get more money, you know that."

Salli knew all that. The vid was full of it—bad news and more bad news. Shipping of goods was at a standstill. Employers were unable to raise wages quickly enough to keep their employees at subsistence level. Salli glanced back over her shoulder and saw that the bread seller had already forgotten her, and was now busy dickering with a man holding up a handful of fresh vegetables.

What was she going to do? Nothing in her life had prepared her for anything like this—she was slowly coming to the realization that her life had prepared her for little more than child rearing. No skill beyond rudimentary mathematics was required of her in the part-time job she was barely holding onto; she could be replaced in minutes. All her childhood had been spent learning to be dependent on men—her father, her brothers, and then Vin. Which was fine until now, when everything was falling apart, and her father and brothers were on the other side of the planet with no way to get to her or she to them. She was suddenly on her own, scared to death, and helpless.

Why am I like this? she thought, then snorted cynically. Why is the world like this? Why isn't Vin's money worth anything?

Vin—the name conjured up a vision of her husband's earnest face, and the worry lines that seemed to have become a part of his features over the past few years. She had never understood what had been plaguing him all this time. He had always acted as a buffer between her and the real world, taking the blows, absorbing them, and allowing only a few vibrations to disturb her. Now he was gone, and so was her insulation. And now she knew first hand the malaise of impotency that had so afflicted his psyche. She felt trapped in a world she had not made. On the surface it was physically similar, but everything had changed. Neither she nor anyone in the street around her had any control over what was happening to them. Powerless, all of them.

And yet, we're to blame, she thought. No one out here made this world, but they all sat around idly or looked the other way while it was being made for them. It could have been stopped way back when, before things got too pushed out of shape, too far out of line. But it was too late now. Salli had an eerie feeling that giant forces were swinging back into balance again, impervious now to whatever was thrown up to block their return.

But she would cope. Anger would help her. Anger at the Imperium for causing this. Anger at herself and her society for leaving her so ill-equipped to cope with this or any other challenge outside the security of the nest. How many other women were caught in her situation right now? How many were losing the fight?

Salli wouldn't lose. She was learning fast. Today she would spend every last one of the remaining four thousand marks before they depreciated further. But not all at once. A little here, a little there, with frequent trips back to the apartment, hiding the purchases within her garments while in transit. It wouldn't do to have someone get the idea that she was stocking up on food; that was a sure way of inviting robbery. No, she would buy whatever was available, whatever was the least perishable, and then keep to her apartment, venturing out only for work and for absolute necessities. Yes, Salli would survive and hold out until things got better and Vin got back . . . she was somehow sure the latter would lead to the former.

And if things ever did get better—she set her mouth in a determined line—something would have to be done to see that this never happened again. She wanted a family, but no child deserved to grow up and face something like this.

Never again! she thought. This must never happen again!

Ω

LaNague held his position until the recorder cycled off, then rose and stretched. "There. That ought to do it." He glanced at Radmon Sayers, who said nothing as he dismantled the vid recorder. The warehouse was empty except for the two of them. "What's the matter, Rad?"

"Nothing," Sayers replied, removing the recorded spool and handing it to LaNague. "It's just that I don't think this will work."

"And why not?" LaNague snapped. "They have to be presented with a choice, and in order to make that choice they've got to know what their alternatives are."

"I still think you could go about this differently. You're placing too much emphasis on these recordings. And frankly, I'm not impressed."

LaNague bit back a terse reply. It angered him to be questioned at this point. With effort he kept his tone measured. "Do you still doubt me? I had to put up with enough of that from you and the rest before the floor fell out from under the mark. And then all of a sudden I was 'brilliant,' a 'genius.' When are you going to learn that I have been planning this, preparing it for years. I've had a lot more time to think things out than you or Zack or Metep or anyone on the Council of Five. I've out-thought them all. I know what I'm doing."

"I don't doubt that," Sayers replied. "You've proved it over and over again. But that doesn't make you infallible. That doesn't mean you're immune to an error of judgment, a miscalculation, just like the rest of us. Are you beyond a second opinion?"

"Of course I'm—"

"Then here's mine: I think the final phase of your plan is too personally dangerous to you, is subject to too many variables, and rests precariously on the persuasive power of these recordings . . . which, in my opinion as a professional in this area, is slight."

"I appreciate your concern," LaNague said softly after a short pause.

Sayers read his expression. "But you're not going to modify your plans, are you?"

LaNague shook his head. "I'm going to have to go with my record, and that's been too accurate so far to ignore." He reached within his vest and withdrew a fifty-mark note. "Look at that!" he said, handing it to Sayers.

"What about it?" He glanced down at the face and could see nothing of any great significance.

"Turn it over."

The reverse side was blank. "Counterfeit!" Sayers cried.

"No. That's the way the mint is releasing them. Not only is

the supply of *keerni* paper getting short, but so's the dye. It's the ultimate ignominy. And fifty marks is now the lowest denomination. It's a mere three months since the crash and already the mark is approximating its true value: that of the paper it's printed on! Three months! None of you believed me when I told you things would happen this fast, so I don't expect any of you to believe me now.'' He held up a vid spool. ''But this will work—I guarantee it!''

''And if not?''

''It will! That's the end of discussion on the matter. And remember: Mora and the others are to know nothing of this next step until it's past the point of no return. Especially Mora!''

Sayers was about to add further comment when Broohnin's abrupt entry through a side door cut him off.

''Just heard from Seph Wolverton over at the Project Perseus Comm Center,'' Broohnin said as soon as he caught sight of them. ''That probe ship just popped into the system and is heading for Throne. Seems to be following instructions to the letter.''

LaNague cursed silently. If only he had another month! The Imperium would be gone by then and there would be no one left in power to manipulate the hostile aliens in Perseus into a war threat. But that wasn't to be, and it was probably just as well that the probe returned now when he was able to deal with it personally, rather than leave it to the others. Their narrow vision was disconcerting, their lack of faith discouraging. If left to handle the probe pilot alone, they'd probably botch it.

''All right,'' LaNague said through a sigh. ''Tell Wolverton to do all he can to keep the ship's presence in the system a secret. It can't remain a secret forever. The closer it moves, the more monitors it will alert. But we, at least, will have the most time to prepare.''

''Why don't we just find a way to blow it out of the sky?'' Broohnin said with a grin. ''That'll solve the problem very nicely, I think.''

LaNague paused for an instant, horrified by the realization that the very same solution had already occurred to him. He had discarded it, naturally, but the idea that his mind might even briefly follow a line of thought similar to Den Broohnin's was chilling.

''We have to get to him first,'' LaNague said, ostensibly deaf to Broohnin's suggestion. ''We have to meet him, spirit him away, and see to it that nobody from the Imperium knows where to find him. After there's no more Imperium, he can tell all of Occupied Space what he found out toward the Perseus arm."

"That sounds like a tall order," Sayers said.

"Don't worry," LaNague told him. "I'll see that it's done. Just leave it to me. I'll take care of everything. As usual."

Wafting briefly through his mind as he spoke was the thought that he sounded like a stranger to himself. He was acting like a pompous ass, impatient, intolerant of any challenge to his notions, of any opinion that deviated from his own. The thought became a question: were these symptoms of some occult malignancy devouring him from within, endangering not only himself, but the revolution and all who had worked for it? He brushed it away like an annoying insect. Nonsense. The revolution was secure. Victory was at hand. Nothing could stop him now. Nothing!

THE ROBIN HOOD READER

Don't Recall Metep!

There is talk all over Throne of organizing a recall of Metep
and his mob. Don't participate! Petitions are being passed.
Don't sign them!

The "free election" resulting from a successful recall
movement will offer you three or four clones of Metep VII.
They'll have different names, different faces, different
genotypes, but once in office they'll follow the same stupid,
irresponsible, reckless policies that have brought the outworlds to their present state.

DO NOT VOTE!!! As presently set up, it's a meaningless
franchise even if the votes are counted with scrupulous
accuracy. Because nowhere on the ballot is there a place for
you to indicate your dissatisfaction with *all* the candidates.
A ballot means nothing, is an utter fraud, unless you can
say "None of the above."

Don't recall Metep . . .
Recall the Imperium!

The Economic Weather Eye

PRICE INDEX (using the 115th year of the
Imperium—when the Imperial
mark became mandatory legal
tender—as base year of 100) 12,792.4
MONEY SUPPLY (M3)   167,322.1
UNEMPLOYMENT LEVEL   31.0%

	Imperial Marks	Solar Credits
GOLD (Troy ounce)	21,500.2	133.3
Silver (Troy ounce)	1,320.7	6.2
Bread (1 kg. loaf)	51.0	1.71

XIX

The Paternalistic State does give its
people a sense of security. But a snug,
secure populace tends to resist movement—especially *forward* movement.

from THE SECOND BOOK OF KYFHO

From this far out, Throne looked like any other Earth-class
planet: blue, brown, swirled with white. Not too impressive,
but it was home. And Salli was there. Vincen Stafford wondered what was going on planetside. Something was wrong,
that was certain. He didn't know what it was, and he didn't
knownd how big it was, but something tricky was going on.
How else to explain the crazy orders he had received?

Part one of the instructions had been logical—return directly to Throne at top speed, stop for nothing; use tight beam
to signal comm center immediately upon arrival in Throne
System. No problem. That's what he had expected to be told,
and was exactly what he wanted to do. One encounter with the
Tarks was quite enough, thank you.

The remaining instructions were the crazy ones. After noti-
fying the comm center of his presence in the system, he was to
proceed with all haste to Throne and establish an orbit that
would pass over Throne latitude eighty degrees north and
longitude ninety degrees east. At no time—this was repeated

202

and doubly emphasized—was he to have further contact with anyone. *Anyone.* No matter who tried to contact him, he was neither to answer nor to listen. He was not to identify himself to anyone else. The Project Perseus Comm Center knew who he was and that was all that mattered. He would be met in orbit by a shuttle and taken down for debriefing.

Something was up, but he couldn't imagine what. Were they afraid he'd cause a panic down below by telling scare stories about the Tarks? They should know him better than that! Maybe they were just being careful, but the precautions seemed extraordinary. Why?

He shrugged. The orders had come from Project Perseus Comm Center . . . his boss. Not his worry. Not his to reason why. He just wanted to get his feet planted firmly on Throne, find Salli, and celebrate the bonus due him for being the contact ship . . . an extra twenty thousand marks. They could do a lot of living on that.

It would be good just to be home again.

He slipped into Throne's gravitational field on a flat trajectory early the next morning, ship's time. The retros slowed him enough to allow the delicate but intractable fingers of the planet's gravity to wrap around the ship and hold it at arm's length. He had plotted the approach carefully during the three days since his arrival in the system, and now he smiled as he made the final minor course adjustments. Perfect! The probe ship's orbit would pass right over the desired co-ordinates with hardly a second's drift. He hadn't spent all those years in navigation school for nothing!

A small blip showed on his screen. He cued the image intensifier to home in on it and . . . there it was. An orbital shuttle, rising to meet him. He upped the intensity. Funny . . . no Imperial markings. But that sort of went with all the other craziness. If the Project Perseus heads were being so secretive about his return, it wasn't all that strange to bring him down to the surface in an unmarked craft.

The comm indicator flashed again. It had been doing that repeatedly for the past day and a half. But like a good soldier, he had followed orders and steadfastly ignored it. At first there had been a strong temptation to disconnect the light, but he had decided against it. Let it flash. Who cared. He was going home.

Ω

"Still no answer from that ship?" Haworth asked.

The tiny face on the vidscreen in his hand wagged back and forth. "None, sir."

"Is there any sign that the ship may be out of control? Is the flight pattern erratic? Could the pilot be hurt?"

"If he's hurt, sir, I'd love to see him fly when he's well. The ship seems to have a definite course in mind. His communicator console could be malfunctioning, but with all the fail-safes built in, it seems unlikely, unless there's major damage. And the ship handles like an undamaged craft. I don't know what to tell you, sir."

"Why weren't we aware of his presence in the system sooner?"

"I don't know, sir."

"You're paid to know!" Haworth gritted. "What good are you if you don't know!"

The insolence in the shrug was apparent even on the miniscule screen. "Not much, I guess." His smile was insolent, too. No one seemed to have any respect any more.

"We'll find out soon enough," Haworth said, passing over the veiled insult—he'd deal with the man later. His name was Wolverton. He wouldn't forget. "Send a shuttle up there immediately and bring that pilot directly to me. I'll debrief him personally. And then we'll get to the bottom of all this."

"There's already a shuttle on the way. You should know that, sir."

Haworth felt a brief, deep chill. "Why? How should I know?"

"You sent it yourself." The man glanced down at something off screen. "I've got the message right here from the shuttle. Said it was under direct orders from you to intercept the probe in orbit and bring the pilot to you."

"I gave no such order! Stop that shuttle!"

"I don't know if we can do that, sir. It looks like it's already made contact."

"Then intercept it before it lands!" He looked at the man's laconic expression and suddenly came to a decision. "No. Never mind. I'll arrange that myself." With no warning, he broke the circuit and began punching in the code for the commander-in-chief of the Imperial Guard. If he had to scramble a fleet of interceptors, he'd do it. He had to interrogate that probe pilot!

Ω

The man who came through the lock was not with the Imperial Guard. He was dressed in Lincoln green hose, a leather jerkin, and a feathered cap. And he held a blaster.

"Quick! Through here. We're taking you down!" He spoke without moving his lips.

Stafford hesitated. "What's going—"

"Move!"

It was suddenly clear to Stafford just whom he was dealing with. The drawings had been flashed on the vid often enough: this was either Robin Hood himself or one of his Merry Men. A closer look revealed a barely perceptible shimmer along the edges of the man's form, a sure sign of a holographic disguise.

"Are you Robin Hood?" he asked, already moving toward the hatch. Despite the menacing presence of the blaster, he did not feel threatened. In fact, the blaster gave him good excuse to go along.

"You'll find out later. Hurry!"

Stafford ducked through the lock and was propelled along a narrow corridor into an even narrower cubicle with a single seat.

"Strap yourself in," the figure said. "We may have a rough ride ahead." The door slid shut and Stafford knew he was locked in. There was a jolt that signaled release of the probe from the shuttle, and increasing drag toward the rear of the cubicle as the craft picked up speed. Stafford decided to strap himself in. He had ridden many a shuttle, but could not remember any that could accelerate like this one.

Ω

"We lost them," Commander-in-chief Tinmer said flatly. There was enough of an edge of anger in his tone to warn Haworth against too much abuse. The man was looking for someone to lash out at, someone to trip his hammer. Haworth decided to let him save his wrath for the interceptor pilots who had evidently flubbed their mission. And besides, Haworth wanted the commander on his side.

"How is that possible?" he said, employing concerned disappointment to mask his growing rage at the incompetence that confronted him at every turn.

"For one thing, that shuttle was not exactly a standard

model. It must have had a special drive or something because it pulled a few tricks that left our men sitting up there like hovercraft. Some of the men think it's the same craft we've chased before on suspicion of smuggling—they were never able to catch that one either. Anyway, the ship went down in the western hinterlands and we've got search teams out now. But even if we find it, there'll be no one on board.''

Haworth closed his eyes in a moment of silent agony. How could this be happening to him? Everything was going wrong! He opened his eyes.

''Find that pilot! It is absolutely imperative that we contact him and find out what he knows. Get the identification number of the probe, check with the Project Perseus center to get the pilot's name and address. Track him down, bring him to me, and no more mistakes! I don't care if you have to mobilize every Imperial Guardsman under your command and send them all out beating bushes and going door to door. That man must be found!''

The commander stiffened visibly. ''Everything that can be done will be done.''

''See to it, Tinmer.''

Daro Haworth stared at the screen after it had gone dark. He knew they would never find the pilot. The guardsmen who would be used for the search were worse than useless. Primus City and the surrounding garrisons were swollen with them; they were bored, inactive, and the less duty they were given, the less they wanted. At least they were assured of shelter and food and clothing, more than could be said for most of the civilian population now. It was costing a fortune to support them, but they had to be kept on ready . . . martial law was no longer an if, but a when. And that when was drawing nigh.

He had thought the time had come yesterday when the dolee section of Primus had its first food riot. By the Core, that had been frightening! It took him back to his student days on Earth when he had almost been caught in one of those frequent outpourings of unfocused rage. If the fellow student with him hadn't been an Earthie, and hadn't developed a sixth sense for the riots, and hadn't pulled him into a building . . . he didn't allow his imagination to venture into the possibilities of what would have happened to a well-dressed outworlder trapped in the middle of that frenzied torrent of humanity. But yesterday's riot had been broken up by a few low-flying troop transports from the garrison out by the mint, and by a few well-placed warning blasts.

Next time would not be so easy. With Food Vouchers being refused everywhere, the dolees were starving. The legislative machinery couldn't raise their allotments fast enough to keep up with prices. And with all the people on the dole now, the mint was hard-pressed to put out currency fast enough to meet the demand. Haworth had heard of runaway inflation but had never thought he'd see it. Nothing he had read could even come close to the reality, however. Nothing. It was like a grossly obese dog chasing its tail . . . futility leading to fatality.

That's why the guardsmen had to take priority. The dolees had been the big power block before with their votes, but votes were no longer important. Blasters were going to be the legislature soon, and Haworth wanted to keep the men who had them happy. Keep them happy, keep them fed, keep them ready to run around and shoot their toys to keep the mobs in line. They weren't good for much else.

They'd certainly never find that pilot. The brazenness of the abduction—if in fact it really was an abduction—along with the perfect timing and daring escape maneuvers . . . all pointed to Robin Hood. It fit his *modus operandi*. And it was clear now that Robin Hood was more than an economic gadfly and tax rebel; he was steadily revealing himself as a full-fledged revolutionary. No mere wild-eyed bomb-thrower, but a crafty conspirator who had anticipated all the ills that had befallen the Imperium and had taken advantage of them. How had he seen it coming? How had he known? Unless . . .

Ridiculous! No one man could kill the Imperial mark! Not even Robin Hood!

If only they could capture *him*! That would be a boon to the Imperium's cause! Take Robin Hood out of the picture—or even better, keep him in the picture and turn him to the Imperium's advantage—and perhaps something could be salvaged. Haworth knew he'd like to sit down and have a long discussion with Robin Hood, whoever he was . . . find out where he was getting his funds, what his final goals were. It would be the most fascinating conversation he had ever had in his life, he was certain. And after it was over, it would be an even greater pleasure to kill Robin Hood.

Ω

"Are you Robin Hood? I mean, *the* Robin Hood?"

LaNague smiled, warmed by the glow of awe and open admiration in the other man's face. "We never really decided who was actually Robin Hood. It's been a group effort, really."

"But you seem to be in charge. Was the Robin Hood idea yours?"

"Well, yes."

"Then you're him." The pilot thrust out his hand. "I'm proud to meet you."

LaNague grasped and shook the proferred hand in the age-old ceremony of greeting and good will, then watched the probe pilot as he walked around in a tight circle, taking in the interior details of the Angus black warehouse. The man was short, slight, and dark, with an appealing boyish face, now filled with wonder.

"So this is the center of operations . . . this is where you plan all those raids and put out *The Robin Hood Reader* . . . never thought I'd ever see it." He turned to LaNague. "But why am I here?"

LaNague put a hand on his shoulder and guided him toward the back office. "To keep you out of Haworth's hands. Once he gets hold of you he'll turn your information into a war scare to keep the outworlds in line behind the Imperium. And especially to keep the people of Throne looking to the Imperium as protector from whatever might be coming out of the sky, rather than as culprit for all the misery they're suffering. We can't allow that to happen. Things are too close to the end point."

Stafford's mouth opened to reply as he entered the back office ahead of LaNague, and remained open but silent when he saw the occupants of the room. The two Merry Men who had shuttled him down from his probe ship had retreated to this office soon after depositing him in the warehouse. They were gone now, replaced by two black-robed figures.

"Flinters!" Stafford squinted his eyes to detect a telltale shimmer along their outlines.

"Those aren't holosuits," LaNague told him. He was watching Stafford's reactions closely. "Does it bother you that Robin Hood is associated with Flinters?"

Stafford hesitated, then: "Not really. It shows you mean business . . . that you aren't just playing games and looking for attention." He finally tore his eyes from Kanya and Josef and looked at LaNague. "Does this mean that I'm a prisoner?"

"A guest," LaNague said. "You'll be kept comfortable and well treated for the next few weeks, but we must keep you out of Haworth's hands."

Stafford's features slackened. "But I won't tell him anything! If you say he's going to use the information to keep himself in power, I'll see that he doesn't get it."

"I'm afraid you can't guarantee that," LaNague said with a weary smile. "Haworth knows you know *something*, and a simple injection is all it will take to have you answering in minute detail every question he asks. I know you may mean well, but Haworth is quite ruthless."

"But my wife—"

"We'll bring her here and set up quarters for the two of you. We'll do anything we can to make your stay as pleasant as possible."

"But I *must* stay," Stafford said. There seemed to be a catch in his voice. He turned away and slumped into a chair, staring at the floor.

"You all right?" LaNague asked.

Stafford's voice was low. "For some reason, I thought things were going to be different. When I saw Merry Men operating the shuttle, I figured Metep and all the rest were on the way out, that things were going to be different now. Better. But they're not. And they never will be, will they?"

"I don't understand."

"I mean, you're going to set yourself up as another Metep, aren't you?"

"Of course not!"

"Then let me go home."

"I can't. You don't seem to understand that I—"

"All I understand," Stafford said, rising to his feet and gesturing angrily, "is that I had it better under Metep VII! I could walk the streets. I could sleep in my home. I can't do that now!"

"You wouldn't be able to do it if Haworth found you, either," LaNague replied. "Think of that."

"The only thing I'm thinking is that I'm a prisoner and you're my jail keeper. Which makes you no better than anyone else in the Imperium. In fact, it makes you worse!"

The words struck LaNague like so many blows. He mentally fought the implications, but finally had to accept them: he had put aside everything he believed in, his entire heritage, in order to further the revolution.

Above all else: Kyfho . . . Adrynna's words came back to him . . . *forget Kyfho in your pursuit of victory over the enemy, and you will become the enemy . . . worse than the enemy, for he doesn't know he is capable of anything better.*

"The enemy . . . me," he muttered, feeling weak and sick. Stafford looked at him questioningly. "You wouldn't understand," he told him. He glanced at Kanya and Josef and saw sympathy there, but no help. It was his battle, one that could only be won alone.

So close . . . so close to victory that victory itself had become his cause. How had he let that happen? Was this what power did to you? It was horrifying. He had always felt himself immune to that sort of lure . . . above it. Instead, he had placed himself above all others, ready and willing to subject their personal desires to his ultimate vision—the very reason for which he so loathed the Imperium!

When had he begun to yield? He couldn't say. The onset had been so insidious he had never noticed the subtle changes in perspective. But he should have realized something was wrong that day by the mint when he had been willing to risk the lives of some of the guards inside rather than delay activating the Barsky box. Since when had a Robin Hood caper meant more than a human life? He should have known then. He was embracing the "can't make an omelet without breaking eggs" attitude that had brought the outworlds to the brink of ruin. Ends had never justified means for him in the past. Why had he let them do so now?

If not for Mora that day, he might have killed someone. And life was what his whole revolution was about . . . letting life grow, allowing it to expand unhindered, keeping it free. The revolution he had originally envisioned was for everyone on all the outworlds, not just a few. And if his revolution was to be everyone's, it had to be for the men in the Imperial Guard, too. They had to have their chance for a new future along with everybody else. But dead men weren't free; neither was a probe pilot locked up in a warehouse.

He wanted to run, to kick down the doors, and flee into the night. But not to Mora—anywhere but to Mora. He felt so ashamed of himself now, especially after the way he had been treating her, that he couldn't bear the thought of facing her . . . not until he had made things right.

"You can leave," he said, his voice barely audible as he

leaned back against the office doorframe.

Stafford took an uncertain step forward. "What? You mean that?"

LaNague nodded, not looking at him. "Go ahead. But be warned: Primus City is not as you left it. It's night out there now, and the streets belong to whoever feels strong enough or desperate enough to venture onto them. You won't like it."

"I've got to get to my wife."

LaNague nodded again, stepping away from the doorway. "Find her. Bring her back here if you wish, or take your chances out there. I leave the choice up to you. But remember two things: the Imperium is looking everywhere for you, and we offer you and your wife safety here."

"Thank you," Stafford said, glancing between LaNague and the two Flinters. Hesitantly at first, and then with growing confidence, he walked past LaNague, across the warehouse floor, and out the side door. He only looked back three times before he was out of sight.

LaNague was silent for a while, gathering his thoughts. The next steps would have to be moved up, the schedule accelerated. "Follow him," he told Kanya and Josef. "Make sure he's left with a choice. If a few Imperial Guardsmen should get hold of him, let him go with them if that's what he wants. But if he decides he'd prefer to stay with us, then see to it that they don't get in his way."

The Flinters nodded, glad for an opportunity to do something besides sit and wait. They adjusted their holosuits to the middle-aged male images, and started for the door.

"One thing," LaNague said as they were leaving. "Don't bring him back here. Take him and his wife to my apartment. Under no circumstances bring him back here."

LaNague could see no expression through the enveloping holograms, but knew the Flinters must have looked puzzled.

"Trust me," he said. The words tasted stale on his tongue.

They were not gone long when Broohnin entered. "Where's the probe pilot?" he asked, his head swiveling back and forth in search of Stafford.

"Gone." LaNague had taken over the seat Stafford had vacated.

"Where'd you hide him?"

"I let him go."

It took a moment for the truth of that statement to register on Broohnin. At first he reacted as if to an obvious and rather silly attempt at humor, then he looked closely into LaNague's face.

"You *what*?"

"I don't believe in imprisoning a man completely innocent of any wrongdoing."

The small amounts of facial skin visible above Broohnin's beard and below his hairline had turned crimson. "You fool! You idiot! Are you insane? What he knows could ruin everything—you said so yourself!"

"I realize that," LaNague said. An icy calm had slipped over him. "I also realize that I cannot allow one unpleasant fact to overcome a lifetime's belief."

"Belief?" Broohnin stormed across the office. "We're talking about revolution here, not belief!" He went to the desk and started rifling through the drawers.

"What *do* you believe in, Broohnin? Anything?"

Pulling a hand blaster from a drawer, Broohnin wheeled and pointed the lens directly at LaNague's face. "I believe in revolution," he said, his breathing ragged. "And I believe in eliminating anyone who gets in the way of that belief!"

LaNague willed his exterior to complete serenity. "Without me, there is no revolution, only a new, stronger Imperium."

After a breathless pause that seemed to go on forever, Broohnin finally lowered the blaster. Without a word, he stalked to the far exit and passed through to the street.

LaNague lifted his left hand and held it before his eyes. It was trembling. He could not remember being exposed to the raw edge of such violent fury before. He let the hand fall back to his lap and sighed. It would not be the last. Before this thing was over, he might well come closer to even greater physical danger. He might even die. But there was no other way.

He heaved himself out of the chair and toward the disheveled desk. Time to move.

Ω

"Why don't you calm down?" Metep VII said from his form-fitting lounger as he watched Daro Haworth pace the floor. There was an air of barely suppressed excitement about the younger man that had grown continually during the few moments he had been present in the room.

"I can't! We've just heard from the municipal police commissioner. They've had a tip on the whereabouts of Robin Hood.''

"We've been getting those ever since the first currency heist. They've all been phony. Usually someone with a grudge on somebody else, or a prankster.''

"The commissioner seems to think this is the real thing,'' Haworth said. "The caller gave the location of a warehouse he says is the center of all the Robin Hood activities. Says we'll find Robin Hood himself there along with enough evidence to convince a dead man that he's the genuine article.'' Haworth's hands rubbed together as if of their own will. "If only it's true! If *only* it's true!''

Metep coughed as he inhaled a yellow vapor from the vial in his hand. He had always liked the euphorogenic gases, but appeared to be using them with greater frequency and in greater quantities lately, especially since the recall talk had started. The calls for votes of confidence in the legislature recently had only compounded his depression. "I'm not so sure the commissioner is the right man to oversee such a project. After all, the municipal police lately have been—''

"I know that!'' Haworth snapped. "That's why I've told them to wait until Tinmer, our illustrious commander-in-chief of the Imperial Guard, can arrive with reinforcements and redeem himself after bungling the capture of that orbital shuttle this morning.''

"Let's hope so,'' Metep said. "Speaking of the shuttle incident, you still have men out looking for that pilot?''

"Of course. I've also got them waiting at his apartment here in the city just in case he shows up looking for his wife.'' Haworth smiled. "Wouldn't that be nice: Robin Hood himself, and our elusive probe pilot in hand before daybreak. That would change everything!''

Ω

Vincen Stafford had never seen the streets of Primus dark before. Glo-globes had always kept the shadows small and scarce. But someone had decided to smash every globe up and down the street, and no one had bothered to replace them. As he walked on, the intersections he crossed gave dark testimony to the fact that this was not the only street to be victimized so. Every street was dark, lined with useless pedestals supporting dim, shattered, useless fragments.

He was not alone on the street. There were dark forms huddled in doorways and skulking in the deeper shadows. He was also aware of other pedestrians ahead of him and behind; not many, but enough to make him feel that he could at least count on some help should there be any trouble.

As Stafford walked on, he had the distinct impression that he was under scrutiny. But by whom? He could detect no one following him. Soon the sensation passed, replaced by a gnawing fear.

Robin Hood had been right. This was not the Primus City he had left a year ago. That city had been bright and lively —dingy on the edges, true, but nothing like this. The streets were choked with litter; ground-effect vehicles were virtually absent from view, and only one or two flitters crossed the night sky. After walking two kilometers, he gave up hope of ever seeing a taxi. He'd have to try the monorail.

As he entered the business district of town, he was in for an even greater shock. A number of the stores stood dark and empty, their fronts smashed open, their insides either stripped of their contents or gutted by fire. The ones that were intact but closed had left their lights on. Stafford peered into the window of one and saw a man sitting conspicuously under a light in a chair against the rear wall of the store. A short-range, wide-beam blaster rifle rested across his knees. When he noticed that Stafford did not move on immediately, he lifted the weapon and cradled it in his arms. Stafford moved on.

Only one store on this street was open. Before he had left on his probe ship mission, every store would be open and busy this early in the evening. Tonight the lights from the front of the open store—a food store—shone out on the street like a beacon. People were clustered around the front of it, waiting to get in. Some carried luggage cases, other shopping bags, some nothing.

Drawn by the light and by other people, Stafford decided to take a quick look to see what the attraction was. As he approached, he noticed armed guards on either side of the doorway, and more inside. On closer inspection, he could see that many of the customers were armed, too.

Since he was not interested in getting through the door, he found it easy to push through the press to the window. A careful, squinting inspection revealed only one product for sale in the market: flour. The center of the floor was stacked with transparent cylinders of it. Stafford gauged their probable weight at fifty kilos each. One by one, people were being allowed to go to the pile, heft a cylinder to a shoulder, and exit through the rear.

But first they had to pay. At a counter to the left, an armed man was counting bundles of currency, stacking it, then dumping it into a bin behind him when the proper amount was reached. The bin was half full; another toward the rear was completely full, and an empty one waited. An armed guard stood over them. Customers were allowed into the store one at a time; a guard frisked them, removed their weapons at the door, and returned at the exit. There was a strong family resemblance between the guards and the storekeeper—father and sons, most likely.

Fascinated, Stafford watched the strange procession for a while, watched the customers empty sacks and satchels of currency onto the counter, watched the second bin behind the man grow full. And then two men were allowed to enter at once. Both were empty-handed. The first caused a stir at the counting table when he produced a handful of what looked like old silver marks, extinct from general circulation for half a generation. The storekeeper studied them, weighed them on a scale, and placed them in an autoanalyzer one at a time. Apparently satisfied with their metal content, he nodded to the two men. Each claimed a cylinder and exited through the rear.

"Nice what a little silver can do these days," said a man beside him at the window. Stafford stepped back for a better look at the speaker. He saw a shabbily dressed man of average build with greasy hair who was giving his flight jumper an appraising glance. There was a bulge under the man's coat that probably meant a weapon, and an overloaded suitcase in his left hand from which a few stray marks protruded at the seam.

"What are they charging for that flour in there?" Stafford asked.

The man shrugged and glanced through the window. "Around ten thousand marks, I'm told." He saw Stafford's jaw swing open. "A bit expensive, I know—a whole day's pay —but I'll be glad to get it at all, what with the surface and air transport unions on strike again."

"Strike? *Again*?"

"I don't blame them though," the man said, seeming to look right through Stafford as he continued speaking in a tremulous monotone. "I wouldn't want to get paid by the week, either. They say they're going to stay out until they get daily pay. Otherwise, it's not worth working." Without warning, tears began to slip down his cheeks and he began to cry. "It's not really worth working, anyway. The money loses value faster than you can spend it . . . and nobody cares any more . . . we're all just putting in our time . . . used to like my job at the bureau . . . used to like my house . . . and my family . . . nothing matters now 'cause I don't know how much longer I'm going to be able to keep any of them . . ."

Embarrassed by the display of naked despair, Stafford pushed away from the window and out to the open sidewalk with a single worrisome thought in his mind: *Salli!* Where was she? How could she have survived this insanity on her own? She could be dead of starvation by now! His only hope was that she had somehow got to her family, or they to her. He never should have left her on her own! He broke into a run. He had to get back to the apartment.

There was a monorail station at the next intersection. The glo-globes that usually surrounded it were shattered like all the rest he had passed, but he did see a light at the top of the platform where the ticket booth would be. On his way to the float-chute, he passed half a dozen loitering men who eyed him with little interest. He quickened his pace and was about to hop into the chute when something stopped him. Pausing at the threshold, he thrust out a hand—no breeze. There was supposed to be an updraft. The sound of derisive laughter made him turn.

"Almost got him!" The loiterers had known the chute wasn't operating but had chosen to wait and see if he fell down the shaft. Stafford took the stairs two at a time up to the platform and gave a crosstown station as his destination to the man in the ticket booth.

"Fifteen hundred," a voice rasped from atop the blaster-proof compartment.

Stafford gulped. "Marks?"

"No, rocks!" the man within snarled.

Stafford turned and walked slowly down the stairs. He had a grand total of forty marks in his pocket. He'd have to walk. It would be a long trek, and he was already weary—a year in a probe ship, despite artificial gravity and a conscientious exercise program, had left him out of condition and short on stamina—but it was the only way.

First, however, he would have to pass through the knot of

six or seven idle men blocking the end of the stairway.

"Nice suit you've got there," said the one in front. "I rather think it would fit me better than you." He smiled, but there was nothing friendly about the grimace.

Stafford said nothing. He glanced around and saw no one he could call upon for help.

"Come on, now. Just take it off and give it to us—and whatever money you've got on you, too—and we'll only rough you up a little. Make us chase you and we'll have to hurt you." He glanced up to the monorail platform ten meters above. "We may try and see if you can really fly in that fancy flight suit."

"I—I have no money," Stafford said in as stern a voice as he could manage. "I didn't even have enough for a ticket."

The man's smile faded. "No one who runs around in that sort of outfit is broke." He started up the steps toward Stafford. "Looks like you want to do this the hard way."

Stafford vaulted over the railing and landed on the ground running—and collided head-on with a darkened glo-globe pedestal. Before he could regain his feet, they were upon him, fists and feet jabbing at his face, his groin, his kidneys.

Suddenly the weight on him lessened, the blows became less frequent, and then stopped. Using the pedestal for support, he struggled to his feet, gasping. When the agony caused by the brutal pummeling subsided to a bearable level, he opened his eyes and looked around.

It was as if there had been an explosion during the assault on him and he had been ground zero. His attackers were strewn in all directions, either sprawled flat on the pavement, slumped on piles of debris, or slung over the stairway railing. Someone or something had pulled them off him and hurled them in all directions, battering them unmercifully in the process. No one was moving—wait—the one who had done all the talking was slowly lifting his head from the ground. Stafford limped over to see if there was to be more trouble. No . . . apparently not. The man grunted something unintelligible through a bloody, ruined mouth, then slumped down again, unconscious.

Stafford turned and lurched away, gradually forcing his headlong gait into some semblance of a trot. He could only guess at what had happened, but after seeing two Flinters back at Robin Hood's warehouse and knowing of Robin Hood's concern for his safety, it seemed reasonable to assume that he had acquired two incredibly efficient bodyguards. He just hoped that they stuck with him past Imperial Park and to his apartment.

After that, he'd no longer need them. He hoped.

The journey through the city became a blur of surreal confusion as his legs and arms became leaden and the very air seared his lungs. But he persisted despite the physical agony, for the mental agony of not knowing what he might find at home was greater. He moved through a city that had lost all resemblance to the place where he had dwelt for years, past people who were not like any he had ever known. There were times when he wondered through the haze of his oxygen-starved brain if he had landed on the wrong planet.

Finally, he found himself before the entrance to his own apartment building, gasping, weak, nauseated. The door was still keyed to his palm, for it opened when he pushed against it. Inside was an oasis of light and warmth, shelter from the dark, silent storm raging behind him. As he trudged to the float-chute, he thought he caught a hint of movement behind him, but saw nothing when he turned, only the entry door slowly sliding closed.

The chute was operating, further testimony to the wisdom of some ancient designer's insistence on decentralized power; each building had its own solar energy collectors and amplifiers. The anti-grav field was a physical joy for Stafford at this moment—he would have spent the rest of the night in the chute if he had not been so frightened for Salli. The fifth floor was his. He grasped a rung and hauled himself out into the real world of weight and inertia.

The door to his apartment was to the right and slid open when it recognized his palm. He saw Salli sitting in a chair straight ahead of him, watching the vid. She gasped and rose to her feet when she saw him, but did not come forward. So Stafford went to her.

"You're all right?" he asked, slipping his arms slowly, hesitantly around her. Her coolness puzzled him. "How did you possibly survive all this alone?"

"I managed." Her eyes kept straying away from his.

"What's the matter?"

Salli's gaze had come to rest at a point over his right shoulder. He turned. Two members of the Imperial Guard were approaching from the inner corner of the room, weapons drawn.

"Vincen Stafford?" said the one in the lead. "We've been

waiting for you. You're under arrest for crimes against the Imperium.''

Ω

"We've got the pilot, sir."

It was all Haworth could do to keep from shouting with joy. But he had to maintain his bearing. After all, this was just a callow trooper on the screen. "Very good. Where is he?"

"Here at his apartment with us."

"You mean you haven't brought him to the Complex yet?" He heard his voice rising.

"We were told to call you directly as soon as he was in custody, sir."

True—he had demanded that. "All right. How many with you now?"

"Just one other."

"Did he resist at all?"

"No, sir. He just walked in and we arrested him."

Haworth considered the situation. As much as he wanted to interrogate that pilot, he doubted the wisdom of allowing a pair of unseasoned Imperial Guards to escort him in. Who'd have ever thought he'd be stupid enough to return to his own apartment?

"Wait there until I send an extra squad to back you up. I don't want any slip-ups."

"Very well, sir." The guardsman didn't seem to mind. He didn't want any slip-ups either.

Haworth arranged for the extra squad to go to Stafford's apartment, then he turned to Metep and clapped his hands.

"This is the night! We've already got the pilot, and within the hour Robin Hood will be in custody, too!"

"What's taking so long with Robin Hood?" Metep asked. His words were slurred from the excess inhalant in his system.

"I'm not leaving a single thing to chance with him. All the city maps have been combed for any possible underground escape route. Every building around the warehouse is being taken over by Imperial Guards; every street is being blocked; even the air space over that building is being sealed off. When we finally close the trap, not even an insect will get through unless we let it! This is it, Jek! Tonight we start getting things under control again!"

Metep VII smiled foggily and put the open end of the vial to his nose again. "That's nice."

Ω

The door chimed and one of the two Imperial Guardsmen approached it warily. It was much too early for the backup squad to arrive. The viewer set in the door revealed two rather plain-looking middle-aged men on the other side. They kept shuffling around, turning their heads back and forth.

"We know you're in there, Mr. Stafford, and we want our money." The guardsman wasn't sure which one of them spoke. They kept wandering in and out of the range of the viewer.

"Go away! Stafford is under arrest."

There was laughter on the other side. "Now *that's* a new one!"

"It's true. This is a member of the Imperial Guard speaking."

More laughter. "We'll have to see that to believe it!"

The guard angrily cycled the door open. "Now do you—"

He was suddenly on the floor and a figure was vaulting through the door, a stunner aimed at the other guard's head. There was no sound from the attacker, the guard, or the weapon, but the guard closed his eyes and joined his comrade on the floor.

"If you wish to go with them, you may," said the bland-looking male invader in a female voice as the pistol was holstered. "We are only here to give you a choice. Someone is offering you and your mate a safe place if you want it. Otherwise, you may wait until they regain consciousness."

"We'll go with you," Stafford said without hesitation.

"Vin!" It was Salli.

He turned to her. "It's all right. We'll be safer with them than with anybody else. I know who they are."

Salli made no reply. She merely clung to him, looking physically exhausted and emotionally drained. She watched as the two newcomers closed the apartment door and arranged the two guardsmen neatly on the floor.

Ω

Broohnin floated in the chute, holding his position with a foot and a hand each hooked into a safety rung. Popping his head into the hall, he took a quick look up and down, then arched back into the chute. He had no idea what lay on the other side of Stafford's apartment door, but he had to go through. He had to be sure Stafford had not told what he knew—would never tell what he knew.

As he prepared to thrust himself into the hall, he heard the whisper of a door cycling open . . . it came from the direction of Stafford's apartment. Broohnin had two options: he could let go of the rungs and float up to the next floor, or he could step out and confront whoever it was.

He chose the latter. If nothing else, he'd have surprise and a drawn weapon on his side. Placing his right foot flat against the rear wall of the chute, he gave a kick and catapulted himself into the hall.

Broohnin almost vomited when he saw Stafford's escort. The holosuit images were all too familiar to him. But it was too late to do anything but act.

"Stop right there!" he said, pointing the blaster at the middle of the pilot's chest. "Another step and he dies!"

They stopped. All four of them—the pilot, a woman, and the two Flinters flanking them. "What is wrong with you, Broohnin?" said a male voice that appeared to be coming from the left: Josef's voice. "There's a squad of Imperial Guard on its way here now. Let us by without any further trouble."

"I'll let three of you by," Broohnin said warily, watching the Flinters for any sign of movement. He was far enough away that no one could reach him before he fired, and he was too close to miss if he did. He had to play this scene very carefully. There would be time for only one blast; the Flinters would be on him after that. The blast would have to kill the pilot, and then Broohnin would have to drop his weapons immediately. There was a chance they'd let him live then, and return to LaNague, who would do nothing, as usual. But at least the pilot would be dead. The thing he had to be absolutely sure *not* to do was to hit one of the Flinters with the blast, because there was no telling what the other one would do when he or she got hold of him.

"What do you mean, 'three'?" It was Kanya's voice.

"The pilot's got to die."

"You don't have to worry about that," Josef said. "He's decided to stay with us. We're taking him back to LaNague."

"I don't care what he's decided or where you're taking him. He could change his mind and walk out again . . . or Metep

could publicly offer him a huge reward if he turns himself in."
Broohnin shook his head. "No . . . can't risk it. He could ruin
everything. You know that."

Broohnin didn't realize what had happened until it was too
late. While he was talking, the Flinters had edged closer and
closer to Stafford and his wife. Then, with one quick sideward
step from each, they had placed themselves in front of the couple, completely eclipsing Broohnin's intended target.

"Don't do that! Move aside!"

"Best to give us the weapon, Broohnin," Kanya said. Moving in unison, they began to approach him, one slow step after
another.

"I'll fire!" he said, aching to retreat but finding himself
rooted to the floor. "I'll kill you both, and then him!"

"You might kill one of us," Josef said. "But that would be
the last thing you would do. Ever."

The blaster was suddenly snatched out of his hand. He saw
it in Kanya's, but the exchange had been a complete blur. He
hadn't seen her move.

"Quickly, now," Josef said, turning to Stafford and his
wife and motioning them toward the drop-chute. "The
backup squad will be here any time now."

As Stafford passed, Kanya handed him Broohnin's blaster.
"Put this in your waistband and forget about it unless we tell
you to use it."

"What about me?" Broohnin asked, fearing the answer
more than he had feared anything in his life.

Kanya and Josef merely glanced his way with their expressionless holosuit faces, then followed the pilot and his wife
down the chute. Broohnin hurried after them. If Imperial
Guardsmen were on their way, he didn't want to be caught
here and have to explain the pilot's empty apartment. He was
right behind them when they all pushed their way out to the
street and came face to face with the backup squad as it
debarked from a lorry flitter. The squad leader recognized
Stafford immediately—no doubt his features had been
drummed into their brains since his escape earlier in the day.

"What's going on here?" he yelled and readied the blaster
rifle he had been cradling in his arms. "Where are the others?
Who are these?"

Kanya and Josef edged toward the front of their group.
Josef's voice was low but audible to the rest of the civilians.

"Be calm, stand quiet, let us handle everything. There's only six of them."

"I asked you a question!" the squad leader said to anyone who would listen. "Where are the two Imperial Guardsmen who are supposed to be with you?"

"I assure you we don't know what you mean," Josef said. "We are not with these others."

The squad leader leveled his blaster at Josef as the other five members of his squad arrayed themselves behind him. "Show me some identification. It had better be perfect or we're all going upstairs to find out what's going on here."

Broohnin felt panic welling up within him, shutting off his air, choking him. This was it—they were either going to be killed or wind up Metep's prisoners. One was as bad as the other. He had to do something. He saw Stafford standing just ahead and to his left, his arms folded cautiously across his chest. His wife was clinging to his left arm and his attention was on her. Peeking out from under his right elbow was the butt of Broohnin's confiscated blaster.

Without thinking, without a conscious effort on his part, Broohnin's hand reached out and snatched at the weapon. He had to have it. It was floating debris on a storm-tossed sea, a chance for survival. No guarantee that it would carry him to safety, but it seemed to be all he had right now.

Stafford spun reflexively as he felt the weapon pulled from his waistband and grabbed for it. "Hey!"

Now was as good a time as any to get rid of the damn pilot, so Broohnin squeezed the trigger as soon as his finger found it. But Stafford's reflexes were faster. He thrust Broohnin's arm upward and Salli screamed as the beam flashed upward, striking no one.

Josef was not so lucky. At the sound of the scream and the sight of a blaster held high and firing, the squad leader responded by pressing his own trigger. There was a brief glare between the guardsman and Josef, illuminating the features of the former, briefly washing away the holosuit effect of the latter. Josef fell without a sound, a few of the accouterments on his weapons belt detaching with the impact, seeming to pop right out of his body as they passed through the holosuit image and landed on the pavement.

Everyone dropped then, including Broohnin. Kanya was the exception. She dove into the midst of the squad of guardsmen and began to wreak incredible havoc—punching, kicking, swirling, dodging, making it impossible for them to fire at her for fear of blasting a fellow guardsman. Broohnin found himself in sole possession of his blaster again. Stafford had rolled on top of his wife and both had their hands clasped protectively and uselessly over their heads. He was about to put an end to the pilot's threat once and for all when something on the pavement caught his eye.

A white disc with a small red button at its center lay beside Josef's inert form. Broohnin could not tell how badly the Flinter was hurt, or even if he were still alive, because of the camouflaging effect of the holosuit. There was no pool of blood around him, but then there seldom was much bleeding from a blaster wound due to the cauterizing effect of the heat. Deciding to risk it, he crawled over to Josef on his belly, reached for the disc, then began to crawl away. A glance over his shoulder revealed that Kanya had just about disposed of the entire squad, so he rose to his feet and sprinted in the other direction, into the safety of the darkness down the street.

With the disc in his left hand and the blaster in his right, Broohnin ran as fast as his pumping legs would carry him, through back alleys, across vacant lots, changing streets, altering direction, but always heading away from the center of town, away from Imperium Park and the Imperium Complex that surrounded it. He no longer needed LaNague or the Flinters or anyone else. The destruction of the Imperium was clutched in his left hand.

XX

> In the constant sociability of our age
> people shudder at solitude to such a
> degree that they do not know of any
> other use to put it to but . . . as a
> punishment for criminals.
>
> *Søren Kierkegaard*

"Josef dead?"

LaNague wanted to scream. The quiet, pensive man who had been with him for nearly five years, who was walking death down to his finger tips and yet so gentle and peace-loving at heart, was dead. It was easy to think of Flinters as nothing more than killing machines, living weapons with no personalities, no identities. Yet they were all individuals, philosophically sophisticated, profoundly moral in their own way, human, mortal . . .

"How?"

Calmly, briefly, Kanya explained it to him, her face on the vid-screen displaying no trace of emotion. Flinters were like that: emotions were not for public display; she would suffer her grief in private later.

"I tried to bring his body back to the warehouse for storage until it could be returned home," she concluded, "but there was no access. They have the building surrounded—on the

225

street level and in the air, with infra-red monitors every twenty meters. I could not approach without being detected."

"Poor Josef," LaNague said, his mind still rebelling at the news of his death. "I'm so sorry, Kanya." He watched her on the screen. How do you comfort a Flinter? He wished he could put an arm around her, knew there would be no steel or stone beneath his hand, but soft, yielding flesh. He sensed her grief. He wanted to pull her head down to his shoulder and let her cry it out. But that would never happen, even if she were standing next to him. Absolute emotional control was an integral part of Flinter rearing. A being skilled in a hundred, a thousand, ways of killing could not allow emotions to rule, ever.

Kanya was demonstrating that control now as she spoke. "Didn't you hear me? You're trapped. We've got to get you out."

LaNague shook his head. "I know what's going on outside. I've been watching. I'll wait for them here . . . no resistance. How's the pilot?"

"He and his wife are safe with Mora."

"And Broohnin? Is he safe where he can cause no more trouble?"

Kanya's face darkened for an instant; lightning flashed in her eyes. "Not yet. But he will be soon."

LaNague stiffened involuntarily. "What aren't you telling me, Kanya?"

"Josef is dead because of Broohnin," she said flatly. "If he had not delayed us at the pilot's apartment, we would have been gone before the squad of Imperial Guard arrived. Even after we were halted in front of the building, if he had followed directions and stood quietly, there would have been no shooting. Josef would be alive and beside me now."

"Let him go, Kanya. He can only harm himself now. You can settle with him later when your grief is not so fresh."

"No."

"Kanya, you pledged yourself to my service until the revolution was over."

"He must be found immediately."

LaNague had an uneasy feeling that Kanya was still not telling him everything. "Why? Why immediately?"

"We dishonored ourselves," she said, her eyes no longer meeting his. "We circumvented your authority by planting a fail-safe device in Imperium Park."

LaNague closed his eyes. He didn't need this. "What sort of device?" He had a sinking feeling that he already knew the answer.

"A Barsky box."

Just what he had feared. "How big? What's the radius of the displacement field?"

"Three kilometers."

"*Oh no!*" LaNague's eyes were open again, and he could see that Kanya's were once more ready to meet them. "Didn't you trust me?"

"There was always the chance that you might fail, that the Imperium would reassert control, or that Earth would move in faster than anyone anticipated. We had to have a means to ensure final destruction."

"But a radius that size could possibly disrupt Throne's crust to the point where there'd be global cataclysm!"

"Either way, the Imperium or the Earthie conquerors who replaced it would no longer be a threat."

"But at a cost of millions of lives! The whole purpose of this revolution is to *save* lives!"

"And we've co-operated! The device was only to be used in the event of your failure. A new Imperium or an Earth take-over would inevitably lead to an invasion of Flint as well as Tolive. I do not know about your planet, but no one on Flint will ever submit to outside rule. Every single one of us would die defending our planet. *That* would be a cost of millions of lives! *Flinter* lives! We prefer to see millions die on Throne. We will never allow anything to threaten our way of life. *Never!*"

LaNague held up his hands to stop her. "All right! We'll have this out later. What's it all got to do with Broohnin?"

"There were two triggers to the device. Broohnin now has one of them."

LaNague sat for a long, silent moment. Then: "Find him."

"I will."

"But how? He could be anywhere."

"All the triggers are equipped with tracers in the event they're lost. No matter where he goes, I'll be able to locate him."

"He's crazy, Kanya. He'll set that thing off just for the fun of it. He's got to be stopped!" After another silence, shorter this time: "Why couldn't you have trusted me?"

"No plan, no matter how carefully wrought, is infallible.

You *have* made miscalculations."

LaNague's heated response was reflexive. "Where? When? Aren't we right on schedule? Isn't everything going according to plan?"

"Was Josef's death in the plan?"

"If you had trusted me a little more," he said, hiding the searing pain those words caused him, "we wouldn't have this threat hanging over our heads now!"

"If you hadn't insisted on keeping Broohnin around against the advice of everyone else concerned—"

"We needed him at first. And . . . and I thought I could change him . . . bring him around."

"You failed. And Josef is dead because of it."

"I'm sorry, Kanya."

"So am I," the Flinter woman replied coldly. "But I'll see to it that he causes no further harm." Her shoulders angled as she reached for the control switch on her vid.

"Don't kill him," LaNague said. "He's been through a lot with us . . . helped us. And after all, he didn't actually fire the blast that killed Josef."

Kanya's face flashed up briefly, inscrutably, then her image faded. LaNague slumped back in his chair. She had a right to hate him as much as she did Broohnin. He was responsible, ultimately, for Josef's death. He was responsible for all of Broohnin's folly, and for his eventual demise at Kanya's hands should she decide to kill him. She could certainly feel justified in exacting her vengeance . . . Broohnin seemed to be acting like a mad dog.

All his fault, really. All of it. How had he managed to be so stupid? He and Broohnin had shared a common goal—the downfall of the Imperium. He had thought that could lead to greater common ground. Yet it hadn't, and it was too clear now that there had never been the slimmest hope of that happening. There was no true common ground. Never had been. Never could be.

At first he had likened the differences between Broohnin and himself to the differences between Flinters and Tolivians. Both cultures had started out with a common philosophy, Kyfho, and had a common goal, absolute individual sovereignty. Yet the differences were now so great. Tolivians preferred to back away from a threat, to withdraw to a safer place, to fight only when absolutely necessary: *leave us alone or we'll move away*. The Flinters had a bolder approach;

although threatening no one, they were willing to do battle at the first sign of aggression against them: *leave us alone or else.* Yet the two cultures had worked well together, now that Tolive had finally decided to fight.

He had once thought a similar rapprochement possible with Broohnin; had at one point actually considered the possibility of convincing Broohnin to surrender himself to the Imperium as Robin Hood, just as LaNague was about to do.

He smiled ruefully to himself. Had he been a fool, or had he deluded himself into believing what was safest and most convenient to believe? In truth, he wished someone—*anyone*—else were sitting here now in this empty warehouse waiting for the Imperial Guard to break in and arrest him. The thought of giving himself over to the Imperium, of prison, locked in a cell, trapped . . . it made him shake. Yet it had to be done . . . one more thing that had to be done . . . Another part of the plan, the most important part. And he could ask no one else to take his place.

Wouldn't be long now. He slid his chair into the middle of the bare expanse of the warehouse floor and sat down, his hands folded calmly before him, presenting an image of utter peace and tranquility. The officers in charge of the search-and-seizure force would be doing their best to whip their men up to a fever pitch. After all, they were assaulting the stronghold of the notorious Robin Hood, and there was no telling what lay in store for them within.

LaNague sat motionless and waited, assuming a completely non-threatening pose. He didn't want anyone to do anything rash.

Ω

"It is utterly imperative that he be taken alive! Is that clear? Every task assigned to the Imperial Guard today has been a catastrophic failure! This is a final chance for the Guard to prove its worth. If you fail this time, there may not be another chance—for any of us!"

Haworth paused in his tirade, hoping he was striking the right chord. He had threatened, he had cajoled; if he had thought tears would work, he'd have somehow dredged them up. He had to get across to Commander Tinmer the crucial nature of what they were about to do.

"If the man inside is truly Robin Hood, and the warehouse is his base of operations—and all indications are that it may very well be—he must be taken alive, and every scrap of evidence that links him with Robin Hood must be collected and brought in with him. I cannot emphasize this strongly enough: he must be taken alive, even at the risk of Guard lives."

Lacking anything more to say, or a clearer, more forceful way of saying it, Haworth let Tinmer, who had taken personal command of the Robin Hood capture mission, fade from the screen. He turned to Metep and found him deep in drugged sleep in his chair, an empty gas vial on the floor beside him.

Haworth shook his head in disgust as he found his own chair and sank into it. Metep VII, elected leader of the Outworld Imperium, was falling apart faster than his domain. And with good reason. He, Haworth, and the other powers within the Imperium had spent their lives trying to mold outworld society along the lines of their own vision, no matter how the clay protested. And had been largely successful. After establishing a firm power base, they had been on the verge of achieving a level of control at which they could influence virtually every facet of outworld life. It was a heady brew, that kind of power. One taste led to a craving for more . . . and more.

Now it was all being taken away. And Jek Milian, so at home in his powerful role as Metep, was suffering acute withdrawal. The Imperium had gradually stolen control of the outworlds from the people who lived on them, and now that control was, in turn, being stolen from it. Everything was going crazy. Why? Had it all been circumstance, or had it been planned this way? Haworth bristled at the idea that some individual or some group had been able to disrupt so completely everything he had striven to build. He wanted to believe that it had all been circumstance—*needed* to believe it.

And yet . . . there was a feather-light sensation at the far end of his mind, an ugly worm of an idea crawling around in the dark back there that whispered *conspiracy* . . . events had followed too direct a pattern . . . *conspiracy* . . . situations that should have taken years to gestate were coming to term in weeks or months . . . *conspiracy* . . . and every damaging event or detrimental situation consistently occurring at the worst possible time, always synergistically potentiating the ill effect of the previous event . . . *conspiracy* . . .

If it were conspiracy, there was only one possible agent: the man who had mocked the Imperium, derided it, made it look

foolish time after time, and eluded capture at every turn—
Robin Hood.

And it was possible—just possible—that the man or men
known as Robin Hood would be in custody tonight. That
bothered him a little. Why now? Why, when it looked as if all
was lost, did they get a tip on the whereabouts of Robin
Hood? Was this yet another part of the conspiracy against the
Imperium?

He slammed his hand against the armrest of his chair. That
was not a healthy thought trend. That sort of thinking left you
afraid to act. If you began to see everything as conspiracy, if
you thought every event was planned and calculated to
manipulate you, you wound up in a state of paralysis. No . . .
Robin Hood had finally made a mistake. One of his minions
had had a falling out with him or had become otherwise disaf-
fected and had betrayed him. That was it.

Tonight, if all went right, if the Imperial Guard didn't make
fools of themselves again—he shook his head here, still unwilling to believe that the probe pilot had slipped through their
fingers twice in one day—he would face Robin Hood. And
then he would know if it had all been planned. If true, that
very fact could be turned to the Imperium's advantage. He
would not only know whom and what he was fighting against
and how they had managed to get the best of him, but he
would have undeniable proof that the blame for the current
chaos did not lie with the Imperium. He would have a scape-
goat—the Imperium badly needed one.

Robin Hood was his last chance to turn aside the tide of
rage welling up around the Imperium. He had apparently lost
the probe pilot as a possible source of distraction. Only Robin
Hood was left to save them all from drowning. And only if
taken alive. Dead, he was a martyr . . . useless.

Ω

The doors blew open with a roar that reverberated through the
empty warehouse. Imperial Guardsmen charged in through
the clouds of settling dust and fanned out efficiently in all
directions. So intent were they on finding snipers and booby
traps that LaNague went temporarily unnoticed. It wasn't
long before he became the center of attention, however.

"Who are you?" said someone who appeared to be an officer. He aimed his hand weapon at the middle of LaNague's
forehead as he spoke, making this the second time in one day

he had been at the wrong end of a blaster.

"The name is LaNague. Peter LaNague. And I'm alone here." He held his palms flat against his thighs to keep his hands from shaking, and worked at keeping his voice steady. He refused to show the terror that gnawed at him from within.

"This your place?"

"Not exactly. I lease it."

An excited young guardsman ran up to the first. "This is the place, sir! No doubt about it!"

"What've you found?"

"High speed duplicators, stacks of various issues of *The Robin Hood Reader,* and boxes full of those little cards that were dropped with the money. Plus a dozen or so holosuits. Should we try one on to see what kind of image we get?"

"I doubt that will be necessary," the officer said, then turned to LaNague. The other members of the unduly large assault force were slowly clustering around as their commander asked the question that was on everyone's mind: "Are you Robin Hood?"

LaNague nodded. His throat was tight, as if unwilling to admit it. Finally: "I go by that name now and then."

An awed murmur rustled through the ranks of the guardsmen like wind through a forest. The officer silenced his command with a quick, angry glare.

"You are under arrest for crimes against the Imperium," he told LaNague. "Where are the rest of your followers?"

LaNague looked directly into the officer's eyes. "Look around you."

He did, and saw only his own troops, each struggling to peek over the other's shoulder or to push his way to the front for a glimpse of the man who was Robin Hood. And suddenly the meaning was clear.

"To your posts!" the commander barked. "Start packing up the evidence immediately!"

After the duty assignments were given, the officer turned the task of overseeing the warehouse end of the operation to a subordinate while he took personal command of a squad of Guard to lead LaNague back to the Imperium Complex.

In a state of self-induced emotional anesthesia, LaNague allowed himself to be led away. Fighting off a sudden awful feeling that he would never return, he cast a final backward glance and saw that every guardsman in the building had stopped what he was doing to watch Robin Hood's exit.

Ω

Finally! Finally something had gone right!

"And there's proof?" Haworth said. "Incontestable proof?"

Tinmer beamed as he spoke. "Ten times more than any jury could want."

"He'll never see a jury. But how do we know he's *the* Robin Hood, not just one of his lackeys? I'm sure he gave you a good story as to why he happened to be there."

"Not at all. He admitted it. Said straight out he was Robin Hood."

The elated tingle of victory that had been coursing along every nerve fiber in Haworth's body suddenly slowed, faltered.

"Freely?"

"Yes! Said his name was Peter LaNague and that he had authored the flyers and planned the raids. According to the census computer, though, he doesn't exist. None of his identity factors match with anyone on Throne."

"Which means he's from one of the other outworlds."

"Or Earth."

Haworth doubted that, especially now that he remembered a certain weapon used to save Metep VII's life almost five years ago, about the same time *The Robin Hood Reader* began to appear. A weapon made on Flint. Things were fitting together at last.

"Check with the other planets—the ones still speaking to us. And with Earth." Haworth knew the replies would all be negative, but decided to keep Tinmer busy.

"You going to interrogate him now?"

Haworth hesitated here. The prisoner probably expected to be hustled into the Complex and immediately filled with drugs to make him talk. Let him wait instead, Haworth thought. Let him spend the night in one of those claustrophobic cells wondering when the interrogation would begin. He'd lie awake wondering while Haworth caught up on some much needed rest.

"Throw him in maximum security and tell your men not to be too rough on him. I want him able to talk in the morning."

"That won't be a problem." Tinmer's expression was grim and dour. "They've been treating him like a visiting dignitary, like a V.I.P., like . . . like an officer!"

Haworth again felt a twinge of anxiety, a chill, as if some-one had briefly opened and closed a door to the night air. It wasn't right for the Guard to give the man who had outrun and outfoxed them all these years such treatment. They should hate him, they should want to get even. Apparently they didn't. Inappropriate behavior, to be sure. But why did it bother him so? He broke the connection and slowly turned away from the set.

Haworth didn't bother attempting to rouse Metep to tell him the news. Tomorrow he'd be in much better shape to comprehend it, and Haworth would be in better shape to deal with it. He was tired. It had been a long, harrowing day and fatigue was beginning to get the best of him. There was no chance for Robin Hood . . . no . . . stop calling him that. He was Peter LaNague now. He had a name just like everybody else; time to start de-mythifying this character. There was no chance for Peter LaNague to escape from the max-sec area. What Haworth needed now was sleep. A dose of one of the stims would keep him going, but beyond cosmetics he didn't approve of artificial means to anything where his body was concerned. The closest he got to a drug was the alpha cap he wore at night. It guaranteed him whatever length of restful slumber he desired, taking him up and down through the various levels of sleep during the set period, allowing him to awaken on schedule, ready to function at his peak.

Despite his fatigue, Daro Haworth's step was light as he strode toward his temporary quarters in the Imperium Complex. Members of the Council of Five and other higher-ups had been moved into the Complex last month, ostensibly to devote all their efforts to curing the ills that afflicted the Imperium, but in reality to escape the marauding bands wandering the countryside, laying siege to the luxury homes and estates occupied by the Imperium's top-level bureaucrats. He would not mind the cramped quarters at all tonight. For tomorrow evening, after six hours under the cap, he'd be fresh and ready to face Ro—*No!* Peter LaNague.

Ω

After an hour in the cell, LaNague had to admit that it really wasn't so bad. Perhaps his quaking terror at the thought of prison had been an overreaction. Everything had been routine: the trip to the Imperium Complex and the walk to the max-imum security section had been uneventful; the recording of his fingerprints, retinal patterns, and the taking of skin and blood samples for genotyping had all gone smoothly. Only his entry into the max-sec cell block had held a surprise.

The prison grapevine was obviously better informed than even the established news media. The public was as yet completely unaware of his capture, but as soon as he set foot on the central walkway between the three tiers of cells, a loud, prolonged, raucous cheer arose from the inmates. They thrust their arms through the bars on their cages, stretching to the limit to touch him, to grab his hand, to slap him on the back. Most could not reach him, but the meaning was clear: even in the maximum security section of the Imperium Complex, the area on Throne most isolated from the daily events of the world outside, Robin Hood was known . . . and loved.

Not exactly the segment of Throne society I've been aiming at, LaNague thought as he took his place in a bottom tier solo cell, watching the bars rise from the floor and ooze down from the ceiling, mechanical stalagmites and stalactites in a manmade cave. They met and locked together in front of him at chest level.

After his escort departed, LaNague was bombarded with questions from all directions. He answered a few, evaded most, remaining completely unambiguous only about identifying himself as Robin Hood, which he freely admitted to anyone who asked. Feigning fatigue, he retired to the rear of his cell and lay in the wall recess with his eyes closed.

Silence soon returned to the max-sec block as the celebrity's arrival was quickly accepted and digested. Conversation was not an easy thing here. Max-sec was reserved for psychopaths, killers, rapists, and habitually violent criminals . . . and now for enemies of the state. These breeds of criminal had to be isolated, separated from the rest of the prisoners as well as the rest of society. Each was given a solitary cell, a synthestone box with five unbroken surfaces, open only at the front where bars closed from above and below like a gaptooth grin, separating them from the central walkway and from each other.

There was no chance of escape, no hope of rescue. LaNague had known that when he called in the tip that led to his arrest. The walls were too thick to be blown without killing those inside. There was only one exit from the section and it was protected by a close mesh of extremely tight ultrasonic beams. No human going through one bank of those beams could maintain consciousness long enough to take two steps. And there were five banks. Should there be any general disturbance in the max-sec block, another system would bathe the entire area with inaudible, consciousness-robbing sound, forcing a half-hour nap on everyone.

LaNague didn't want to get out just yet anyway. He had to sit and hope that Metep and the Council of Five would play into his hands . . . and hope that Sayers would be able to play one of those recordings on the air . . . and hope that the populace would respond. So many variables. Too many, perhaps. He had shredded the outworlders' confidence in the Imperium, now he had to mend it, but in a different weave, a different cut, a radical style. Could he do it?

Somewhere inside of him was a cold knot of fear and doubt that said no one could do it.

LaNague had almost dozed off—he had a talent for that, no matter what the circumstances—when he heard footsteps on the walkway. They stopped outside his cell and he peered cautiously out of his recess toward the bars. One of the prison guards stood there, a flat, square container balanced on his upturned palm. LaNague gently eased his left hand into his right axilla, probing until he found the tiny lump under the skin. He desperately hoped he would not have to squeeze it now.

"You hungry?" the guard said as he caught sight of LaNague's face in the darkness of the recess.

Sliding to the floor and warily approaching the front of the cell, LaNague said, "A little."

"Good." The guard tapped a code into the box attached to his waist, a code LaNague knew was changed three times a day. The central bar at the front of his cell suddenly snapped in two at its middle, the top half rising, the bottom sinking until about twenty centimeters separated the ends. After passing the container through the opening, the guard tapped his box again and the two bars approximated and merged again.

It was a food tray. LaNague activated the heating element and set it aside. "I would have thought the kitchen was closed."

"It is." The guard smiled. He was tall, lean, his uniform ill-fitting. "But not for you."

"Why's that?" LaNague was immediately suspicious. "Orders from on high?"

The guard grunted. "Not likely! No, we were all sitting

around thinking what a dirty thing it was to put someone like you in with these guys—I mean, most of them have killed at least one person; and if not, it wasn't for not trying. They'd kill again, too, given the chance. We can't even let them near each other, let alone decent people. A guy like you just doesn't belong here. I mean, you didn't kill anybody—or even hurt anybody—all these years. All you did was make the big boys look stupid and spread the money around afterwards so everybody could have a good time. We don't think you belong here, Mr. Robin Hood, and although we can't do much about getting you out of max-sec, we'll make sure nobody gives you any trouble while you're in here."

"Thank you," LaNague said, touched. "Do you always second-guess your superiors this way?"

After a moment of thought: "No, come to think of it. You're the first prisoner I ever gave a second thought to. I always figured you—you know, Robin Hood—were crazy. I mean, dropping that money and all. I never got any. My sister did once, but I work the night shift so I never had a chance. Did read that flyer of yours though . . . that *really* seemed crazy at the time, but from what I've seen lately, I know you're not crazy. Never were. It's everybody else that's crazy."

He seemed surprised and somewhat abashed at what he had just said. He gestured to the tray, which had started to steam. "Better eat that while it's hot." As LaNague turned away, the guard moved closer to the bars and spoke again. "One more thing . . . I'm not supposed to do this, but—" He thrust his open right hand between the bars.

LaNague grasped it and shook it firmly. "What's your name?"

"Steen. Chars Steen."

"Glad to know you, Steen."

"Not as glad as I am to know you!" He turned and quickly strode toward the exit at the end of the walkway.

LaNague stood and looked at the tray for a while, moved by the small but significant gesture of solidarity from the guards. Perhaps he had touched people more deeply than he realized. Sitting down before the tray, he lifted the lid. He really wasn't hungry, but made himself eat. After all, it was a gift.

He managed to swallow a few bites, but had to stop when Mora drifted through his mind. Since his arrest he had been doing his best to fend off the thought of her, but lost the battle now. She would be learning of his capture soon, hopefully not from the vid. Telling her beforehand would have been impossible. Mora would have done everything in her power to stop him; failing that, she would have tried to be arrested along with him, despite the way he had been treating her.

A short spool had been left explaining everything . . . a rotten way to do it, but the only way. With his appetite gone, he scraped the remaining contents of the tray into the commode and watched them swirl away, then crawled back into the recess and forced himself to sleep. It was better than thinking about what Mora was going through.

"How could you let him do it?" Mora's voice was shrill, her gestures frantic as she twisted in her seat trying to find a comfortable position. There was none. Her mind had been reeling from the news about Josef—now this!

"How could I stop him?" Radmon Sayers said defensively as he stood before her in the LaNague apartment. He had waited until the pilot and his wife had fallen asleep in the other room, then had put on the spool and let LaNague explain it himself.

"Someone else could have gone! One of his *loyal*"—she hated herself for the way she snarled the word—"followers could have taken his place! No one in the Imperium knows what Robin Hood looks like!"

"He didn't feel he could allow anyone else to be placed in custody as the most wanted man in the outworlds. And frankly, I respect that decision."

Mora sank back in her chair and nodded reluctantly. It was unfair of her to castigate Sayers, or to call into question the courage of any of the Merry Men. She knew Peter—although with the way he had been behaving since her arrival on Throne, perhaps not as well as she had thought. But he had never been good at asking favors of anyone, even a simple favor that was due him. He preferred to take care of it himself and get it out of the way rather than impose on anyone. So the idea of asking someone else to risk his life posing as Robin Hood would have been completely beyond him.

"I'm sorry," she mumbled through a sigh. "It's just that I had the distinct impression he had someone else in mind as the public's Robin Hood."

"That may have been a calculated effect for your benefit."

"Maybe. What are we supposed to do now?"

Sayers fished in his pocket and came up with three vid spools. "We wait for an opportunity to play one of these over the air."

"What's on them?" Mora asked, rising from her seat.

"Your husband . . . making an appeal to the people of Throne to choose between Metep and Robin Hood."

"Are they any good? Will they convince anyone?" She didn't like the expression on Sayers' face.

"I can't say." He kept his eyes on the spools in his hand. "A lot of the public's acceptance will depend on the fact that he's been identified as Robin Hood. The news bulletins should be breaking just about now, although hardly anybody's watching. But all of Throne will know by breakfast."

"Play one for me."

"There's three, one for each of the contingencies he thought possible."

"Play them all."

Sayers plugged them into the apartment holovid set, one after another. Mora watched with growing dismay, an invisible hand making a fist with her heart in the middle, gripping it tighter and tighter until she was sure it must stop beating. Peter's messages to the people of Throne were beautifully precise and well reasoned. They pointed out the velvet-gloved tyranny of the Imperium, and the inevitable consequences. No one living in the economic holocaust engulfing Throne could deny the truth of what he said. He appealed on the grounds of principle and pragmatism. But there was some vital element missing.

"He's doomed," Mora said in a voice that sounded as hollow as she felt. The third spool had just finished throwing out its holographic image of Peter LaNague, alias Robin Hood, sitting at a desk and calmly telling whoever might be listening to rise up and put an end to the Outworld Imperium once and for all.

Sayers puffed out his cheeks and exhaled slowly. "That's what I told him when we recorded these. But he wouldn't listen."

"No . . . of course he wouldn't. He expects everyone in the galaxy to respond to pure reason, now that he's finally got their attention." She gestured toward the vid set. "A Tolivian or a Flinter would understand and respond fiercely to any one of those spools. But the people of Throne?"

She went to the window. Pierrot sat on the sill, drooping heavily over the edge of his pot in the morose *kengai* configuration. She had watered the tree, spoken to it, but nothing she did brought it upright again. She looked beyond to the dark empty streets awaiting dawn, and thought about Peter. He had become a different man since leaving Tolive—cold, distant, preoccupied, even ruthless. But those spools . . . they were the work of a fool!

"Why didn't he listen to you, or check with me, or take *some*body's advice? Those spools are dry, pedantic, didactic, and emotionally flat! They may get a good number of people nodding their heads and agreeing in the safety of their homes, but they won't get them out in the street, running and shaking their fists in the air and screaming at the tops of their lungs for an end to Metep and his rotten Imperium!" She whirled and faced Sayers. *"They won't work!"*

"They're all we've got."

Mora saw the three spools sitting in a row beside the vid set. With one swift motion she snatched them up, hurled them into the dissociator in the corner, and activated it.

Sayers leaped forward, but too late. *"No!"* He stared at her in disbelief. "Do you realize what you've done? Those were the only copies!"

"Good! Now we'll have to think of something else." She paused. It had been necessary to destroy the spools. As long as they remained intact, Sayers would have felt duty-bound to find a way to broadcast them. But with them now gone beyond any hope of retrieval, he was free to act on his own—and to listen to her. Mora had already concocted a variation on Peter's basic plan. But she would need help—Flinter help. With Josef dead and Kanya gone she knew not where, Mora would have to turn to other Flinters. They were available, filtering down in a steady stream over the past few weeks, setting up isolated enclaves, waiting for the time when their services would be needed. Mora knew where to find them.

Ω

He was almost there. Gasping for breath, Broohnin stopped on a rise and looked back at the dim glow that was Primus City. Last year it would have lit up half the sky at this distance, but with glo-globes fast becoming an endangered species on its streets, the city was a faint ghost of its former self. He sat down for a moment and scanned the terrain behind him, watching for any sign of movement as his lungs caught up to his body.

After a long moment of intense scrutiny, he was satisfied. His eyes were adjusted to the darkness and he saw no one on his trail, not even an animal. He had come a long way; his muscles were protesting as much now as they had on the Earth jaunt. He had allowed himself to get soft again . . . but he had to push on. A little farther out from the city and he'd feel safe.

The trigger was still in his hand, although the activating button was locked. No problem there . . . not many small locks could stand for long against his years of experience in by-passing them. He bet it wasn't even a true lock . . . the trigger was most likely protected by a simple safety mechanism. When he reached a spot he considered safe, he was sure he could release it with a minimum of ado.

Heaving himself again to his feet, he forced his protesting muscles onward. Not far now. Not too much longer. Then it was good-by Imperium. He had originally planned to hold the trigger back, use it as a trump card in his continuing battle with LaNague. But that was out of the question now. Somewhere along the path of his flight from Primus he had stopped to rest in an all-night tavern near the city limits. He could have used an ale but there was none to be had. As it was, nearly all of his cash went for a small wedge of cheese anyway. It was in the tavern that he learned of Robin Hood's arrest.

At first he thought it was a hoax or a mistake, but the face that filled the projection field of the tavern's holovid was LaNague's. Caught him red-handed, they said, and were holding him under heavy guard in the Imperium Complex. Broohnin had rushed out of the tavern then, continuing his flight from Primus at full speed.

The revolution was over. Without LaNague to direct things, it would sputter and stall and die. Broohnin hated to admit it, but the ugly truth wouldn't go away: only LaNague had the power to marshal the various forces necessary to bring the tottering Imperium all the way down. Only he had the authority to command the Flinters and who-knew-what-other resources. Only he knew what the final phase of the revolution was to be.

Broohnin had nothing except the trigger for the giant Barsky box he had seen buried in Imperium Park. That would be enough to literally decapitate the Imperium by sending Imperium Park and the entire Imperium Complex surrounding it to some unspecified point in time and space. Wherever it ended up, Broohnin was sure it would be far from Throne. Everyone within the Complex—Metep, the entire Council of Five, all the myriad petty bureaucrats—along with a few early risers in the park, would vanish without a trace, without warning.

He had an urge to stop where he was, find the way to release the trigger, and activate the box *now*. But that might mean a less than completely satisfactory result. He had to wait until mid-morning when the Complex was acrawl with all the lice that kept the huge bureaucracy functioning. To destroy the Imperium Complex before then was to risk missing a key person, perhaps Metep himself.

He'd have to wait, and wait out here, far from the city. Much as he would have loved to see the Complex and all it represented flash from view and existence, he preferred to keep a safe distance between himself and the event, and stroll into Primus later to see the open pit where the Imperium had been.

He smiled as he thought of something else: he would also be looking at the spot where Peter LaNague had been.

Ω

Haworth awakened with a start. The vidphone had activated the auto shut-off in his alpha cap, thrusting him immediately up to consciousness. He pulled it off and leaned over to activate the receiver. He would accept the call once he saw who was on the other end.

"Daro!" It was Jek. Metep VII had finally come out of his stupor. "Daro, you there?"

Haworth keyed in his transmitter so Metep could see and hear his chief adviser. "Yes, Jek, I'm here. What is it?"

"Why wasn't I told of the Robin Hood capture immediately?" His manner was haughty, his voice cold. He was in one of his Why-wasn't-I-consulted-first moods, a recurrent state of whenever he felt that Haworth and the council were making too many independent decisions. Fortunately, they were short lived.

"You were sitting not two meters away from me when the word came." He kept his tone light but drove his point home quickly and cleanly: "Trouble was, you weren't conscious."

"I should have been awakened! It had been a long day and I was dozing, waiting for the news. I should have been told immediately!"

Haworth looked closely at Metep's image. This was not the anticipated reaction. A quick comment about Jek's overindulgence in one gas or another was usually sufficient to deflate him, eliciting a nervous laugh and a change of subject. But this was something new. He seemed to have puffed up his self-importance beyond the usual level, to a point where he was impervious to casual barbs. That worried Haworth.

"Well, that's not important," he said easily. "What really matters is—"

"It *is* important. It is of paramount importance that Metep be kept apprized of all developments, especially where enemies of the state are concerned. I should have been awakened immediately. Precious time has already been wasted."

"I'm sorry, Jek. It won't happen again." *What's he been sniffing now?* Haworth wondered. *Acts like he thinks he's really running things!* "I'm going to get the interrogation procedures started as soon as I've had some breakfast. After we've learned all we can from him, we'll have a quiet little trial and have done with him."

"We can't wait that long!" Metep said, his vocal pitch rising, his lips twitching. "He must be tried and convicted *today*! And in public. I've already made arrangements for proceedings in Freedom Hall this afternoon."

The same odd sensation that Haworth had experienced last night upon learning that the prisoner had freely admitted to being Robin Hood, and again when told of the deferential treatment given him by the Guard, came over him again. He could almost hear the crash, feel the vibrations as giant tumblers within some huge, unseen cosmic lock fell into place one by one.

"No! That's the worst thing you could do! This man has already become some sort of folk hero. Don't give him the extra exposure!"

Metep sneered. "Ridiculous! He's a common criminal and his own notoriety will be used against him." His face suddenly softened and he was the old Jek Milian again. "Don't you see, Daro? He's my last chance to save my reputation! We have evidence aplenty that he's Robin Hood; we just have to manufacture a little more to link him to Earth and blame him for this runaway inflation that's ruining everything. He'll get us all off the hook!"

"I'm calling a meeting of the council," Haworth said. "I can't let you do this!"

"I thought you'd say that!" Hard lines formed in Metep's features once more. "So I did that myself. If you think you can get enough votes to override me, you're wrong!" His face faded away.

$$\Omega$$

Broohnin awoke cold and stiff with the light. After an instant of disorientation, he remembered his circumstances. He had been running on stims the past few days, and had left the city with none on him. The crash had come before dawn, and now the sun glowered hazily from its mid-morning perch in the sky.

Pulling himself erect, he immediately reached for the trigger. Wouldn't be long now. Everything had gone wrong and got pushed off the track. But now everything was going to be set right. A brief inspection in the light of day showed the safety mechanism to be of rudimentary construction, geared more toward the prevention of accidental firing than determined tampering. Easy to circumvent it. He'd just have to—

The trigger disappeared from his hands in a blur of motion. Broohnin whirled around as best he could from a sitting position, pulling his blaster out as he moved. That too was torn from his grasp as soon as it cleared his belt. When he saw who was behind him, all his sphincters let go in an uncontrolled rush.

Kanya dropped the trigger device and blaster at her feet and struck him across the face, sending him reeling into the dirt. As he tried to scramble to his feet and run away, she tripped him and knocked him sprawling again. Each time Broohnin caught a glimpse of her face it was the same: expressionless, emotionless, with neither anger nor mercy in her eyes, only cold, intense concentration. And silent. She uttered no sound as she hovered over him like an avenging angel of death.

With each attempt to rise, she would knock him flat again, bruising a new area of his body with unerring accuracy. He pleaded with her at first, but she might as well have been deaf. He gave that up soon. And when he gave up trying to escape her, she began to lift him up and hurl him against the ground or a boulder or a tree trunk. Always hurting him, always damaging him, always increasing the agony a little more each time. Yet never enough to cause him to lose consciousness. He became a broken-stringed marionette in the hands of a mad puppeteer, hurled limply from stage right to stage left.

Soon his eyes were swollen shut, and even if he had wanted to look at Kanya, he would have been unable to. And still the systematic beating continued. When he had seen her drop the blaster before she hit him the first time, Broohnin had been afraid Kanya intended to beat him to death. Now he was afraid she wouldn't.

XXI

A leader . . . is one of the things that
distinguishes a mob from a people. He
maintains the level of individuals. Too
few individuals and a people reverts to
a mob.

Stilgar

One look at the expressions on the faces around the table and
Haworth knew he was wasting his time. The members of the
council were disposed toward Jek in the first place, not only
because he was the current Metep, but because they considered
him one of their own. Haworth had always been an outsider.
They were as frightened and confused as Jek, and he had their
ear. So the Council of Five—*sans* Daro Haworth—was
squarely behind Metep VII. He considered turning at the
doorway and leaving them to approve Metep's proposal
blindly, but forced himself to enter. He had to try. He had
spent too many years clawing his way up to his present position to let everything go without a fight.

"Now that we're all here," Metep said as soon as Haworth
had crossed the threshold, "the question will be brought to a
vote." He wasn't even going to wait until Haworth was
seated.

"Isn't there going to be any discussion?"

"We *have* discussed it," Metep said, "and we've decided, all of us, that a speedy public trial is the only sensible course. Documents are at this moment being prepared to show incontrovertible proof of Robin Hood's link with Earth. We'll show that Earth hired him and financed him, and even show that it was his theft of millions upon millions of Imperial marks that sparked the whole inflation spiral. And to demonstrate to the people that I am still their leader—a strong leader—*I* will personally conduct the trial."

Haworth sat down before answering. "Did it ever occur to any of you that this may be exactly what he wants you to do?"

Over rumbling comments of "Ridiculous!" and "Absurd!" Metep said, "No man in his right mind would turn himself over to us for trial. And I think you'll have to admit that this Robin Hood fellow—LaNague, isn't it?—is hardly insane. Nor is he stupid."

"Nor is he Robin Hood." The chatter stopped. Haworth had their attention now.

"He admits to it!"

Haworth smiled. "Very well: *I'll* admit to it, too, But that doesn't mean I'm Robin Hood. And one of Robin Hood's so-called Merry Men could have volunteered to stand in for him. Remember, we don't have a single physical characteristic by which to identify Robin Hood. I'm willing to bet this man Peter LaNague is a fraud. I'm willing to bet he's been planted here just to make fools of us, to make us convict him and sentence him in public; and then he'll come up with evidence to prove that he wasn't even on Throne when the raids occurred. Keep in mind that there's no verifiable identity for the prisoner. We can't even prove he's someone called Peter LaNague, let alone Robin Hood!"

He watched their faces as they considered his words. He had been speaking calmly, softly, hiding his inner tension. He didn't believe a word of what he had just said, but he knew he had to stop the public trial and was throwing out every suspicious thought that popped into his head, anything that would muddy the water and keep the council members confused. He personally believed the man who called himself LaNague to be Robin Hood, and for that reason wanted him kept out of the public eye.

"But we *need* him to be Robin Hood!" Metep said into the ensuing silence. "He *must* be Robin Hood! It's the only way we can salvage *anything*!" His tone became plaintive. "The trial will draw attention from us to him. Discontent will focus on him and Earth. That will give us time—"

"No trial," Haworth said firmly. "Interrogate him quietly, execute him secretly, then announce that he has been released due to conflicting evidence and that the search for the real Robin Hood continues. No public trial is going to give us breathing room of any consequence."

"But that leaves us where we are now!" Metep said through quivering lips. "Don't you understand? They're out there getting ready to recall me! And when they kick me out, you'll all go with me!"

"You can declare martial law due to the economic crisis," Haworth said into Metep's growing hysteria. "They can't recall you then."

"But I don't want to be known as the only Metep who had to call out the Guard to stay in office! If I have to, I will, certainly. But the trial—"

"The trial is a trap!" Haworth was on his feet, shouting. It was a release of the pressure that had been building within him since Metep had awakened him this morning. It was also a last resort. "Can't you get it through those neutronium skulls of yours that we're dealing with a genius here? I know for certain in my mind that Robin Hood—whoever he is—is responsible for everything bad that had happened to us. I don't know how he did it, I don't know why, I don't know what his next move is, but I am certain a public trial is just what he expects of us. *Don't do it!* Let me interrogate him for a few days. The right combination of drugs will start him talking and then we'll know everything—perhaps even the identity of the real Robin Hood."

He paused for breath, watching their impassive faces. "Look . . . I'll compromise: when I'm done with him you can have your little show if you still want it. But let me break him first!"

"It must be now. Today." From Metep's tone, Haworth knew he was beyond persuasion. "All in favor?" Metep said, raising his right hand and not bothering to look around the table. The other four members of the council raised their hands.

Haworth wheeled and stalked toward the door. "Then it's on your heads! I'll have no part of it!"

"Where do you think you're going?" Metep asked in a flat, cold voice.

"Off this planet before you send it up in smoke!"

"Earth, perhaps?" Krager said, his lined face beaming gleefully in the wake of Haworth's defeat.

"You are under house arrest," Metep said. "You will be confined to your Complex quarters until the trial, at which time you will be escorted to Freedom Hall with the rest of us. I knew you'd try to run out on us and cannot allow it. It is crucial that we keep up appearances of unity."

"You can't do that!"

Metep smiled wanly as he pressed a stud on the table top. "Can't I?" The outer door cycled open and two guardsmen entered. "Take him."

Ω

By the time the guard stopped in front of the cell, LaNague had the lump in his right axilla trapped between his thumb and forefinger, ready to squeeze.

"Well," the guard said—this one was as portly as Steen had been lean, "the fecaliths on top must want to get you out of the way real bad, Mr. Robin Hood."

LaNague's fingers tightened on the lump. "What makes you say that?"

"They scheduled your trial for this afternoon . . . in Freedom Hall. It's all over the vid."

"Is that so?" LaNague released the lump, actually a pea-sized wad of jelly encased in an impermeable membrane, and relaxed. It was all he could do to keep from laughing aloud and doing a jig around the cell. He had dreaded the thought of squeezing that little packet, and now it looked as if he wouldn't have to. It contained a neuroleptic substance that would leak out into the surrounding subcutaneous fat when the membranes was ruptured. From there via the bloodstream it would eventually find the way to its only active site in the body, the Broca area in the right hemisphere of his brain, where it would cause a membrance dysfunction in the neurons there, effectively paralyzing his language function for two weeks. He would be incapable of verbalizing any of his thoughts; any questions asked verbally would be perceived as incoherent sound; written questions would be seen as a meaningless jumble of marks, beyond comprehension; anything he tried to write would come out the same way. The condition was known as total receptive and expressive aphasia. LaNague would be rendered incapable of giving his interrogators truth or fiction, no matter what drugs they pumped into him.

"I swear by the Core, it's the truth!" the guard said. "Never seen anybody brought to trial so fast. They're really going to make an example of you, I'm sorry to say."

"You don't think they should?"

The guard shook his head. "You had the right idea all along, from what I can tell. But how'd you know all this was going to happen?"

"History," LaNague said, refraining with an effort from quoting Santayana. "This has all happened before on Earth. Most of the time it ended in ruin and temporary stagnation. Occasionally it gave rise to monstrous evil. I was hoping we'd avoid both those roads this time."

"Looks like you're not going to be around to have much say either way," the guard said resignedly.

"What's your name?"

"Boucher. Why?"

"You could help me."

Boucher shook his head. "Don't ask me to get you out, because I couldn't, even if I decided to risk it. It's just not possible." He smiled. "You know, I could lose this job just for talking to you about it. Not that it would matter much. The money I get doesn't buy enough food for me to feed my kids. If it wasn't for the stuff I sneak out of the kitchen a couple of times a week, we'd starve. Imagine that! I'm getting paid a thousand marks an hour and I'm losing weight! And they missed paying us yesterday. If that happens again, we're going to start demanding twice-a-day pay periods or we'll walk. *Then* there'll be trouble! But no, I can't get you out. Even if I gave you my blaster, they'd stop you. They'd let you kill me before they'd let you out."

"I don't want that kind of help. I just want you to see that I get to the trial alive."

Boucher laughed. "No one's going to kill you, at least not until they give you the death sentence!" He sobered abruptly. "Look, I'm sorry I said that. I didn't mean—"

"I know you didn't. But I'm quite serious about that. Someone may try to see that I don't get to trial . . . ever."

"That's—"

"Just do this one favor for me. Get some of the other guards you know and trust, and keep careful watch. After all, I'm not asking anything more than what the Imperium pays you to do: guard a prisoner."

Boucher's eyes narrowed. "All right. If it'll make you feel better, I'll see to it." He walked away, glancing back over his shoulder every few paces and shaking his head as if he thought the infamous Robin Hood might be crazy after all.

LaNague wandered the perimeter of his cell. Adrenalin was pounding through his system, causing his heart to race, his underarms and palms to drip perspiration. Why? Everything was going according to plan. Why this feeling of impending doom? Why this shapeless fear that something was going to go terribly wrong? That he was going to die?

He stopped and breathed slowly and deeply, telling himself that everything was all right, that it was a stress reaction due to the swift approach of the trial. Everything would come to a head at the trial once Sayers played the designated tape sometime today, beaming Robin Hood's pre-recorded message out to the people. LaNague would then know if he had wasted the last five years. If he had, the Imperium would see to it that he had no further years left to waste.

$$\Omega$$

Twelve ought to be enough, Mora thought. Even if the building down there were loaded with armed guards on full alert, twelve Flinters would be more than enough. As it was, according to Sayers, only a few unarmed and unsuspecting security personnel would be scattered throughout the three floors of the broadcasting station. No problem taking over.

That wasn't what filled her with dread. It was her own part in the little escapade about to be launched. Could she measure up? Maybe she shouldn't have destroyed Peter's spools. Maybe she had been overly critical of them. After all, Peter had been so right all along, why shouldn't he be right now? Mora clenched her teeth and closed her eyes in silent determination. *Don't think like that!* She had to follow through with this. She had burned her bridges, and the only way left was straight ahead. Peter *had* been wrong about those tapes and only she had had the courage to do something about them.

She glanced around at the impassive faces of the six robed figures crowded into the tiny flitter cabin with her. Six more hovered in the flitter behind. All were in full ceremonial battle dress, fully aware that their appearance alone was a most effective weapon.

The tension was making her ill. She wasn't used to this.

Why did everyone else look so calm? Come to think of it, she looked calm, too. All her turmoil was sealed under her skin. She wondered if the Flinters beside her were equally knotted up inside. Probably not. No one could feel like this and be a Flinter.

It was time. The two craft swooped down to the roof of the broadcast station and the Flinters poured out of their flitters and through the upper entrance Sayers had arranged to leave open. They all had their assignments and would make certain that Mora had a clear path to her destination.

Sayers himself was in his studio on the second floor doing a well-publicized news special on Robin Hood. He had given her specific directions on how to reach his studio. The Flinters had cleared the way and no one questioned her presence in the building. She swung out of a drop-chute, turned left. There was a Flinter at the door to the studio, motioning her forward. This was it. Sayers was inside waiting to put her before millions of Throners. Her mind was suddenly blank. What was she going to say? Peter's very life depended on what she would be doing in the next few minutes.

I'm doing this for you, Peter, she thought as she crossed the threshold. *Neither of us is the same person we were when this began, but right or wrong, this is my way of saying I still believe in you.*

Ω

It was midday when Boucher returned, hurrying down the walkway, carrying something in his hand.

"You married?" he shouted from half the length of the corridor.

Filled with an unstable mixture of curiosity and dread, LaNague hesitated. "Yes," he finally managed to say. "Why?"

"Because somebody who says she's your wife is on the vid!" Boucher said, urging his bulky frame into a trot. "And is *she* going to be in trouble!" He puffed up to LaNague's cell and held out a hand-sized vid set. It was a flat screen model and Mora's face filled the viewplate.

LaNague watched with growing dismay as Mora sent out a plea for all those who had come to believe in Robin Hood to come to his aid. She was saying essentially what LaNague himself had said on the second pre-recorded spool—the one to be played for the trial contingency—but not the way he had said it. Her appeal was rambling, unfocused, obviously unrehearsed. She was ruining everything!

Or was she?

As LaNague listened, he realized that although Mora was speaking emotionally, the emotion was clearly genuine. She was afraid for her man and was making an appeal to any of his friends who might be listening to help him now when he needed them. Her eyes shone as she spoke, blazing with conviction. She was reaching for the heart as well as the mind, and risking her life to do it. Her message was for all Throners; but most of all, for her husband.

As she paused briefly before beginning her appeal again, Boucher glanced at LaNague, his voice thick. "That's some woman you've got there."

LaNague nodded, unable to speak. Turning his face away, he walked to the far corner of his cell and stood there, remembering how he had so bitterly resented Mora's very presence on Throne, his cold rejection of the warmth, love, and support she had offered. Through the thousand tiny insults and affronts he had heaped on her during the past few months, she had remained true to him, and truer than he to the cause they shared. He remained in the corner until he could breathe evenly again, until the muscles in his throat were relaxed enough to permit coherent speech, until the moisture welling in his eyes had receded to a normal level. Then he returned to the bars to watch and listen to the rest of Mora's appeal.

Ω

They may have confined him to quarters, but at least he wasn't incommunicado. He had turned to the vid to see what Sayers would be saying to the public on his Robin Hood news special; but instead of the vidcaster's familiar face in the holofield, there was a strange woman calling herself Robin Hood's wife, pleading for revolution. He immediately tried to contact the studio, but no calls were being taken through the central circuits at the building. Checking a special directory, he found a security code to make the computer patch him through to the control booth in Sayers' studio.

A technician took the call. He did not look well. Although he recognized Daro Haworth immediately, it seemed to have little effect on him.

"What is going *on* over there? I want that transmission cut immediately! *Immediately!* Do you hear?''

"I can't do that, sir."

"Unless you want this to be the last free day of your life,"
Haworth screamed, "you will cut that transmission!"

"Sir . . ." The technician adjusted the angle on his visual
pickup to maximum width, revealing a number of black-
cloaked figures with red circles painted on their foreheads and
weapons belts across their chests arrayed behind him. "Do
you see my predicament?"

Flinters! Was Robin Hood a Flinter? "How did they get
in?"

The technician shrugged. "All of a sudden they were here
with the woman. Radmon seemed to be expecting them."

Sayers! Of course he'd be involved! "What about security?
Didn't anyone try to stop them?"

The technician glanced over his shoulder, then back to
Haworth. "Would you? We got an alarm off immediately but
no one's showed up yet."

At that point, one of the Flinters leaned over and broke the
connection. Shaken, but still functioning, Haworth immediately stabbed in the code to Commander Tinmer over at
the Imperial Guard garrison. The commander answered the
chime himself, and his expression was far from encouraging.

"Don't say it!" he said as soon as he recognized Haworth.
"I've been personally trying to muster a force big enough to
retake the broadcast station ever since we received the alarm."

"You've had plenty of time!"

"We're having some minor discipline problems here. The
men are letting us know how unhappy they are with the way
their pay has been handled recently. There's been a delay here
and there in the currency shipments due to breakdowns in
machinery over at Treasury, and the men seem to think that if
the pay can be late, *they* can be late." His sudden smile was
totally devoid of humor. "Don't worry. The problem's really
not that serious. Just some flip talk and sloganeering. You
know . . . 'No pay, no fight' . . . that sort of thing."

"What are they doing instead of obeying orders?"

Tinmer's smile died. "Instead of scrambling to their
transports as ordered, most of them are still in their barracks
watching that whore on the vid. But don't worry. We'll
straighten everything out. Just need a little more time, is all.
I—"

Haworth slammed his fist viciously against the power plate, severing the connection. He now saw the whole plan. The final pieces had just angled into place. But there was no attendant rush of triumph, only crushing depression. For he could see no way of salvaging the Imperium and his place within it. No way at all, except . . .

He pushed *that* thought away. It wasn't for him.

Gloom settled heavily. Haworth had devoted his life to the Imperium, or rather to increasing its power and making that power his own. And now it was all slipping away from him. By the end of the day he would be a political nonentity, a nobody, all his efforts of the past two decades negated by that man down in max-sec, that man who called himself Robin Hood.

It no longer mattered whether or not he was actually Robin Hood. The Imperium itself had identified him as such and that was good enough for the public. They were ready to follow him—Haworth could sense it. No matter if he were the true mastermind behind the colossal conspiracy that had brought the Imperium to its present state, or just a stand-in, the public knew his face and he would live in the battered and angry minds of all outworlders as Robin Hood.

Or die . . .

The previously rejected thought crept back into focus. Yes, that was a possible way out. If the proclaimed messiah were dead, the rabble would have no one to follow, no rallying point, no alternative to Metep and the Imperium. They would be enraged at his death, true, but they would be leaderless . . . and once again malleable.

It just might work. It *had* to work. But who to do it? Haworth could think of no one he could trust who could get close enough, and no one close enough he could trust to do it. Which left Haworth himself. The thought was repugnant— not the idea of killing, *per se*, but actually doing it himself. He was used to giving orders, to having others take care of un- pleasant details. Trouble was, he had run out of others.

He went to a locked compartment in the wall and tapped in a code to open it. After the briefest hesitation, he withdrew a small blaster, palm-sized with a wrist clamp. He had bought it when civil disorder had threatened, when street gangs had moved out to the more affluent neighborhoods, oblivious to the prestige and position of their victims. He never dreamed it would be used for something like this.

Hefting the lightweight weapon in his hand, Haworth almost returned it to the compartment. He'd never get away with it. Still . . . with an abrupt motion, he slammed the door shut and clamped the blaster to his right wrist.

As far as he could see, there was no choice. Robin Hood had to die if Haworth's life was to retain any meaning, and an opportunity to kill without being seen might come along. The tiny blaster could be angled in such a way that he could appear to be scratching the side of his face while sighting in on the target. With caution, and a great deal of luck, he could get away with it.

If he didn't get away with it—if he killed LaNague but was identified as the assassin, he would no doubt be torn to pieces on the spot. Haworth shrugged to no one but himself. It was worth the risk. If Robin Hood lived, the goals Haworth had pursued throughout his life would be placed far beyond his reach; if he killed him and was discovered, Haworth's very life would be taken from him. He could not decide which was worse.

Allowed to run its conclusion, the Robin Hood plan would mean the end of everything Haworth had worked for. He would lose the power to shape the future of outworld civilization as he saw fit. He would be reduced from a maker of history to a footnote in history. Without ever standing for election, he had become a major guiding power within the Imperium . . . and perhaps should take some blame for guiding it into its current state. But he could fix everything—he was sure of it! All he needed was a little more time, a little more control, and a lot less Robin Hood.

Ω

There were fully a dozen guards escorting LaNague to Freedom Hall. He noticed Boucher in the lead and Steen among them, even though it wasn't his shift. The prisoners on maxsec all shouted encouragement as he was led away. So did the remaining guards.

"Boucher told me what you said about someone trying to kill you," Steen whispered as they marched through the tunnel that passed under the Complex and surfaced at the private entrance to Freedom Hall. "I think you're crazy but decided to come along anyway. Lots of crazy people around these days."

LaNague could only nod. The eerie feeling that he would

never leave Freedom Hall alive was stealing over him again. Attributing it to last-minute panic didn't work. Nothing shook it loose, not even his fervent disbelief in premonitions of any sort.

His escort stopped in a small antechamber that opened onto the dais at the end of the immense hall. The traditional elevated throne for Metep, a diadem-like structure with a central pedestal six meters high, had been set up center stage with five seats in a semi-circle around it at floor level. To the right of it, closer to LaNague, a makeshift dock had been constructed, looking like a gallows.

All for me, he thought.

Although he could catch only meager glimpses of it between the heads of his escort, it was the crowd that caught and held LaNague's attention. There were people out there. *Lots* of them. More people than he ever thought could possibly squeeze into Freedom Hall. A sea of humanity lapping at the dais. And from what he could gather, there were thousands more outside the building, trying to push their way in. All were chanting steadily, the various pitches and timbres and accents merging into a non-descript roar, repeating over and over:

"...FREE ROBIN!...FREE ROBIN!...FREE ROBIN!..."

When the Council of Five finally made its appearance, its members looked distinctly uneasy as they glanced at the unruly crowd surging against the bulkhead of Imperial Guard, three men deep at all points and fully armed, that separated them from their loyal subjects. Haworth came in last, and LaNague had the impression that he was under some sort of guard himself. Had the chief adviser been threatened, or had he decided to skip the public trial and been overruled? Interesting.

The noise from the crowd doubled at sight of the council, the two words of the chant ricocheting off the walls, permeating the air. And it trebled when Metep VII, dressed in his ceremonial finest for the vid cameras sending his image to the millions of Throners who could not be here, was led in and rode his throne up the pedestal to the top of the diadem.

All six of the Imperium's leaders appeared disturbed by the chant, but in different ways. The council members were overtly fearful and looked as if nothing would please them more than to be somewhere else, the farther away the better.

Metep VII, however, looked annoyed, angry, suitably imperious. He was taking the chant as a personal affront. Which, of course, it was.

When his seat had reached the top of the diadem's central pedestal, Metep spoke. Directional microphones focused automatically on him and boomed his amplified voice over the immense crowd within, and out to the throngs surrounding Freedom Hall and choking the streets leading to it.

"There will be silence during these proceedings," he said in a voice that carried such confidence and authority that the crowd quieted to hear what he had to say. "Any observers who cannot conduct themselves in a manner suitable to the gravity of the matter at hand will be ejected." He looked to his left. "Bring out the prisoner."

As LaNague was led to the dock, the crowd rustled and rippled and surged like the waters of a bay raised to a chop by a sudden blast of wind. People were pushing forward, craning their necks, climbing on each other's shoulders for a look at the man who had made it rain money. The Imperial Guardsmen assigned to crowd control had their hands full, but even they managed a peek over their shoulders at the dock.

There were a few cheers, a few short-lived, disorganized chants of "Free Robin!" but mostly a hushed awe. LaNague looked out on the sea of faces and felt a horrific ecstasy jolt through him. They were for him—he could feel it. But they were so strong, so labile . . . they could wreak terrible damage if they got out of control. Much would depend on pure luck from here on in.

"The prisoner's name is Peter LaNague, and he has freely admitted to being the criminal known as Robin Hood. He is to be tried today for armed robbery, sedition, and other grievous crimes against the state."

The crowd's reaction was spontaneous: multiple cries of "No!" merged smoothly and quickly into a single, prolonged, deafening, *"NOOOOO!"*

Metep was overtly taken aback by the response, but with a contemptuous toss of his head he pressed on, fumbling only on the first word when he spoke again.

"Due to the extraordinary nature of the crimes involved, the trial will be held before a tribunal consisting of Metep and the Council of Five, rather than the traditional jury. This is in accordance with the special emergency powers available to the Imperium during times of crisis such as these."

"NOOOOO!" Clenched fists shot into the air.

Metep rose in his seat. From the docket, LaNague could see that the man was clearly furious, his regal mien chipping, cracking, flaking off.

"You admire Robin Hood?" he said to the crowd in a voice that shook with anger. "Wait! Just wait! Before we are through here today, we will have presented irrefutable evidence that this man who calls himself Robin Hood is in truth an agent of Earth, and an enemy of all loyal outworlders!"

The "Nooooo!" that rose from the audience then was somewhat diminished in its resonance and volume, due not to a lessening of conviction in the crowd, but to the fact that many people in the hall had begun to laugh.

"And the penalty for this"—there was a touch of hysteria in Metep's voice as it climbed toward a scream; sensing it, the crowd quieted momentarily—"is death!"

If Metep VII had expected utter silence to follow his pronouncement, he was to be bitterly disappointed. The responding *"NOOOOOOO!"* was louder and longer then any preceding it. But the crowd was not going to limit itself to a merely verbal outburst this time. Like a single Gargantuan mass of protoplasm leaving the primordial sea for the first time, it flowed toward the dais shouting, "FREE ROBIN! FREE ROBIN!" The Imperial Guardsmen could do no more than give ground gracefully, pushing with the sides of their blaster rifles against the incredible mass of humanity that faced them, retreating steadily rearward despite their best efforts.

"Order!" Metep shrieked from his pedestal. "Order! I will have the Guard shoot to kill the first man to set foot on the dais!"

On hearing this, one of the guardsmen backed up toward the diadem throne and looked up at Metep, then back to the crowd. With obvious disgust, he raised his blaster rifle over his head, held it there momentarily, then hurled it to the floor in front of him.

That did it. That was the chink in the dam. Within the span of a single heartbeat, the rest of the guardsmen threw down their own weapons, leaving nothing between the crowd and the dais. Most of them joined in the forward rush, shouting "FREE ROBIN!" along with everybody else.

The crowd divided spontaneously, part surging toward Metep's throne, the rest rushing in LaNague's direction. He knew their intent was to rescue him, but he was frightened all the same. Their movements were so wild and frantic that he feared they would unintentionally wash over and trample him to death.

They didn't. Their laughing faces surrounded the dock, calling his name, tearing the side railings away with bare hands, pulling him from the platform and hoisting him onto their shoulders.

A much grimmer scene was being played at center stage as the other half of the crowd—the angry half—stormed the diadem throne. The members of the Council of Five on the lower level were completely ignored as they scattered in all directions. The crowd wanted only one man, the man who represented the Imperium itself: Metep VII. Seeing his angry subjects approaching him, Metep had wisely locked his seat into position at the top of the pedestal. All attempts to start his descent failed until someone thought of shaking him loose.

The diadem throne was a huge, gaudy structure with considerable mass. But the crowd, too, was huge and considerably determined. At first the thone moved imperceptibly as the group on one side pushed while the other pulled, both quickly reversing their efforts. Soon the entire structure was swaying back and forth, with Metep VII, bereft of every shred of dignity, clutching desperately to his seat to the accompaniment of wild laughter from below. And when he finally decided to start his seat back down the pedestal, it was too late. He suddenly lost his grip and tumbled screaming to the waiting crowd below. The roar of human voices that arose then was deafening.

LaNague's immediate concern was that the crowd would beat Metep without mercy. Fortunately, that was not to be. Metep's scrambling efforts to maintain purchase on the rocking throne had been comedic enough to raise the general mood of his tormentors, averting a potentially ugly confrontation. He was hauled by his arms and his legs like so much baggage to the dock that had just been vacated by his former prisoner, while LaNague was carried shoulder-top to the now empty throne. The seat had reached floor level by this time and LaNague was thrust into it. Someone reversed the controls and it began to ascend the pedestal again, this time with a new occupant. As he rode toward the top of the diadem, a new chant arose from below:

"METEP EIGHT! METEP EIGHT! METEP EIGHT! . . ."

LaNague ignored it, expecting this kind of response. It was

naïve, it was shortsighted, it was all too typical. It was why history repeated itself, over and over. What he had not expected was to be raised on this idiotic throne. He felt ridiculous and naked, like an oversized blaster target. For that feeling was back; the feeling that he was going to die.

He brushed it off again. It was just that he hadn't heard from Kanya, which meant that Broohnin could still be loose with the trigger to the big Barsky box. If activated, it would mean instant death for LaNague and everyone in sight.

He looked around at the undulating mass of upturned faces, all joyous, all filled with unhoped for hope, all sensing that they were midwives at the birth of something new. Just what it might be, they didn't know, but it had to be better than what they had been living through recently.

Not all faces were smiling, however. He spotted Haworth looking up at him, his right hand pressed against his forehead —injured, perhaps?—a look of utter concentration on his face, his left eye squinted closed. The crowd seemed to be ignoring him despite his outlandish appearance. Metep had held the title and was therefore the power in the Imperium as far as the public was concerned. Only a few knew Haworth as the real decision-maker.

LaNague looked away from the chief adviser, back toward the huge expanse of the crowd stretching to the far end of Freedom Hall and out into the growing darkness beyond. As his head moved, however, he caught a glint at Haworth's wrist out of the corner of his eye, and realized what the man was doing.

Pointing below, LaNague rose to his feet and shouted, "Daro Haworth!" The remote directional microphones, automatically trained on the seat's occupant, Metep or not, amplified it to a *"DARO HAWORTH!"* that shook the walls.

Silence descended on Freedom Hall like a muffling cloak as Haworth was immediately grabbed and his arms pinned to his sides by a familiar middle-aged male figure.

"Release him," LaNague said, his voice still amplified, but not to such a degree now that he was speaking in a more subdued tone. "And give him room."

The crowd either would not or could not move away from Haworth. They kept pawing at him, shoving him.

"Give him room, please," LaNague said from almost directly above the scene. When the crowd around Haworth still did not move back, he nodded to the middle-aged man who then touched a hand to his belt. The holosuit flickered off and suddenly there was a Flinter female in full battle regalia beside Haworth. And just as suddenly there was a circle of empty space around Haworth as people backed away. Kanya had returned.

"Go ahead, Mr. Haworth," LaNague said in a soft voice audible to the end of Freedom Hall. "Kill me. That's what you were about to do, wasn't it? Do it. But bring your blaster out into the open so everyone can watch. When this mock trial was over and I was found guilty—the verdict was never in doubt, was it?—I was to be executed. But you were going to let someone else do the actual deed. Now that won't be necessary. The pleasure is yours alone. Do it."

LaNague felt dizzy standing there six meters in the air, watching a man with artificially darkened skin and artificially whitened hair pull a blaster from his sleeve and point it in his direction. But he had to stand fast, hoping Haworth would miss if he fired, that Kanya would be able to ruin his aim. Hoping above all that he would be able to face Haworth down. The scene was being played to every operating vid set on the planet, and being recorded for replay on all the other outworlds. Metep, slumped useless and ruined in the prisoner's dock, had already been made to look like a fool. All that was left now was Haworth, who had to be faced and disgraced, otherwise he might become a rallying point for the few royalists who would remain active in the wake of the revolution.

Haworth looked as frightened as LaNague felt. And although the weapon was pointed upward, he was not sighting on his target. Instead, his head swiveled back and forth, oscillating between the flesh and blood Flinter beside him, to the silent, fearful, hostile ring of faces that enclosed him.

LaNague's voice became a booming whisper. *"Now,* Mr. Haworth. Now, or drop it."

With an agonized groan or equal parts fear and frustration, Haworth swung the blaster away from LaNague and placed the lens at the end of the barrel against his forehead. Members of the crowd behind him winced and ducked, fully expecting the back of his head to explode over them. Haworth glanced quickly about and saw that only Kanya was standing within reach of him. She had the ability to snatch the weapon from his hand before he could fire, but she did not move.

Neither did Haworth. Even the perfunctory courtesy of forcible restraint from committing suicide was to be denied him. He was on his own, completely. No one was going to pull the trigger for him, no one was going to prevent him from pulling it himself. It was all up to him. As centerpiece in the grim tableau, with all Throne—and soon all of the outworlds—watching, he stood naked, stripped of all pretense, split from throat to pubes with all his innards steaming and reeking in the air for everyone to see.

An utterly miserable and despairing sob broke from his lips as he let his arm slump to his side and the blaster fall unused to the floor. Kanya scooped it up immediately. As she led him away, the chant began again.

"METEP EIGHT! METEP EIGHT! METEP EIGHT!"

LaNague sat down heavily in the chair to take the weight off his suddenly wobbly knees. As he gathered his thoughts, gathered his strength, and hoped that he had been looking death in the eye for the last time that day, he heard the chant falter. Looking up, he saw the crowd dividing down the middle. Like a vibe-knife through a haunch of raw meat, a wedge of a dozen or so Flinters was cleaving a path toward the dais. Watching the group move closer, he saw that someone was shielded within that wedge: Mora.

As soon as he recognized her, LaNague started his seat into descent. By the time it reached the floor of the diadem, Mora was standing there, waiting for him. She leaped to his side in the chair, and as they embraced, the chair began to climb the pedestal again.

At that point, the crowd within and without Freedom Hall dissolved into a veritable frenzy of jubilation. None of LaNague's carefully calculated ploys to win support from the people of Throne could even approach the impact of seeing him and his wife embrace on the diadem throne. All present had seen Mora on the vid; most were there in response to her plea. And now they saw her together with her man and felt that had played a part in reuniting the couple. They were cheering for themselves as well as for Robin Hood and his gutsy wife.

"I love you," LaNague whispered close to Mora's ear. "I never stopped. I just . . . went away for a while."

"I know," she said in a voice as soft as the body he clutched against him. "And it's good to have you back."

Gradually, the cheers organized into the bothersome chant: "METEP EIGHT! METEP EIGHT! METEP EIGHT! METEP EIGHT!"

Would they never tire of calling for a new Metep? As he looked down into the thousands of hopeful eyes, the thousands of happy, trusting faces, he knew that the past five years had all been a prelude. Now the *real* work began. He had to take all the horrors these people had experienced and wash them away; he had to convince them that although it could happen again, it need not; that there was another way . . . a better way. Doing that might prove more difficult than the revolution itself.

He had to convince all these good people that he was not the new Metep. More, he had to convince them that they did not want another Metep. Ever again.

Epilogue

Still one more thing, fellow citizens:
a wise and frugal government, which
shall refrain men from injuring one
another, which shall leave them otherwise free to regulate their own pursuits
of industry and improvement, and
shall not take from the mouth of labor
the bread it has earned. This is the sum
of good government.

Thomas Jefferson

He threw the clothes into the shipping canister with sharp,
angry motions. Had they been objects made of something less
pliant than cloth they would have shattered or bounced off to
the other side of the room. A full standard year ago he had
been brought to the Imperium Complex a prisoner; he had remained within the Complex after the revolution of his own ac-
cord. Now he was leaving. Leaving Throne altogether, in fact.
For good.

By the window, Pierrot's trunk was in a constant state of
slow, confused flux. The tree appeared healthy, with new
growth a lighter green against the dark of the old. The trunk
was now held in a neutral position, balancing LaNague's
joyous anticipation of returning to Tolive against his anger at

the piece of news he had just received.

A long year, this last one, and ultimately frustrating. It had begun so well in Freedom Hall, telling the assembled multitudes there and all the millions watching on the vid that a new Metep was not the answer, that the Imperium was dead and should gratefully be allowed to remain so. The enthusiastic cheers that greeted this were repeated when LaNague broached his idea that the outworlds band together within a totally new structure, one of unique design, with many-doored walls and no roof—an alliance that would allow each member planet to pursue its own course in whatever direction its inhabitants desired, and yet still feel a part of the whole of humanity. In the bright afterglow of Metep's downfall, anything and everything seemed possible.

A call was sent to all the sibling outworlds: the Imperium is dead . . . send us someone you trust to help form a new organization, a new alliance—a Federation. And while the people of Throne awaited the arrival of the representatives, the task of restoring social and economic stability was begun.

Muscle was provided by the planet Flint. For the first—and doubtlessly the last—time in outworld history, Flinters became a common sight on the streets of another planet. They were especially visible on the streets of Primus City. And when there were none in view, it was highly possible that an innocent-looking civilian was actually a holographic patina under which lurked an armed Flinter, ready to strike if attacked.

Such tactics were necessary. Too many street gangs had formed during the holocaust; too many had come to think of the streets they roamed as their own private preserves, had become accustomed to taking whatever they wanted, whenever they wanted it. They had to be dealt with . . . sometimes harshly. Gang members either learned that violence was no longer a means to anything on Throne, or died trying to prove otherwise. The word was out: peace or else.

Soon, there was peace.

Coincident with the Flinter efforts, Tolive took on the massive task of correcting the economic chaos that was the underlying cause of the social upheaval. Freighterloads of gold and silver coins, minted on Tolive and stamped with the now familiar star-in-the-ohm insignia that had become so intimately associated with Robin Hood, were delivered to Throne. Exchange rates were established for trading the new coins for the worthless paper marks glutting the economy.

Someday the Tolivians hoped to be paid back, at least partially. There was no hope of full reimbursement, ever. But this was the price they were willing to pay. They were, in effect, buying a secure future for their way of life. To their minds, it was money well spent.

The effect of a new, stable medium of exchange was almost miraculous. Within days, the transport unions were back to work, raw materials were reaching manufacturers, staple commodities were flowing into the cities. Gone were demands for daily and twice-daily pay periods, gone was the fearful drive to spend whatever one had as soon as it was in hand, gone the urge to hoard. Old businesses reopened, and a few new ones started up, all looking for workers. During the holocaust it had been futile to manufacture or offer a product for sale—if it wasn't stolen first, the money received in exchange would be depreciating in buying power so rapidly that it became a losing proposition even to consider any sort of commerce. Now, it was different.

The hope and feeling of security engendered by the hard currency went a long way toward restoring a sense of normalcy. Tomorrow was no longer feared, but eagerly anticipated. Myriad problems needed attending, however. Despite the resurgence of industrial activity, there remained a huge body of unemployed, many of them former employees of the Imperium. The dole was temporarily maintained for their sake, and those able were put to work cleaning up the debris of the breakdown. As new businesses sprung up to tend to the tasks no longer being done by the Imperium's endless arrays of bureaus, the former government workers gradually found places for themselves.

Throne was undergoing an amazing transformation. Someone had answers; someone was in charge again and everything was going to be all right. The people were ready to follow Robin Hood anywhere, do anything he said, just as long as they didn't have to go through *that* again. LaNague found no comfort in their blind devotion. Had he been a different sort of man, he could have forged the outworlds into a totalitarian regime the likes of which human history had never seen. Throners especially were so vulnerable during the aftermath that they would have done anything he asked as long as he kept food on the shelves and the monorails on schedule. It was sad. It was terrifying.

The representatives from the other outworlds finally began

arriving, in an uncertain trickle at first, then in a steady stream. LaNague gathered them all together in Freedom Hall and presented them with a blueprint for a new alliance, a charter for a commonality of planets that would provide a nucleus for defining the goals and common interests of the member worlds, yet would stay out of all planetary and interplanetary affairs as long as aggression was not involved. The Outworld Federation, as LaNague called it, would serve mainly as a peace-keeping force and would be strictly bound by the limits of the charter, a document written, rewritten, and refined by generations of the LaNague family.

No planet could initiate force against another planet without risking immediate reprisals by the Federation Defense Force. The Federation would be a voluntaristic organization; member planets would pay dues and would have a voice in Federation policy—a tiny voice, for the charter put strict limits on what the organization could do; in turn, they would receive the full protection of the Defense Force. Planets not wishing to join could go it alone, but could not expect any aid from the Federation at any time.

Only one internal requirement was mandated of every planet: all inhabitants of said planet, who were not fugitives from justice, must be free to emigrate at will. A planet could place whatever restrictions it wished on ingress, but free engress with all legally acquired possessions was an absolute necessity for membership. Penalties for infringement of this rule ranged from fines to expulsion.

Beyond containing the aggressive tendencies of its more acquisitive members, and protecting the free movement of trade between all the planets in its jurisdiction, the charter left the Federation with little to do. Unless someone somewhere initiated force against a member planet or its citizens, the Federation merely stood by and watched humanity go about its business. Many of the representatives found this sort of radical noninterventionism profoundly disturbing. It was something completely beyond their experience, beyond their education, as alien as the Tarks had seemed when news of their existence was announced. In the minds of many representatives, the form of government envisioned in the LaNague Charter was simply not enough. It didn't really . . . govern.

And that's when the trouble began.

LaNague realized now that he should have seen it coming. Even Broohnin foresaw it when LaNague had visited him in the hospital where he was recovering from the not-quite fatal beating Kanya had administered to him. After reading through the charter, Broohnin had laughed derisively.

"I always said you were a dreamer, LaNague! They'll cut this thing to pieces the minute you turn your back! They'll hack away at it, bit by bit by bit until you won't recognize it. They won't be able to keep their hands off it!"

LaNague hadn't believed him then; he was sure the outworlds had learned their lesson. He was wrong. A significant percentage of the representatives who appeared intelligent turned out to be ineducable in certain areas of life. There followed a battle that took up the remainder of the year, between the purists who wanted the charter accepted as it was, reactionaries who wanted significant changes, and centrists who proposed a compromise—leave the charter as is, but attach an emergency clause to be activated only in times of crisis to give the Federation special powers to deal with an unexpected and grave threat to the member planets.

Despite LaNague's months of pleading, cajoling, threatening, warning, and begging, word had just come through that the charter had been accepted *in toto*—with the emergency clause firmly attached by an overwhelming majority of the representatives. The Outworld Federation, which many were now calling the LaNague Federation, had been born. Throne was to be renamed Federation Central, and a new era was beginning for the outworlds.

Peter LaNague's anger was fading to despondence now as he continued to pack. He had sent word to the representatives that he wanted his name completely expunged from the violated version of the charter. He disowned it and the Federation itself, and would have no further contact with anyone connected with the organization. The new president of the General Council sent his regrets, but said that as far as everyone was concerned, it was still the LaNague Charter.

Privately, LaNague knew he might one day change his mind, but for now he was too angry, too discouraged. All those years . . . all that work . . . had it all been for nothing? He saw the emergency clause as a ticking bomb sitting under the charter and the organization it guided, a constant temptation to all the Daro Haworths and would-be Meteps of the future.

The vidphone chimed. It was Broohnin. With his beard gone, he looked almost handsome, his features marred only by the triangular scar on his cheek and the leering smile twisting his lips.

"Just heard the news. Looks like they've already started tearing up your little dream. What're you going to do now?"

"Leave. Right behind you."

"Oh, I'm leaving all right," he said, his eyes squinting in anger. "But don't think I'm just going to sit around and get fat on Nolevatol. I'll be getting together a few people who think like me, and when your *Federation*"—he spat the word—"steps out of line, I'll be ready to make life miserable for it!"

"Good," LaNague said tiredly. "Because I won't. I'm through." He cut the transmission.

Broohnin had been allowed to remain on Throne to recuperate as long as LaNague and Flinters remained to watch him. Kanya had broken nearly every bone in his body, and although fully mended now, he would have aches and pains and stiffness as lifetime reminders. With LaNague's departure, Broohnin was being deported to Nolevatol, his homeworld.

LaNague's own homeworld, and all it held, awaited him. He and Mora had returned to Tolive shortly after the revolution. He still could not get over how Laina had grown and changed. After a few weeks of getting to know both his wife and his daughter again, he had returned to Throne, leaving them behind. His next homecoming was to be his last.

He went to the window and looked out at the quiet, green expanse of Imperium Park, wondering what they were going to rename it . . . not LaNague Park, he hoped. The sunlight, the sight of children playing, of couples walking slowly along, leaning together, making plans, lightened his mood.

Perhaps he was being too hard on his fellow outworlders. Perhaps it was possible the emergency clause would never be invoked. Perhaps the outworlds had truly learned their lesson. He hoped so. He had given them their chance. The rest was up to them and their children.

Peter LaNague was going home.